The
Night
of the
Mi'raj

The
Night
of the
Mi'raj
Zoë
Ferraris

Little, Brown

LITTLE, BROWN

First published in Great Britain in 2008 by Little, Brown

Copyright © Zoë Ferraris 2008

The moral right of the author has been asserted.

A CIP catalogue record for this book
is available from the British Library.

Hardback ISBN: 978-0-316-02749-6
C-Format ISBN: 978-1-4087-0095-2

Typeset in Caslon by M Rules
Printed and bound in Great Britain by
Clays Ltd, St Ives plc

Little, Brown
An imprint of
Little, Brown Book Group
100 Victoria Embankment
London EC4Y 0DY

An Hachette Livre UK Company

www.littlebrown.co.uk

The
Night
of the
Mi'raj

Marriage is my practice.
One who forsakes this practice of mine is not from me.

—the Prophet Mohammed, praise be upon him,
sallalahu alayhi wasallam.

I

Before the sun set that evening, Nayir filled his canteen, tucked a prayer rug beneath his arm, and climbed the south-facing dune near the camp. Behind him came a burst of loud laughter from one of the tents, and he imagined that his men were playing cards, probably *tarneep*, and passing the *siddiqi* around. Years of travelling in the desert had taught him that it was impossible to stop people from doing whatever they liked. There was no law out here, and if the men wanted alcohol they would drink. It disgusted Nayir that they would wake up on Friday morning, the holy day, their bodies fouled with gin. But he said nothing. After ten days of fruitless searching, he was not in the mood to chastise.

He scaled the dune at an easy pace, stopping only once he'd reached the crest. From here he had a sprawling view of the desert valley, crisp and flat, surrounded by low dunes that undulated in the golden colour of sunset. But his eye was drawn to the blot on the landscape: half a dozen vultures hunched over a jackal's carcass. It was the reason they'd stopped here – another false lead.

Two days ago, they'd given up scouring the desert and

started to follow the vultures instead, but each flock of vultures brought only the sight of a dead jackal or gazelle. It was a relief of course, but a disappointment too. He still held out hope that they would find her.

Taking his compass from his pocket, he found the direction of Mecca and pointed his prayer rug there. He opened his canteen and took a precautionary sniff. The water smelled tinny. He took a swig then quickly knelt on the sand to perform his ablutions. He scrubbed his arms, neck and hands, and, when he was finished, screwed the canteen tightly shut, relishing the brief coolness of water on his skin.

Standing above the rug, he began to pray, but his thoughts kept on turning to Nouf. For the sake of modesty he tried not to imagine her face or her body, but the more he thought about her, the more vivid she became. In his mind, she was walking through the desert, leaning into the wind, black cloak whipping against her sunburned ankles. *Allah forgive me for imagining her ankles*, he thought. And then: *At least I think she's still alive.*

When he wasn't praying, he imagined other things about her. He saw her kneeling and shovelling sand into her mouth, mistaking it for water. He saw her sprawled on her back, the metal of a cell phone burning a brand onto her palm. He saw the jackals tearing her body to pieces. During prayers, he tried to reverse these fears and imagine her still struggling. Tonight, his mind fought harder than ever to give life to what felt like a hopeless case.

Prayers finished, he felt more tired than before. He rolled up the rug and sat on the sand at the very edge of the hill, looking out at the dunes that surrounded the valley. The wind picked up and stroked the desert floor, begging a few grains of sand the better to flaunt its elegance, while the earth shed its skin with a ripple and seemed to take flight. The bodies of the dunes changed endlessly with the winds.

2

They rose into peaks or slithered like snake trails. The Bedouin had taught him how to interpret the shapes to determine the chance of a sandstorm or the direction of tomorrow's wind. Some Bedouin believed that the forms held prophetic meanings too. Right now, the land directly ahead of him formed a series of crescents, graceful half-moons that rolled toward the horizon. Crescents meant change was in the air.

His thoughts turned to the picture in his pocket. Checking to see that no one was coming up the hill behind him, he took the picture out and allowed himself the rare indulgence of studying a woman's face.

Nouf ash-Shrawi stood in the centre of the frame, smiling happily as she cut a slice of cake at her younger sister's birthday party. She had a long nose, black eyes, and a gorgeous smile; it was hard to imagine that just four weeks after the picture was taken she had run away – to the desert, no less – leaving everything behind: a fiancé, a luxurious life, and a large, happy family. She'd even left the five-year-old sister who stood beside her in the picture looking up at her with heartbreaking adoration. *Why?* he wondered. Nouf was only sixteen. She had a whole life in front of her.

And where did she go?

When Othman had phoned and told him about his sister's disappearance, he had sounded weaker than Nayir had ever heard him. 'I'd give my blood,' he stammered, 'if that would help find her.' In the long silence that followed, Nayir knew he was crying; he'd heard the choke in his voice. Othman had never asked for anything before. Nayir said he would assist.

For many years, he had taken the Shrawi men to the desert. In fact, he'd taken dozens of families just like the Shrawis, and they were all the same: rich and pompous, desperate to prove that they hadn't lost their Bedouin birthright even though, for most of them, the country's dark wells of petroleum would always be more compelling than its landscape. But Othman was different. He was one of the few men who loved the desert as much as Nayir and who had the brains to enjoy his adventures. He didn't mount a camel until someone told him how to get off. He didn't get sunburn, didn't get lost. Drawn together by a mutual love of the desert, he and Nayir had fallen into an easy friendship that had deepened over the years.

On the telephone, Othman was so distraught that the story came out in confusing fragments. His sister was gone. She had run away. Maybe she'd been kidnapped. Because of their wealth, it was possible that someone wanted ransom money – but kidnappings were rare, and there was no ransom note yet. Only a day had passed, but it seemed long enough. Nayir had to pry to get the facts. No one knew exactly when she had left; they only noticed she was missing in the late afternoon. She had last been seen in the morning, when she told her mother she was going to the mall to exchange a pair of shoes. But by evening, the family had discovered that other things were gone too: a pick-up truck, the new black cloak she was saving for the honeymoon. When they realized that a camel was missing from the stables, they decided she'd run away to the desert.

Her disappearance had taken everyone by surprise. 'She was happy,' Othman said. 'She was about to get married.'

'Maybe she got nervous?' Nayir had asked gently.

'No, she wanted this marriage.'

If there was more to the story, Othman wasn't saying.

Nayir spent the next day making preparations. He refused the lavish payment the family offered, taking only what he needed. He hired fifty-two camels, contacted every desert man he knew, and even called the Ministry of the Interior's Special Services to see if they could track her

4

by military satellite, but their overhead optics were reserved for other things. Still, he managed to compose a search and rescue team involving several dozen men and a unit of part-time Bedouin who wouldn't even look at Nouf's picture, claiming they didn't need to, that there was only one type of woman for whom being stranded in the largest desert in the world was a kind of improvement on her daily life. The men developed a theory that Nouf had eloped with an American lover to escape her arranged marriage. It was hard to say why they all believed the idea. There had been a few cases of rich Saudi girls falling for American men, and they were shocking enough to linger in the collective memory. But it wasn't as frequent as people supposed, and as far as Nayir knew, no Saudi girl had ever eloped to the *desert*.

The Shrawis asked Nayir to focus his search on one area of the desert, with radii extending outward from As-Sulayyil. They stationed other search parties to the north and northwest, and one to the southwest. He would have liked more liberty to expand his operations at his own discretion, but as it was, he was hemmed in by strangers who seldom bothered to communicate with him. So he ignored the rules. Two days in, he ordered his men to follow their own instincts even if it took them into neighbouring territory. If Nouf was still out there, her chances of survival dwindled with every hour of daylight. This was no time to be formal, as if the search were a wedding dinner and the guests should be seated just so.

Besides, his team was the largest, and although he didn't often do search and rescue, he knew the desert better than most. He'd practically grown up in the desert. His uncle Samir had raised him, and Samir kept foreign friends: scholars, scientists, men who came to study the Red Sea, the birds and the fish, or the Bedouin way of life. Nayir spent summers chipping dirt on archaeological digs for rich Europeans who sought the tomb of Abraham, or the remains of the gold that the Jews had carried from Egypt. He spent winters clutching the rear humps of camels, clattering through the sand with tin pots and canteens. He became an archer, a falconer, a survivalist of sorts who could find his way home from remote locations needing only a headscarf, water, and the sky. He wasn't a Bedouin by blood, but he felt like one.

He'd never failed to find a lost traveller. If Nouf had run away, he had to assume that she didn't want to be found. For ten days they scoured the dunes in Rovers, on camels, from airplanes and choppers, and in frequent cases they found each other, which caused some relief, hard as it was to find anything living in all of that sand. But they did not find Nouf, and finally the reports that Nayir's men placed before him began to suggest alternative theories in which she'd taken an overnight bus to Muscat, or boarded an airplane for Amman.

He cursed the situation. Maybe she'd spent a night in the wild and decided it was too uncomfortable, too dirty, and she'd moved on. Yet Nayir feared that she had stayed, and now it was too late. It took only two days for a man to die in the desert. For a young girl from a wealthy family, a girl who had probably never left the comfort of an air-conditioned room, death would come faster than that.

The sunset showered the landscape in a warm orange light, and a stiff sirocco troubled the air. It stirred a sharp longing that reached beyond his concerns for Nouf. Lately, he'd been overcome by thoughts of what was missing in his life. Irrationally, he felt that it wasn't only Nouf he'd lost, it was the possibility of finding any woman. Closing his eyes, he asked Allah once again: *What is Your plan for me? I trust in Your plan, but I'm impatient. Please reveal Your design.*

6

Behind him came a shout. Quickly stuffing the picture back in his pocket, he stood up and saw one of his men at the bottom of the hill, pointing at a pair of headlights in the distance. Nayir grabbed his rug and canteen and scrambled down the dune. Somcone was coming, and a desperate foreboding told him that it was bad news. He jogged along the bottom of the dune and waited as the Rover drove into the camp. It stopped beside the largest tent.

Nayir didn't recognize the young man at the wheel. He looked like a Bedouin with his sharp features and dark skin. He was wearing a leather bomber jacket over his dusty white robe, and when he stepped out of the car, he regarded Nayir with apprehension.

Nayir welcomed the guest and extended his hand. He knew he was too big and imposing to put anyone at ease, but he tried. Nervously, the boy introduced himself as Ibrahim Suleiman, a son of one of the Shrawi servants. The men gathered around, waiting for the news, but Ibrahim stood quietly, and Nayir realized that he wanted to speak in private.

He led the boy into the tent, praying that the men hadn't been drinking after all. There was no worse way to disgrace oneself than to lead a man into a tent that smelled of alcohol. But the tent doors were open and the wind blew in, along with a generous spray of sand.

Inside, Nayir lit a lamp, offered his guest a floor cushion, and began preparing tea. He refrained from asking questions, but he hurried through the tea-making because he was eager to hear the news. Once it was ready, Nayir sat cross-legged beside his guest and waited for him to drink first.

Once the second cup had been poured, Ibrahim leaned forward and balanced his teacup on his knee. 'They found her,' he said, his eyes lowered.

'They did?' The tension drained out of Nayir so suddenly that it hurt. 'Where?'

'About two kilometres south of the Shrawi campsite. She was near a wadi.'

'They've had men there for a week. Are they certain it's her?'

'Yes.'

'Who found her?'

'We're not sure. Someone who wasn't working for the family. Travellers.'

'How do you know this?'

'Tahsin's cousin Majid came to our camp and delivered the news. He'd spoken to the Coroner.' Ibrahim took another sip of his tea. 'He said that the travellers took her back to Jeddah. She was already dead.'

'Dead?'

'Yes.' Ibrahim sat back. 'They took her to the Coroner's office in Jeddah. They had no idea who she was.'

It was over. He thought about his men outside, wondered if they would feel relief or disappointment. Probably relief. He wasn't sure what to tell them about the girl. It was odd that the family's own search party had been stationed near the wadi. A group of cousins and servants must have been right on top of her, yet they missed her completely. They also missed whoever had been travelling through the area. The travellers must have returned her body to the city before the Shrawis had even figured out that they'd passed through. All of this made Nayir uneasy, but he would have to double-check the information; it wasn't exactly reliable.

'How did the family find out about it?' Nayir asked.

'Someone at the Coroner's office knows the family and called them to break the news.'

Nayir nodded, still feeling numb. The teapot was empty. Slowly he stood and went to the stove. He poured more water into the pot and lit the match for the stove with a clumsy twitch, burning the tip of his thumb. The sharpness of the pain lit a spark inside him, a quick, fierce anger. The urge to find her was still strong. *Forgive me for my pride*, he thought. *I should think about the family now.* But he couldn't.

He went back and sat down. 'Do you know how she died?'

'No.' There was a sad acceptance in the boy's eyes. 'Heat stroke, I imagine.'

'It's a terrible way to die,' Nayir said. 'I can't help thinking there's something we could have done.'

'I doubt it.'

'Why?' Nayir asked. 'What do you think happened to her?'

The Bedouin looked him straight in the eye. 'Same thing that happens to any girl, I think.'

'And what's that?' Nayir asked. *Love? Sex? What do you know about it?* Ibrahim's face told him that it had been wrong to ask; the boy was blushing. Nayir wanted to know more, to pry the answers out of him, but he knew, too, that if Nouf's death had happened because of love or sex, then any truthful reply would be less proper still. Modestly, he waited for an elaboration, but Ibrahim merely sipped his tea, resolute in his silence.

2

Dank and grubby, Rawashin Alley could not have less resembled a depot of Paradise, a way-station for bodies on their way to Allah. Yet the Coroner's building was there, tucked between two ugly office buildings and looking rather like a cousin of both. The upper part of the Seventies-era structure was grey and boxy with round concrete protrusions that partially shielded a column of tinted windows. Iron bars crisscrossed the façade. The effect was like viewing cracked eggshells in a cage. The lower floor was windowless, a sheer slab of concrete interrupted only by a pair of metal doors and a security-code panel. Nayir had tried the doors already, spoken to an elderly guard, and been directed to a stairway at the side of the building.

Incongruously, the basement exterior was like an advertisement for the Old Jeddah Restoration Society. It ran the length of the building and contained some of the famous bay windows for which the street was named. The *rawashin* displayed teak latticework and shallow arched headings. Peeling paint curled from the stone walls beneath them. At the bottom of the stairs, a single wooden door was propped open, revealing folds of darkness within.

Loitering at the foot of the stairway, Nayir gathered his wits by chewing a peppery miswak and spitting its bristles onto the ground. He told himself that he had to go inside, there was no way around it. The sun beat down, and he was sweating in a painful way, as if his skin were oozing nails. This visit wasn't just a favour for the Shrawis – which was what he had been telling himself the whole way there; this was, he now realized, an invasion of privacy. Nouf's corpse was inside, and it was his job to take her home.

He had spent all night in the desert wrestling with his failure. While his body sought much-needed sleep, his mind gnawed stubbornly on the myriad decisions he could have made, commands he could have issued, instincts he could have followed that might have saved her life. He'd finally fallen asleep around 5 a.m. only to wake abruptly an hour later to find that his frustration had dissolved into pity and guilt. There was nothing he could do for Nouf now, but however unlikely it was that he could still assist her family, he felt compelled to try.

He'd spent his morning prayers meditating. The Shrawis were too modest, too private to appreciate a display of condolence. It had to be something useful and quiet. As he packed up his equipment, loaded his Jeep and drove back into the city, he scoured his thoughts for the perfect gesture, but the exhaustion of the past week was taking its toll. It was only when Jeddah came into view that his energy began to return, and with it a tentative idea: Nouf's body might still be at the Coroner's. The Shrawi sons would have just returned from the desert themselves; they would be distraught and exhausted. They would probably send servants to pick up the body, or perhaps someone from the mosque. How degrading to think of the parade of strangers' hands and eyes that had already swept over her corpse. Would the family not prefer that someone close to them handle Nouf's final trip home?

From the Jeep he phoned Othman and fumbled through the question: *Would you need – would it be all right, I thought I might help, if she's still at the Coroner's . . .?*

'Thank you so much,' Othman said quietly. 'It would be an enormous help.'

The tone of relief in his voice prompted Nayir to say: 'Just tell me what to do.'

Now staring at the bay window's intricate latticework, his body weary but his mind perversely growing sharper as the minutes ticked by, Nayir confronted the less pleasant reasons he'd come. Morbid curiosity. The need for a sense of closure. A desire to prove himself capable of *something*. It was the selfishness of this last reason that weighed on him most.

The family is waiting.

Flicking his miswak into the gutter, he marshalled himself and entered the building only to find another set of stairs. He descended these with both hands pressed firmly to the wall. After the nuclear white of the day, the darkness was sudden and total.

Once his eyes adjusted, he saw a security guard reading at his desk. The sight of the plain brown uniform and the surly face above it unsettled him. This was the building's real security. Slicing and prodding a dead human body was forbidden by law, and while the government quietly sanctioned autopsies, there would always be vigilantes hunting for un-Muslim behaviour.

Seeing Nayir, the guard narrowed his eyes. Nayir approached the desk and looked behind its occupant, down a single long hallway that was dimly lit with fluorescent lights. 'I'm here to pick up a body.' He fished in his pocket for the official release form he'd received from one of the Shrawi servants that afternoon.

The guard studied the paper carefully, folded it, and handed it back. 'She's down the hall,' he said.

'Which—?'

The man raised an eyebrow and pointed behind him to the only corridor in view. Nayir nodded. He tried to relax. He wiped the sweat from his neck and approached a pair of swing doors at the end of the hall. When he opened them, the smell hit him like a slap: ammonia, death, blood, and something else just as foul. Forcing a swallow, he thought he could taste sulphur from the brimstone that the Bedouin sometimes used to purify departing souls. *No*, he thought, *that's my imagination.* The room was sterile and bright. In the centre stood a medical examiner bent over a body on the table. He was a lanky man with a cap of grey hair a shade darker than his lab coat. He looked up. '*Salaam aleikum.*'

'*W'aleikum as-salaam.*' Nayir felt dizzy and tried not to look at the body. He turned his gaze to the cabinets, packed with textbooks, gauze, empty glass jars.

'Can I help you?' the examiner asked.

'I understand you have the girl who—'

'Are you family?'

'No, I'm not. No.' Irrationally, Nayir felt like a pervert. He had the urge to explain that he was there out of duty, not desire. The air was hot and close; he could smell the corpse and it was making him sick. The edges of his vision flickered with darkness. He took a deep breath and turned to see a blood-smeared smock hanging on the wall.

'Then you're not allowed in here,' the examiner said.

'I have permission to see the body. I have to see – I mean, I have to pick it up.' He ran a hand down his face. 'I'm here to pick up the body.'

The examiner dropped his scalpel in a silver tray and regarded Nayir with frustration. 'We're not done with it. You're just going to have to wait.'

Nayir was vaguely relieved. 'Before I take her, I'd like to make sure that it's really her.'

'It's her.' The examiner, seeing Nayir's reluctance, came around the table. 'Let me see your papers. Nouf Ash-Shrawi, right?' He took the papers from Nayir and read them carefully. 'Yes, she's the one.' He motioned to the table behind him.

Nayir hesitated, uncomfortable with his next remark. 'I'd like to see her face.'

The examiner stared at him, and Nayir realized that he'd crossed a line, that the examiner now thought he was a pervert even if he did have the right papers.

'Only because it's a matter of principle,' Nayir said.

'She's already been identified.'

Nayir read the man's nametag: *Abdullah Maamoon, Medical Examiner.* He was just about to speak again when the door opened behind them, and a woman entered the room. There would, of course, be female examiners to handle the female corpses, but seeing one in the flesh was a shock. She wore a white lab coat and a *hijab,* a black scarf on her hair. Because her face was exposed, he averted his gaze, blushing as he did so. Uncertain where to rest his eyes, he let them fall on the plastic ID tag that hung round her neck: *Katya Hijazi, Laboratory Technician.* He was surprised to see her first name on the tag – it should have been as private as her hair or the shape of her body – and it made her seem defiant.

Worried that the older man might think he was staring at her breasts, Nayir dropped his gaze to the floor, catching sight of two shapely feet ensconced in bright blue sandals. He blushed again and turned away from her, trying not to turn completely but just enough to indicate that he wouldn't look at her.

The woman's shoulders drooped slightly, which seemed

to indicate that she'd noticed Nayir's discomfort and was disappointed by it. Reaching into her pocket, she took out a burqa, draped it over her face, and fastened the Velcro at the back of her head. Pleased by the action, but still uncomfortable with her presence in the room, Nayir watched her from the periphery of his vision. Once the burqa was on, and it was all right to glance at her, he dared a peek, but a slit in the burqa showed her eyes, and she looked right at him. He quickly glanced away, disturbed by her forwardness.

'*Salaam aleikum*, Dr Maamoon,' she said, approaching the examiner. Her voice was challenging. 'You haven't been giving Mr Sharqi a hard time, have you?'

Nayir hoped his confusion didn't show. How did she know his name? And what sort of woman wielded a strange man's name so confidently? The guard must have told her. But why?

The examiner was piqued by her forwardness and grumbled unintelligibly. She must have been a new employee, not yet used to dealing with the more traditional old man.

'Oh, good,' the woman said, 'because he's here to pick up the body.'

Maamoon shot Nayir a suspicious look. 'So he said.'

Miss Hijazi turned to Nayir. She was standing right next to him, a little closer than was appropriate, he thought. 'How are you going to transport her?' she asked.

He hesitated, unwilling to speak directly to her. He glanced down and caught a glimpse of her hand. She was wearing a wedding band, or perhaps an engagement ring; he couldn't tell. The fact that she had a husband made her presence here slightly easier to take – but only slightly.

Nayir spoke to the examiner. 'I have a Jeep parked outside, but I'd like to identify the body before I leave with it.'

'All right,' Miss Hijazi answered. Nayir thought it was brazen of her to talk when she was not being spoken to, but her professional manner surprised him. Women, even the forward ones, usually regarded him as an animal of some sort – his tall and hulking frame, his deep, rough voice. But this one, although she stepped carefully around him, seemed at ease. 'We've already identified her, you know.'

Nayir's stomach flopped. She seemed determined to start a conversation, but he kept his eyes on Maamoon, wishing the old man would talk to him. Instead he stood there looking suspicious. 'I want to see the body myself,' Nayir said, thinking: *At this point, all I really want to do is leave.*

'She's on the table now. You can have a look.'

Miss Hijazi led him to the metal table where Nouf's body lay and pulled the sheet from her face. When Nayir looked down, he felt another wave of dizziness but remembered to breathe. At first, he didn't see any resemblance to Nouf, but as he studied the contours of her face, he began to see it – the small, careful mouth, the high Shrawi cheekbones.

'I think it's her.' He coughed as the smell rose up and engulfed him. Poor girl. Her face was half-charred from the sun, and the other half was a ghastly grey. She must have been lying on her side for days; the burns were extreme. The grey side, however, was spattered with mud. 'Thank you,' he said, stepping back.

Miss Hijazi inspected Nouf's head. Nayir noticed something sticky in her hair just above the left ear. He turned to Maamoon and asked: 'Is that blood?'

Maamoon simply shrugged while Miss Hijazi continued inspecting the wound. 'Yes,' she answered finally. 'There's bruising. It looks like someone hit her pretty hard. And there's something else . . .' With a pair of tweezers, she plucked a tiny sliver from the wound and held it up. 'Looks like a wood chip.'

Nayir felt a strange agitation. He kept his eyes on the examiner. 'Was that wound the cause of death?'

'No,' said Maamoon. 'She drowned.'

A silence ensued, but Maamoon, his eyes flashing with a professional delight, pointed to an X-ray on the wall that showed Nouf's chest. Nayir studied the X-ray, not sure what to make of it. 'She drowned?'

'That's what I said. A classic case. Foam in the mouth. Her lungs and stomach were filled with water.'

The simplicity of 'drowning' begged all sorts of questions. At least, when a woman drowns in the largest sand desert in the world, there ought to be an equally remarkable explanation.

'If she drowned,' Nayir said, 'then how do you explain the wound on her head?'

The examiner bristled. 'She must have bumped it.'

'While she was drowning?'

'Yes, *while she was drowning*.'

During this exchange, Miss Hijazi continued to probe Nouf's scalp. Nayir noticed that her hands were unsteady. He dared a look at her eyes and saw a frown. 'If this wound is from the drowning,' she said finally, 'then there must be other wounds like it on her body.'

Nayir marvelled at her audacity and wondered how the examiner could put up with it. He glanced at her nametag again, noticing this time that she was a lab technician, not a medical examiner. What exactly was the difference?

'It rained a week ago, did it not?' Maamoon asked.

'Almost two weeks ago,' Nayir answered. 'The day she disappeared there was rain. How long has she been dead?'

'It's difficult to say.'

Nayir could feel the woman's gaze on his face, but he kept his attention on Maamoon. 'Is it possible to say whether the bump on her head occurred when she was still alive?'

'Yes,' the woman said.

Nayir waited for an elaboration but she didn't provide one. A silence ensued, and Miss Hijazi gently moved the sheet from Nouf's arms. When she turned her attention to a series of bruises on the wrists and hands, Nayir allowed himself to watch. She swabbed one of the lesions. 'Looks like sand,' she said. 'There's something beneath her fingernails, too. These look like defensive wounds.'

'No, no, no,' Maamoon clucked, pushing her aside and pointing to one of Nouf's wrists. 'Those marks are from a camel's reins. Don't you see the pattern?'

Nayir studied the wounds more closely. They weren't uniform, and Nouf had scratches on her fingertips as well. 'They look like defensive wounds to me.'

Maamoon grew stern. 'I *said* they're from leather *straps*.'

Miss Hijazi placed a swab in a glass tube and set it gently on the counter. Turning back to the body, she paused for a moment and then gingerly lifted the edge of the grey sheet that covered Nouf's legs. She held it in the air and studied the body for a long time. Nayir watched her eyes move over it, as carefully and sensitively as her hands, and it surprised him to see that she was touched by this death. There was a sadness in her eyes that spoke of personal loss, and he wondered if she had known the family and if she was the one who had informed them.

Finally, she laid down the sheet. When she spoke, her voice was questioning, reluctant, a sharp contrast to her words. 'I see no evidence that she touched a camel. No hairs on the body, no abrasions on her thighs.' Maamoon tried to interrupt her but she continued: 'I don't have much experience estimating time of death, but I'd guess she's been dead at least a week.'

'Of course!' Maamoon snapped. 'Considering how often it rains in the desert, I'd say she died when it rained. Here's what happened. The wadis filled up, she was crossing the desert through one of those wadis and – *shack!* – it started to rain. She tried to swim, but a flash flood carried her away. She banged her head; she hurt her wrists. *Yanni*, she drowned.'

Nayir studied the examiner. 'But she had a camel.'

'So what?' he cried. 'Camels can't swim!'

Which was completely untrue. Gorillas were the only animals incapable of swimming. Camels, despite infrequent contact with water, happened to excel at the sport. Nayir had seen it himself at the Dromedary Rehabilitation Centre in Dubai, where the therapists encouraged their patients into pools to heal broken bones and soothe arthritic joints. Once in the water, the camels frolicked like children and even grew angry when the sessions ended. *Why*, they seemed to ask, *did Allah craft our bodies to live out of water?*

'Camels swim,' he said. 'And the camel would have saved her life.' Nayir fumbled in his pocket for another miswak and stuffed it into his mouth, grateful for the spicy taste which took away some of the odour of death. He chewed for a while and circled the table. Nouf's right hand stuck out from under the sheet. The wrist was splattered with a brownish mud. It seemed to have been baked into her skin by the heat. 'What is this?' he asked.

'It looks like mud,' Miss Hijazi said. She scraped samples of the skin into a jar.

Maamoon snatched the jar. 'She *drowned*, my friends. Mr Sharqi, are you convinced that it's her?'

Nayir stopped chewing. 'Yes, it's her. But that's strange about the camel.'

Maamoon shrugged. 'Maybe they got separated, say, before she entered the wadi?'

'No one loses a camel in the desert. That's suicide.'

'I did not suggest suicide!' the old man yelped.

'Neither did I,' Nayir said.

The examiner narrowed his eyes. 'Don't even *say* it. It's ridiculous! You think she was murdered?'

Nayir raised his eyebrows.

'How? I mean . . . *how*?' Maamoon choked on his spit and coughed. 'Someone would have to wait for the particular condition of this woman being in a wadi, alone, in the middle of the desert, without any camel, and it would have to rain and there would also have to be a flash flood at the very same time. And then this killer, who is by Allah a very patient man, would have to find a way to drown her in the flood without actually drowning himself. Who would do that? Why not just stab her and be done with it?'

No one replied. Nayir stole a glance at Miss Hijazi's eyes and found them inscrutable. The examiner was right – murder by drowning seemed far-fetched. Had Nouf found a water source and died in her desperation to take a drink? Perhaps she'd entered a flooded wadi. The rain had been strong, and he remembered being grateful for it, thinking it might just give her a chance to survive.

'Is there anything else?' the old man snapped, glaring at Nayir.

'I just wondered if everything else was okay?' he said. 'With the body, I mean . . . was she *okay*?'

Maamoon grimaced. Nayir realized that the examiner felt deeply pressured by his question. It gave him an odd feeling of power, even if it was only the result of the authority conferred upon him by the family.

'I know what you're asking,' the examiner said, 'and we haven't got that far. Although she is not actually a medical examiner, Miss Hijazi' – he said the name pejoratively – 'is here to do an ultrasound.' Abruptly, he whipped back the sheet to reveal Nouf's whole body. Nayir blanched and lowered his eyes, but it didn't prevent him from catching sight of everything – the hips, the legs, the pubis. Searching desperately for somewhere to rest his gaze, he caught sight of a tube of jelly, a syringe, and a metal instrument that looked dangerously like a phallus.

'Thank you,' he said abruptly. 'I think I'll wait outside.' As he turned to the door, he stopped. The room was spinning. He sucked in a chest full of air and bent over, hands gripping his knees, forehead pounding. His heart felt like a stone in a can. He imagined that single chasm between the girl's legs but that moment bled strangely into the next, in which he found himself lying on the floor, head thumping.

'Mr Sharqi!' Maamoon was kneeling beside him, holding a bottle of camphor to his nose. 'Mr Sharqi, Allah protect you, you're an honest man.'

'Water,' Nayir croaked.

'I'll get you some!' Shaking his head, Maamoon stood up and left the room.

Nayir struggled to his feet, pausing as he stood to make sure he wouldn't faint again.

Miss Hijazi seemed upset. 'I'm sorry, Mr Sharqi.'

He was too embarrassed to reply, but at least she had the decency to go about her business. She took a fingerprint kit from the cabinet and, pulling a chair up to the table, she sat down and began taking Nouf's prints.

A long silence went by and he looked down at Nouf, or what used to be Nouf. The body was now safely beneath the sheet, but he still felt nauseous and had to look away.

'Why do you need to do an ultrasound?' he asked, keeping his eyes away from Miss Hijazi's face.

'Maybe you'd better sit down?' she suggested.

He was too startled by her forwardness to give a reply.

'You're here to pick up the body,' she said, 'so pick up the body and forget about the rest. The case is closed; they've decided it was an accidental death. As Maamoon said, I am not really an examiner. The real examiner is on maternity leave. I'm only here because they couldn't find a replacement, and they need a woman to supervise the job. But because this is an important case, they brought Maamoon in from Riyadh, and he decided the death was caused by drowning. So drowning it is. No need to ask questions. It's done.'

The sarcasm in her voice surprised him. 'You think it is a cover-up?' he asked. She shrugged. If it were true, then the family would have to be behind it. They were the only people powerful enough. He could think of a few reasons the Shrawis would want to hide the truth, but the biggest reason of all was right in front of him.

He hesitated before asking. 'She wasn't a virgin?'

Miss Hijazi finished the fingerprints and packed up the kit. She stood and returned the kit to the wall. Nayir waited, hoping she would give him something, but when she turned back in his direction, he quickly looked away. He wished there were a way he could persuade her to trust him, but she was right not to. He was a stranger, and a man. Grudgingly, he acknowledged the decency of her silence, rebellious though it seemed.

He looked at his watch. It was three-fifteen. Nouf had to be in the ground by sunset. He had less than an hour to get the body to the Shrawi estate; the family would need another hour to prepare it for burial.

Maamoon came bustling in with a glass of water. It tasted like soap, but Nayir didn't complain. The old man clapped him on the back and gave a sympathetic frown. 'It's not that bad when they're alive, you know, don't let it spoil you.'

☽

The best of women, the Prophet said, *is the one who is pleasing to look at, who carries out your instructions when you ask her.* The phrase ran through his mind as he pulled his Jeep out of the cargo bay at the back of the building and took a left into traffic. Although the Prophet was right, it seemed there was also a way of being righteous without being obedient. Miss Hijazi's silence at the end of the visit weighed on him.

He thought back on her earlier behaviour, which he still considered brazen, although he wondered if that, too, was conducted in the spirit of protecting Nouf. Miss Hijazi had argued with Maamoon about how Nouf had died, about her camel, about the cause of the wound on her head. Nayir couldn't be sure whether her boldness was in Nouf's best interests, or whether it was carried out because of professional egotism, or because that was simply the sort of person she was. His instincts told him that the former was the case, and that she was guarding secrets for Nouf's sake.

Anyway, she was right about one thing. Defensive wounds. Head trauma. Drowning, no camel. It sounded strange. The camel part was especially troubling, because if he knew anything, he knew that no one lost a camel in the desert.

3

Driving south along the beachfront road, Nayir watched the city's skyscrapers and urban jumble give way to a lazy desert sprawl. To the left, tiny cottages dotted fields that lay barren in the afternoon sun, and over to the right, the sea fluttered like a blue satin scarf. Keeping his eyes on the landscape, he was hoping to forget that Nouf's body was in the back, yet how could he ignore it? He drove slowly, took turns carefully, and obeyed every traffic light despite an absence of traffic, for though it might not be possible to upset the dead, it would be a grievous act to upset the living by injuring or mauling a beloved daughter's corpse.

He left the freeway and turned onto an access road that followed the shoreline south. Here a magnificent mosque stood alone by the beach, its dome pure white, its minaret slim. The road turned into a private drive, marked by a wooden 'No Trespassing' sign, and he drove until he reached the tower gates, two white concrete sentinels with an iron fence between them. An ancient, broken video camera hung askew from one of the gates.

Nayir took a few deep breaths and tried to focus. A two-kilometre bridge stretched out before him. It was narrow – barely wide enough for a pick-up truck – and from the shoreline perspective it appeared to be made of rubber. Under the glare of the heat, the macadam rippled like a roller-coaster. The chain-link railing gave him no comfort – in some places it had been ripped apart, exactly as if a car had blown through it. This was the only motor access to the estate. Over the years, he'd crossed this bridge a hundred times, but it still made him uneasy.

He drove forward slowly, eyes fixed on the road, taking one breath after another until he picked up a rhythm. He tried to suppress his usual image – blowing a tyre, crashing through the fence, dropping into the murky sea – and soon the Shrawis' island grew larger. Glancing up, he could see the soft contours of the whitewashed palace set among jagged rocks.

Once on the island, he followed the gravel road that led to a small, seldom-used service entrance on the estate's west side. Two men were waiting there. They took Nouf's body out of his trunk, thanked him curtly, and told him to drive back around to the front. Watching his cargo disappear through the gate, Nayir felt a surprising sense of loss.

He thought of calling Othman to let him know that the body had arrived, but he hesitated, wondering what the family already knew about the cause of her death. It occurred to him that he might be asked to explain what he'd learned at the Coroner's office. The examiner had said that someone from the family had already identified the body and come to collect Nouf's belongings, but that could have been a servant or an escort, not someone who would press for sensitive information. Nayir wasn't sure what he would say to them. He might explain that Nouf had died in a flood, but he was wary of saying anything that implied she was murdered, in case they had been responsible for the cover-up, if that's what it was. Looking up at the house, he felt disoriented. He'd never really noticed it from this perspective before; the outside walls were the same shiny white, but the windows were smaller, their screens a solid black, nothing like the elaborate wooden screens at the front of the house through which it was possible to view certain things, if one looked carefully. *This must be the women's part of the house.*

He got into the Jeep and drove away from the service gate. It occurred to him that Nouf would have driven down this road. Othman said she had stolen a truck from the parking lot in front of the house, although Nayir had to imagine the rest himself. There were dozens of cars in the lot that the family owned but seldom used. It would have taken days for anyone to notice the absence of an old Toyota pickup. All of the car keys hung in the cloakroom by the front door. They were meticulously labelled. Nayir often fetched them himself while preparing trucks for the men's desert trips. When no one was looking, Nouf could have stolen the keys from the cloakroom, sneaked outside and taken the truck.

From there, she had to drive down the access road, past the small service entrance to the rear gate, a large wooden door that was usually open. She would hardly have been noticed on the road. It was bordered by hedges and trees. The house itself sat so high above, and was surrounded by such steep cliffs, that most of the time it was difficult to see the road even from the terraces. The stables were just inside the rear gate. He imagined that she drove right up to the stable door, took the camel out of her stall, and encouraged – forced? – her into the back of the truck. How that happened was a mystery to him. Once it was done, she would have driven back along the service road and past the front parking lot, where she could have got onto the bridge with very little chance of being seen. It wasn't a foolproof plan for running away, but she'd left while most of the men were at work. The women seldom ventured outside, and so probably hadn't noticed anything. Only the servants might have seen her, but Othman had already told him that no one had.

Nayir pulled into the marble-topped parking lot near the estate's front entrance. A multitude of town cars, Cadillacs and Rovers crowded the lot, forcing him to circle back toward the bridge for a spot. He didn't mind parking so far from the house – there was less chance that people would notice his ugly, rusted-out Jeep – but as he walked across the lot, shoes clacking loudly, he began to wish there'd been a spot by the door. The heat was intense, and in his suit it was excruciating. He wondered for the millionth time how much the family had paid to construct a polished marble parking lot. The glare was so bright that Nayir, who prided himself on never needing sunglasses, was forced to place his hand across the bridge of his nose to shield his eyes.

Othman's mother, Nusra, met him at the door. Like many older women, she had relinquished a face veil and wore a simple black scarf to cover her hair – hers fastened so tightly that it looked like a skullcap. Her deeply lined face posed no threat to strange men, was certainly no cause for erotic alarm, but her sons complained anyway, fussing over the impropriety of exposing herself in public. Nayir suspected that their protests were not about propriety; he believed they were repulsed by her eyes.

Inexplicably blinded while giving birth to her first child, Nusra refused to wear sunglasses. She liked to feel the light on her face and claimed it could illuminate the darkness in her head. One day, she said, her vision would snap on as abruptly as it had snapped off thirty-three years ago, and when that day came, how would she notice the miraculous change if her eyes were hidden?

When she opened the door, Nayir looked away out of respect and because the sight of those enamelled, blue-rimmed eyes made his spine seize up. He was surprised that she would answer the door. She should have been sur-rounded by comforting women, suffering paroxysms of silent grief.

'Nayir,' she crowed. (How did she know? She always knew.) '*Ahlan wa'Sahlan*. Please come in.'

He stepped through the giant doorway and remembered himself. 'Many blessings on you, Um-Tahsin. I'm deeply sorry for your loss.'

'Thank you.' She fumbled for his hand, took it in her own and stroked the flat of his palm, her rough, dry fingers catching his skin. 'Thank you for everything. Your search for Nouf brought us hope when we had none.'

'It was an honour.'

'Please come in.' She led Nayir down the hallway, her steps as confident as a child's. 'I always know when it's you because the air in the house becomes fresher, happier. And I can smell the desert on your skin.'

'What does it smell like?' he asked.

'Sunlight.' She opened a door and motioned him into the sitting room. 'And dust.'

He looked around. The crowd was thinning, and he didn't see Othman among the men. Small groups of cousins and uncles, most wearing headscarves and long white *thobes*, were wandering onto the terrace that surrounded the house, whispering to one another, their faces stoic and respectful. Nayir had half expected to find the brothers sitting quietly with tear-stained faces, but that was ridiculous. Of course they wouldn't let their feelings show.

'The ceremony begins soon,' Nusra said. 'But mean-while, rest.'

Nayir turned to thank her, but she'd slipped away.

☽

The Shrawi women had cleaned Nouf's body and wrapped it in the *kafan* she'd worn on the Hajj the summer before. The white sheet, long and unbroken by stitching or seams, circled her slender body in three tight bands. The women placed the body on a wooden board in the central courtyard of the family's mosque, the cleanest room on the island.

Nouf's head was facing Mecca by the precise calculations of the GPS system that the builders had used to construct the mosque. The entire room jutted at an awkward north-easterly angle from the house, but the builders had promised that the room was in perfect alignment with the Ka'aba in the Holy Mosque, some hundred kilometres distant.

The right side of the room was closest to Jeddah, to the mountains and the desert beyond that. This was where Nayir stood, waiting for the prayers to begin. Just ahead of him, the Shrawi brothers formed a dignified crowd. Nayir was the only non-family member in the group – at least among the men – and this distinction pleased him almost too much on so grim an occasion. Behind them, the women stood in a cluster. From the corner of his eye, Nayir noticed that some were not veiled completely – their eyes were showing – and he kept his gaze firmly on the men.

Suddenly, the imam put his hands to his ears and invoked one of the ninety-nine names of Allah, *Al-Haseeb, the Reckoner.* As his prayers began, all the members of the congregation placed their hands on their bellies, right over left, and began to whisper their own versions of the prayer. As the prayer expanded, the chanting grew fiercer and the women grew louder, some even breaking from traditional prayers to utter spontaneous pleas. Above the clamour Nayir heard Nusra repeating the prayer: *Oh Allah, make the end of my life the best of my life, and the best of my deeds, their conclusion, and the best of my days the day on which I shall meet Thee.* Her voice was so powerful that the men began to hush. It reverberated through the open room and overcame the crashing waves on the rocks below.

When she was finished, she called out one last thing, her voice rising to the roof like a scurrilous wind: *Works are accomplished according to intentions. A man receives only what he intends.*

It was not clear why she uttered this phrase; surely Nusra would never send her daughter to the gates of Paradise with a thought as cynical as that one. It must have been meant for somebody else. Unable to turn around and look at her face without humiliating himself, Nayir made assumptions about her meaning by studying the faces of her sons, who stood nearby in a militant row. Even from the side, they projected the same anger that had shocked Nayir in their mother's voice, and in that precise moment he realized that the family must have known that someone killed Nouf, and that the killer was still at large.

Othman caught his eye, and Nayir quickly returned to his prayers. Once they were finished, he followed the procession out to the burial grounds. Nouf was the first Shrawi to be laid in the earth on that Red Sea isle, but the family had constructed a spacious graveyard, fenced by a black stone wall. A thick layer of cedar chips covered the earth except where the diggers had opened her grave.

Once the diggers had laid the body in the hole and climbed back up to join the living, the family lined up to pay their final respects. From the back of their hands, each person tossed a portion of sand onto her body, which was still wrapped in the *kafan*. A coffin would be vanity.

From a white ceramic bowl, Nayir scooped out a tea-spoon of sand and spread it on the back of his hand. It was a very fine grain, a shade lighter than his skin. The diggers must have carried it up from the beach. The sand's touch brought back memories of the desert, when he'd still believed that Nouf was alive, when he imagined she might be in hiding.

Reaching the grave, he noticed something odd. The sand had not obscured the position of the body. She was wrapped completely in the *kafan*, but a slight bend in the knees indicated which way she was facing. He tossed his sand into the hole and fumbled in his pocket for his compass. A quick glance determined that he was right: Nouf's back was turned to Mecca. Not her feet, but her *back*. He mumbled a blessing and turned away.

The image disturbed him. If what he suspected was true, why hadn't Miss Hijazi told him?

A family buries a woman with her back to Mecca only when she carries a baby in her belly, a baby whose face, in death, must be turned in the direction of the Holy Mosque.

4

Nayir entered the men's sitting room and stood for a moment facing the courtyard. A network of hand-carved mahogany screens laced the room, and through their geometric web flowed the sound of gurgling fountains. In the centre of each screen was a religious phrase carved in the shape of a spinning hawk. The letters and diacritics wrapped around one another like wings and feathers, clouds and sun. For most men who entered the room, the screen's picture was simply a hawk; but a searching, patient eye would find the phrase that Nayir had deciphered long ago: *Whoever pays the tax on his wealth will have its evil removed from him.*

It was a reference to the Shrawi business, the First Muslim International Cooperative, a network of charitable organizations whose income flowed from the ancient principle of *zakat*, religious almsgiving. Saudis gave two and a half per cent of all monthly earnings as alms, a practice enforced by law. Every year some ten billion dollars passed from rich to poor. It was money for needy Muslims, not for hospitals or mosques or religious schools, and so, under law, the Cooperative could accept donations only for the poor.

And accept they did. They acquired nearly a quarter of

the cash and assets that the citizens of Jeddah found fit to donate. Over the years, the Shrawi Cooperative had become so renowned, the family so respected, that the donors began to heap money on the Shrawis themselves, which allowed them to live very well.

But in honour of their Bedouin ancestry, their furnishings were elegant and plain. Except for a glass globe that hung from the ceiling, the sitting rooms where they welcomed guests had none of the typically ostentatious décor of the wealthy. The carpets were flat and white, the sofas well used. Even the water tray was simple: white ceramic mugs, a bamboo tray. *God himself is graceful*, the Prophet said, *and elegance pleases Him.*

The Shrawi sons lived by this code, which their father taught them with unrelenting drive. Abu-Tahsin was a Bedouin who'd grown up in the desert, where a man kept only what he could carry. He believed that nothing material was worth having. 'You can't take it with you when you die,' he would say. 'Remember that! No baggage on the final journey.' He was well known for giving things away, not just money, but cars and boats and purebred horses. The sons, too, gave their belongings away, so that the family was, in effect, a channel through which vast treasures flowed but never quite rested.

And that, thought Nayir, *is why I can stand them.*

He heard shuffling in the hallway. The door opened and the Shrawi brothers entered the room with two other men, whom Nayir vaguely recognized as cousins. The brothers greeted him with hugs and a kiss on each cheek. Had he been blind, he could have identified them by their colognes alone – Tahsin wore Gucci, Fahad wore Giorgio. But when he kissed Othman, he smelled a musk that suggested a sweaty sleep.

The eldest brother, Tahsin, introduced the cousins, one

of whom shook Nayir's hand with a jerk and said: 'You're the Bedouin I'm always hearing about!'

'Nayir's not a Bedouin,' Othman remarked.

'Oh, what are you then?' the cousin asked, his tone suggesting the existence of a new and fantastical race that would be even funnier and more backwards than the Bedouin.

'Palestinian,' Othman said, pre-empting Nayir.

'Ah, Palestinian.' The cousin plunked onto a sofa and glanced up at Nayir, who stood uncomfortably in the centre of the room. There was nothing funny about a Palestinian. All eyes scanned his ill-fitting suit, and Nayir wondered for the thousandth time what it was about him that made people stare. Perhaps it was his size, which, coupled with a stern manner, made him seem unfriendly. Either that or he looked like a dolt, a dusty, under-stimulated man who had spent too long in the stupefying heat.

'It's good to see you, Nayir. Please, sit down.' Tahsin spread his arm in a generous arc, gathered his robe in his fist, and settled onto a sofa. He laid his manicured hands on his lap, one hand poised to fidget with the mammoth ring on his pinky. 'We would offer something, but—'

Nayir raised a hand. It was gauche to offer well-wishers food until three days after the funeral. Othman motioned him to sit on one of the white foam cushions that hemmed the room, and Nayir accepted with relief.

He dared a glance at Othman. He was the only brother wearing trousers – the others wore robes – but he looked no more formal; in fact, his shirt was wrinkled and one sleeve was rolled up. Normally, he did his best to look and act like his brothers. He was an adopted son, and perhaps more inclined to prove that he belonged, or at least to prevent anyone from noticing his difference. He was taller than the others, thinner too, and his large grey eyes were certainly a rarity among the brown-eyed Shrawis. But in his sitting-room behaviour he was an impeccable Shrawi – cool, reserved, quietly pious.

Once water had been served, Nayir felt the familiar gloom of etiquette descend. He knew his place here. He was the desert guide, the outside friend whose presence imposed the burden of *noblesse oblige* on the family's sons. Nayir glanced at Othman, his only ally. Othman looked sallow and tired, but he met Nayir's eye with a look that seemed to say: *We have much to discuss.*

Nayir had a million questions for him, but he wouldn't ask them in front of the others. He wondered especially what would happen with Othman's wedding; he was supposed to be married next month. Had they decided to postpone?

Politely, Nayir enquired about Othman's father, Abu-Tahsin, who had undergone heart surgery a week ago – some said because of his daughter's flight – and was politely informed that Father would be home by next week, Allah willing.

Abu-Tahsin's attack had taken everyone by surprise. In all the years Nayir had known him, he'd seemed as healthy as a man half his age. He worked tirelessly for his charities, and in his spare time raced camels, motorcycles, and all-terrain vehicles. His interest in his sons had never flagged, and he took them wherever he went. By the time they were men, they knew their world well and were just as easy in the palaces of Riyadh as they were in scuba gear at the bottom of the sea. It was because of Abu-Tahsin that the family made twice-yearly excursions to the desert.

Tahsin turned to Nayir. 'Brother, thank you for coming. What you've done for Nouf puts us in your debt. I hope you'll give us the chance to return the favour one day.'

Nayir cleared his throat. 'May the day never come.'

'Indeed,' Tahsin said. Whenever Nayir sat with the brothers, Tahsin did the talking. He was the oldest, and perhaps used to taking charge of things, but in appearance and manner he came across as an oddly self-effacing man. He never looked Nayir in the eye but kept his gaze down. He spoke clearly but softly, and his face reminded Nayir of prey, that delicate mouth unused to vicious acts, the eyes widely spaced to keep watch for danger. Nayir went back and forth between thinking that Tahsin was humble and thinking that it was all an act, because when Tahsin wanted a certain result, he got it.

'I regret the outcome of my search,' Nayir said. Tahsin clucked his tongue, but Nayir pushed on. 'I had hoped to find her.'

'We rest assured of your intentions!' Tahsin exclaimed.

Nayir weighed his next words carefully. 'I had also hoped to satisfy your curiosity about why she left.' He glanced at his company and saw that their faces were impenetrable masks. Only Othman showed discomfort, but he didn't meet Nayir's eye.

'We will never understand why she ran away,' said Tahsin, settling his bulk deeper into the cushion's folds. 'A girl like my sister, so naïve and pristine, so *untouched* by the world. Do you know I never saw her cry? Or frown? Or even turn down her lip? She was bliss in a girl's body, as virtuous as her mother, *ism'allah*, my Nouf. It's not real. Not even now, with her body as evidence.'

'Yes,' Fahad added, his voice whiskery and shy. Everyone turned to him, surprised that he'd spoken. 'We thought she'd been kidnapped. We thought: *She'd never leave on her own!* But then it became obvious when we discovered the camel . . . gone. She'd run away.'

'There was never a clue,' Tahsin continued. 'Some passion drove her, but I can recall no evidence of passion in my sister. None!'

'None confided, at least,' Othman remarked.

An awkward silence took hold. No one looked at Othman, and the brothers seemed to draw into themselves.

Nayir was inclined to agree with Othman's assessment. Of course Nouf had passions, they just didn't know what those were. He felt no empathy for brothers who had only the vaguest, most superficial impression of their sisters. Certainly, women had other concerns. They lived in a different manner, in other parts of the house. He imagined that their lives barely intersected except during meals, holidays, excursions. But there was no taboo against talking to a sister. A sister, he imagined, should be the most comforting of women – an accessible female with whom one could speak openly, who could explain sensitive things where others might shy from trying. Nayir had no siblings, but he had longed for a sister his entire life. To have seven and no knowledge of them! Did the brothers simply ignore their sisters? Impossible. *One* of them must have spoken to Nouf *sometime*. They must have taken at least a passing interest in her schooling, hobbies, her taste in shoes.

He studied them. Tahsin, with a wife and nine children, and his enormous work responsibilities; he was probably too busy, or acted as if he was. Fahad, too, worked all the time. He and his wife had three young girls, but they didn't live on the island any more; they had a house in the city and probably didn't see Nouf very often. Only Othman would have seen her regularly. He still lived at home. But on the phone he'd been unable to tell Nayir anything. Perhaps he'd been in shock.

It wasn't odd that the brothers were being so reserved – they kept their feelings buried, or shared among themselves – and on any other occasion, he would have thought nothing of it. But as the minutes ticked by, questions sprang forcefully into his mind. If Nouf had seemed so happy at home, wasn't it still likely that she'd been kidnapped? The kidnapper could have stolen the camel to make it look as if

37

she'd run away. Had she ever talked about leaving? If not to her brothers, then to her sisters or a friend? And most important, did they know about the pregnancy before she ran away? He couldn't find a way to raise his concerns; he couldn't even come up with a subject for idle chatter. He studied each of them in the hopes that they would speak, but their silence was heavy and conscientious. It wasn't his place to force the issue. Would any among them ask the difficult question: what had happened to Nouf? Would anyone take responsibility for, if not her death, then at least the circumstances leading up to it?

A servant came in with a lighted hookah and set it down beside Tahsin. With a cloth at his waist, the servant wiped the hookah's nozzle and handed it to Tahsin, who accepted it sternly. The servant bowed and left.

Tahsin held the hookah to his mouth. Everyone stared at him, waiting for the first inhalation. Nayir found himself longing for the comforting slap of water as it bubbled in the pipe, the soft crackle of charcoal lighting the tobacco, any sound to break the silence. Tahsin finally took a drag, and it seemed for a moment that his long exhalation of sweet-smelling smoke was matched by the relieved exhalations of everyone.

Slowly, the hookah made its way around the circuit. One of the cousins praised the tobacco and asked where it was from, which started a light conversation. Nayir realized that the brothers were done talking about Nouf. He leaned back against the wall. The disappointment of his failed search still troubled him. Why hadn't he sent a team to check out the family's campsite to make sure they knew what they were doing? Accident or not, her death had been preventable. He felt determined to find out what had happened to her. *Allah, am I prying? Am I doing this to satisfy my own sick curiosity?* No, he thought. It was the right thing to do, and he felt, somehow, that he owed it to Othman.

On the other hand, solving a problem like this would mean learning everything he could about Nouf, and that would be nearly impossible. Only her sisters would have known very much, but he wouldn't be allowed to speak with them, nor ask personal questions. He had never met the older one, but he had seen a few of the others when they were still young enough not to wear veils. On one occasion years ago, when he'd come to the house to prepare the men for a desert trip, the girls had met him with quiet awkwardness. They'd been a well-behaved bunch, and in the absence of notable personality traits he'd found it hard to tell them apart. Perhaps he'd even met Nouf back then. But the only one he remembered was the infant he'd held. For a brief anguished moment, that little creature had struck him with a sense of his own terrific power. She'd screamed, and he'd quickly handed her back.

There must be a lot of official cases like this, he thought. Cases where a man has to understand a woman's life; to know the details of her last few days, weeks, months; to know where she spent her time, and why, and with whom; to know her desires, her secrets. But the job's disappointment was probably sharp: women, so used to secrecy, undoubtedly took their mysteries to their graves.

Othman caught his eye. 'Shall we walk?' he asked.

This was their typical manoeuvre – taking polite leave to talk alone. Gratefully, Nayir nodded, and they rose and stepped onto the terrace.

A balustrade snaked around the house. Dusk was beginning to fall, wrapping the sky in a hazy pink. Nayir followed Othman along the winding terrace. Eventually, it turned into a dirt stairway with two black walls on either side. Down they went, interminably lower, until they heard the faint grunting of animals settling into sleep.

5

At the bottom of the stairs they entered a courtyard, and Nayir realized he had been here before, many times in fact, but had always come at it by a different route. Now he recognized the low bower of figs that hung near the stone stables. To his left was the estate's most informal entrance, the rear gate that Nouf must have used. It was a giant wooden door through which two trucks could pass without touching. The door served as a docking bay for the family's foodstuffs and receivables. It was also where Nayir and his men came to load the camels and various accoutrements that the Shrawis brought with them to the desert.

But Othman led Nayir off to the right, through an iron gate and into a garden encircled by hedges. A gravel pathway twisted through the shrubs and trees, and they walked along it, slowing their pace.

'I still can't believe this is happening,' Othman said.

'I'm sorry—'

'I know you did everything you could,' he interrupted, and then added: 'And thank you for bringing Nouf to the house.'

'No problem,' Nayir said, noticing the tension in

Othman's face. They came upon a stone bench and an empty fountain, but kept on walking. 'The examiner didn't release any paperwork,' Nayir said. 'I take it that he called you.'

'Yes.'

Nayir thought back on the examiner's office, uncertain whether to tell Othman that he'd seen the body and learned about the manner of her death. He decided to wait for Othman to speak; he seemed to have something to say.

They walked in a circuit through the gardens, exchanging a few words when the silence grew awkward.

'I spoke with the examiner just before the service,' Othman said abruptly. 'I was surprised that she drowned.'

Nayir nodded. 'The way he saw it, she must have been stuck in a wadi. The floods happen fast. It can be hard to get out in time.'

'You've heard of this happening before?'

'Yes, but it's rare.'

'Seems to me she should have been able to see it coming.'

'It's possible she might have been unconscious,' Nayir said, 'maybe because of the heat. By the way, did you ever find the camel?'

'Yes. She's here,' Othman said. 'Although apparently she's not doing well.'

'What happened?'

'I don't know. She nearly injured one of the stable hands, so they shut her in a dark room. It's the only thing that keeps her calm.'

'Where did they find her?'

'One of the search parties found her not too far from where the body was found, I think. You'd have to look at the map.'

They passed another empty fountain; the conversation

threatened to dry up. 'So you've accepted that her death was accidental?' Nayir ventured, hoping to sound as casual as he could.

There was a slight hesitation. 'Well, murder seems unlikely.'

Nayir decided to push ahead. 'Did the examiner mention that Nouf had defensive wounds on her wrists and a bump on her head?'

Othman didn't reply.

'The wounds on her wrists might have been from a camel's reins,' Nayir said, 'but they didn't seem uniform enough to one of the examiners. There was bruising and scratching almost as if someone had grabbed her, and she'd fought back.'

'They could have been accidental wounds,' Othman said finally. 'But if they weren't . . . I don't know. Someone may have grabbed her, but did they drown her? I don't think they could do that without drowning themselves as well.'

He was right: defensive wounds did not mean murder. But they could mean rape or kidnapping. Nayir wanted to say it, but he felt he'd already gone far enough, and he was running out of nerve.

'But no,' Othman admitted suddenly, 'I'm not sure her death was accidental. The truth is, my brothers asked the examiner's office to classify it that way, for the family's sake.'

Nayir stopped walking. 'They paid for a cover-up?'

'Tahsin did.' Othman looked awkward for a moment. 'He doesn't trust the police. And we all felt it would be easier for my mother if she didn't have to explain things to our relatives. It's bad enough for her with my father being ill.'

'I understand,' Nayir said, 'but the cover-up makes your whole family look suspicious.'

'I know. But I have someone in the lab who is collecting

the necessary evidence. She's going to treat this as if it were an open investigation.'

Nayir felt a strange coupling of relief and unease – relief at the family's interest in finding out the truth, even if it was done in an illegal manner, and unease because of the pronoun 'she'.

'Is it . . . Miss Hijazi?' he asked.

'Yes,' Othman said. 'You met her?'

For a blinding moment, Nayir couldn't understand why Miss Hijazi hadn't told him about her connection to the family. He'd suspected it, of course, but he remembered that she'd seemed upset about the cover-up – of which, apparently, she was a part. 'She was there,' he said. 'How do you know her?'

'She's my fiancée.'

If there was something more surprising he could have said, Nayir couldn't imagine it. The wedding had come up in conversation many times – Nayir knew, for example, that the bride's surname was Hijazi – but there were plenty of Hijazis, and Othman referred to her as 'my fiancée' otherwise. He also knew that Othman met her privately; she came with an escort. The girl's mother was dead and Um-Tahsin had taken a maternal role with her, helping to organize the wedding details like the dress and the rings. But Nayir had lacked the nerve to pry any further. He didn't know what sort of family she was from or what kind of personality she had, and he certainly didn't know what she looked like. He'd simply assumed that she was sweet and decent, a girl from a wealthy family. He had not guessed that she might have a job, especially one where she would interact with men.

'Oh, well . . .' he said, feeling flustered. 'I'm sorry, I hadn't made the connection. Is she a cousin of yours?'

'No, she's not family.' Othman seemed embarrassed. 'We met through a friend. She didn't tell you who she was?'

Nayir shook his head. It was probably proper of her to keep her identity hidden, but he couldn't help feeling embarrassed himself. He wondered how well Othman really knew her. Certainly he would have noticed her boldness. Or was she less bold with him? She'd been too forward for Nayir's comfort, and he couldn't imagine Othman tolerating that sort of behaviour either. He was curious to know his friend's thoughts, but he couldn't find a delicate way to broach the subject.

'Does it surprise you so much?' Othman asked.

'No, no. She's just – you didn't tell me she worked at the examiner's office.'

Othman actually blushed. 'Well, I didn't think it was necessary.'

Nayir turned away, but he was intrigued by Othman's shame. *He must really love her*, he thought, *to tolerate her having a job.*

'Congratulations,' Nayir said finally, realizing he should have said it sooner.

Othman chuckled.

'I mean it.'

'Please try!' Othman was grinning. He continued walking.

'So I take it you're pursuing this case on your own?' Nayir asked, steering the focus away from Miss Hijazi.

'Yes.' Othman stopped smiling. 'Actually, I was hoping you would help. We've hired a private investigator, and he wants to see where she was found. We have a map, but I was hoping you could help him find the place.'

Nayir felt another wash of dismay. A private investigator? The family should have asked him first; they knew how well he knew the desert. *But this is pride*, he told himself. *Forgive my pride.* 'Of course I'll help.'

'Thanks.'

44

'The private investigator – was that your brother's idea, too?'

'No, that was mine. My family has not decided whether her death was accidental or not.' Othman shook his head. 'I think we just want answers.'

Nayir sensed a chance for transparency. 'What about you? What do you think happened?'

Othman stopped walking. He sighed and crossed his arms. 'Ever since I discovered she was gone, I've felt that someone took her. We've talked to her escort, Mohammed, but he said Nouf had called him that morning and told him she didn't need him that day, so he went out with his wife. Meanwhile, Nouf told my mother that she was going to the mall to exchange her wedding shoes.'

'How did she manage to leave without an escort?' Nayir asked. 'I mean, I'm just wondering why no one noticed that Mohammed wasn't here that day.'

'Well, my mother doesn't follow her every time she leaves the house. Usually, Nouf met Mohammed round by the stables. She went to the stables by herself all the time – usually in the mornings. She liked spending time with the camels. When she was ready to leave, she'd call him and he'd drive around to the back gate and pick her up there.'

Nayir nodded. 'So she could have been gone long before anyone thought she had even left the house.'

'Yes. Nouf told my mother she'd be at the stables that morning, and meet Mohammed around noon. For all we know, she could have left right after talking to my mother.'

'Did any of the servants notice her hanging around the stables?'

Othman shook his head. 'They didn't see anything.'

'Who discovered she was missing?'

'My mother. She expected Nouf back around five, and when she didn't show up, my mother called Mohammed. He

45

told her what Nouf had said that morning. That set the house in an uproar. My brother went down to check the stables; we questioned all the servants; my mother sent them to look for her jet ski. Sometimes Nouf would ski around the island on her own, but the jet ski was still at the dock. None of the servants had heard or seen anything unusual.'

Nayir had heard some of this before, but he wanted to hear it again. 'She didn't leave a note?'

'No.'

'And you don't have any idea where she might have wanted to go?'

'None. Honestly, she spent a lot of time shopping. She was preparing for her wedding. That's why I couldn't believe that she would have run away on her own.'

Nayir nodded. 'So it was natural for your mother to think that Nouf would spend five or six hours at the mall.'

'Yes, certainly. It takes a good hour just to get downtown from here, and that's when traffic is good.'

Nayir nodded reflectively.

'Believe me,' Othman said, 'she was eager to get married. I don't believe she would jeopardize her future.' He shut his eyes, and for a moment seemed overcome with exhaustion. He rubbed his forehead vigorously and let his hands slide down his face. Nayir waited for him to continue. 'Even if she harboured a secret desire to escape this life, it just doesn't make sense. She was not that deceptive.'

'I can't imagine anyone wanting to escape this life.' Nayir motioned to the house. 'She must have lived very comfortably here.' The distant roar of an engine broke into their conversation. It sounded like a speedboat.

'When she first disappeared,' Othman said, 'Tahsin thought that she was frightened by the prospect of marriage. That she'd had a change of heart. Sure, marriage is intimidating for a sixteen-year-old girl, but we all believed that she wanted it badly, and she wouldn't have spoiled her plans. At the same time, why would anyone kidnap her and then not demand ransom? Nothing makes sense.'

The engine's roar grew louder and then abruptly receded. Nayir glanced idly at the ground. It was certainly a confusing situation, but his thoughts kept returning to the bruises on Nouf's wrists, and to the fact that she'd lost her camel.

Othman's cell phone jangled. Hastily, he excused himself, answered the phone, and walked away, stopping beside a row of hedges out of earshot from Nayir. Nayir imagined it was Miss Hijazi calling, and he felt a stab of guilt. Having met her without Othman's being present now felt like a betrayal. It occurred to him that Miss Hijazi was probably at the house right now. A strange envy struck him when he thought of the women's sitting room and of Othman's ability to penetrate that room, even if it was only through the telephone. What would she say? Would she tell him what the women were discussing? Would they be talking about Nouf, as Nayir and the brothers had done, or would they steer clear of the subject for fear of upsetting Um-Tahsin?

His thoughts circled back to the problem of her boldness, and he wondered if he should tell Othman that his fiancée had been so forward with another man. Othman glanced in his direction with what Nayir thought was a curious look, and with a touch of embarrassment Nayir turned away. *No, he thought, better to leave the whole thing alone.*

Beside him, an iron gate led down a short path to a terrace overlooking the sea. Intrigued by the engine's roar, he slipped through the gate, walked down to the terrace and stood at the edge of the balustrade. It was a breathtaking view. The sea spread to the horizon, oscillating between the cobalt of day and the soft red of twilight. The Shrawis were lucky to own property like this, far from the noise and dust of the city and its burgeoning suburbs. Jeddah was swelling rapidly, expanding up and down the coast and pushing its way deep into the desert to accommodate its two-million-strong population. One day it would become a suburb of Mecca, ninety kilometres to the east. The Shrawis, he knew, had grown tired of living in a metropolis of such monstrous proportions. Their island was paradise, close enough to be part of city life but far enough to provide a sense of privacy and calm. The royal family owned many of the habitable islands off the Jeddah coast; the rest were designated as natural preserves for rare bird species. This island had once belonged to the King's brother, but in a notable act of generosity, the Crown Prince had given it to Abu-Tahsin for reasons that no one would tell.

The sound of the engine grew louder and Nayir looked down. A sheer rock wall fell down to the beach, and when his eyes grazed the shore, he spotted the source of the noise. A woman was riding a bright yellow jet ski. She wore a black cloak, but it looked as if her headscarf had blown off and was whipping around her neck. A long, thick ponytail hung down her back.

She had to be a Shrawi. There were no other islands nearby, and certainly no woman would ski this far from the mainland by herself without a veil. It didn't seem likely that the Shrawis would let their daughters race around, especially on the evening of the funeral, but who else could it be? No servant could afford a jet ski, and anyway he doubted that the servants would let their women expose themselves at work.

He glanced over his shoulder to make sure no one was watching, then he turned back to the woman with unguarded interest. She stayed close to the island, and the ski's loud roar echoed off the rocks as she headed around to the southern dock. Even from a distance he could see the controlled angle of her body as she ripped through the water, slicing up waves and churning foam in her wake. He imagined that Nouf had skied like this, and that if this was one of her sisters or cousins, this angry cavorting was a fitting expression of grief.

'What—?' Othman was behind him, staring down at the woman on the jet ski. He looked horrified.

'What is it?' Nayir asked.

Othman continued to stare, unmoving, until the woman turned back toward the island, exposing her face. Slowly his hand went to his chest. His other hand clutched the railing. He bent forward, shutting his eyes tightly and breathing with the deep, intentional inhalations of a man trying to keep himself from fainting.

Nayir stared at him. '*Bismillah ar-rahman ar-raheem,*' he whispered.

Othman took a deep breath that seemed to shudder in his whole chest. Nayir turned away, feeling that his gaze was an invasion of privacy. He watched the jet ski turn to the north and disappear beneath the overhanging rocks.

A few moments later, Othman put both hands on the balustrade and pushed himself up. His skin was the colour of sesame paste. 'I thought it was Nouf,' he said. His arms were shaking. 'That was her jet ski, but it was only Ab – one of my other sisters.'

Nayir looked down; the engine was now a distant hum.

Othman's arms fell to his sides. 'She shouldn't be out.'

'Perhaps she's upset.' Nayir gazed at his friend. The colour was slowly returning to his cheeks. 'People do strange things when they're grieving.'

'I know,' Othman murmured. 'But it's going to upset my mother.'

'Does your sister jet-ski often?'

'Yes. No.' Othman checked his watch. The gesture seemed more like a nervous tic than a genuine desire to know the time. 'Since Nouf disappeared, Tahsin won't let the girls go anywhere, and that includes riding on the water. If you'll excuse me, I'd better go and straighten this out.'

'Yes, go ahead. I can find my way ba—'

Othman turned away before the sentence was finished and hurried towards the gate.

Nayir left the alcove and walked along the gravel path, wondering what exactly had happened. Nearly fainting at the sight of a perceived ghost seemed normal. But in the little episode that had just played out, the look of perfect terror on Othman's face when he'd seen his sister's jet ski approach had struck a strangely dissonant note. It wasn't the terror as much as the sudden plunge into a suspended reality that was, for Othman, not natural at all.

I said it myself, Nayir thought ruefully. *People do strange things in their grief.*

☽

Nayir arrived at the courtyard just as the outdoor lights were coming on. The camel keeper, Amad, was standing at the stable door, staring at Nayir with a myopic squint.

Nayir approached. 'I recognize you now,' Amad said, walking forward and stumbling on a shattered brick. He kicked it aside. 'You're the desert guide. It's been a while.'

'Yes, Nayir ash-Sharqi.' He extended his hand for a shake. 'It's good to see you again.' He seemed to remember that the man was desert born. He recognized something Bedouin in him, although he wasn't sure what. The firm cut of the jaw, the steady posture, a certain choppiness of speech. Or perhaps it was the man's incessant blinking.

'Will you take the family out again soon? The camels miss the desert, you know.'

'I miss it myself,' Nayir said. He'd come back into the

50

city only this morning, but this trip out had not restored him in the least. All the fruitless searching had worn him down, and that, followed by the blow of Nouf's death, had created a tight knot in his gut – anger at the family for being so secretive, and at himself for not having found her. A strong part of him wished he could go back to the desert tonight and spend a few days relaxing with no one to bother him. But he would keep his word to Othman and wait for the private investigator to call.

They were standing in front of a wide wooden door that led into the stables.

'How is the camel they found in the desert?' Nayir asked. 'I heard she was having some problems.'

Amad hesitated. Nayir could tell that he'd raised an awkward subject. 'No problems,' the keeper said. 'She's fine. Who told you that?'

'My mistake.' Nayir reached into his pocket for a miswak. Amad squinted, watching his movements. It was a wonder the old man didn't wear glasses.

'It's terrible what happened to the girl,' Nayir said.

'Yes. I'm sorry for their loss.'

Nayir was struck by the man's sudden reserve. He put the miswak in his mouth and took another look at the courtyard. 'The Shrawi girl who disappeared – she spent a lot of time with the camels,' he said.

Amad eyed him, suspiciously, he thought. 'She liked animals. She was down here a lot, with her escort usually. Or she came with her brother. All the girls come down to visit the camels, but that one especially.' Amad peered vaguely at the gate.

'But it's strange, isn't it?' Nayir said. 'I can't imagine how she managed to get a camel into, what, a pick-up truck? That seems a big job for a young girl like that.'

'Well, don't go looking too carefully now.' Amad spat on

the ground and looked up at the house. 'Ask me, this is one of those things better left in the dark.'

'Why do you say that?'

'I've learned one thing here: when you enter the house of the blind, you put out your eyes. Now if you'll excuse me. I have to unload the last of the feed.'

Nayir watched Amad enter the stable with one hand touching the wall and the other groping nervously. 'Got to fix that light,' he muttered as the darkness swallowed him.

Feeling oddly exposed, Nayir looked back at the garden gate, but Othman had not returned. From behind, he heard a scratching noise and turned to see a woman striding out of the stables. She had a sturdy build, about as wide as Nayir, and her movements had a confidence that he recognized in people who spent time in the desert. She was, he felt certain, the keeper's daughter.

When she saw him, she raised a hand to her face, which was unveiled. A black crest of hair fell over her cheek. Nayir couldn't help noticing the enormous bruise above her left eye before she skittered through a doorway in the stone wall to his right and disappeared.

Perhaps someone had overpowered her to steal the camel, but who would knock out the daughter when the father would have been so much easier to handle, being elderly and half-blind as he was? It might have been a matter of necessity. Maybe the daughter stumbled on Nouf – or her kidnapper. He wondered, anxiously, if Othman knew anything about it, and if so, why he hadn't mentioned it. Nayir wished there were a way he could talk to the girl.

The camel, however, wasn't taboo. Glancing one last time at the garden gate, Nayir crept behind the stable door and waited for Amad to leave. Propped against the building were half a dozen long planks and a clutch of lead pipes. The planks were lighter than they looked; it would have been easy for Nouf, or someone else, to use them as a ramp for getting a camel into the back of a truck. Nayir picked up a pipe. It was heavy enough to knock someone out. He studied each one, but none of them had traces of blood. It also looked as if none had been cleaned recently. They were covered with thousands of tiny, soft splinters from the cedar chips that were strewn on the ground, just like the chips Miss Hijazi had found in Nouf's head wound.

He heard Amad grumbling within. Moments later the keeper came out, calling his daughter's name and taking off in the direction she'd gone. Grabbing a handful of sugar from a sack by the door, Nayir slipped into the stables.

The interior was as dark as the folds of a woman's cloak. He fished out his penlight and switched it on against his palm in case he was standing too close to the animals. He didn't want to startle them. The scent of manure lodged in his throat.

Once his eyes had adjusted, he raised the penlight, approached the first stall and peered inside. A camel was asleep on its belly. Nayir backed away and an instinct kicked in, telling him to speak softly to the beasts; they weren't awake but they would hear him anyway and know he was friend not foe. He whispered as he crept down the aisle. He passed stalls on each side, most of them locked, some stirring with life. Peeking into each one, he saw its prisoner sleeping, and he crept on to the next. He was looking for the camel that wasn't asleep, the camel who was too anxious to rest. He picked his way through the stable, annoyed for once that the Shrawis kept so many camels on a useless island in the middle of the sea.

Finally, he found her. The camel was white, her fur yellowed by the penlight. Nayir stood back from the stall door, murmuring a soft lure for the animal inside. It seemed to take a very long time, perhaps a full ten minutes, for the camel to climb to her feet with a rustle and a groan, blowing another whiff of dung in his direction. He continued to whisper phrases until he heard the beast nudge the stall door. He stopped whispering. The camel nudged again.

With enormous care he unlatched the door and let it drift open. He kept his eyes on the floor and mumbled pleasantries until the camel shook her head with a delicate whinny, indicating that Nayir could approach.

He looked at her then and saw an elegant lady, standing knock-kneed on a tuft of straw. Thick lashes accentuated her wide brown eyes, and she seemed to gaze at him with a mixture of bashfulness and curiosity.

'*Salaam aleikum*,' he said. She nuzzled his arm. The keeper was right: this was not a traumatized camel, so who had told Othman otherwise? Nayir didn't think he would lie about the camel; it seemed more like the natural exaggeration of rumour.

He opened his palm, revealing sugar tablets in the glow of his penlight. She threw back her muzzle and gave another ladylike snort. When he raised the sugar to her nose, she gobbled it down faster than he'd ever seen a camel eat, and when she finished she let him stroke her shoulders where the nerves and joints merged in a sensitive knot. She was tense – not as tense as he'd expected, but she'd had some exercise lately, more proof that she hadn't been kept in a cage. Finally, standing close enough to inspect her, he went over every inch of her fur with his light, looking for signs of injury or abuse. He found nothing. She was as happy and fit as if she'd just won a race, save for a lingering sense of alertness that had been easily quelled by a few soft words.

He patted her, stroking the nape of her neck, the shoulder, and down the left foreleg, where his fingers encountered something odd. It felt as if gelatin had dried in

54

her hair, but a closer look revealed that the marks were not for lack of grooming. He drew the penlight to the spot and, pushing aside the longer hairs, he found a place where the hair was shorter than the rest. It was a series of lines – five, to be exact, each no longer than his thumb. They looked like burns.

Five lines on the leg of a camel meant what? He thought for a moment, then it came to him. After tucking her in again and saying goodnight, he crept back out to the empty courtyard, baffled by his find.

6

Katya Hijazi sat in the back seat of the Toyota as her driver Ahmad steered through the darkened streets. He stopped fully at every corner, sipped coffee from his favourite white mug, checked the side streets (which were always empty) and eased forward, content to crawl like a snail. At one intersection, he rolled down the front window to let in the cool air, and stealthily, Katya rolled down the back window too, just enough to reveal a patch of night sky.

There was always a hazard heading out into the world, but on this morning in particular she was in a watchful, darkly expectant mood. The night before, she had called Ahmad to ask if he would pick her up before dawn. She didn't say why, and Ahmad, as usual, didn't ask.

But her father did. She had awoken to a quiet house and managed to tiptoe out without waking Abu, but just as soon as the car had reached the corner of her street, her cell phone rang and she'd spent five minutes explaining to her father that she had to be at work early, that she would be paid overtime, and that her boss wouldn't make a habit of placing such inhumane demands on her time. Lie piled upon lie, and even then Abu would worry. His concern, however remote, now hung in the car and made her guilt even heavier.

She didn't want him to know just how much she was working on the case. He supported her pursuit of the truth about Nouf's death, but she didn't want to have to explain that she was going to be sneaking around the laboratory and hiding things from her boss and co-workers. Abu wouldn't like it – because he didn't like the idea of Katya breaking the rules and also he didn't approve of the way the examiner had closed Nouf's case without looking carefully at all the facts. Either way, he would have something negative to say, and the less criticism he directed at her job, the better.

She had stashed the biological samples from Nouf's body in her purse, and she wanted to process them, which she could do only when no one else was in the lab. But she had never been to work so early and wasn't sure that the women's entrance to the building would even be open, or that the security guard would let her pass. She had the skin sample from beneath Nouf's fingernails, the wood chips from her head wound, the mud from her wrist, and some mud traces from her skin and hair. She also had a blood sample from the fetus. Processing it all surreptitiously would take a few days. The women's section of the lab didn't open until eight, but it might give her enough time to prepare the evidence.

If her boss found out that she was running samples from a case that had been closed, she would lose her job. It didn't matter that it was the family who had asked them to close the case, and that she was in fact working for the family at Othman's request. There were too many problems with the situation. Could the examiner admit that he had been bribed? Could Tahsin admit to paying him? Could the family admit that they'd hired a woman? There was no discussing any of it.

Ahmad crept along, the Toyota's headlights glowing weakly. As they left the old town, the streets grew wider and felt emptier, the buildings newer and less friendly. The comforting sight of old wooden window screens and elaborately ornamented doors gave way to the travesty of rusty iron grilles and decayed air conditioners hanging from windows like crooked teeth dripping with saliva. There were street lamps here, but they gave off a dull grey light.

'Everything all right?' Ahmad asked.

'Yes, Ahmad. Thank you.'

At once he turned left and they entered what felt like a women's street. All the storefronts displayed perfumes and sweet oils, abaayas, jewellery and baubles. Lights filled the shop windows, but as the Toyota crept past, they flickered off here and there in preparation for morning prayers. The only other movement came from black shapes flitting through the streets. Normally, men inhabited these sidewalks, but this early in the morning there were women, as quiet and alert as deer, stealing the opportunity to wander unmolested. A man would be a blot on the picture, his robe glowing whiter than the moon, chasing away the dark shapes of night.

Ahmad stopped at a corner. Katya asked him to inch into the intersection and wait. Down the length of the cross street she could see the palest foam of light rising up like a wave on the horizon. She watched it, waiting for the translucent ghostly glow that would mark the technical first point of dawn. Thanks to college astronomy, everything she knew about the universe had some relevance to the calculation of prayer times. It was a monumental task, that calculation. For such things one had to understand latitudes, solar declinations, azimuths, apparent solar times, and equations of time. Armies of men spent their lives observing the heavens just to calculate and predict the exact moment of dawn and the precise number of minutes and seconds that would elapse between dawn and sunrise, for it was in those minutes that Fajr prayers were performed. She held her breath, still staring at the horizon, curious to see if the muezzin's call would synchronize with the break of dawn.

Indeed, the distant glimmer of light appeared just as the first *Allahu akbar* rang from the speakers of a nearby mosque. *God is great.* The simultaneity of events sent a chill through her.

Then, less happily, she thought that while those armies of men had turned their eyes toward the heavens, the great sky was only ever visible to her from her rooftop or through the slit of an open car window.

Ahmad drove through the intersection, pulled over to the kerb, and grabbed his prayer rug from the passenger seat. He got out and spread his rug on the pavement, standing to begin his prayers. Katya watched, feeling uneasy. She hadn't stopped thinking of Nouf all night; and now, like the flickering of storefront lights, she felt illumination dying inside her. The day before, she'd been certain that Nouf had been murdered, but what if the scratches on her arms and the wound on her head had happened during the drowning? Or been caused by an accident? Katya had also felt certain that she understood the family. They wanted to handle the investigation quietly; she respected their need for privacy. But what if they were hiding something?

They might never have told her about the cover-up had she not called Othman to warn him that the examiner had done a shoddy job. Othman quickly asked for her help. She agreed, of course, but technically it was too late to collect evidence – Nouf's body was already being returned to the house. Surreptitiously, Katya had saved samples from the examination, but Othman didn't know she was going to do that. He didn't even know she was stepping in for the regular examiner. Did he just assume that she was all-powerful at work?

She hated having these thoughts. Inevitably, they led her to wonder if she was doing the right thing, marrying a man she'd chosen herself. A man her father didn't like.

Katya looked up and saw two young women about to leave a nearby store. Seeing Ahmad on the sidewalk, they stopped and retreated from the shop's glass door, perhaps afraid that Ahmad was one of those men who, seeing a woman after performing his ablutions, would have to do them again. Katya wanted to tell them that Ahmad wouldn't mind them walking past, and that anyway he was the blindest man on the planet – he had the special talent of being able to look at a woman and not see her face at all. But she couldn't motion to the women; they were behind a curtain now, and the dark-tinted windows were impenetrable from without. So she watched Ahmad pray, watched him turn his head and whisper his *tasleem*, 'peace be upon you and the mercy of God,' while admiring the serenity that stole over his face.

It was that same look of goodness, of calm and security, that made her father trust him. The two men had been childhood friends back in Lebanon and had emigrated to Saudi when they were both twenty-one. It was after Ahmad's wife, a long-dead but once beautiful Russian émigrée, that Katya had been named. Katya had never met her, but there was a picture of her in the glove compartment, an old snapshot taken in the mountains of Syria. The snow on her hat, the bushy scarf around her neck, were the perfect accessories for the pale, blonde-haired, wintry woman. Katya couldn't imagine her in any other setting, and, it seemed, neither could Ahmad. He started every story about her: 'I remember the vacation we took to Syria. How much she loved the cold . . .' Occasionally Katya reminded herself that Ahmad's wife had lived in Jeddah too. She had died here of cancer in the summer of 1968.

But whereas Abu had gone on to a successful career as a chemist, Ahmad had been content to be a taxi-driver, and eventually a women's escort, arguing that his chosen profession, while it didn't always pay the bills, at least gave him the satisfaction of protecting young virgins from wily men, the religious police included. Being with Ahmad felt a bit like being with a watered-down version of her father, someone who was reliably concerned for her safety but whose worry lacked the bite of parental anxiety. Most of the time he treated her like royalty, but for all his display of servitude and kindness, Katya knew that in her own small world, Ahmad was king. Were it not for him, she wouldn't be able to get around at all. There were taxis for women, with nice immigrant drivers, but her father would never allow it.

Far down the street, she saw men coming out of their homes, answering the call to prayer. It was time to roll up the window. Turning, she looked up one last time at the blushing sky, hoping for a taste of the awe that had struck her, but all she felt was guilt. Guilt for lying to Abu, for not having done her Fajr prayer, for making Ahmad come to work before the light hit the sky. Guilt for doubting Othman. There was only one thing she was determined not to feel guilty about, and that was her work on Nouf's case.

Her mother used to say that *salat* was a generous verb. It meant to pray, to bless, to honour, to magnify, but its underlying meaning was 'to turn towards'. So when she was unable to pray – because of sickness or menstruation – she was still obliged to turn her thoughts to Allah. And wasn't that what she was doing now, turning her mind toward the mysteries of His creation? Especially as they pertained to prayer times and Nouf? Allah, at least, was with her on that, for in the Quran it said: 'If there be but the weight of a mustard-seed, and it were hidden in a rock, or anywhere in the heavens or on earth, Allah will bring it forth: for Allah understands the finest mysteries, and is well acquainted with them.'

Still, she knew that it was cheating. She had missed her prayers.

Ahmad rolled up his prayer rug and brushed the dirt from its fringes. He got back into the car and they sat, waiting for the prayers to be done. Down the street, men were crowding into a mosque. Some were praying on the sidewalks in front of their stores. Ahmad picked up his mug and resumed his sipping. She watched his comforting face in the rear-view mirror, wishing she could confide all her doubts about Othman and his family. But inevitably he would tell her father, and she didn't want Abu to know that there was any doubt in her mind. They waited until the prayers were done and the men came pouring back out of the mosque.

Ahmad started the car, and took a turn at the next corner. Every day he took a different route to the lab to show her something new. Even though there were a finite number of ways to get to work, the streets changed so quickly that each trip seemed fresh. Not two weeks before they had gone down this street, the one with the palm trees, both plastic and real, the real ones chattering with one another over the smaller plastic ones' heads. It had been bustling with construction workers, mostly Yemenis and Asians. A concrete-mixing truck had been churning loudly next to an empty plot, and across the street a wrecking ball was tearing down a gutted apartment building. Now nothing was left but a gaping space and a huge drum with cables coiled around it. The workers had sprayed the ground with oil to keep the sand from encroaching on the street.

Ten minutes later, Ahmad pulled up to a small metal door that looked like an old service entrance but was actually the women's entrance to the lab. She thanked him, checked that her burqa was securely fastened, and quickly got out of the car. Glancing around just long enough to see that the parking lot was empty, she descended the stairs to the doorway and swiped her ID tag. A green light flashed, and the door swung open. She let out a sigh of relief.

There was no security guard – or perhaps he was sleeping somewhere – and she tiptoed past his desk into a hallway lit with its usual grey fluorescence. Her new sandals squeaked on the floor as she scurried down the corridor to the laboratory door. Inside, she switched on the lights and went quickly to her primary workstation, a small white desk in the corner which she kept meticulously clean. She set her purse on the desk and fumbled inside for the baggies containing skin and trace substances, and two small vials with samples from the fetus. She stuffed the baggie with the skin samples into the pocket of her skirt.

Her hands were shaking as she hastily opened the desk drawer and put the remaining items inside, tucking them beneath a neat stack of tissues so they wouldn't roll around. She had taken the precaution of labelling them all with false ID numbers and names from the other cases she was working on. *At-Talib, Ibrahim.* A construction worker who'd been poisoned. *Roderigo, Thelma.* A housemaid who'd died of blunt-force trauma to the head. She shut the drawer and locked it.

It took a few minutes to prepare the skin sample from Nouf's fingernails, but just as she was sliding it into the microscope, there was a noise behind her.

'*Sabaah al-khayr!*'

It was a simple good morning, but the shock of it, the loudness and sharpness of the voice, nearly made her cry out. She managed to keep from dropping the sample. Turning, she saw her co-worker, Salwa.

Katya let out a strangled reply: '*Sabaah an-nur.*' *The light of morning to you.*

'Who is it?' Salwa demanded. The loudness of her voice always made Katya feel caught, even when she wasn't guilty.

Katya realized that she hadn't removed her burqa. She lifted it now, showing Salwa her face.

Salwa frowned. Self-appointed chief of the women's section of the lab, she was a short, quick, sturdy woman who strode about with a pencil behind her ear and her burqa flipped up. It rested on her crown like a coronet; and she wore it just as imperiously. In the rare event that a man peered in at the door, the other women always scrambled to find their burqas and fasten them on, whispering apologies and hiding their faces in fear. But Salwa, whose burqa was always at the ready, would stare defiantly at the intruder. If she determined that the man was someone who might report back to her boss, she would grudgingly draw the pencil from behind her ear and use it to roll the burqa down, just as a medieval mullah might unscroll a parchment for an illiterate king.

Even when her burqa was down, there was no sequestering the mighty voice with which Allah had blessed her. It was a voice to shake the tables and make the beakers sing. It was in constant use, its resonant power augmented by the building's clean lines and plain surfaces. Once it had even interfered with the muezzin's call to prayer. Half the time, Katya suspected that Salwa got her way because so many people around her were so eager to keep her quiet.

'What are you doing here so early?' Salwa asked, drawing closer to Katya with a look of frank suspicion on her face. 'Take off your abaaya. Let me see your arms and shoulders.'

Katya felt irrationally panicked. 'My abaaya?'

'Yes. Do it.'

She unzipped the front of the black cloak and slid out of the garment, revealing a white button-down shirt and a long black skirt. Salwa came closer, unbuttoned Katya's cuffs and used her pencil to raise the sleeves. Katya realized she was looking for bruises.

'I'm fine,' she assured her.

Salwa dropped her arm and looked straight into Katya's eyes. 'The only reason women come here early is to escape their husbands or fathers.'

Katya felt her cheeks flush. Despite the gloss of concern, Salwa had managed to make her feel like an abused woman anyway. 'Nobody hits me,' she said.

'So what are you doing here?'

Katya rolled down her sleeves and slid back into her abaaya. 'I couldn't sleep.'

Salwa eyed her with a satisfaction more maternal than penal. 'Ah. Is this about your upcoming wedding?'

Katya knew better than to trust her with personal information. Now that their boss, Adara, was on maternity leave – for the second time in a year – Salwa seemed to think that she was permanently in charge. She had been there longer than any of the other women, but she didn't actually do anything except bully the other workers. Her real power resided in the fact that the division chief, Abdul-Aziz, was her brother-in-law. And because he was family, Salwa could talk to him in person, an advantage that no one else shared. If someone did her job well, Salwa took the credit. If she was sloppy, she made sure that someone else took the blame. With Abdul-Aziz she was obsequious, rushing to his office whenever he called, attending to his dry cleaning, his lunches, his meeting schedule, and bringing presents for his children at least once a week, but that subservience swung a pendulum of compensation when, returning to the female section of the lab, she subjected the women to her tyrannical demands. Segregated in the building's smallest wing, the female technicians lived in the dark air of her recycled moods. Frustration. Cloying kindness. Privately, they called her the Daughter of Saddam.

But right now, Katya had to say something. 'I am nervous,' she admitted. 'Honestly, I can't sleep. I think work is the best remedy for me right now.'

Salwa stuck her pencil back behind her ear and cogitated. Finding this excuse plausible enough, if not wholly satisfying, she drew herself up and said: 'Fine. I've got plenty for you to do. But you're not being paid overtime, I hope you understand that.'

'Of course,' Katya said, biting back her resentment. As if she expected overtime. As if money were her only concern.

'What are you working on now?' Salwa asked.

'Skin cells from the Roderigo case.'

Salwa glanced down at the microscope as if it were a dirty dog. 'All right, put that aside. I've got two other cases that have a rush priority.'

Katya nodded, sat down at the microscope and slid the tray out and set it on the table. She cursed her bad luck, and wondered suddenly why Salwa was here so early. It wasn't as if she ever did any work herself. Maybe *she* was avoiding an abusive man. Or, more likely, avoiding her responsibilities at home – a disabled husband, three young children, and, according to Salwa at least, the most impudent Indonesian housemaid on the planet. Maybe for her, work really was an escape.

Still, Katya couldn't help admiring certain of Salwa's qualities. She was strong enough to demand raises for the women. When Abdul-Aziz was absent, and she could get away with it, she assigned men's jobs to her charges. She had sent Katya to fill in for Adara on Nouf's case. And it was Salwa who, in the spirit of making women strong in the workplace, had encouraged her not to wear her burqa. 'Men don't respect you when you follow the rules all the time. Sometimes you have to address them directly and show them your face, even if you put your burqa down later.'

Then Katya wondered what Salwa would have done with her if she *had* discovered bruises on her arms. Would she have fired her? Consoled her? Sent her to a clinic? Most likely she would have reported it to Abdul-Aziz, and there was no telling what he would have done. He existed as a cold, distant authority whose professional decisions – if they were truly his – occasionally angered her.

Salwa came back and dumped two massive folders on the table. 'Process these as soon as possible.' Before Katya could reply, she turned and left, muttering something about needing to dust Abdul-Aziz's office before he arrived. Katya suspected she wanted to use his Italian coffeemaker and perch herself on his thousand-riyal massage chair, where she could watch the news and maybe catch an Oprah rerun before the working day began. Katya and her co-worker Maddawi had once peeked into his office.

Katya opened the folders and inspected their contents. She felt crushed. It would take her days to cover it all. She had assured Othman that she would do everything possible. She hadn't told him about the risks to her job; he hadn't asked. But he was waiting for answers. The family was waiting. And even if it was done in the open, the DNA analysis was bound to take some time.

She glanced at the door. Salwa wasn't coming back. There were no windows in the room, so Katya couldn't see when someone was coming, but equally, they couldn't see her. Turning back to the counter, she pushed the folders aside, took Nouf's sample from the table, and was just about to slide it under the microscope when the door opened and Salwa came back in. She bustled around, humming to herself, and came over to make sure that Katya was doing her job.

Katya managed to hide Nouf's evidence and make an earnest show of plunging into the new cases, but as she rolled her swivel chair back to the microscope and began to prepare a sample for the plate, she glanced up at the clock – 6.15 a.m. – and realized that it was going to be a very long day.

7

Nayir chewed a miswak and stared through binoculars across the vast expanse of desert. To the south reached a great sheet of sand, firm enough to drive on but in places so rough it could pop a man's tyres. Some distance to the north, the foothills of the Hijaz flickered yellow against the brilliant morning light.

He lowered the binoculars. Just three feet away, blocking his perfect scope of the natural world, stood Suleiman Suhail, Private Investigator and owner of the Benson & Hedges Detective Agency. In the hour they'd spent driving out here, Nayir had expected him to light a cigarette, but apparently he wasn't a smoker.

'Where are we?' Suhail asked.

At the beginning of the journey, Suhail had given him the map, saying: 'Take this Bedouin map and tell me if you understand it.' Nayir wanted to tell him that 'Bedouin map' was an oxymoron, that real Bedouins didn't use or need such tools, but he saw Suhail's point. It was a topographical chart of the western desert with nothing but the Red Sea coastline to orient the casual reader. Someone had pencilled GPS coordinates in the margin and a note saying: 'girl's body' with a date and time. Nayir hoped that the Bedouin had written the note, although it didn't seem likely that they would use GPS coordinates to identify a spot. It was about as likely as the Bedouin owning such a fine map in the first place. It looked rather like the contents of the atlas that Nayir had seen in Othman's duffel bag when they went to the desert, a folder filled with the kind of serious maps he would receive, now and again, as a gift from someone in the oil ministry or an Aramco geologist. Something another man would frame and hang above his desk, but that Othman, being Othman, would actually want to use. Nayir now imagined that Othman had provided the current chart, pencilling in the coordinates when the Bedouin had showed the family where they'd found the body. Curiously, there was a small icon suggesting an oil platform. Nayir knew this part of the desert fairly well – well enough to know that there weren't any oil drilling sites in the vicinity – but perhaps a new research station had gone up. He would have to call Aramco to find out.

'This is the spot the Bedouin marked,' Nayir said, checking the coordinates against his own GPS.

He glanced to the west and saw Mutlaq's truck approaching, churning up a thick cloud of dust in its wake. Mutlaq was the best of the Bedouin trackers who'd assisted in the search for Nouf. His coming today was a favour, and although Nayir trusted him completely, he was anxious about the meeting between him and the investigator. Mutlaq could be eccentric, and Suhail didn't seem like the sort of man who would have much patience with or respect for a Bedouin.

'I thought she died in a wadi.' Suhail squinted through his sunglasses. 'Where's the wadi?'

Before them lay a shallow groove in the land running north to south as far as they could see. Nayir motioned to the length of the groove.

'This whole thing?' Suhail cried. Nayir noticed that his dress shirt was soaked in sweat. 'Do you see a crime scene?' Suhail forced a laugh and put a finger on his temple. 'These are city eyes, and they don't see a crime scene.' He squinted against the sun as well as through the beads of sweat that dripped over his brow. Nayir noticed that his face was dangerously red. He probably never left the quiet of an air-conditioned office.

'You think cell phones work out here?' Suhail asked.

'Sometimes.'

Suhail reached in the Jeep's window and took out his cell. It wasn't working. He threw it on the seat. 'By the way, these are her things,' he said, taking a black plastic bag from the back of the Jeep and bringing it to Nayir. 'The Bedouin found them with the body. Maybe there's a clue in there.'

Surprised that the Shrawis had given Nouf's belongings to the investigator, Nayir took the sack. It would have been even better if he could have spoken to the men who found her, but according to the family they had disappeared just as soon as they'd left the body at the Coroner's. Nayir poked his nose into the sack. It held a dirty white robe – a man's robe. He took it out and unfolded it. One side was blackened, probably from overexposure to the sun, and the whole thing smelled like the examiner's office. There was a spatter of blood on the left shoulder, probably Nouf's. In the bag he also found a narrow gold wristwatch, studded with diamonds, and a single bright pink shoe. He took it out of the bag. It had a six-inch stiletto heel. Although it was water-stained, no sequins were missing from the strap, and the sole was not scuffed.

'Not exactly a walking shoe.' Suhail grinned. 'There's only one thing you do with that kind of shoe.' Nayir gave him a look. 'Sorry,' Suhail said, chuckling, 'but it's always been my philosophy that the dead shouldn't interfere too much with the pleasures of the living. Don't get me wrong – I think it's terrible that she died. I'm only saying, screams don't disturb the severed head.'

Annoyed and vaguely offended, Nayir decided not to encourage him. He took a last look inside the bag. At the bottom was a crumpled, yellow piece of paper. He took it out and tried to peel it open but in the unpeeling realized that the folds were intentional. Judging by the crease marks, it was supposed to be a bird – a stork, perhaps, with those slender legs. A very strange object. How had it survived the flood? She must have kept it close to her skin – in her shoe, perhaps, the *real* shoes she wore, for no one ventures into the desert without a pair of shoes, if only to protect their feet from the sun.

'Find anything?' Suhail asked.

'No.' Nayir took the bag to the Jeep and tucked it into his duffel bag. Suhail didn't seem bothered that Nayir was keeping Nouf's belongings; he was studying Nayir's face.

'Stop looking so grave,' the investigator said. 'Do you really think we're doing something wrong, talking about the girl this way? Insulting her family's honour? Oh, come on. You don't really believe that, do you?' He actually looked worried, but Nayir kept his face as neutral as possible. 'Forgive me, brother,' Suhail went on, incredulous. 'I didn't realize how righteous you were. I'm a Muslim too, you know, but in Syria we don't practise this strict form of Islam. We're a happier bunch, I'd say.'

'I'm Palestinian,' Nayir said, as if that explained everything.

'You are? Well, you looked Bedu to me.'

'I'm not a Bedu.'

Nayir walked away from the Jeep, trying to shake off his disgust. Over the course of his desert career, he had worked

72

with many Bedouin tribes. It was impossible not to rely on them for advice, directions, and the occasional life-saving assistance. There was a time when being mistaken for a Bedouin had pleased him, and for a while he had cultivated the image of a harsh, unrefined man of the desert who had no interest in the trivial concerns of urban life. He'd kept a rifle on his shoulder, a curved dagger on his belt. He'd even wrapped his *shumagh* into a turban. But he'd never felt that he belonged. The Bedouin were hospitable but extremely clannish, and while they had opened their doors to him, he had always been a guest. It had stung him especially to realize that he would never be allowed to meet their daughters, sisters or wives. And the truth was that he spent most of his time in Jeddah, so that the more he was mistaken for a Bedouin, the more he was reminded that he was not a Saudi either. The recognition was instant: *You must be a Bedouin.* It meant: *You can't be a Saudi.* And people were right. He wasn't a Saudi. He belonged nowhere, and like most Palestinians he was essentially stateless.

Mutlaq's truck arrived with a crackle of tyres on dirt and a billow of dust. Moments later, the man stepped out, brushing his robe with a harsh whip of his palms and kicking sand from his sandals. Seeing Nayir, his dark eyes lit with amusement. 'There's too much dust around here.'

Nayir grinned and embraced his friend. Mutlaq greeted him with the traditional kiss on the nose, the only Bedouin gesture Nayir had never dared to imitate. Mutlaq was imposing; tall and broad-shouldered. His hands were precise and forceful in their habits, and he had the proudest face that Nayir had ever seen. He kept it clean-shaven and was so compulsive about it that he kept a pair of tweezers in his car to pluck stray hairs at traffic lights (when he stopped for them). When Nayir asked him why he didn't grow a beard like every other Bedu, Mutlaq pointed at the mirror and said: 'That's my grandfather's face, Allah's mercy be upon him; it shouldn't be covered.'

Once they had finished their greeting, Nayir stood back. 'Thank you for coming,' he said.

'It's no problem, brother.'

'According to the map, they found her here.' He pointed to the wadi behind them. 'But we haven't really looked. And I don't know how much we're going to find anyway. The rain might have washed everything away.'

'Yes, but most likely the water travelled in the wadi.' Mutlaq swept his arm to the north. 'Just because it rained over there, doesn't mean there won't be footprints here.'

Suhail approached them, and Mutlaq stiffened. He greeted the investigator with a firm handshake and an intense scrutiny that took in every wrinkle and fold, every bead of sweat on his body. Nayir introduced the two men, but Mutlaq was already peering over the investigator's shoulder at the footprints he had left in the sand. Suhail turned slowly and looked behind him as if expecting to encounter a lynx.

'What's he doing?' Suhail asked as Mutlaq moved away.

'Studying your footprints,' Nayir said.

'He's walking all over them.'

'It doesn't matter. He'll remember them anyway.'

'Is he tracking *me*?' Suhail asked.

'Think of it as being fingerprinted. In case your tracks get mixed up with the others, he'll know which ones are yours.' Nayir felt the urge to brag. He wanted to tell him that Mutlaq never forgot a footprint. He might forget a name, or the particulars of their meeting, but if, five years from now, he came across Suhail's print on a dusty Jeddah street, he would remember the face – and footwear – that went with it.

But opting not to push the limits of credibility, he

explained instead that Mutlaq was from the Murrah tribe, a group renowned for its tracking skills. Suhail seemed to know what it meant to be a Murrah. He waved off any further explanation and gazed at Mutlaq with new interest.

Mutlaq had finished with Suhail's tracks, and now his full attention was focused on the wadi.

'Has he found the girl's footprints?' asked Suhail.

'Not yet,' said Mutlaq over his shoulder. 'But I will know when I see them.'

Suhail wiped his forehead and shot Nayir a sceptical look.

Mutlaq turned to face them. 'There are many girls in the desert, but I bet you only one of them was running scared in a pair of city shoes.'

'All right,' Suhail said after a pause. 'But how do you know when footprints belong to a girl? Maybe she had man-shaped feet?'

Mutlaq grinned, but he didn't reply. Instead, he went back to his truck and began to rummage through the truck bed. Nayir watched him expectantly. He knew that it was possible to identify the gender of a footprint, but he had never seen it done.

'I have seen it all,' Mutlaq said. 'People trying to disguise their tracks with every sort of trick. Women wearing men's shoes; men wearing women's shoes. People use old car tyres and cardboard. They use a broom to brush away their tracks, forgetting that a broom has a footprint of its own. After a while, you learn to tell the difference between the foot and the footwear. You can change your shoes, but you cannot change the way your feet carry you through the world.'

Nayir had to admit that Mutlaq made him wish he were a Bedouin. Not only to be an excellent tracker, but to know women well enough to perceive their difference from men in the brush of a foot.

Certainly, given a choice, he would have chosen to be a

Murrah. Every police station and counter-terrorist unit in the country had at least one tracker working in its ranks, and chances were that he was a Murrah. Mutlaq had once worked for the Jeddah police, but the pay had been terrible. He made more now owning a shoe store at the Corniche shopping centre. But he liked to go back to the desert when he could. He was a specialist in *firaasa*, the ancient skill of identifying blood relationships based on the study of feet. Years ago, that had seemed like a questionable talent to Nayir, but Mutlaq had proven it worthy. While he'd worked for the police, he had used his skill to find thieves, terrorists and missing persons, to assist in inheritance disputes, and to save innocents from charges of adultery. He'd even restored a stray donkey to its rightful owner. Sometimes it was hard to believe the things he could do simply by studying disruptions in the sand, but, Nayir thought, in a country so covered in dust, there was always a footprint somewhere.

Mutlaq took a handful of thin wooden stakes from his truck. Striding away from their vehicles, the men approached the wadi's rim and Nayir caught sight of something odd: colour, first muted pinks and purples, then a splash of bright yellow. Reaching the rim, they beheld a magnificent carpet of flora. Plants lined the wadi in every direction, bursting with young, fertile greens and jostling one another for a space in the sunlight. In a week or two, the flowers would bloom, but already they could see the nascent cornflower blues, magentas, pinks and pearly whites, minuscule buds and baby globe thistles, succulent leaves and prickly green stems. Nayir had seen deserts bloom before, but never anything as plentiful as this.

'Amazing,' he said.

'This,' whispered Mutlaq, pointing down into the wadi, 'is the footprint of the rain.'

Gingerly, he stepped down the wadi's banks and Nayir

followed, squatting for a closer look. He found borage shoots growing near a purple bed of wild iris, and a peculiar kind of mint that the Bedouin used to treat stomach ailments. He remembered with a poignant mix of pleasure and shame the time a young Bedouin woman and her father had taken him on a walking trip to harvest medicinal plants. The young girl, whose name he never learned, had chatted freely with him from behind an ornate burqa rimmed with gold coins. As she'd bent to pluck a milkweed stalk, her burqa had fallen forward, and he'd caught sight of her face. He stared unabashedly, overcome by the innocence of her expression, a look that seemed to mirror his feelings for her. But, noticing his gaze, the girl stood up and turned away. She ignored him for the rest of the hike.

Looking at the flowers now, his own marvel was dampened by the memory of Nouf. The rainwater was gone, but its legacy thrived in the riot of flora. It was testimony, he thought, to the volume of the rain, and the likely force of the flood that had killed her.

The wadi's banks weren't steep in either direction, which meant that if Nouf had seen the waters coming she would have been able to scramble out of the riverbed. And most likely, she would have noticed a coming flood. She must have been unconscious when the water hit – deeply unconscious, because the water's roar would have been enough to shake the earth.

Nayir looked down at the plants. They weren't old enough for Nouf to have seen them. So what drew her into the wadi in the first place?

Suhail climbed out of the wadi and went back to the Jeep for a drink of water. Nayir followed Mutlaq down the riverbed, stepping erratically to avoid trampling the flowers and stopping now and then to inspect an odd plant. The men walked for a good quarter-mile, Mutlaq keeping to the wadi's rim to look for tracks on the banks, and Nayir staying well within the wadi to keep out of his way.

'Anything interesting?' Nayir asked.

'Fox tracks, some mice. Nothing out of the ordinary. But what's this?' He climbed onto the bank and wandered about. Nayir wanted to follow but didn't dare move for fear of disturbing the sand. Mutlaq came back to the wadi's edge. 'Bedouin were here. One truck. Four young men. No camels.' He was scanning the flowerbeds in the wadi. 'There,' he said, pointing just to the left of Nayir's feet.

Nayir looked down and saw nothing but a dense cluster of green. Mutlaq came down, squatted beside him, and began moving stalks aside, studying the dirt beneath them.

'This is where they found her,' Mutlaq said. He stood up and, using the stakes, outlined an area the size of a body.

'Hasn't the plant growth disturbed the area?' Nayir asked.

'No, no. This was a heavy indentation. You see, she was brought here by the rain, and then, when she stopped moving, the rain sank into the earth. And so did she. Come closer.'

Nayir squatted and saw that indeed there was a significant depression in the ground. 'You're right.'

'Impressions in wet sand make the easiest reading. Look here, you can even see her fingers.'

He was right: the outline of her hand was nearly perfect. She had been lying on her side, and when they studied the spot where her face had been, they saw the shape of her jaw. It gave Nayir a chill. If the flood had been as strong as he thought, Nouf would have been carried downstream. She might have travelled a good distance before ending up here.

'Can you tell how much water there was?' Nayir asked.

Mutlaq considered it, but shook his head. 'You want to know how far she travelled with the flood?'

'Yes.'

'It's hard to say.' He stood and gazed up the wadi's length. 'It would depend on the volume of the water. We'll have to follow the wadi to see how far the flood might have taken her.'

They marked the place with a stake on the bank and continued up the wadi. Suhail lingered behind and kept stumbling on the sand. Twice they stopped to make sure he was drinking enough water, but he insisted he was fine. Eventually, Mutlaq sent him back to the Jeep, and Suhail went willingly, clearly exhausted.

They headed up the wadi, walking slowly for an hour. Judging by the condition of the sand on the banks, it hadn't actually rained in this part of the desert. They decided it could be a much longer walk than they had thought, so they went back to the vehicles to drive further up the wadi's banks. They retraced their steps. The sun was reaching its zenith, and as their shadows shrank around their feet, so their steps grew slower and heavier in the sand. Mutlaq pointed this out. 'Tired feet,' he said, 'can announce the time of day.' Nayir wondered if they would also be able to read Nouf's mood by the prints she had left.

Back at the Jeep, he was surprised to find Suhail asleep. He reached in the window and touched his forehead. The investigator awoke with a jolt, staring blankly back at him. Nayir withdrew his hand. 'You'd better drink some water.'

'I already did.'

Nayir spat out his miswak and went to the back. A sudden gust of wind blew sand in his face. He took his scarf, wrapped it around his head, and pulled the loose end across his mouth. After hauling the water jug out of the back, he refilled his canteen, all the while studying the wadi. It would be a bumpy trip, he guessed, but they'd drive upstream as far as they could. This might be where the

Bedouin found her body, but it wasn't where she died. That was the real crime scene.

☽

Nayir followed Mutlaq's truck, wondering how his friend could see anything amidst all of the dust blowing about. Suhail kept his head out of the window, dutifully studying the sand for signs of recent rain. They drove until Nayir spotted acacia trees in the distance. They were set back from the wadi, a semicircle of trees enclosing a large boulder.

The sight sparked a sudden familiarity. He had come here recently with Othman. He remembered the spot because of the boulder, and the mysterious presence of trees in an otherwise total vista of gravel and sand. They had wanted to do a week-long excursion, but Othman was too busy to be away for more than two nights, so they'd set up a small camp and spent the afternoons hiking down the wadi's trail, looking for signs of life. They'd spotted a fox, or so they thought.

Nayir drove up to the trees and motioned for Mutlaq to stop. Everyone climbed out.

'What is it?' Suhail asked. Nayir went closer, inspecting the trees, the boulder. It was indeed the same place. The stone had a distinct groove for sitting that could accommodate only one man. They had both preferred to sit on the sand. Mutlaq came up behind him and studied the ground.

'These look like your prints.'

'They are,' Nayir said, studying the tangle of prints in the sand. Despite knowing Mutlaq so well, he was still impressed.

'Who was with you?' Mutlaq asked.

'Othman ash-Shrawi. The brother of the victim.'

'Ahhhh. Yes.' Mutlaq took a closer look, walking around

the boulder and following the tracks, one hand held forward like a divining rod. 'He's a nervous man.'

'Othman?'

'Yes. But he follows you.'

Nayir couldn't make anything out of the prints. He was hot and tired. He sat on the boulder, grateful for the thin slice of shade. Unscrewing his canteen, and giving it a sniff, he took a long drink and stared out at the wadi. Perhaps sensing Nayir's sudden discomfort, Mutlaq wandered off.

Nayir took another drink. It was shocking that Nouf's body had been found in the vicinity of a spot he'd come to with Othman. What were the chances? It was the last visit they'd made to the desert – aside from the search for Nouf.

He saw Suhail coming. He was carrying a shoe. 'I spotted this beneath one of those flowers,' he said as he approached.

It was a rugged shoe with a well-worn sole. Nayir inspected it. He couldn't be sure, but a mild running of the colour on the heel suggested that it had been wet and then dried. It was a size 36, the same as the stiletto.

'It might be hers,' Nayir said. 'It could have been knocked off in the flood. I'll take it back to the family, see if they recognize it.'

Suhail nodded and walked off again as Mutlaq returned.

'May I see?' Mutlaq asked. Nayir offered him the shoe, and he studied it carefully but without comment. He handed it back to Nayir.

They spent the next few minutes walking up and down the place where Suhail had found the shoe, looking for foot-prints, animal prints, anything. Aside from a few bird tracks, the ground was smooth.

'Look,' Mutlaq said with excitement. 'A houbara was here.'

Nayir saw the telltale claw prints in the sand and felt

strangely comforted that at least something survived out here.

'So how can you tell the difference between a man's and a woman's prints?' Nayir asked.

Mutlaq lifted his head and regarded him.

'I mean,' Nayir waved his hand, 'I'm sure women tend to have smaller feet, but what else?'

'It's not just the size of the feet,' Mutlaq replied. 'It's never one thing.' He took a quick drink from his canteen and looked out over the heat-distorted horizon. 'I've been doing this for so long, I don't remember the rules any more. I judge on instinct. When I see a woman's footprints, I just know it's a woman.'

'They walk differently from men?'

Mutlaq squinted. 'Well, yes. Their bodies are different. Their hips are different. But I would say they walk differently for other reasons as well.'

The three men got back in their vehicles and drove on. They had gone only a few kilometres when Mutlaq stopped and leaned out of his window, calling over to Nayir: 'The rain fell here, so we won't find more footprints beyond this.'

Disappointed, Nayir got out of the Jeep, leaving Suhail asleep in the passenger seat. Mutlaq was right, the sand had been smoothed down by the rain. Mutlaq got out and joined him. They went to the edge of the wadi and peered down. It wasn't very far – a ten-foot drop to the bottom. Someone could have tossed her down there after hitting her on the head, in which case she would have woken up and started walking down the wadi, not realizing that it was going to rain . . .

Or perhaps she never woke up.

He and Mutlaq scanned the area one last time for footprints. They walked slowly, following the wadi. Fifty metres downhill, they saw a lump of fabric lying by a shrub, but it turned out to be a man's scarf, and judging from the dust and the fading, it had been there much longer than Nouf. Beyond that, there was no sign of activity.

'I'm sorry I can't be more help,' Mutlaq said. 'I suspect that the shoe you found is hers. If you can verify that, I'll be glad to help you hunt around for more prints. She had to have left them somewhere.'

Back at the Jeep, they found Suhail awake and fidgeting with the GPS. The investigator's fingers were shaking, and he seemed to be having trouble with hand–eye coordination. Nayir studied his skin; he wasn't sweating any more. Reaching through the window, he took Suhail's wrist.

'What are you doing?'

Nayir took his pulse rate. It was 135.

'Something wrong?' Suhail asked.

'Yes. You're dying.'

Suhail let out a sarcastic snort. Mutlaq went to the back of his truck and took out a two-gallon jug of water. He brought it back, opened it, and dumped it on Suhail.

'Damn you!' Suhail wiped the water from his face. 'This was a nice shirt!'

Nayir gave him a bottle and told him to drink it, a little at a time, until they reached Jeddah.

The sun was setting as Nayir said goodbye to Mutlaq, started the Jeep, and drove back down to the road. It wasn't very often that the desert depressed him. The day had brought back all the frustration he'd felt searching for Nouf, and it taunted him.

It wasn't until he was back on the freeway that he realized Suhail was unconscious. Well, there was nothing he could do except take him to the hospital when they got back to Jeddah. Some investigator, this one, little Benson & Hedges. It was going to take a bigger man to find Nouf's killer; this shrimp couldn't find water in a cooler.

8

Although Nayir's uncle Samir had devoted his life to science and baulked at superstitions – 'a regrettable heritage' he called it – that used possession by the djinn to explain and treat every ailment, he kept one conviction intact: he believed in the power of the evil eye.

It was much more than a malicious gaze. The effects ranged from ailments as innocuous as hiccups to those as deadly as an embolism in a healthy young man. Because Samir was a chemist, his friends and neighbours considered him wise in matters relating to anything that required a good education – medicine, law, religious philosophy – and they often sought his advice. Over the years, people had discovered that he wasn't much use for setting broken bones or understanding the nuances of jurisprudence, but he knew nearly everything about the Human Gaze, its history, its power, even its cultural peculiarities. Word spread that he was wise on this matter above all, and before long he could count upon three to four visits a week, mostly from strangers, and most of them complaining of the evil eye.

Samir obliged anyone who came to his door with the same serious questions a doctor might ask a patient. If he found it ironic that he, a legitimate scientist, should be delving into a subject with a greater history of fraud than witchcraft, telekinesis and faith healing combined, he never shared this thought with his guests. He recorded their complaints and took care in transcribing each disease from its start. While he could generally offer his visitors nothing more practical than a pendant for protection and the name of a good Bedouin exorcist, he did manage, with his kindly tone and general air of professionalism, to assuage some of their suffering. He also pursued his favourite pet subject at no great cost to himself. And with that he was pleased.

Much as a doctor builds immunity from a constant exposure to germs, Samir had never suffered from the evil eye himself – although he claimed that this resulted from his excellent use of protection. He wore a blue glass amulet beneath his shirt, but more important, he preempted every threatening gaze with a subtle sign of five. It could come in any form. He scratched his chin five times, blinked five times, drew five strokes down his arm with his hand. On occasion he even protected Nayir, giving him five soft pats on the shoulder, or repeating his name five times.

For Nayir, the habit had never stuck. He had a secret scorn for impractical gestures; they generally drew attention and invited more evil. But a quiet part of him was willing to concede that the evil eye was not a mere myth.

He was sitting in his uncle's study on the leeward side of a titanic oak desk, just where the ceiling fan dropped a gentle caress. They had lingered over a very late dinner, and the musky smell of lamb still clung to their robes. He could feel the miswak in his pocket jabbing his thigh, but he didn't take it out – there was nowhere to spit bristles in Samir's house – so he looked at the walls, at the map of the world and the *Bombyx mori* specimens all perfectly framed and labelled. To the right loomed a shelf of textbooks of various shapes and sizes, their only commonalities a certain outmoded chemistry topic and a very thin layer of dust.

On the other side of the desk, Samir sat smoking a Western pipe, a stubby brown artefact that a British archaeologist had given him in 1968. He blew a smoke stream toward the ceiling fan – which blew it back down toward Nayir – and tapped the pipe's mouthpiece on his carbuncular nose.

'How was the desert?' he asked.

'Good,' Nayir said, and they fell into one of the comfortable silences they often shared.

After Nayir's parents had died in an accident when he was a baby, Samir had raised him. He was Nayir's father's brother, and the only family member wealthy enough to take in a young boy. Samir had fought the state for the privilege of raising Nayir. The only other option was to let him grow up in Palestine with Samir's sister Aisha, who already had seven children, but no husband and no money. Samir liked to remind Nayir that Palestine was a terrible place to raise a child, and that, had he grown up there, he would likely be dead or imprisoned by the Israelis today.

Samir had long ago found a niche for himself working with archaeologists all over the Middle East, analysing artefacts and training archaeologists to use the latest chemical analysis equipment. Nayir remembered his childhood as a series of digs. They typically lasted for months at a time, and he often missed school to accompany Samir to the desert. As Samir had always been too preoccupied with work, Nayir had been left to take care of himself. He became a loner but also an adventurer, even as a boy sneaking off on his own to explore the desert.

Despite the independence, or perhaps because he had too much of it, his childhood had provoked an intense

86

longing for a family, a longing that lasted well into adult-hood and which, he was certain, would never be satisfied. His deepest fear was that he'd never marry. Parents arranged marriages. Parents had brothers and sisters who had children who needed to be married. They organized the complicated social visits in which a man got to meet a prospective bride (veiled, of course) – but the groom could at least study her fingers and feet (unless she was socked and gloved as well) and learn what he could from those extraneous parts. (The best insight, of course, was a thorough study of her brother's face.) Samir could provide him with none of these things – there were no cousins to marry, not in Saudi at least – and even if he could have arranged a marriage for Nayir, Samir felt strongly that a man should 'do some living' before settling down. Samir himself, now aged sixty-five, was still doing some living.

Nayir often remarked that the Quran encouraged marriage, in fact made it imperative, saying: 'Marry those among you who are single.' But Samir always replied with another verse: 'Let those who find not the wherewithal for marriage keep themselves chaste until Allah gives them means out of His grace.' And Nayir couldn't argue with that.

He sometimes felt that what his childhood had most lacked was the presence of a woman. A mother or an aunt, even a sister. Samir had known one or two women in his time – foreign women who didn't think it was inappropriate to befriend a non-family man – but those relationships had been brief. The archaeology digs were almost completely male; it was rare to meet a woman in the desert, even rarer than meeting one in Jeddah. Nayir joked with his friends that everything he knew about women had been gleaned from rumour, the Quran, and an assortment of bootleg television videos: *Happy Days, Columbo,* and *WKRP in Cincinnati.* Although his friends laughed, it was sadly true, and Nayir was left with the depressing sense that the world of women was one that he would never be allowed to enter.

It was Samir who had first set him up as a desert guide, arranging for him to take the Shrawis to the desert. Samir had met the Shrawis because the family donated huge sums of money to archaeological research. Soon, other families began to request Nayir's services, and now he was involved in the business full-time, escorting tourists and wealthy Saudis to all ends of the map. Being a desert guide was satisfying – it gave him a sense of community and allowed him to live well, even if he chose to live on a boat, which was, in Samir's oft-stated opinion, 'living like a teenager in a tin can'. Nayir's job with the Shrawis had been intended as recreation, not a career, and however much he was enjoying himself now, there was the future to think about. Once he realized that he was no longer sixteen, he would have to get a proper house and a job that involved books, desks, and framed diplomas. Nayir would rather have suffered lifelong hiccups *and* an embolism than gone into a 'legitimate' career, but he never said so to his uncle.

That afternoon, Nayir had brought some samples from Nouf's body that he had managed to obtain, hoping that Samir could help him analyse the finds in his basement laboratory.

Samir broke the silence with a gentle cough. 'So you think the Shrawi girl didn't run away?' he asked. They had discussed Nouf at dinner, but only briefly.

'It's confusing,' Nayir said. 'All of the evidence points to a kidnapping. She was hit on the head. The family thinks that she overpowered the camel-keeper's daughter on the estate, but I caught a glimpse of the daughter ...' He pressed a finger to his cheek to control a sudden twitch. 'She was as tall as me, maybe even as strong, and Nouf was short. And how could she have driven off on her own? She would have had to navigate a whole network of freeways to reach the desert road. She could drive a jet ski, but a truck? Honestly . . .' He shook his head.

'Have they found the truck?'

'No, not yet. Then there's the camel. She wouldn't have let it go; that camel meant the difference between life and death.' He leaned back and sighed. 'Maybe she was kidnapped with the camel to make it look like she ran away. The kidnapper dropped her in the wadi, hit her on the head, and the camel wandered off.'

'And then what?' Samir asked.

'Then the kidnapper drove back to Jeddah? I don't know. I discovered the sign of the evil eye on her camel's leg. It looked about two weeks old, maybe less. It's possible that Nouf made those lines in the desert, but that would mean that she wasn't alone. She would have wanted to protect herself, and the five lines don't protect you from the desert or the sun; they only safeguard against the human eye.'

'That's not strictly true,' Samir said. 'Recite the Two Takings of Refuge for me.'

Nayir sighed. As far back as he could remember, Samir had asked him to recite the last two surahs of the Quran in a situation of need. 'I know the verses,' he said.

Samir began to recite. '*I seek refuge with the Lord of the Dawn, from the mischief of created things; from the mischief of Darkness as it overspreads; from the mischief of those who practise Secret Arts: and from the mischief of the envious one as he practises envy.* Do you hear that? *From the mischief of Darkness as it overspreads.*' He ignored Nayir's sigh of annoyance and carried on. '*I seek refuge with the Lord and Cherisher of Mankind, the Ruler of Mankind, the Judge of Mankind, from the mischief of the Whisperer of Evil who withdraws, after his whisper, who whispers into the hearts of Mankind, among Djinns and among Men.* And djinns can take other forms, not just human. Remember, they are invisible forces of evil.'

Nayir suppressed his exasperation. They were indeed two beautiful surahs; they were also the only true wards against the evil eye, because they were the only charms that directly invoked Allah's assistance. 'So why didn't Nouf just recite the Two Takings of Refuge?' he asked. 'And for that matter, why would anyone use a symbol or an amulet when the Two Takings are always with them?'

Samir sighed and sat back, a signal that he was about to launch into a lecture. Nayir sat up. 'The short version, please.'

Samir chuckled. 'Most symbols of protection rely on the number five. Five fingers. Five words. Some people even recite the Two Takings five times.'

'I know that.' Nayir waved his hand. 'Five pillars of Islam. Five prayer times a day.'

'The perfect Ka'aba in heaven is made of stones from the five sacred mountains: Sinai, al-Judi, Hire, Olivet and Lebanon.' Samir looked as if he were preparing to discharge the longest list – or at least round it off to five examples – but Nayir was impatient.

'All right,' he said snappishly, 'I know the magic meaning of the number. It doesn't answer my question.'

'You can only whisper the prayer during a moment in time, but a visual symbol is always with you, on guard even when you are not.'

'Isn't that Allah's job?' Nayir asked.

'Yes, it is. But symbols are comforting, too. So perhaps your Shrawi girl wanted that comfort. Perhaps she was afraid. It's even possible that she was trying to protect herself from a human eye. I think the question you want to ask is: who was with her in the desert?'

'A kidnapper, a stranger, or someone not from the family.

It would have to mean she was with someone she didn't trust. Or didn't know she could trust. If she did run away, then it was with someone she trusted enough to be alone with in the desert, but didn't trust entirely. She could have made the lines just in case.'

'So you think she wasn't kidnapped,' Samir said.

'I don't know.'

'Why would someone kidnap her?' Samir asked. 'There was no ransom demand.'

'Possibly to silence her. She was pregnant.'

Samir nodded. 'Don't you find the cover-up suspicious?'

'They want to solve this one alone. That makes them just like every other rich family, it doesn't mean they're guilty.'

'But you must consider that a woman of Nouf's station would not have known anyone but her brothers.'

Nayir frowned deeply. 'Don't be ridiculous. You *know* her brothers. They wouldn't do this.'

'You're defending them as if you fear their guilt.'

Nayir bristled. Of course he feared their guilt. Whoever stole the camel knew the estate well enough to steal the camel. But he hadn't known it that well – he'd stumbled across the camel-keeper's daughter.

Samir's face was hard with annoyance, but slowly it resolved into a patient calm. 'I have known the Shrawi men for many years, and you're right – this isn't the sort of thing they would do. But my logic stands: a woman like Nouf, who was from a good family, would have known only her brothers.'

Nayir sat regarding his uncle, the pipe, the coif of grey hair and the diplomas that hung on the wall behind it. A vague halo of smoke clung to the view. He couldn't help feeling that he was still a young boy taking lessons from a patient old man.

'Can we check on those samples now?' he asked impatiently.

The corners of Samir's mouth lifted. He laid his pipe on its stand and rose to his feet, wobbling slightly. Without the desk to shield him, he suddenly seemed frail, but he regarded his nephew with a thoughtful eye.

'I'm glad you're doing something productive with your time.'

Nayir bit his tongue.

☽

The basement was a dimly lit space with low ceilings and dusty stone walls. These days, Samir spent most of his time in the cool, secluded room, conducting research into an obscure branch of chemistry that Nayir had never bothered to understand. The lab was an odd mix of old and new: a mass spectrometer stood beside a shelf of decaying books, while rows of sterile vials and pipettes shared space with an iron-plated boiling apparatus that might have been a relic from the Ottoman Empire. Above it all hung a faded poster of Jerusalem, lit at night.

It was here that Samir had spent the afternoon processing the samples that Nayir had brought. There were several samples from Nouf's body, swabs of dirt from her wrist, and sand and other traces from her skin and her head wound, courtesy of Benson & Hedges, who'd received them from Othman, who'd apparently received them from Miss Hijazi.

'The samples are interesting,' Samir said. He handed Nayir a print-out, but Nayir set it on the table.

'Just tell me what it says.'

'The first one is dirt.'

'Yes, thanks.'

'*And* manure.' Samir regarded his nephew with a thoughtful eye. 'The sample was contaminated by blood and sand, but manure is manure.'

The darkened substance on Nouf's wrist had contained traces of manure? 'Can you tell if it's from a camel?'

'Only if camels eat *Apocynaceae*. In the manure, I found traces of cardiotonic glycosides, prussic acid, and rutin, the active poisons in the Nerium plant, commonly known as oleander.'

'What?'

'It's a flowering plant. It's not indigenous to Jeddah, but I'm sure you can find them here and there.'

'I know what it is. I'm just surprised.'

'Ah. Well, they don't need a lot of water. They're sturdy plants; they like sand and sunshine, but you probably won't find them in the desert.' He hauled a textbook down from the shelf and fluttered through the pages. 'This is oleander.'

Politely, Nayir glanced at the black-and-white sketch. 'So whatever ate this plant probably ate the sample in Jeddah.'

'Yes. In a sandy place with little water.'

'That should narrow it down.'

Samir disliked sarcasm, and he frowned deeply. 'It's a poisonous plant. Highly toxic.'

Nayir registered this piece of information with mild interest.

'The second sample may be more helpful,' Samir went on. 'I looked at the sand from her head wound. It was rough, almost like gravel, and dark orange in colour.'

'I didn't see any dark sand in the wadi,' Nayir said. 'How dark was it?'

'Well, I only had a small sample, but it was darker than most sand. There were traces of clay in the mixture as well.'

'So sand and dirt?'

'It seems that way.' One by one, Samir began shutting down his machines, and as he traversed the room he also began collecting items for Nayir: a box of plastic gloves, sterile swabs, baggies and hard plastic containers. 'You'll need these,' he said, piling the items into Nayir's arms. 'There's more work to be done.'

Distractedly, Nayir let his uncle stuff the goods into any pocket that would take them. 'Thanks, that's enough. I really don't need all this.'

'What's wrong?' his uncle asked, studying his face.

'What kind of animal eats a poisonous plant?'

Samir gave the question some thought. 'It must have been a desperate act.'

9

The next morning, Nayir stood in the cabin of his boat, the ~~Fatimah~~, and tried to forget his dream from the night before. He'd dreamed of Fatimah again. It had been almost four years since he'd seen her, but the dreams were more vivid every time. She was the only woman he'd ever courted.

His desert friend Bilal had introduced them, saying that Fatimah was the sort of woman who wanted to choose her own husband. Nayir was hesitant about meeting a woman, but she was Bilal's cousin, and Bilal assured him that she was a good Muslim. Right away, Nayir saw that he was right. Fatimah lived modestly in a two-bedroom flat with her mother. She did a yearly Hajj and lived by her prayer schedule. Her calm disposition and the sweet, ticklish way she laughed at his jokes gave him the sense that she was decent and modest.

They spent a few weeks getting to know each other. They met in her sitting room, a cool, quiet gallery overlooking a courtyard. On the coffee table was a gorgeous leather-bound Quran, open to a different surah every day. Despite the nerve-racking presence of her mother, Nayir was grateful for the chaperone; it made the visits feel less awkward. But as he got to know Fatimah, and he realized just how virtuous she was, the motherly chaperone seemed superfluous. Fatimah loved to debate the finer points of Islamic interpretation, like whether or not the veil should cover the face or just the hair. She quoted generously from the Quran without ever touching the book. One time she recited the whole four-page section from surah *An-Nur* that dealt with the veil: 'Believing women,' it said, should 'draw their veils over their bosoms and not display their beauty except to their husbands . . .' She believed that covering the bosom was a literal prescription, but the rest was up to the individual. She covered her head, she said, because it was the modest thing to do, and then she joked that her face wasn't pretty enough to cause much disturbance among men, but she would veil it to spare them the fright. Nayir smiled at the joke, although he privately disagreed. Her face didn't dazzle, but it drew him in anyway, becoming lovelier as the days went by. She was half his height, and from what he could tell through the black cloaks she always wore, voluptuous as well.

They began to meet more frequently, sometimes twice a day. She was a miracle to him, the first woman he'd ever got to know well, and yet the most perfect woman of all. After seeing her for three months, he couldn't imagine *not* knowing her. She had been meeting other men, however, and one day she announced that she had chosen her husband – a doctor.

He took it with surprising aplomb. After leaving her apartment that day, he stood on the street, looked up at her shuttered window, and realized that he would never go back inside. She would become another man's wife. He wanted to preserve something, anything of their friendship, but it was simply too improper. Oddly, he was proud of himself. It felt as if his rationality existed to sustain him through difficult times. Over the next few weeks he spent long hours in prayer, and thought that maybe his isolation was Allah's real plan for him – to what greater purpose he didn't know, but he would have faith.

The heartbreak happened only slowly, over the course of years. He began to think of her with ever-greater sadness, so that each time he did, the wound opened wider. His dreams of her grew more frequent. She appeared exactly as she'd been in the sitting room: questioning, sweet-tempered, cloaked in black with the Quran open on the table before her. Sometimes she was having sex with gentlemen callers while Nayir watched. She would strip for them, tease them. He wanted her, and he would try to have her, holding her, crying, begging her to turn to him, but she never did. The men always noticed Nayir's failure and laughed. The dreams were so real that they left him feeling that he'd actually travelled in a ghostly body through the night and seen the real Fatimah by dream magic. When he woke, it was with a deep disgust for his yearnings and, later, for the way he had been fooled.

Now, swaying gently with the water's rhythm, he stared into the tiny closet that held all the clothing he never wore. Most of the items were piled on the floor, but a few remained on hangers, and among those, he stared at one in particular, the brown suit he'd often worn to Fatimah's house. He took it off the hanger and thought about his dream, trying to chase away the shame. Quranic interpretation said that the body was like a garment for the soul; it was good and pure, endowed with gorgeous flaws. Only in excess did the human delve into sin, and he was certainly not guilty of that, unless one considered his chastity excessive.

He smelled the suit; it was musty, no trace left of the frankincense she sometimes burned in the sitting room.

Searching the pockets, he found a miswak, a spare key for the boat, and his old misyar. The latter he took out with an ache of nostalgia. It was a fake marriage licence signed by a sheikh and left blank for the casual bride and groom; it protected a hedonistic couple in case they were discovered having sex out of wedlock – they could hand it to a cop as proof of marriage. The law was not kind to unmarried lovers. The punishment for having sex out of wedlock – for even being caught with a single woman – was arrest, charges of prostitution and public indecency, a trial without a lawyer, and, if the parties were found guilty, a public beheading. Of course, the chances of being found with Fatimah in her apartment were practically zero, but he'd always dreamed of taking her somewhere, to the desert perhaps, or a quiet beach. It was for such an outing that he'd bought the misyar.

It looked flimsy now, wrinkled from sweat and worn from being folded and tucked away. In the box for 'groom' he had long ago printed 'Nayir ibn Suleiman ash-Sharqi' in his finest handwriting, but the box for 'bride' had been empty since he bought it, four years ago, from an Egyptian sheikh who doubled as a butcher in the old town.

How many times had he almost penned Fatimah's name in the box? How close had he come to marrying her? He must have been crazy, trusting a woman he had no reason to trust. But with a vividness that stung him, he remembered the coolness of her sitting room. It was the reason he'd bought the jacket in the first place. No matter the weather, the room was always cool, as if she didn't really live in this sweltering world where everything else wilted and died.

☽

He had spent the night before thinking about Nouf. Now that his dealings with the private investigator were finished, his interest in the case no longer seemed legitimate. But he wanted answers to the questions that were bothering him: Why had she died so close to the family's campsite? If she'd driven out there, why hadn't anyone found the truck? Where had they found the camel? Why did Othman think the camel had been traumatized? Each question about Othman seemed to spawn a dozen others: Were his brothers pressuring him to keep quiet? Was he hiding something, even from his family? Or did he not trust Nayir?

Nayir's cell phone rang. He spent a surprised moment staring at it, but he answered.

'What did you do to my detective?' Othman asked by way of greeting. Nayir heard the amusement in his voice. 'He's out of the hospital, but he came by this morning to apologize. He's quitting. I tried talking him out of it, but he wouldn't listen.'

'Stubborn guy.'

'I wish he'd been as stubborn about the case,' Othman said. 'What are you doing right now?'

'Oh . . . staring at my closet.'

'I'm free this morning; my meeting fell through, but I have to buy clothing for my fiancée's trousseau. Jackets – can you believe it? These days they want jackets.'

Nayir was too embarrassed to admit that he had heard about wedding jackets. 'Do they come with instructions for handling heat stroke?'

Othman laughed. 'And not just one, but *many* jackets. I think they come with a promise of travel to cooler climates.'

'Ah.'

'Actually, I could use a jacket myself. I can't find my desert parka.'

Nayir looked into his closet again, wondering what had happened to the parka Samir had given him for his birthday one year. He'd dragged it out to the desert once, but the weather hadn't been cold enough, and he hadn't seen it since then. 'I know about a good jacket bazaar,' he said. 'There's one at Haraj al-Sawarikh, but the better one is south.'

'You've been to a jacket bazaar?' Othman's voice was bright with amusement. 'I didn't think you were the type.'

Nayir chuckled uncomfortably. Wearing a coat in the heat obviously meant you were not wearing anything else. 'Yes, that sounds like me.'

'So I'll meet you at the marina in an hour?' Othman asked.

He hesitated. 'Sure. That should give me time for morning prayers.'

As he hung up, he wondered if he was doing the right thing. On the phone it was easy to pretend that things were normal, but it wouldn't be so easy in person. He picked up the brown suit. It was such an ugly thing, faded and dusty. One hem was ripping so that even if it hadn't reminded him of Fatimah, it was too worn and out of fashion to wear again. He dropped the suit in the trash and went to the bathroom to wash.

☾

The jacket bazaar was on the outskirts of town, nestled inside a larger market that sold CDs, cassettes, hairpins and sunglasses. Nayir always thought there must be a connection, but he had never figured it out. The whole area was cordoned off by high stakes strung together with floating green lights and red-tasselled twine. A neon sign at the entrance, lit even in daylight, gave the motto of the place: *The Royal Bazaar, We Always Have Change.*

They were in Othman's car, a silver Porsche. Although Nayir loved the car's looks, he was simply too large to enjoy its sweet size and his knees knocked on the dashboard. They'd been silent for most of the ride. At the marina,

Nayir had shown Othman the walking shoe they'd found at the wadi, and Othman had recognized it as Nouf's. The information had dampened both their moods.

Othman steered through the unpaved parking lot, tyres kicking up gravel and dust, until he found a spot in the shade of an SUV and parked. Struggling to climb out, Nayir imagined he resembled a crustacean popping out of its shell.

As they crossed the parking lot, a call to prayer rang through the air. They stopped and looked at each other. By royal decree, all the shops would close and any man selling goods would be chastised and sent back to the Philippines, or Singapore, or Palestine, his permits and visa for ever revoked.

'You want to pray?' Othman asked.

'I just did.'

'Me, too.' They headed toward a small wooden kiosk which, had it been open, would have sold them two ice-cold, orange Mirandas, but which could now offer them only a triangle of shade. They stood in silence, waves of heat rolling over their bodies. Nayir wished he could provide the right kind of light banter, but he knew Othman disliked it, being forced to engage in it himself all the time. He'd once told Nayir that he liked the way the desert made silence seem honest.

'The private investigator told me that you didn't find much at the wadi.'

Nayir was relieved that Othman had raised the subject. He explained what he'd learned from Samir – that the sand from the wadi didn't match the dirt found on Nouf's wrist.

Othman seemed agitated. 'So what is it you think happened to her?'

'I wish I knew.'

'I need to talk to her escort again. I've tried already, but he wouldn't open up. He's sticking to his story, but I'm sure he knows more than he's saying.'

'He says he only spoke to her on the phone,' Nayir prompted.

'Yes. She called him on the day she disappeared and said she didn't need him. He saw nothing. We don't get along. We never have, since we were kids. Perhaps he'd talk to someone else.'

'I'd be glad to do it,' Nayir said. Despite himself, he felt a twinge of pleasure that Suhail had proven such a wimp, and that Othman still welcomed his help. The conversation was beginning to dispel his doubts.

'You've done a lot already,' Othman said.

'It's no problem. I know you want to find out what happened. By the way, the camel I saw at your stables wasn't traumatized at all.'

'Oh.' Othman looked surprised. 'Well, I didn't actually see her myself. One of the servants told me about it. Did you find anything else in the desert?'

Nayir hesitated. 'The place was familiar. It was the campsite we chose a few months ago.'

His remark was met with a long, heavy silence. 'Our campsite?' Othman asked finally. 'With the boulder?'

'Yes. The same one.'

'Are you sure?'

'Yes.'

Nayir watched his face closely, relieved to see it awash with confusion. Othman clearly had no idea how such a coincidence could have happened.

'That's not where they found her body,' Nayir said. He explained that although they'd found nothing at the campsite, he guessed the flood had washed her downstream to the place the Bedouin had marked on the map.

Othman stared at the ground. 'You didn't find my jacket, by any chance?'

'Your jacket?'

'It's missing. The one I always take to the desert. I hadn't thought it was suspicious until now, but the maps from our last trip were in the pocket. There was also my portable GPS, salt tablets, all that stuff. Maybe she took it. That would explain how she ended up there, or anywhere near where we'd gone camping.'

Nayir crossed his arms. It was possible that Nouf had stolen the jacket, but the person most likely to have used it was Othman. Who else would know about it? Did Nouf typically poke through his closet? Would she have known about his maps? It was an unfortunate irony that in being transparent, Othman had managed to make himself look more suspicious.

Allah, forgive my doubting mind. 'How long has the jacket been missing?' he asked.

'I just noticed it yesterday.'

'Who else would know about it?'

'A lot of people have seen me wear it, but who knew what I kept in it? I can't be sure.'

The prayers finished, and Othman motioned him into the bazaar. They slid beneath a string of tasselled lights and found themselves in the fluorescent glow of a children's toy boutique – the only one in the bazaar – which sold *Star Wars* beach towels and GI Joe balloons and plastic Barbie umbrellas by the case. Cutting to the left, they passed a row of vendors hawking pirate cassettes of Um-Kalthoum. Nayir stared distractedly at his surroundings as they headed into the jacket quarter.

Dozens of jacket stalls spread out before them. Othman started to laugh. 'I'll never get over a sight like this.'

Nayir had to admit: buying outerwear in the world's

hottest climate was a little weird. The vendors didn't seem to realize the futility of their profession, because they embraced it with a passion rivalled only by that of the fireplace and central heating vendors in a separate market on the other side of town. The coat vendors kept their racks lined with sable, mink, rabbit and fox. Trench coats were always in fashion, as were faux Dalmatian swing coats, grey and black pea coats lined with fibre stiffeners, and woollen suit coats in sizes that ranged from tiny to utterly grotesque. Each vendor had a flat stall that faced the pedestrian traffic, their jackets in a neat row like a herd of elephants with their trunks hanging over the street.

Of the many vendors, Nayir had come to know the Qahtani brothers. He preferred their stalls. They had the biggest selection, they never complained when he tried things on, and they didn't seem to mind that he never actually purchased their goods, just wandered through the racks every few months in search of an intangible something.

Just as they approached the Qahtanis' stall, an entourage of bachelors – rich Saudi men in their spanking white robes – descended on the ladies' section. They spread out like soldiers occupying space, their manicured hands deftly fingering the goods. Nayir watched them with disgust and wondered if they too were buying coats for their fiancées. Seeing Othman move into the crowd of bachelors made him uneasy; he looked and acted just like them. They were all hypocrites, because every man knew that the anticipation of travel – the hallmark of any marriage proposal – was in fact its greatest delusion. None of these buffoons had any intention of taking his new wife anywhere, at least not if they could help it. What had Othman promised Miss Hijazi?

Nayir moved in his own direction. He browsed through the coats and tried to imagine which of the many would fit his own future wife. The Russian fur? Too showy. The bomber jacket with the American insignia? In what fantasy world would he ever take a woman to America? No, he would never buy a woman a coat. If she did own a coat, it would have to be one that she purchased herself.

'Bedu!' Eissa came around the cash register to greet him. His brother Sha'aban, seated on a folding chair behind the counter, poked his head up and smiled.

'Nice to see you!' Eissa said. 'It's been a long time. Tell me, you're not here because it's wedding season, are you?'

'No.' Nayir gave a dry laugh. 'No, thank you.'

'What – you don't want to get married?' Sha'aban asked, standing up now. 'Why not?'

Nayir shrugged. Eissa and Sha'aban exchanged a look.

'My wife drives me crazy,' Sha'aban said, 'but I can't live without her. Who else would take care of me?'

'Sha'aban, you are lazy.' Eissa turned to Nayir. 'He doesn't even know how to make his own tea. What can we do for you, brother?'

'I'm here with a friend. He's shopping for his fiancée.'

Eissa's eyebrows shot up. 'Well, while you're waiting let me show you our latest thing.' He slid behind the register and withdrew a plastic dry-cleaning bag through which Nayir saw the ugliest jacket on earth, a cropped leather affair with a fitted waist and a flared, tasselled hem. The stitching on the chest reminded him of something.

'Cowboy,' Eissa said. 'This is genuine ranch wear.'

Seeing the hesitant look on Nayir's face, Sha'aban slapped his brother's arm. 'I told you it's ugly.'

'It's not ugly!' Eissa lifted the plastic wrap and fingered the tassels with enthusiasm. 'Look at the quality. I sold one yesterday. It's just *you*, Sha'aban.'

'I think I'm looking for something different,' Nayir said.

Eissa laid the cowboy jacket on the counter and motioned at the coats with a sweep of his arm. 'It's all yours.'

Nayir went back to prowling the racks, pausing at the raincoats, admiring the colours until he came to the trench coats. One in particular caught his eye – beige, lightweight, a classic cut.

Eissa noticed and laid a hand on his belly. 'Look, Sha'aban, the Columbo coat.'

'Is that what he wants?'

'What did you call it?' Nayir asked.

'You know, Peter Falk.' Eissa cocked a non-existent gun. 'Bang, bang, private eye.' He did some fancy shooting while Nayir slid into the coat. Eissa gasped. 'Ye-e-es! It's you! One hundred per cent man!' This last was in English, which made them all laugh.

Nayir went to the cash register and stood in front of the mirror. The coat fitted perfectly. He stuck his hand in the pocket, which was lined with satin and a few grains of sand that would be for ever jammed in the bottom corner. He buttoned it, unbuttoned it, flipped up the collar, and ran his hands down the front to smooth out the wrinkles.

Othman came over, a grin on his face. 'Buying something?' he asked.

Nayir turned away from the mirror. 'It's not exactly my style.'

'Sure it is.' Eissa snorted. 'What is this – Eissa Is Stupid Day?'

'It's true.' Sha'aban shook his hands at Nayir. 'You're Columbo!'

'I don't know.' He slid the coat off.

'No!' Eissa seized the coat and held it to Nayir's shoulders. 'Come on, it's you! I mean, it's remarkable. I hadn't thought it at first, but that's the way it is with the things that surprise you: you are convinced not because someone tells you to be convinced, you're convinced *because you discovered it yourself.*' He pinched his fingers together and poked the air. 'It's yours from then on. It's your own secret island. Your America! You know, I would have put you in Armani Thug, maybe Moscow in Winter, but not Columbo. But now that I've seen with my own eyes, for me, it is a *fact*.' Eissa was earnest, and Sha'aban nodded, apparently too convinced by fact to say anything. Nayir looked from one to the other, surprised by their unusual excitement.

'I didn't really come here to buy a coat.'

Eissa grew stern. 'That's fine. I know you're a modest man, but I'll give you the right price.'

Nayir hedged. It was ridiculous to buy a coat. What was it? A showy garment, and wasn't it one of the greatest sins to wear garments with pride? He couldn't wear it in the desert. He couldn't wear it in the city, except on those two or three days a year when the temperature dropped to the 80s and it actually felt cold. And wasn't it a raincoat after all? In Jeddah, it rained once a year, for approximately five minutes if they were lucky. But he liked it, he *wanted* it. Besides, the Quran said that garments were bestowed upon man to cover his shame, but also to adorn him. There was no sin in self-adornment. *Oh Children of Adam! Wear your beautiful apparel at every time and place . . . but waste not by excess.*

Othman came up beside him. 'It is a modest coat. I think it fits you.'

Tentatively, Nayir turned back to the mirror. Othman was right: it was a simple coat.

Othman set his own purchases on the counter, half a dozen women's jackets, from leather to fur. Nayir noticed that he was also buying a desert parka. Othman showed him all of the jackets for Miss Hijazi, fussing over each one. 'I honestly don't know if they're going to fit her.'

Nayir wanted to ask if that really mattered, but he kept his thoughts to himself. The choice amazed him. If the jackets were any indication of their travel plans, the couple would be going to Antarctica for their honeymoon.

'So you're buying the Columbo coat?' Eissa asked.

'Yes,' Nayir grumbled. 'Why not.'

The brothers charged him fifty riyals. As he stood at the register, waiting for Eissa to give him change, he began to feel foolish. He was buying a *coat*. The heat bore down on his head. He looked around for the nearest beverage kiosk, and what he saw drained the blood from his face. Beyond the next stall was a woman, alone. The front of her cloak hung open to expose a naked, well-formed body. She was the softest brown, caramel pudding, glistening with sweat in the neon lights. She smiled at Nayir. A second later she melted into the crowd.

Nayir froze. He tried to counter with another image – Um-Tahsin's blind eyes, Samir burping at dinner – but he could see only the woman, her glistening thighs spread slightly apart, her long, firm finger stroking her groin. He glanced around, but it had happened too fast and no one else had noticed. His cheeks burned red. He instinctively reached to cover his groin. If he had been wearing his robe, he could have leaned forward and avoided the show, but with these dratted trousers clamping his crotch he couldn't even tuck it up and squeeze.

'What's wrong?' Othman asked. 'You look sick.'

Nayir ducked into the shade behind the register and waved his hand at the crowd. 'I just got flashed.'

Othman looked around, horrified. 'By a man?'

'No, a woman.' And as he said it, he thought of the smug look in her eyes, the vanity and self-adoration. He wanted to call the police.

Othman's look of horror slowly resolved into amusement. He started to laugh. 'I'm sorry.' He tried to stop but couldn't, and the more he suppressed his laughter, the redder his face grew, until even Eissa and Sha'aban noticed. Nayir forced a chuckle.

'I'm sorry,' Othman said, taking a breath.

'No problem.'

They thanked the brothers and left, pushing back through a crowd that thickened around them like cream. The sun was fierce, and they stopped to buy Mirandas, but by the time they'd cracked open the cans, the drinks were already warm. Heading back into the crowd, they found the toy boutique and ducked beneath the tasselled lights. When they reached the parking lot, Nayir suffered another image of the woman stroking her groin, and this time it caused an even greater explosion of anger. He couldn't believe it had happened, and now that they were leaving, he wished he had called the police.

Just as abruptly, Nouf appeared in his mind, Nouf on the metal table, sheet slipping away from her thighs, and all at once his anger deflated.

Othman seemed to have sobered as well. 'Don't take it personally,' he said. 'I've heard that it happens here quite frequently.'

'You're talking about the flasher?'

'Yes.'

'Oh.'

Othman pursed his lips. 'Think about it – all these people trying on coats. What better camouflage for a flasher?'

'They must pick their victims,' Nayir said with a sudden heat. 'They probably have a secret sense that tells them which men will be most offended.'

'Have you ever been flashed before?'

'No.'

'Then it was random,' Othman said. 'Although I do think it's true that when people see you, they see a good man.'

Nayir shot him a sceptical look. 'That's not what I meant.'

'Brother,' Othman said, smiling, 'I would never accuse you of vanity or pride.'

Nayir nodded, feeling awkward, still wondering if he had somehow invited the flasher, if she had known that he would be more offended than most men, and had preyed on him like a devil. Or was it a sign? A warning that perhaps he was going too far, and that in buying a coat, he, too, was falling prey to vanity?

He thought about vanity the whole way home, and as an antidote to his growing shame, he said the prayer that the Prophet Mohammed always said when putting on a new garment, *O Allah, to You be all praise. You have clothed me with this. I ask You for the good of it, and the good for which it was made, and I seek refuge with You from the evil of it, and the evil for which it was made. Praise be to Allah.*

He said the prayer twice, because the more he looked at it, the more he liked the coat.

IO

That afternoon, Nayir drove to Kilo Seven and parked on the block that Othman had described. The street was nearly deserted, and the sun beat down on the narrow dirt road, reflecting off the buildings and creating the sort of light that made it possible to see through shut eyes. At the corner, a group of Sudanese women sat on woven blankets, selling pumpkin seeds in tiny plastic bags that weighed less than the dime it cost to buy them.

He was wearing the coat. At first, it had made him feel deeply self-conscious, but he had worn it to the supermarket already and discovered a new feeling of authority. There was a devilish pride in that, but he reminded himself that it was for a good cause, and that the pride would disappear soon enough. It always did.

He found the house he was looking for, but when he rapped on the door he got no reply. The knocks echoed on the other side, a courtyard perhaps. He rapped again, then stepped back and looked up. From the roof, a veiled face peered down at him.

A few minutes later, the door swung open. A young man stood there. He looked to be in his twenties. A week-old growth shadowed his jaw and gave him a dishevelled look. He wore a rumpled white oxford shirt and loose linen trousers. Because of the sun's glare, Nayir found it difficult to read his expression.

'I'm looking for Mohammed Ramdani,' Nayir said.

'Who are you?' The voice squeaked with youth.

'My name is Nayir ash-Sharqi. Does Mohammed live here?'

'Who told you that?'

'Are you Mohammed?'

The man didn't move. 'What do you want?'

'I want to talk to you about Nouf ash-Shrawi. I'm told you were her escort.'

The man's face rippled with unease. 'Did the family send you?'

'No.'

'Are you police?'

'No, I'm an investigator.'

Mohammed blinked nervously, and after long, stern scrutiny, he stepped aside, motioning Nayir indoors.

Nayir passed through a courtyard and into the relative darkness of a foyer. A cloak hung on a peg, and a dozen shoes were lined against the wall. He caught a curious, comforting smell. Manure.

'Do you keep animals?' he asked.

'No.'

'Nothing? No chickens?'

Mohammed looked confused. 'No. Why?'

Nayir realized that his questions were slightly offensive. 'Never mind,' he said.

Mohammed ushered him down a narrow hallway and into a sitting room. Beside the sitting-room door was the entrance to the main part of the house, and just above that doorframe was a Khamsa hand, a five-fingered symbol of protection against the evil eye. A pile of threadbare pillows were stacked in a corner, and three bamboo mats were spread on the floor. Mohammed offered his guest the cleanest of the mats and called someone to bring a pot of tea. The two men sat together, legs crossed.

They waited in silence. The shutters were closed, but the heat seeped in. In a nearby room, a baby began to cry.

Mohammed relaxed. It happened with a surprising speed. Nayir sensed that he was used to quietude. Now he seemed to have an easy confidence. It was no wonder he worked as an escort.

A rap on the door and Mohammed stood and went into the hall. Nayir heard a woman's voice. 'We're out of dates!' she whispered. 'All I have is stew. I'm so embarrassed! Shall I serve it?'

'No. Tea is fine, *habibti*. Thank you.' Mohammed backed into the room holding a tea service. He shut the door with his foot. 'My wife, Hend,' he explained with a nervous smile. After sitting down, he poured two thimble cups, passing one to Nayir and setting the other on the floor by his feet. Now the baby screeched, but Mohammed ignored it.

Nayir sipped his tea and marvelled at the casual way that Mohammed had spoken of his wife. There had been no need to explain who she was, and telling Nayir her name was something else entirely. It put Mohammed squarely in the category of young infidel wannabe. Gone were the days of calling one's wife 'the mother of Mohammed Jr'; today women had first names, last names, jobs and whatnot. He wondered how many men had known Nouf's name.

Nayir set down his cup and Mohammed refilled it.

'My condolences for Nouf,' Nayir said.

'Thank you.'

'I know what it's like to suffer a loss.'

'I'm devastated.' Mohammed ran a hand through his hair.

Once again, the scent of manure wafted into Nayir's nose. 'How long have you worked for the family?' he asked.

'Since I was a boy. My father was a driver for Abu-Tahsin when he was my age.' Mohammed shook his head. 'Father died last year.'

'Allah's peace be upon him.'

'Thank you.'

'Was he happy with the family?' Nayir asked.

'Yes. The Shrawis treated him well. I grew up on their old estate, the one they had before they moved to the island. When they moved, I got married, so I got my own place.' He waved a hand at the bare walls. 'Ugly as it is. I used to think I should have stayed on the island, but I'm glad I didn't.'

'Oh?' Nayir glanced at his host.

'I wasn't happy there. Except with Nouf. She was different.'

'Different how?'

Mohammed shrugged. He narrowed his eyes. 'Are you close to the family?'

'Only in an official capacity. I'm their desert guide.'

'Ah. I think I've heard of you. You're the Bedouin guy.'

Nayir pressed his lips together. 'The family hired me to find Nouf when she ran away.'

Mohammed nodded thoughtfully. 'So no one's paying you now?'

'No.'

'Then why are you here?'

'I'm not satisfied that her death was an accident.'

Mohammed motioned sidelong to Nayir's coat and gave a faint smile. 'You sure look the part. But I have to admit, I didn't think there was anything strange about her death. It was tragic, but nothing made me think of murder.'

'Murder?'

'Oh. I . . . Isn't that why you're here?'

Nayir eyed his host. 'Do you think she was murdered?'

'I didn't. I don't. I mean, I just assumed that's what you meant.'

'Not exactly.'

Mohammed wiped the sweat from his temple. 'Then why did you come?'

Nayir paused. 'Tell me what happened on the day she disappeared. You must have seen her that day.'

He shook his head. 'She called and said she didn't need me.'

'Was that normal?'

'Well, I don't know. She's done it before, if that's what you mean.'

'She told her mother she was going to exchange her wedding shoes,' Nayir said. 'And you didn't take her to the mall?'

'No.'

Nayir sat forward. 'How did she leave the house if you didn't take her?'

'I don't know. If I'm not there, she'll usually go out with her mother, or her sisters-in-law and one of their escorts...' Mohammed opened his hands. 'Look, I've already told Tahsin and Othman everything I know. We've gone over it a dozen times.'

'I want to hear your side of the story. When did you realize that she'd run away?'

Mohammed blinked the sweat from his eyes. 'That evening, her mother called me. I told her everything I knew. I went to the estate right away, but of course, by then there was nothing I could do...'

Nayir waited but nothing came. 'What did you do that day?'

Mohammed flinched. 'I had to run errands with my wife.'

'Was she with you all day?'

'Yes, and her sister was there, too.'

115

Nayir knew that he should talk to Mohammed's wife and her sister to confirm his story, but it wouldn't be proper. He set his teacup on the floor. 'I wonder why a woman like Nouf would run away. It doesn't seem likely, does it? She had everything – money, a good family, a fiancé. Maybe you can help me make sense of it. You knew her.'

Mohammed poured Nayir another cup of tea, but the water was gone and the leaves spilled out. Abruptly, he set the teapot down and pressed his fingers against his eyes. A long silence went by. When he lowered his hand, his face was dark red and puffy. 'Please forgive me. I was supposed to *protect* her.'

Nayir felt his host's pain but wondered just how much was professional guilt.

'Look,' Mohammed said, 'it's obvious that Nouf ran away because she was sick of her life.' He forced himself to look into Nayir's eyes. 'You may not want to believe me, but let me tell you, she wasn't the only one who wanted to escape. Most of the girls feel that way. They hate it on the island. They're always out shopping, or riding their jet skis. *Yanni*, I never thought she would actually *do* it. Not like – not like that.'

Nayir could see tears welling in Mohammed's eyes. He reached into his pocket and pulled out a new miswak. 'Do you mind if I . . .?'

'No. Go ahead.'

With his thumbnail, Nayir scraped off the top inch of bark and dumped the pieces on the tea tray. He stuck the miswak in his mouth. 'They say that women suffer here,' he said. 'But as far as I know, only one woman suffered enough to run out to the desert and get herself killed. So what made her actually do it?'

Mohammed swallowed hard. 'I don't know.'

'You said she was different. What did you mean?'

'I don't know.' Mohammed let out his breath. 'I just meant – she was Nouf.' He couldn't find a place for his hands, and the sweat poured so freely from his face that his collar was damp. Another silence went by, and Nayir studied him.

'You knew Nouf for what – sixteen years? Long enough, I think, to know quite a bit about her.'

'Yes, of course. We were practically family.'

Family. The word hung in the air. 'Long enough to develop a . . . relationship with her?' Of course, Nayir thought, a *true* relationship devoid of the stifling proprieties of kinship and marriage. How easy would it have been for Mohammed to fall in love with Nouf? She was pretty. A rich girl who had everything he lacked. He had known her better than anyone else, and yet she was forbidden.

The escort stared at the floor, blinking rapidly. His face was a ghastly grey. 'I had nothing to do with her death,' he said.

'There's something else I don't understand,' Nayir went on. 'If it's true she drove away from the estate – how did she learn how to drive?'

Mohammed continued to stare at the floor. 'I taught her. It was something we did for fun. The other girls do it, too, even Zainab, and she's only six. I know it's crazy, but they would do it anyway, and I figured it was better if I taught them how to drive safely and if I made a few rules. They have to practise on the dirt road behind the house, where nobody can see.'

'All right. But let's say she ran away. She would have needed to prepare for it. She would have had to determine where she was going. Did she have maps? A GPS system? How would she get such things? I wonder. Would she steal them? Or would somebody help her?'

'It wasn't me.'

'Why not? You helped her learn how to drive, which is a lot more dangerous than stealing. It's illegal, too.'

Mohammed looked frightened. 'I know, but it's not—'

'How did she know where to find the keys to the truck, for that matter? And how did she get the camel into the truck? That's a pretty big job; it requires a little muscle. Someone also hit the camel-keeper's daughter on the head, but that girl was bigger than Nouf. How did Nouf manage to knock her out? I think someone helped her, someone who knew she was running away.'

'*Ya Allah, Allah, Bism'allah.*' Mohammed looked as if he would cry.

'And how did she get out to the desert?'

Mohammed rocked back and forth, hands clutched in a knot on his lap. 'I don't know.'

'And her . . . condition—'

'*Allah!* I would never touch her!'

'Someone did. As far as I can tell, you were the only man she saw regularly.'

Mohammed's shoulders began to shake. 'No, no. Listen. There was this guy. Eric. Eric Scarsberry. I used to take her to see him. She wanted to go to America and he was going to help her.'

Nayir sat up. 'America? How?'

'She gave him a million riyals. He was going to set her up in New York with an apartment, a green card, I don't know what else. It was what she always wanted. She wanted to leave.'

Nayir stared at his host. Nouf was going to run away with an American? Despite everything, he was surprised. How was it possible? Women were not allowed to leave the country without an exit visa signed by their husbands or fathers. Certainly Abu-Tahsin would never allow her to travel anywhere. She would have needed a husband, but it couldn't have been Eric. Muslim women were not allowed to marry infidels.

'How was she going to leave?' Nayir asked.

'On her honeymoon. She was going to New York with Qazi.'

'Her fiancé?'

'Yes. She was going to leave him in the hotel and meet Eric somewhere.'

'She was going to marry Qazi and then run off with the American?'

Mohammed stopped shaking and buried his face in his hands. He mumbled something.

'What?'

He dropped his hands. 'I know it's my fault. I should never have allowed it. I knew it was wrong, but she wanted it so much . . .'

'What did she want?' Nayir held his breath.

'She . . . she wanted to live in America.' Seeing Nayir's horrified look, he explained. 'She saw this programme on television one day, about a woman who studied wild dogs in Africa. She wanted to be just like that woman, even though the woman lived with these dogs – dogs! She was dirty. She'd been in Africa for three months, but she loved her life. I think that impressed Nouf more than anything else, that this woman could live like a dog and be so happy. More than Nouf, at least.' He swallowed hard. 'All her friends at school get to go to London and New York. They're rich kids, just like Nouf, and they go wherever they want. But Nouf's parents would never let her leave the country, especially to go to America! All she wanted was to go to school, to study zoology, and then she was going off to live in the wild somewhere. Africa maybe. But she couldn't do any of that here, her father wouldn't allow it. It was something she wanted more than anything else and I . . . I couldn't say no!' The tears began to fall. Nayir looked away, but Mohammed's quiet sobs disturbed him anyway.

'I'm sorry,' he said, not sure what else to say.

Angrily, Mohammed wiped his cheek. '*Bism'allah*,' he hissed. 'I almost feel like I killed her.'

'Tell me,' Nayir said, 'how did she communicate with Eric?'

'She met him at the Corniche mall. I don't know where he lived.'

'Did you go with her?'

'Yes.'

'When did you see Eric last?'

'About three weeks ago. He gave her a key and the address to his apartment in New York.'

'His apartment?'

'Yes.' Mohammed reached into his pocket and produced a thick key ring. 'This is a copy of the key; she gave it to me in case she lost her own, or in case something happened. She was going to stay there for a while until her own apartment was ready.'

'May I borrow the key?'

'You're not—'

'I won't show this to the family.'

Mohammed slid it off the key ring and handed it to Nayir. 'Listen, you've got to believe me,' he said. 'I've been crazy with guilt. I had the feeling that Eric might be somehow involved in her death, but I have no idea where to find him. I don't know where he lives, what company he works for, or if he's still in the country.' For a moment his eyes were wild.

Nayir didn't want to ask the next question, but he had no choice. 'Do you think she was serious enough about Eric . . . serious in the way that—'

'That she would be intimate with him?' Mohammed

looked disgusted, or offended, or both. 'When I took her to see Eric,' he tapped his cheek below the eye, 'she never left my sight. He never even saw her *face*.'

Nayir tried to decide whether he was telling the truth. His gut told him yes, even if it seemed improbable.

Mohammed dropped his hand. 'You're going to tell the family.'

'For now,' Nayir said, 'I'll keep your secret in my fist. But let me ask you this: Nouf disappeared three days before her wedding. Now if what you say it true, then why would she give up her plan and run away before the wedding? She couldn't leave the country without Qazi.'

'Eric must have promised her a way. I don't know how, but it wasn't impossible. He had connections at the docks, he even had his own boat! He could have smuggled her out.'

'Did she say that might happen?'

'No.' Mohammed fell into a thoughtful silence. He shut his eyes. 'I always figured that if she were leaving for good, she would have said goodbye.'

The tragic tone caught Nayir in the throat, but he forced it down. Mohammed, after all, had been complicit in her plan of escape. He had helped her meet Eric and then withheld the truth from her family. He was, by all accounts, an untrustworthy escort.

And the details of Mohammed's story bothered him. Why did she want to live in America? Why not Europe? Or Egypt? In Cairo, she would have many of the freedoms she could have found in America without the difficulty of a language barrier. But maybe it was too close; it was just across the sea, and going to Egypt was not as dramatic as going to America, land of infidels. She must have wanted to leave her family for good, and to leave with a loud statement. Going to America was not a slap in the face, it was a knock-out blow to a righteous family like the Shrawis.

He found that he was tapping his miswak against the back of his hand, and he stopped.

'Did Nouf ever go into the men's side of the house – her brothers' bedrooms? Or their former bedrooms? Their offices?'

'No, I don't think so. Why?'

'You never saw her go into the men's bedrooms?'

'To be honest, I don't go in there myself, so I don't know where she went. Why would she be interested in their old bedrooms?'

'Did she ever talk about her brothers' clothing? A jacket, perhaps?'

Mohammed had to think about it, but he shook his head. 'She hardly talked about her brothers at all. She was nervous around them. They weren't exactly affectionate with her.'

'How were they?'

'Distant.'

'One more thing,' Nayir said, hearing noise in the hall. 'Was Nouf superstitious?'

Mohammed looked sceptical. 'No, not really.'

'The camel she took to the desert had a mark on its leg – a sign of protection against the evil eye. Why would she make that mark?'

'I don't know,' he said. 'It seems strange.'

'I noticed a Khamsa hand on the door frame—' Nayir motioned to the hallway, and Mohammed turned with a jerk. 'Are you superstitious?'

'My wife put that—' Suddenly, the door opened and Mohammed's wife came in. She held a baby asleep in her arms. She was wearing a scarf, but her face was exposed, and she wore a radiant, mischievous grin. Nayir looked away, but Mohammed stood up. He kissed his wife on the cheek and took the baby, turning to show Nayir, who climbed to his feet.

'My daughter,' he said, beaming. 'She's as loud as a plane crash, but we can show her off when she sleeps.'

Nayir stroked the baby's cheek. *'Ism'allah, ism'allah.'*

He wanted to ask Mohammed's wife to confirm her husband's alibi, but he was seized with shame at the idea of it. He kept his eyes resolutely on the baby and wondered if Mohammed's wife had ever met Nouf and what she had thought.

'Please don't leave,' the wife said. 'I'm serving dinner.'

'Oh, no thank you.' Even though it made the couple feel awkward, Nayir spoke to Mohammed. His wife seemed to understand Nayir's discomfort and, quietly, she took the baby and slipped out of the room.

Mohammed showed him out. 'Let me know if you find Eric,' he said.

☽

Back on the street, the Sudanese women had gone. Nayir stuck the miswak in his mouth and returned to his car, which had acquired a new layer of dust. He opened the doors to let out the heat and leaned against the fender, perplexed and disturbed by his revised understanding of Nouf. The fact that she wanted to run away to America set her in a category beyond what he had previously believed: that she was a nervous bride escaping an arranged marriage. Although he had imagined that she had been dishonest with her family, the new Nouf in his mind was starkly deceptive, plotting a scheme to satisfy her desires and hurt her family. She was not fearful; she was ambitious. She was going to appal her family, perhaps even damage their reputation, and all for what? A chance to live with dogs? He struggled to re-envision her and realized that, until now, he had always thought of her as a victim.

Yet this version of things presented its own problems. If

Mohammed had known her better than her brothers, and she had trusted him so much, wouldn't she have at least tried to say goodbye to him? Or had she been deceiving Mohammed too?

As Nayir climbed back into his Jeep, one thought disturbed him above all else: it was odd that Mohammed would go out of his way to help Nouf leave Saudi, but do nothing to find her killer.

I I

There were many reasons to love the marina. Waking up in the morning to the smell of the sea and the delicious view of a blue horizon. Spending the day in the fresh air, cooled by the water and the wind. Watching the pedlars who wandered by hawking prayer rugs and miswak, brass pots and cotton sandals from China. A vendor's large silver truck was always parked at the marina gates, and at precisely 6 a.m. the smell of fresh pita, of *ful* beans cooked in garlic, and of the best coffee in the world came wafting out of the truck's windows. At 6.15 the truck's side flipped up like a mother dog's leg and the men who were queued there scrambled round for their breakfasts, falling on the vendor's window like a litter of pups. The neighbours kept their eyes open; there was zero crime here. No one fought over parking spots. At night, the cabin's lullaby rocking was a magical thing, suggesting motion within immobility. But perhaps the finest thing about the marina was the constant lap of water against the hull and the gentle clatter of boats against their docks, a reminder that this was not the prison of a house and that it was merely a matter of slipping the rope and starting the engine, and

Nayir and his entire existence would float free on a vista of waves.

And yet, people always wanted to know: how had the devoted desert man come to have such an affair with the sea? He had no answer, really. He had learned to love the desert as a boy, but as an adult he had come to desire a newer version of the wild. On the sea he found a curious replication of the sandy waste. There was vastness, quietude, hidden life, and the challenging paradox of monotony and uncertainty. There was also the ability to get away from your neighbours. If it ever became too difficult to avoid their scrutiny, their questions about his career, his family, his possibilities for marriage, he could simply relocate to a different slip and voilà – a whole new set of strange eyes, not yet comfortable enough to begin spying, would keep their modesty behind curtained portholes. Since coming to the marina, he had not actually moved, but knowing that it was an option brought him a tremendous sense of freedom and made having neighbours more bearable.

This morning, he stood on the dock gazing up at the western sky, Columbo coat draped over his arm. He was trying to abate a terrible mood by contemplating the goodness of his world, and he might have contemplated further had it not been for his neighbour, Majid.

'*Salaam!*' Majid called from the opposite slip. He was standing on his bow looking curiously at Nayir.

'*Sabaah al-khayr.*' Standing alone with a strange item of clothing on his arm was – he realized only too late – an invitation to comment.

'What's the news?'

'*Al-hamdulillah,*' Nayir replied.

Majid was the dock's other frustrated bachelor, and as such served as both a comfort and a warning. Between them there was a hint of disgust at this uneasy parallel, enhanced by the fact that they were of the same height and age, their faces were uncannily similar in structure, and they both carried Palestinian blood. The great difference between them was that Majid was the youngest son of a very large family – and not just his immediate family; his female cousins numbered in the dozens – and yet he had managed never to marry. He was a pedantically devout man, but apparently no woman was righteous enough to have him.

Majid stepped onto the pier. 'Heading out this morning?' he asked.

'Yes. I've got some things to do.'

'What is this?' Majid motioned to the coat. 'Let me see. Did you buy yourself a coat?' He drew out the arm and inspected the buttons. 'Is it a raincoat?' He smiled. 'Tell me, where are you going that you might encounter rain?'

'I'm not going anywhere.'

Majid grinned. 'Are we expecting rain *here*?'

The wickedness of his grin was a satisfying reminder that Nayir and Majid were as different as dogs and cats. Nayir thought, too, that this was a man who, precisely five times a day, performed his ablutions and strutted down fifty feet of parking lot to the marina mosque. If, in his short walk through sparse pedestrian traffic, he should spot a woman (and therefore ruin his ablutions by witnessing the unclean), he would shout at the woman at the top of his lungs, march back to his boat, bang open the cabin hatch, climb below, and with great rocking and splashing, perform his ablutions again. He would then emerge, cleaner of soul and body, and gaze up and down the pier in an awkward way as if hoping to detect a woman at the very periphery of his vision, which would not be quite the same thing as *seeing* her. And then, detecting none, he would flip a pair of prophylactic sunglasses onto his nose and march down the pier. Nayir had never seen him bump into a woman twice in one outing. Usually his first explosion was enough to drive the women – not to mention all the birds – from the dock, and Majid would stride confidently back to the mosque.

He looked into Majid's eyes. These were precisely the judging eyes that would worry him the most, and for that reason it was always worth being polite. 'And what's your news? How is work?'

Majid shrugged. 'The same. What about you – how is it in the desert these days?'

'Fine.' Nayir began heading down the pier, calling abruptly over his shoulder: 'Have a good morning.' But the tone of condescension in Majid's question rankled him all the way to the Jeep.

The morning only got worse. Traffic was terrible. He stopped for coffee and eggs at a roadside vendor, but the air was so thick with exhaust fumes that he couldn't breathe, so he went back to the Jeep and drove recklessly off, forgetting his plans for the day, desperate only to get away from the honking traffic and the gagging smell of diesel. But there was no getting free, even when the buildings thinned out and there was nothing near the freeway but fields of sand. In a fury he drove onto the hard shoulder, switched to four-wheel drive and veered off into the sand, heading for nowhere. When the freeway was only a thin line at the horizon, he stopped the Jeep and ate his breakfast and then, checking his prayer schedule, got out with his rug to pray on the sand.

It was only then that his anger dissipated. He finished his prayers, sat back on the sand in the shade of the Jeep, and considered the cause of his mood. A new dread had cropped up since the conversation with Mohammed. Nouf had made plans to run away. To *America*. She had died in the desert, but her running to America would have been another kind of death. And that was what caused the dread. That America represented all that was free and exciting, that it was a destination worth erasing your life for, that this place, this city, this desert, this sea, could not nourish a young girl's dreams.

☽

Qazi ash-Shrawi laid the clipboard on the desk and came to the window to stand closer to Nayir. He had a quiet voice, and the sounds from the warehouse below were causing him to speak louder than was comfortable.

They were in Qazi's office at his father's shoe warehouse. It was a glass-panelled room looking out over row after row of inventory boxes, some stacked so high that only a crane could reach them.

Qazi was almost as tall as Nayir, but half as wide. He wore a clean white robe and an immaculately pressed head-scarf held down by a new black goat-hair *igal*. When he walked, Nayir noticed a pair of battered sneakers peeking out from the bottom of his robe – odd, considering that his father ran the biggest shoe import business in Jeddah which Qazi, the oldest son, was set to inherit one day. Yet the shoes looked comfortable and suggested that, despite his elegance and refinement, Qazi was a hard worker.

'I only saw her once in person,' he said. 'And everyone was there – my uncle, my cousins, my father. There were servants in the room. She wasn't allowed to lift her burqa, so I didn't see her face.'

'Did you talk to her?' Nayir asked.

'I asked her if she was excited about the wedding and she said yes. That was it.'

'Did she sound excited?'

'I don't know. I think she was nervous.' Qazi looked down at his workers and grew thoughtful.

'So you had no idea what she looked like?' Nayir asked.

'Well, I saw a picture. Othman showed it to me.'

129

'What was she like?'

Qazi gave an anxious smile.

Ever since meeting Qazi, Nayir had felt protective of him. There was an air of caution about him, and an immediate impression of grace; he was like a giraffe in the savannah, ears sharply poised to listen for danger, and, like a giraffe, there was something sad and oddly vulnerable about him.

Nayir looked dolefully at the panorama and tried to imagine what had really prompted him to want to marry Nouf. Family pressure? Money? Love? He didn't seem the sort of man who would rush into a marriage unless every detail was right. With his clear brown eyes and square jaw, he was remarkably handsome. Nayir could imagine women lining up to have him. There must have been a reason he chose Nouf.

'Do you know what happened to her?' Qazi asked.

'As I said, it's still under investigation.'

'I thought the police said it was an accident,' he whispered.

'They did.'

A worker opened the door behind them, and seeing them, he apologized for the intrusion.

'It's no problem, Da'ud,' Qazi said. 'Just give me a few minutes.'

'I'm sorry to take your time,' Nayir said.

'No, really.' Qazi raised his hand. 'You sure you don't want coffee?'

'I'm fine, thanks.'

'Then please have a seat. I can give you all the time you need.'

Nayir returned to the desk and Qazi joined him, moving the clipboard aside and putting his elbow squarely on the desk as if to say: *Go ahead, ask me anything.*

'So you never spoke to Nouf except that one time?' Nayir asked.

Qazi pressed his lips together and stared at the desktop with eyes that said: *I take that back, ask me something else.*

'Getting married – that's a big decision,' Nayir said. 'You're young.'

'I'm nineteen.'

'If I'd got married when I was your age, I would have wanted to know everything about the woman before making that kind of commitment.' Nayir saw his face twitch. 'That's a decision for life. I'd want to make sure I was doing the right thing, and then I'd want to make sure again, especially if I didn't know the girl that well.'

'I did kind of know her,' Qazi said. 'We used to play together when we were kids.'

'What was she like then?'

He shrugged. 'I liked her. She was beautiful.'

'That's it?'

'Well,' he smiled wistfully, 'I remember one time she beat me at soccer when we were kids. We were on the roof of my parent's house. I think she was six. Anyway, she threw me on the cement and started pounding on my chest. I was taken by surprise. I'm three years older; I didn't want to hurt her. She was screaming that she'd kill me if I let her win again.' He laughed. 'She thought I was letting her win on purpose.'

'Were you?'

'No. I let her believe it until she beat me again and—' He stopped smiling. 'Well, we were kids, but the only way to protect myself was to take the offensive, throw her on the ground and punch her.' He shook his head. 'I gave her a bloody nose. I still can't believe I did it. She told me later that she didn't hold it against me.'

'So she was a strong girl,' Nayir said. Qazi didn't reply, so he went on. 'People change when they get older. If it were me, I would have been curious to see what she'd become.'

Qazi chewed his lip.

'Look,' Nayir said, 'the family didn't ask me to come here; I just wanted to talk to you. You're the only link I have to understanding her. Her brothers – well, they were older than she was. They didn't know her so well. I was hoping you could tell me more. She would have been different with you, am I right?'

'They didn't ask you to come here?'

'No. And I won't say anything. You have my word.'

'All right,' he said softly. 'I called her once or twice.' He looked up at Nayir. 'It wasn't what you think.'

'What was she like on the phone?'

'She was – I don't know, she sounded sweet.' A secretive look stole over his face and he gave the hint of a smile. 'She asked me if I liked dogs, and I said yes. And she wanted to know if I'd take her to New York for the honeymoon. She made me promise.' He gave a soft laugh. 'At first I was worried about it, because she seemed so excited, but she said that she'd always dreamed of going to New York and that she wanted me to be there when she finally made it.'

Nayir hoped that his face didn't reveal his woe. It was getting to be too much – this tall, careful, considerate man heading off to New York with no idea at all that his new wife was about to abandon him. It seemed impossible that he could have killed her. Even if he suspected that he was being used, it didn't seem like a strong enough motive for Qazi.

'What else did you talk about?' Nayir asked.

'Mostly New York – what we were going to do, where we were going to stay. She kept asking me if it was all right if she left her face uncovered, and only wore her scarf.'

'And what did you say?'

'I said it was okay. I wanted her to be able to see New York.'

Nayir looked at his lap to conceal a wince. He hated what was happening; he felt his anger coming back, and all the pity he'd felt for Nouf seemed pathetically misplaced. He had to remind himself that she'd probably been murdered and that if anyone stood to be humiliated by her behaviour, it would have been Qazi.

'I realize that she was beautiful, and that's what drew you in. But what was it that made you want to marry her?' Nayir asked. 'There must have been something special about her.'

Qazi gave a soft smile and bowed his head. 'Yes. She was beautiful, that's what attracted me, but once I started getting to know her, she seemed happy.' He looked up. 'She's the only cousin I had who laughed like she did, and didn't talk about proper behaviour all the time. She talked about her dogs, and taking walks to the beach, and jet-skiing for fun. But she wasn't silly all the time either, she was just – a perfect balance.' He pressed his hands to his mouth. Nayir could see that the loss had affected him deeply and that he hadn't quite dealt with his grief. Tears threatened to fall, but Qazi excused himself and went into a small bathroom adjoining the office. It surprised Nayir to feel so much sadness from him. He had spoken to Nouf on the phone only a few times, had met her once, veiled by a burqa, but he must have become deeply attached to her anyway, or at least to the idea of her. And why not? They shared a childhood connection. She was going to be his wife. He must have thought of her as his wife already.

Qazi returned a moment later with redder eyes. He sat back down at the desk and apologized for the interruption. Nayir gave him some time before plunging into his next question.

'When did you find out about . . . her behaviour?'

Qazi's hands seemed to grow unsteady and he drew them onto his lap. 'My father told me at the funeral.'

'I see. That's late. You didn't have any idea before then?'

Qazi frowned. 'No, of course not.'

'Can you tell me where you were on the morning that she disappeared?'

'I was – actually, I was at their house.'

'The Shrawi estate?'

'Yes. I had to drop off another part of the trousseau.' Glancing nervously at Nayir, he added: 'I was only there for fifteen minutes. Othman can vouch for me.'

'What time were you there?'

'Before noon,' he said. 'You don't think I'm involved in this?'

'And where were you after that?'

'I came back here. But first I stopped for lunch, and I drove around for a while.' He was tense now, his arms rigidly crossed on his chest. 'I had nothing to do with her running away, I hope you know that.'

'How long were you out?'

'About an hour. I do that every day at lunchtime. You can ask anyone.'

'So no one can really vouch for you around the time that Nouf went missing.'

Qazi sighed and sat forward again. 'No,' he said. 'I thought you just wanted to know more about her.'

'I do,' Nayir said gently. He felt bad for pressing, but Qazi seemed to have handled it well. 'But you have to admit, you stood to lose the most from her indiscretions. If anyone found out about her behaviour, they could have told you—'

'But why would they?'

'To stop the wedding.'

Qazi shook his head sadly. 'And my answer to the

134

problem would have been to kidnap her? That's crazy.' He looked straight into Nayir's eyes. 'If I'd wanted to stop the wedding, I would have called off the wedding. It would have been that easy.'

He was right – it would have been easy, and if anyone had asked why, he could have come up with a dozen excuses. He wasn't ready. He'd had a change of heart. No one would have blamed a nineteen-year-old boy for his hesitation. If Nouf's fiancé had kidnapped her, he would have had to be a much more arrogant, prideful man, someone for whom her indiscretion would have been deeply insulting. Qazi just didn't seem like that man.

12

When Katya opened the door, the screech of the blender deafened her. Sighing, she took off her shoes, unwound her scarf, and laid her cloak and purse on the coffee table. A second later, the blender stopped.

'I'm home!' she called.

Her father appeared in the kitchen doorway holding a smoothie in a frozen glass.

'Is that for me?' she asked.

'If you like.'

She collapsed on the sofa and held out her hand – exactly, she thought, like a chick in a nest. Her father came closer and, looking down on her, gently handed her the glass. 'How was work?'

'Good,' she said. He nodded and turned back to the kitchen. 'Thank you, Abi,' she called after him.

'Othman called this afternoon.'

She waited, the smoothie chilling her hands, but Abu was quiet so she stood up and went to the kitchen doorway. He turned on the tap and began to wash the dishes.

'What did you do today?' she asked. He didn't reply. Tentatively, she tasted the smoothie. It was odd and earthy, as if he'd added grass, but she managed to swallow it. 'So what's for dinner?' she asked.

He shrugged. 'The fridge is almost empty, but we do have some eggs.'

She was hungry enough to eat a carton of eggs, but if she asked him to cook them, she knew he would say: 'Do it yourself.'

The frustration of working long hours was finally beginning to catch up with her. When she'd started this job almost a year ago, she'd been so excited about having a job at all that she never felt tired, or if she did, it was satisfying. But now she felt worn out. She'd been up since six this morning and now had no energy to go to the grocery store or cook a meal. Abu ought to have done it.

He's retired, she thought with a stab of frustration. *He has all the time in the world.* But the look on his face told her that he didn't have all the energy in the world. Something was bothering him, and it wasn't just Othman.

After Katya's mother had died, he'd quit his job at the chemical plant and settled quickly into retirement. Almost overnight, his salt-sprinkled hair had gone completely grey, his sharp black eyes no longer looked so keen, and his body, once unusually hearty and tall, had withered somehow. Maybe it was the fact that he no longer wore his well-fitting suits; he only wore his house robe, which made him look permanently unkempt.

Without his job, they had little money. His retirement income wasn't enough to cover expenses. Thankfully, they already owned the apartment, a two-bedroom place in the old town, but some months they couldn't afford to pay the bills, and when their phone got disconnected for non-payment, Katya had decided to find a job.

For years, she'd tutored high-school students in chemistry. All of her students were from the School for Girls just

down the street. They came in pairs with their escorts –
usually brothers or cousins – who waited while Katya helped
the girls with their homework. Every once in a while, as the
girls were leaving, she'd hear their escorts tease them: 'Why
are you studying chemistry? Can you use it for cooking? It's
not like you're going to get a *job*.' The comments hurt her as
much as they wounded her students. She enjoyed the work;
encouraging young girls to become more than good cooks
was meaningful to her. It paid decently and it was something she could do at home. But she had longed for many
years to have a job where she could put her skills to better
use.

She had received a Ph.D. in Molecular Biology from King
Abdul-Aziz University, but like every other woman in her
programme – an all-women's programme – she had finished
her degree with the bittersweet knowledge that, although
she had accomplished a terrific feat, she had precious few
prospects for the future. There were very few jobs for
women, especially educated women. Women were allowed
to work only in places where they wouldn't interact with
men, or so infrequently as not to draw attention to themselves, which limited them to girls' schools and women's
hospital clinics.

Fresh out of college, Katya had taken a teaching job. She
had survived a year. It had been too much work for too little
pay, and she simply wasn't motivated enough. She preferred
the quiet of a laboratory, where she didn't have to be around
people all the time, where she could experience the excitement of discovery, and the pleasures of cleanliness,
organization and control. It seemed that there should be
plenty of jobs for women in environments like that, yet the
country's scientific jobs were filled by men first. Frustrated,
and growing more resentful, she'd stuck to tutoring biology
and chemistry for nearly two years.

Just when it became clear that she had no choice but to find a better job, the city crime lab opened a department for women, and she applied. They accepted her at once, impressed with her educational background. The prospect of working in a laboratory thrilled her, but she dreaded telling her father. He hadn't liked the idea of her teaching, and that was in a strictly female environment. Although the crime lab would be segregated, there was a chance that she would see men on occasion.

She broke the news to him with enormous trepidation. They were sitting at the kitchen table, peeling carrots and sipping tea. The fridge was empty, the stove wasn't working, and they were both feeling down. When she told him about the job, he jerked upright and narrowed his eyes. 'Come on, we're not *that* poor,' he said.

It had stung her so deeply that she'd wanted to cry. Letting a woman work was a desperate thing to do. They had sunk in the world. Her face must have shown her disappointment, because Abu backpedalled.

'Wait,' he said. 'Is this something you *want* to do?'

She nodded, not trusting herself to speak.

'Then for now . . .' he struggled to say it, 'take the job.' He smiled sadly at her just as the tears spilled down her cheeks. She wiped them angrily away, embarrassed by her crying. 'If it doesn't work out,' he added, 'you can always quit.'

She nodded again, feeling deeply relieved. Even though they didn't really have a choice, she was grateful that he'd been big enough not to care what other people would think about his daughter working. It was exciting that she would have a job in the public sphere, but there was still a secret anguish at the thought that, in working, she represented their poverty, and that somehow it shamed him.

He was careful after that. He told her he was proud that

she'd found such a well-paying job and that she was a molecular biologist. Katya suspected that deep down he still felt the shame. It manifested itself as a reluctance to tackle the problem of housework. Every morning, he would stop her at the door. 'Who's going to cook dinner tonight?' he would ask.

She promised that she would still do the cooking and keep up with the housework, the cleaning and laundry and shopping that her mother had done before she'd died. It seemed a reasonable deal, because even though it was patently unfair, for Abu, it was better to take things one step at a time. For now, he was supporting her having a job, and that was enough.

Katya went to work. Although being around death took some getting used to, she delighted in the fact that she was helping solve crimes. Over the course of the year, Abu had realized that she didn't have the time or energy to do everything herself, and he'd begun to take up some of the slack. Now he cleaned and did laundry; he even went shopping, but he cooked dinner only when he was genuinely hungry, and, being sixty-four, he was seldom hungry. *He has an old man's appetite*, she often thought, *and I have an appetite for both of us.*

She realized that he was slightly depressed – who wouldn't be after losing a wife of thirty years and quitting a lifelong job? She had hoped that time would heal his sadness, or at least make it more bearable. Sometimes she'd come home to find a whole dinner laid out for her – lamb, rice, eggplant and bread – and other times it happened like this: eggs in the fridge, an experimental smoothie.

She squeezed the smoothie glass and took a deep breath. 'I've been thinking about Nouf's case all day.' Abu turned to face her. Detergent bubbles dribbled down his wrist. 'I'm beginning to believe she was kidnapped, like Othman said.'

He frowned. She could see in his face that he was struggling with something. 'I wonder how much her family knows,' he said.

She shrugged and set her glass on the counter. 'Othman has told me everything he knows.'

'Let me guess – it isn't much.'

'He's dealing with his grief. And besides, he's so busy with his job . . .' She trailed off, waving her hand to indicate that she'd already said all of this before. 'I want to wash before dinner.'

She left the room, hoping to cut short his inevitable criticism of Othman. Abu disapproved of her marriage plans. His disgruntlement took the form of a steady, low-level grumbling, a build-up of petty discontents about Othman and his family. She knew that he was worried for her, worried that Othman didn't really love her or that he would change his mind, cancel the wedding and discard her, because he was rich and because, if something better came along, he could do whatever he liked. Perhaps Abu simply couldn't believe that she was worthy of a rich man's love – she, a middle-class girl who was too old to be marrying in the first place. The thought made her uneasy, because she sometimes wondered the same thing herself. Did Othman really love her? Was he disappointed that she was twenty-eight? Would he change his mind, once they were married? But in Othman's presence she was always confident of his affection. More likely, the source of Abu's tension was Abu himself and his old-fashioned notion that a child's marriage should be a bargain between the parents. In that regard, he was not an equal to the Shrawis, just a low-status in-law who had been stripped of his bargaining power when Katya and Othman had arranged the marriage themselves.

She had met Othman through her best friend, Maddawi, who had married a close cousin of his and who was herself a distant cousin of the Shrawis. The wedding had been a completely segregated event. In the family's grand suburban home, Katya had crept out onto a narrow balcony to get away from the cacophony of a celebration that involved over five hundred guests, and she'd stumbled on Othman. When he saw that her face was exposed, he didn't avert his gaze. He met her eyes and smiled – sadly, she thought. But he introduced himself, asked her name, and actually *shook her hand*. His self-possession and quiet confidence pleased her. She was nervous at first, not certain what to make of him, but they fell into conversation as naturally as if they were family, and they talked for two hours before he had to leave. Afterwards, she marvelled at the fact that they had laughed like old friends and told each other stories about their families which, she was certain, neither one of them had told anyone before.

Over the next few months, they continued to meet. They drove around in his car, where they could talk without worrying about religious police. They also met in crowded shopping malls, where the air conditioning made it possible to walk around in comfort and where, among the bustle of thousands of shoppers, the chances of being noticed by people they knew were extremely slim. At first, she thought he was attractive in a smouldering kind of way, but after a while she realized that he seemed to have no sexual intentions at all. He was the sort of man who could look at a woman's face, shake her hand, introduce himself, and not a single part of it turned him on. He was warm and funny, sometimes a delightful conversationalist, but she suspected that, deep inside, he was cold. With dismay, she came upon a painful truth: that a modern, enlightened man like Othman, the sort of man who could actually *meet* a woman in public and not think she was a whore, might not have enough within him to sustain a passionate relationship.

142

But when, one evening four months into their friendship, he took her to a secluded strip of highway and finally kissed her, she thought maybe she'd been wrong. He did have passion; he was simply a slow and careful man. And she liked him more than ever. A few weeks later, he asked her to marry him, and she said yes.

Of course, it was a scandal that she'd been meeting an unmarried man in public. She never told Abu, even after she announced her marriage plans. She simply told him that she'd met Othman at the wedding, that he'd been taken with her, and they'd kept up a friendship on the phone. Abu didn't believe her, she could tell, but she couldn't bring herself to admit the truth. In certain ways, Abu was still painfully traditional, insisting that she wear the veil when his friends came to the house (friends he'd had for forty years) and making unkind remarks about her two female cousins who had both chosen their own husbands. But times were changing, and ever so slowly, Abu was changing with them, supporting her job, even doing the housework. She hoped this dislike of Othman was just a last stand of tradition.

And, sometimes, she suspected that her age was the real reason he hadn't outright forbidden the marriage: in Abu's mind – and the mind of nearly everyone else she knew – she was lucky at twenty-eight to have found a man who didn't already have three wives and sixteen kids.

She went into the bathroom, closing the door halfway. She turned on the tap and pinned up her hair, but just as she was about to bend over the sink, she caught sight of Abu in the door frame.

'It's too bad about the girl,' he said, opening the hamper and taking out the dirty laundry. 'You've said she was intelligent. I suspect she would have led a very fine life.'

'I think so, too.' The water rose in the sink, so Katya turned off the tap and pulled up the plug. It was covered in hair and soap. She peeled the glop from the plug, dropped it in the bin, and quickly washed her hands.

'Who do you think kidnapped her?' he asked.

'I have no idea.'

'No suspects?'

'Not yet,' she said. 'And for all we know, she did run away.'

'But you don't think so.'

Katya didn't reply. Dirty towels piled on his arm, Abu leaned against the door frame. 'It seems connected to the fact that she was pregnant. But I ask myself who would be troubled most by the news of her pregnancy? Her mother? Her father? I think Nouf would be troubled the most, don't you think?'

Katya nodded. The question touched on a lurking fear she'd had since she discovered that Nouf had been pregnant. What if she'd been raped? Not on the day she disappeared – the pregnancy was at least a few weeks along – but before that. And what if the discovery of the pregnancy was so horrible that it drove her to run away? Katya had seen Nouf two weeks before she'd disappeared. She would have been pregnant then. It had been no different from any other time Katya had seen her, but she could have been hiding her anguish or despair.

Yet there was no evidence of month-old rape on the body – no cuts or bruises that had already healed.

'Maybe,' Katya said. 'Nouf would have been upset. But I don't think she was suicidal, and the scratches on her wrist mean that even if she did run away, she fought with someone before she left.'

'You may be right,' Abu said, 'but the way that family raises their children bothers me. You know this, so I won't say any more, except that I think Nouf may have been a victim of her upbringing.'

144

'What do you mean?'

'I think she may have wanted to punish herself more than anyone else wanted to. The Shrawis are so intensely focused on appearing righteous. They have to be; it's their job. They take money from everyone in the name of Allah, so they have to be virtuous and absolutely blameless. But that's a lot of pressure, especially for a young girl with a rebellious streak.'

Katya studied her father's big brown eyes. He was right; in some ways the Shrawis were a high-pressure family, but the simple way he'd just described Nouf fascinated her. Is that really what he thought, she wondered – that Nouf was just a regular girl with a 'rebellious streak'? It made her sound charming, innocuous even. This was the same man who, in another mood, might have called her a hoyden or a bad example of a woman. Retirement seemed to be smoothing his edges. She remembered how angry he'd been when, two years ago, after spending weeks arranging a marriage for her, he had discovered that she wouldn't marry the man. He didn't speak to her for a whole day, and when he finally did, his frustration exploded out of him, a blistering tirade in which he'd called her a 'wretched ingrate' and warned that she would become a 'useless woman'. How, she wondered, would he describe her today?

'Perhaps you're right,' she said.

A minute later, drying her face on a towel, she regarded her father slumped in the doorway, a sad look in his eyes.

'Aren't you going to make my eggs?' she asked.

He drew himself up sternly, but then he smiled. 'I'm doing the *laundry*,' he said. 'It's your turn to cook.'

☽

Back in the kitchen, she took off her engagement ring and set it carefully on the window frame. She finished washing the dishes Abu had left in the sink and pondered how to talk about Nouf without bringing Othman into it. The case really *was* beginning to obsess her. Whom had Nouf been fighting with before she disappeared? Was it the same person who had hit her on the head? Why had they found manure on her wrist? And wood flakes in the wound in her skull? This was obviously more than an accidental drowning, and Katya felt compelled to string the facts together, if not to prove murder, at least to satisfy herself – and Othman as well – that it *was* an accident.

But no matter how hard she tried, any theories about Nouf would bring up Othman – or worse, her job.

A few minutes later, Abu joined her in the kitchen. He leaned against the counter and picked up her smoothie. 'Didn't you like it?'

'It was fine,' she said. She could tell that his mood had improved since she'd come home, and she wondered exactly how lonely he was when she was working. 'How was your day?' she asked again.

He shrugged. 'It was all right.' He came and stood beside her at the sink. 'That co-worker of yours isn't still bothering you, is he?'

'No, it's fine,' she said. He was referring to Qasim, one of the lab techs in the men's section, who had come into the women's laboratory one day and demanded that the women start wearing socks. There were too many ankles showing for his comfort.

'Do men often just walk into the women's section?' Abu asked.

'No, no, Abi, it's not like that. And don't worry. They're putting a lock on the door.'

'So you still don't interact with men?'

'That's right.' Instantly, she thought about Maamoon and Nayir and felt a twinge of guilt. Yes, she had met men, but

Maamoon was a grouchy old medical examiner, and Nayir didn't seem to count. He was a lackey for the Shrawis, and, judging by the way Othman talked about him, something of a holy Bedouin guide. Every few months he and Othman went to the desert to commune with nature.

She opened the refrigerator and looked inside – except for the eggs, it really was empty. She plucked four eggs from the box, set a frying pan on the stove, switched on the burner and poured a dollop of oil in the pan. She had to admit that before meeting Nayir she'd been intrigued by Othman's description of him – pure and noble, a romantic Bedouin figure. He'd turned out to be such an ayatollah. He hadn't been able to speak to her without blushing, he wouldn't meet her eye, and he had fainted when he saw Nouf's body, as if he'd been exposed to the face of the devil himself. Nayir was just the sort of man who stopped women on the street to complain that they weren't wearing gloves, or that he could see too much of a face through a burqa.

Meeting Nayir ought to have made her appreciate Othman all the more, but instead it made her apprehensive. Was Othman really so clueless about his friends? Or was Nayir completely different with Othman? Perhaps he really was a spiritual role model, and Othman felt inspired by that. In a way, it disgusted her – not having to worry about right-eousness in your friends was one of the luxuries of being a man.

Abu stood beside her. In silence they watched the eggs until they were done. Skilfully, Katya slid them onto plates, put the frying pan back on the stove, and extinguished the flame. Abu motioned to her hands.

'Reminds me of your mother,' he said. 'The way you handle the pan.'

A sudden spasm in her throat prevented her reply. Her mother had been dead for more than two years, but Katya still couldn't think about her without a threatening grief. These days, when she allowed herself to linger on thoughts of her mother, it was inevitably to mourn the fact that she wouldn't be there for the wedding. Mother, who'd been unable to have more than one child of her own, had wanted grandchildren – as many as possible. She believed that marriage should be a woman's highest goal, and Katya's resistance to the idea had disappointed her profoundly.

They ate in relative silence, and when they were done, they sat on the patio overlooking the street. Abu gave her a mildly reproving look for not wearing a burqa, and she mumbled something about being too tired to go back into the house and get one.

The daytime crowds were gone, the souk vendors' carts were folded away, and now the local residents wandered by, some of them waving or calling greetings to Abu, others avoiding him for fear of seeing Katya's unveiled face. She counted them as they passed – the men who wouldn't say hello to a friend because she was there, because looking at her would have been as dangerous as staring at the sun – and she got to four before she went inside.

Retreating to her bedroom, she decided to call Othman. She wanted to tell him about her discovery that the skin and blood beneath Nouf's fingernails weren't her own. She'd been putting it off because she wasn't sure how to break the news that Nouf had struggled with someone. She'd already had to tell him about the death, then the pregnancy. She didn't want him to associate her with devastating news. Now, every time she mentioned Nouf's name, he fell silent. She knew his sister's death had affected him deeply, and that Othman, in general, was hesitant in expressing his feelings, but it worried her that he was so quiet on the subject. She imagined that it was taking a much greater toll on him than he would ever admit.

When he answered, he sounded tired but he apologized, saying he'd been in meetings all day. 'I want to see you,' he said. 'Can we make time this week?'

She agreed with relief. They had spoken at the funeral but they hadn't been able to see each other. Before that, he'd spent ten days in the desert, searching for Nouf. In that time, she'd become a zombie; she'd lost sleep every night worrying about him.

It took a while before she marshalled the nerve to tell him about the evidence beneath Nouf's fingernails. He grew quiet, as she'd expected, and she felt a sudden guilt. *This could have waited until tomorrow*, she thought. After a lengthy silence, she heard him sigh.

'I'm sorry,' he said. 'I've been thinking about it all day. I really appreciate your help.'

'It's no trouble.'

'Well, I appreciate it anyway.'

'Do you have any idea whom she might have struggled with?'

'No,' he said. 'Not at all.'

'Just one more thing,' she said, 'and then I won't bother you with any more of this tonight. I'd like to get a DNA sample from her escort. I'm wondering if you could talk to him.'

'Why do you need DNA?'

'I think if anyone kidnapped her, it would have been him. I'd like to check his DNA against the trace from her fingernails.'

'That's a good idea,' Othman said. 'But he doesn't like me, you know. It might be better to talk to Nayir. He's going over to talk to Mohammed. Maybe he already has. Let me give you Nayir's number.'

Wanting to protest, Katya reluctantly wrote down the number. She didn't want to call Nayir. He was exactly the sort of man who wouldn't speak to a woman on the phone. 'I'll call him,' she said, 'if you think it's all right?'

'Of course it's all right. He's a bit traditional, but if you explain what you need, he'll be willing to help.'

She was sure he wouldn't be, but she would try.

'If he doesn't answer his cell phone,' Othman said, hesitating, 'you're going to have to go over to his boat. Or send your driver.'

'Oh, I couldn't do that.'

'Believe me, it's no problem. I trust you.'

She was pleased that Othman trusted her modesty, but that wasn't the problem. 'Nayir will be alarmed if I show up at his boat,' she said. He would think she was being highly immodest.

'I know it's not exactly appropriate,' Othman said, 'but sometimes he doesn't answer his cell phone for days at a time. It can be very frustrating when you want to talk to him.'

Katya was silent.

'Just go with your escort,' Othman said, 'and be sure to wear your burqa. It should be fine. Nayir's very Bedouin in his treatment of women, but he's a good man. He'll understand.'

She wanted to explain exactly how horrible it would be for *her* to go to Nayir's boat – she always found it degrading when men ignored her, when they wouldn't meet her eye, and when they acted as if she were a prostitute just for opening her mouth – but Othman held Nayir in such high regard that she didn't want to speak ill of him. 'I'll give him a call,' she assured her fiancé.

☽

That night, she dreamt of baking cookies, warm, luscious sugar cookies exactly like her mother used to make. But when she started to eat them, her mother appeared in the kitchen doorway and warned her not to eat too many. A man doesn't like a fat woman, she said, not until she's had a few children, because otherwise he'll think she eats too much. She'll eat everything, the belching wench, she'll even eat the food for the children, and they'll be skinny, retarded, and a shame to their father. Then what kind of mother will she be?

In the dream, Katya began to cry.

13

Nayir returned to the marina after a morning of fruitless searching for Eric Scarsberry. He had visited three American living compounds but had turned up nothing. As he drove from one to the next, his thoughts kept returning to the idea of Nouf having an American lover and to the ways in which his men had embellished the theory. One evening at the campfire, they had described the sorts of things a man would have to say to seduce a girl like Nouf. 'In America, you can shop any time you want,' and: 'In America, you can have your own car!' The one that stuck in his mind most was: 'In America, a man can't marry a second wife.'

Any mention of a second wife always caught his attention. He liked the idea that it was something to strive for, being an only wife, and in that regard he thought that Nouf might have a good reason to avoid a Saudi marriage after all. He himself rejected the idea of multiple wives. The Quran allowed four, but only with the provision that each wife be treated *exactly the same*, which was, to Nayir's way of thinking, another way of forbidding polygamy, because what man could treat four women in precisely the same way? Give them each the same attention every day, the same amount of money, the same number of children? The same kisses? The same sex? Any man with that much stamina obviously had nothing else to do. When would he find the time to work, raise children, pray? It was ludicrous, and yet he saw these families all the time, these husbands who juggled four wives and twenty children. He saw them picnicking at the Corniche, the children swarming around like small tribes of bandits, their wives bickering while they laid out enormous rugs and set up elaborate outdoor kitchens with camping stoves and dozens of coolers. He would sit on a bench and watch from a distance, studying the wives all cloaked and veiled, and try to determine whether the husband was actually treating them equally. In most cases, the husband would sit on a separate rug with other men, above the fray. If the children approached him, they did so with trepidation. The women never approached except to bring food. At least, Nayir thought, the husband was ignoring them all. Equally.

But no matter how often he saw such families, no matter how commonplace they came to seem, it galled him every time to see a man with four wives. It didn't seem fair that some men could have four when others had none.

Exhausted from the midday heat, he pulled his Jeep into the marina lot. Usually he parked in the shade, even though there was only a single, wandering strip of it, cast by a ramshackle storage shed. Because he had lived at the marina longer than any of the other residents, they always left the space for him. Never mind that the shade lasted only an hour, or that his Jeep was the oldest piece of junk in the lot, their neighbourliness touched him. Today, however, another car had stolen that coveted spot. It was a black Toyota with newish plates and a Quran on the dashboard.

He stood for a moment and puzzled over the car. Perhaps

he had a new neighbour. A businessman or a weekend sailor.

As he walked down the unsteady pier, the old wood creaked beneath his weight, and the boats bobbed in sympathetic rhythm. He scanned the rows for the new neighbour's boat but instead he spotted a woman on the pier. He couldn't see who it was; she wore a black robe and a scarf with a burqa. Only her eyes showed.

When she saw Nayir, she stood up straighter, and he knew instantly that it was Miss Hijazi. He didn't know any other women, and she had recognized him. What was she doing here? He nearly tripped on a coil of rope. As he drew closer, he recognized her eyes and the shape of her shoulders. She waited for him to speak.

'Miss Hijazi,' he said.

'Mr Sharqi,' she replied, pointedly not extending her hand. She stared at Nayir's coat, looked it up and down twice but made no comment.

'*Ahlan wa'Sahlan,*' he said, not sure what to do. If the neighbours saw her, they'd start to gossip – who knows, they might even call the religious police – but he couldn't hide her anywhere; there was nowhere to hide, and inviting her onto the boat was out of the question. It would be like asking her to bed. Just standing beside her made him feel guilty.

'Where's Othman?' he asked, glancing at Majid's boat.

'At work.'

'Does he know that you're here?'

'Yes, he gave me the address.'

'He did?'

'I'm sorry,' she said. 'I've tried calling but your cell phone was off.'

He took the phone from his pocket. It was off. 'Don't you have an escort?'

'I have a driver.' Her voice betrayed a slight annoyance.

'Where is he?'

'Taking a walk.'

He didn't say anything. She lowered her eyes. 'I didn't come here for the wrong reasons, Mr Sharqi. My escort has known me since I was a child. He trusts me.'

He heard a thump in a nearby boat. It was all the spur he needed to spring to action. 'Come,' he said, ushering her down the pier. 'My boat's over there.'

From forty yards, the sight of the ~~Fatimah~~ was a magnificent one. She was a Catalina yacht, thirty feet long with a bright red mainsail and a marine blue jib, both scrolled tightly around their masts. But as they drew closer, Nayir became acutely aware of the state of the harbour. Torn magazine pictures and clumps of trash floated in the water. He led her down the side ramp. Leaping onto the top deck, he offered her a hand, but she ignored it and hopped onto the boat.

'*Tfaddalu*,' he said, motioning to the cabin entrance. Leaping onto the boat was one thing, climbing down the rickety ladder was another. He descended and turned to help Miss Hijazi, but he didn't want to touch her, or appear to be looking up her skirts, so he moved away.

Gracefully, she stepped off the ladder.

'Have a seat,' he said, motioning to the dinette and the small sofa opposite. Quickly, he snatched a pile of navigational charts from the sofa and threw them into the bedroom, but when he returned, he was shocked anew by the discovery of a dried turd on the sofa. It took him a moment to recognize an old cigar, undoubtedly left there by his dear friend Azim. He shoved it into his pocket.

'*Tfaddalu*. Sit down.' He motioned to the sofa. No proper woman would descend on him like this. If the neighbours had seen her, who knew what would happen? *Ya'Allah*, they could be arrested for this. She introduced herself into the space with a cautious drop; she seemed to be holding her breath.

'Something wrong?' he asked. She didn't reply.

He felt guilty for her discomfort even as he was grateful for it – it meant that she at least realized she was imposing on him and that her presence was improper. Remembering his manners, he went into the kitchenette and offered her coffee, sweets and dates, all of which she politely declined. He made coffee anyway, and, while he was at it, tasted one of his dates. It had the texture of freshly poured concrete. Discreetly, he spat it in the sink and dumped the rest in the bin.

He brought the coffee to the table, poured her a cup and went back into the kitchen, so he could speak to her from the safety of distance. 'You didn't say that you knew the family,' he said.

'I didn't want the examiner to know that I was connected to them,' she said. 'He was just looking for an excuse to throw me off the case.'

Nayir felt foolish for not having thought of that.

'I've only come here for business reasons, Mr Sharqi. I hope you realize that.'

Although the comment was spoken modestly, it prompted him to think of the other reasons she might have come. It was, in a way, an accusation: *You think dirty thoughts.* He felt a brief indignation.

'I've already processed the samples,' he said.

'Which samples?'

'The private investigator gave me a dirt sample from her head wound. It looks as if she didn't get hit in the desert. The dirt from her wound was dark orange with clay mixed in. It didn't match the dirt from the wadi.'

'Good.' She nodded. 'Those are the samples I gave to Othman. I haven't had time to process them yet.' She seemed nervous; her fingers worried the hem of her sleeve. 'Othman tells me that you know she was pregnant.'

He nodded, but she wasn't looking at him, so he had to say 'Yes.'

'I was hoping you could help me get some DNA samples,' she said. 'To determine who the baby's father was.' She kept her eyes on the floor, and he kept his on the stove. 'I need them from everyone,' she went on. 'I need samples from her fiancé, her cousins, her escort, any man who's been to the house. I'd like to match them to some skin cells and blood that I took from beneath her fingernails and on her wrists. Whoever fathered the child probably had the strongest motivation to kidnap her.'

'Can't you get the brothers' DNA yourself?'

She seemed surprised, and he realized suddenly what the question implied. He felt a hot flush of shame.

Miss Hijazi was flustered, and she sat in tense silence for a full minute. Finally, she exhaled. 'What are you doing right now?'

He looked around. 'What do you mean?'

'Do you have any plans for this afternoon?'

'Yes, I'm busy. What about you? I thought you had a job.'

'I took the afternoon off,' she said. 'Have you spoken with the escort yet?'

Does Othman tell her everything? he wondered.

'Mr Sharqi.' She drew herself up. 'I realize I'm making you uncomfortable—'

'No, you're not,' he lied.

'Yes, I am, but I'm doing it for Nouf. This is not about you or me. This is about a woman who died, and who needs someone to find the truth. You're the only one Othman trusts, the only one he can count on.'

Nayir crossed his arms and said nothing, but the idea that Othman trusted him softened his mood somewhat.

'I'm only asking because I was hoping you could tell me more about the escort. He seems like a primary suspect.'

'I don't think so.' He gave a brief synopsis of what Mohammed had told him about Eric Scarsberry. Except for a subtle tightening in her shoulders, she did not seem surprised, but neither did she speak. 'I trust you not to repeat this to anyone,' he said.

'Of course not.'

'I was searching for Eric's apartment this morning,' he said. 'I imagine it's on an American compound. I know of six different ones. I've checked three so far, but I haven't found the right one yet.'

For a moment she didn't speak. 'I'd like to come with you,' she said finally, standing up.

'No. No, no. I can do this alone. You just, you go—'

'You don't have to drive me,' she said. 'I have my own transportation, if you'd rather follow me.'

He hesitated. One part of him revolted against the idea of escorting his friend's fiancée – into an American compound, of all places! – but he knew she was right: they were doing this for Nouf, and ultimately, that was what Othman wanted. Still, there was no reason she had to come along, only that she was stubborn, or trying to impress Othman. The more generous part of him suspected that she was genuinely becoming involved in this case. It was no little thing for her to pursue the evidence trail on what had already been classified an accidental death. She was probably going against her boss's wishes, perhaps even jeopardizing her job. Grudgingly, he had to admit that he admired her persistence for the sake of truth.

'All right,' he said. 'Since you have your own transportation.'

14

Following Miss Hijazi's Toyota, Nayir wondered what sort of parents she had who would allow her to work in a mixed environment. They must be Westernized. He could imagine her father wearing a business suit, speaking perfect English; her mother was perhaps one of those women who wrote letters to the King and the ministers complaining about the laws against women. (Why can't we drive cars? Why can't we travel to Mecca without our husbands' permission?) But he had trouble matching this image of the Westernized family with the sort who would socialize with the Shrawis. It was more unusual still that Miss Hijazi herself was marrying into the family. It surprised him that Othman approved of her having a job, not only because it meant she would be interacting with men, but because it implied that she needed the money. The Shrawis might not be too happy about that.

They reached the gates of the American compound. To the left, a neon blue sign read 'Club Jed' in ornate, mock-Arabic script. A security guard approached the Toyota and spent a few minutes talking with the driver. Finally, he waved them through, motioning for Nayir to continue on as well.

Inside the compound, the environment changed. These were mostly Saudi-style homes, bright stucco buildings with ornate shutters and flat roofs, but the gardens were strangely American, bursting with flowers he didn't recognize. Americans lived here, as well as other Western workers who signed up for two, maybe three years of work in Saudi. Most of them came because the work was lucrative and completely tax-free; some companies even paid for their employees to fly back to America once or twice a year. There was a high demand for imported labour – a good many Saudis were wealthy enough not to have to work, and, Nayir thought, they believed that work was beneath them – but despite the necessity for American workers, he still felt a twinge of resentment that they should come here and build their own little worlds, their own private compounds where they lived as if they were still in America.

Nayir followed Miss Hijazi's car along the checkerboard streets to a parking lot that was crowded with pick-ups and SUVs. They climbed out of their cars. To the right was a footpath that led up a short hill.

'According to the guard, that's a club,' Miss Hijazi said, pointing to a building at the crest of the hill. Although the building was squat and grungy, a marble balustrade lent it an air of refinement. 'We can ask about Eric there.'

'It's a women's club?' he asked.

'An everybody club. A bar.'

'A *bar*?' Even on the compound, alcohol was still forbidden.

'No alcohol, of course,' she assured him. 'Come on, let's look inside. We might find him there, or someone who knows him.'

'Isn't your escort coming?' Nayir asked.

She hesitated. 'There's no reason for it. Not while you're with me,' she said, although something about the tone of her voice implied: *Unless I'm mistaken about you.*

160

The club was empty except for a sprinkling of tired customers in peripheral seats. Dim overhead lamps cast a shellacked light. The stillness of the clientele and the odd way the lighting bisected their bodies gave the room a depressing vacuity, like the parts depot of a wax works. A stale smell pervaded the air. They passed a table where three women sat talking. One woman shot him a smile, but he looked away.

Miss Hijazi seemed subdued, perhaps a little nervous. With a casual movement, she lifted her burqa. Nayir tried not to look at her face, but he couldn't help it; it glowed like the moon. He noticed she was pretty in a quirky way – her nose a little long, her lips a bit crooked. If she had a speck of modesty she'd lower her veil in front of all these strangers, but he noticed that no one stared.

They went through a sliding glass door to an outdoor patio where iron café tables were scattered about. There was a border of grass, a heap of unrecognizable flora, and – folly of follies – a swimming pool. The water shone with a cool aqua light, but the air was thick with its chlorine stench.

Beside the pool, two women were sunbathing. Nayir was hardly able to ignore them, so he squinted and raised a hand to his eyes, pretending that the sun was overwhelming him. In the corner a bronzed, wrinkled man sat on a lawn chair. He was sipping ice water and studying the newspaper on the table before him. He saw them and lowered his paper.

On instinct, Nayir approached the man and asked about Eric Scarsberry.

'You mean Scarberry,' the man said. 'Yeah, I know him. He lives here.'

'Do you know the address? We're investigating a crime and we need to ask him a few questions.'

'Sure. He's on Peachtree.' The man gave directions and the house number. 'I haven't seen him in a while. Is he in some kind of trouble?'

'No, but he may be able to help us.' Nayir saw that Miss Hijazi had hung back by the door. Her burqa was down again.

Nayir thanked the man and excused himself. He went back to Miss Hijazi. 'I think I've got it,' he said. 'You can wait with your escort if you like.'

She didn't reply but followed him as he went around the pool and crossed a very green lawn. The grass felt like rubber. Reaching a white fence, they ducked through an arbour and popped out on a sidewalk on a quiet, residential street. They walked along, looking at the buildings.

'The guy said it was down here,' Nayir said, motioning to the left. They turned down a side street. Nayir wiped the sweat from the back of his neck. Miss Hijazi seemed calmer now, strolling easily along, unalarmed that she was alone with Nayir. Perhaps it was the effect of the Americanness around them that made her relax. He was still on edge.

'I'm curious about something,' she said. 'Why is it you never took Nouf to the desert?'

'Her father wouldn't allow it. He didn't think it was safe.'

'Would it have been safe?'

For some reason – perhaps the wind gentled the air around them – her smell drifted into his nose. It was warm and clean, and as it flooded through him, his whole body tingled. She might have felt it, too, because he noticed a sudden drawing back, an awkwardness, a not knowing what to do with her hands.

'She would have been safe with me,' he said. He studied the street around them. This wasn't a Saudi street, there were no religious police here, no one to stop them and demand proof of marriage, yet he felt the skin prickle on his neck.

They found the street sign for Peachtree and cut to the left, into a housing complex that shone a crisp white. It was quiet here, and the loud clack of their footsteps on the side-walk made them step onto the grass.

They approached a row of buildings and found apartment 229-B hidden behind a high stone wall. Henna vines struggled through the cracks, and a lonely lizard clung to the wall, its body stiller than stone. They crept through another arbour. The house was a duplex, and both sides were quiet. The apartment on the right had a small backyard patio littered with oddments: a baseball, a plastic paddling pool, a shattered plate. They made for the left-hand apartment. Through a sliding glass door they saw an empty room. Nayir knocked, but no one responded, so he tried the door, and it opened.

They entered the house. There was a brown recliner in the corner and a 12-inch TV on top of a box.

'Stinky,' he remarked. 'What is that smell?'

'Animal.' She sniffed the air. 'A house pet, maybe?'

Silently, they wandered from room to room. There was little to see. The only room that showed any signs of life was the bedroom. Laundry lay scattered about; the linens were rumpled; empty mineral water bottles crowded the top of the armoire. There were no pictures on the walls.

'I have to say,' Miss Hijazi whispered, 'I don't see a woman's touch.'

They made their way to the study, where a quick scan of the desk revealed paperwork belonging to Eric Scarberry. A pay stub, an insurance form. There were no books or computers, no evidence that he'd spent more than a fleeting afternoon there, paying his bills.

'Do you think someone else has been here already?' she asked.

'No. He probably made this mess himself.'

They moved into the kitchen, where picnic plates and plastic silverware were the utensils of choice. The trash can was empty. Peeking into the refrigerator, they found a plate of mouldy cheese and a month-old carton of milk. Miss Hijazi went into the living room.

Giving the kitchen a final scan, Nayir found a book wedged between the refrigerator and a cabinet. He prised it out. *1001 Recipes From Arabia*, published by the American Ladies of Jeddah. Flipping through the pages, he noticed a few grease stains. Someone had used it, but judging from the dust, that had been a sultan's age ago.

'I found the smell,' Miss Hijazi called out.

He went into the living room. She was squatting by a birdcage on the coffee table. The bird inside was dead. Judging from its size, it was a parakeet. The water bowl was empty. Nayir inspected the food bowl and found that the seeds had all been eaten; only their shells remained.

'I guess he's been gone for a while,' he said. 'It seems strange that a guy this messy would keep a bird.'

'It's the latest thing. Birds are supposed to warn you of a chemical attack. They die first. I've heard that Americans keep them, especially on the compound.'

He looked around. 'Did you see a gas mask anywhere?'

She frowned.

Squeezing his hand through the cage door, he pulled out a section of the newspaper that lined the bottom. He shook off the droppings and flipped the page over. It was the front section of the *Arab News*, dated one full month before Nouf had gone missing.

He set the paper down. 'Eric left here before she disappeared?'

She glanced at the paper. 'Well, maybe he's been back and just forgot to change the paper. He doesn't seem to care about his house very much.'

Miss Hijazi scooped the parakeet into the paper and took it to the bathroom. Nayir stared at the cage, wondering if Eric had run away or if he'd ended up like his bird. In either case, there had to be a way to track him down.

15

Her driver was still waiting when they returned to the parking lot. Nayir half-imagined that he would be upset, or bored, or dead of heat stroke, but he was sitting in the car, leisurely reading the Quran. The Toyota was running. The air conditioning must have been at full blast, because when Nayir opened the rear door to let Miss Hijazi in, a cold burst of air blew over his chest. It gave him a moment's chill.

She didn't climb into the car right away. She seemed reluctant to say goodbye, and it surprised him to realize that his perceptions of her had altered slightly. She was not exactly modest, but not brazen either. She was something in between, shifting like a mirage. Remembering that this was Othman's fiancée, a wall went up in his mind, and he motioned her into the car.

'There's one more thing I wanted to do before heading back to work,' she said. 'My driver has another appointment, so he's going to drop me off, and I don't think I can do this alone.'

'What is it?'

'Um-Tahsin told me that she received a phone call from

an optometrist. Nouf ordered a pair of glasses before she ran away. Um-Tahsin had no idea. She was going to send one of the servants to pick them up, but I offered to do it. I felt that it would mean something to her if I did. I think she wants to have the glasses.'

It struck Nayir as terribly sad that Um-Tahsin would want to keep a pair of glasses that Nouf would have worn, had she lived.

'I can escort you,' he said.

She nodded gratefully and climbed into her car.

As Nayir followed the Toyota downtown, he told himself that he was doing Othman a favour, escorting his fiancée, but a small part of him knew that he wasn't doing any favours, he was committing a sin of *zina*, being in the company of an unmarried woman, and he was committing a sin against a friend who trusted him.

Even though her visit was highly inappropriate, he had to admit that it presented an opportunity. She might be able to tell him things about Nouf that he would otherwise never find out – things even Othman didn't know. She might also know something about the autopsy that the examiner had kept shrouded in the secrecy of the cover-up. And, he admitted to himself, he *wanted* to escort her. He couldn't say exactly why.

When the Toyota pulled over on a busy downtown street, he pulled in behind it and parked. He climbed out of the car, quickly glancing around for religious police. There were a few men on the street, but no one looked suspicious. They were only a few blocks from the Coroner's office.

Miss Hijazi watched her car pull away. 'I think it's that way,' she said as she started to fish in her purse. It was a cavernous bag, and it took her a few minutes to navigate through all of the smaller purses, the keys, the calendars, a freak upswell of change. Annoyed, she flipped up her burqa and went back to searching. In an effort to keep his eyes from her face, he switched his gaze to the purse and saw a cell-phone charger, a prayer schedule, an extra burqa and, surprise of surprises, a bottle of nail polish.

'You paint your nails?' he blurted.

She looked at him, forcing him to look away. She went back to fishing.

Just then, someone laid a sweaty hand on his shoulder. Nayir spun around.

'Excuse me,' the man said, fixing Nayir with a stare and motioning to Miss Hijazi with a tilt of his head. 'In the name of Allah and Allah's peace be upon you. Sir, pardon me, but your wife is not properly veiled.'

Nayir felt a stab of panic, but he gazed coolly at the man. He was clean-cut with short hair, pleated trousers, and a necktie printed with the 99 Names of Allah. He looked entirely too Western to be a religious policeman, yet the man's black eyes, seen through thick glasses, blazed with self-righteous indignation.

Nayir frowned. 'Are you looking at my wife?' he asked. The man opened his mouth, but Nayir interrupted. 'She's *my wife*,' he shouted. 'You'd better have a good excuse for staring at her!'

The man took a step back. 'Apologies, brother, but you understand it's a matter of decency.'

'That's no excuse.' Nayir moved closer with a menacing squint. 'Don't you have your *own* wife to worry about?'

Blushing, the man turned and walked away, ducking around the next corner. Guilt flooded through Nayir, and he quickly asked forgiveness for the sin of lying. It wouldn't have happened if he hadn't been committing a sin of *zina* in the first place. He turned and saw that Miss Hijazi had lowered her burqa.

'Is he gone?' she whispered.

'Yes.' He laid a hand on his chest to still his heart. 'Yes, he's gone.'

'Was he religious police?'

'No. Vigilante.'

'How can you be sure?' she asked.

'He was wearing Armani.'

'Ah.' Relief flooded her eyes. She held up a small business card. 'I found it.'

'*Al-hamdulillah*.' He snatched the card, read the address, and took off.

☽

Dr Ahed Jahiz was once the finest optometrist in Egypt. His business, which began as a microscopic boutique in an alley in downtown Cairo, had blossomed into a three-storey, glass-walled emporium through years and years of persistent labour and his utter devotion to the optical arts. He had his own machines for studying the eye, for cutting lenses and polishing frames. He sold Italian bifocals that cost more than the average automobile. He even offered a scholarship programme to send country yokels to the finest optical academies in Europe, provided they worked for *him* when they returned.

But as militant Islamism spread like a plague of sand fleas through the Muslim world, Cairo, that loose-kneed, sluttish sister, became the victim of frequent outbursts of violence, resulting in, among other things, a Chevy sedan driving through the front windows of Jahiz & Co. and blowing twelve customers, five staff members and three German tourists to Paradise.

Dr Jahiz, who was in Mali at the time, delivering a truckload of cast-off reading glasses to the poor, returned to Cairo to find his building in ruins, gutted the way a pack of hungry children might plunder a birthday cake if left unchecked by adults. The sum of his life's work was strewn over three square blocks of town. (They found frames in the Nile.) People were dead. Good Muslims were angry, bad Muslims vengeful, and Jahiz decided that it was time to begin life anew. He collected the insurance and set off for Saudi, home of the Prophet – peace be upon him – and site of the holiest city in Islam, a country which, he hoped, would not prove as near-sighted as his blessed Egypt.

But if Cairo was myopic, then Saudi went blindfold. Jahiz had assumed that the richest population in the Muslim Middle East would appreciate his skill and dedication, his magnificent vision of an optical empire that would one day be able to adjust and repair every single flaw in the human eye, but his assumptions were wrong. Saudis, it turned out, went to *Saudi* optometrists. Perhaps, thought Jahiz, this was because only Saudi optometrists understood that the Saudis were world-renowned for their excellent vision. Few Saudis wore glasses. It had never been fashionable and it never would be. The wearing of glasses was, he discovered, a sensitive subject, since every Bedouin in creation prided himself on his superior ability to see anything, at any distance, at any stage of life. Although the age of the Bedouin had long since passed away, and the sedentary Saudis had left many customs in their desert past – spitting every five minutes, travelling by night, cleaning their babies with camel urine – they had not yet abandoned the delusion that they were all blessed with perfect sight.

So his business remained a meagre empire at best, and while Jahiz never lost his pious regard for the science of the eye, he felt his passions slowly deflating like birthday balloons weeks after the fête. He was growing old. He was impatient and inclined to bursts of phlegm. Worst of all, he scorned his clientele. They were ridiculous – what else could you say about a wealthy society that consciously veiled half its population and pretended the other half could see through brick?

This morning, Jahiz entertained himself polishing the Calvin Klein sunglasses in the display case near the front window. Sunglasses were his hottest item – a new shipment every week. They kept him from bankruptcy and from turning his miserable life to Allah, Seer of all things.

Miss Hijazi and Nayir entered the shop, stood at the edge of the great Persian rug and greeted Jahiz, who pocketed his rag and rose to assist them, blessing them with the formal greeting he used for every client: *May Allah's peace and ever-lasting mercy be on you.* Nayir explained what they wanted, and Jahiz, sighing, stepped into the equipment room to retrieve the order.

'One pair of Sophia Loren frames, size 12, mauve inlay, brass trim. Clear plastic lenses, no prescription.'

Nayir frowned. 'No prescription?'

'That's what it says.' With a shaking hand, Jahiz pointed to the chart. 'She called in last month and requested glasses *without* a prescription.'

'No prescription?' Nayir rubbed his chin and frowned at Miss Hijazi. 'None?'

She made no sign that she heard them. Her burqa was down, and her hands were tucked into the sleeves of her cloak.

'Okay,' Nayir said. 'If that's what it says.'

'Please ask your wife to sit at the desk.'

'They're not for her,' Nayir said. 'They're for a friend who died.'

'Oh.' Jahiz's shoulders slumped. 'I'm very sorry to hear that.'

'Thank you.' Nayir watched as Jahiz slid the glasses into a hard leather case. He handed them to Nayir.

'I can see that you're squinting,' Jahiz said. 'Tell me, do you spend a lot of time in the desert?'

'Ah . . . yes.' Nayir was taken aback.

'You know, sir, the desert is a very bright place. The sand creates an awful lot of reflected light, which can be damaging to the eyes. Do you clean them regularly?'

'The eyes?'

'Yes, the eyes must be cleaned every week, especially in the desert. All that sand, it gets in the eyes, it *irritates* the lining, it causes bleeding, swelling, eventually infection. It can even lead to certain types of disease. Do you have trouble reading street signs?'

'No . . . well, maybe sometimes at night.'

'Night vision is the first to go. I think it would be in your best interests to have a check-up, just to make sure your eyes are in their best shape.'

'Ah, no,' Nayir said. 'I have perfect vision.'

'Yes,' Jahiz cooed, 'yes, of course. But sometimes the dust can *aggravate* the eyes, and you never know what the effects will be. I have the best machines. High-class machines, imported from Europe. We could do the exam now, if you'd like. It won't take half an hour.'

Nayir glanced at Miss Hijazi, who was pretending to look out of the window. 'I'm busy now.'

'Then maybe we can set up an appointment?'

Nayir continued to decline, but Jahiz was persistent. Finally, the doctor offered him a discount on a pair of Gucci sunglasses that had just arrived from Rome. 'You know,' he said, flapping his hands over his eyes, 'sometimes even the falcons need a rest from the overwhelming sights of the world.'

Nayir hesitated. 'I don't usually wear sunglasses,' he said.

Jahiz gave an exasperated sigh. Nayir paid for Nouf's glasses, thanked Jahiz again, and escorted Miss Hijazi out of the store. They stopped on the sidewalk.

'Why would she buy glasses without a prescription?' he asked.

'Maybe for show?'

He nodded uncertainly and handed her the glasses but realized that she wasn't looking at his hands. 'Here,' he said. 'Take them.'

She accepted the glasses, but she seemed lost in her thoughts. For an awkward moment, Nayir stood there trying not to look at her, not certain how to say goodbye.

'Thank you, Nayir,' she said. 'I can walk myself to work from here.'

He was so surprised to hear her say his name that his goodbye came too late, after she'd turned away. Confused and embarrassed, he went back to his Jeep.

16

A cardboard sign at the doorway read: WOMEN ONLY. Yet the doors were wide open, with people passing in and out – women mostly, all unveiled and smiling. Two Arab men strode blithely into the room. Both wore Western suits and were chatting in English, but one man had a string of prayer beads woven through his fingers.

Buttoning his coat, Nayir followed them inside.

The hotel conference room was cavernous. Thick carpets, heavy drapes and the presence of so many people had a muffling effect, quelling loud voices and the garrulous laughter that always seemed to accompany groups of Americans. Yet the crowd gave off a sense of things having reached their conclusion. A few Indonesian busboys were clearing the wreckage from a dozen banquet tables, while the guests milled about, reluctant to abandon their fun. In passing, Nayir drew a few untroubled glances.

A bazaar curved like a queue through the centre of the room. There were three dozen tables of hand-crafted gifts, art supplies, books, baked goods, children's clothing. Nayir made his way to a table of books. He picked up *How to Survive a Year in Saudi Arabia: A Handbook for Expat Wives* and *Stitching Like a Bedouin: Authentic Patterns for Macramé, Embroidery and Weaving Projects!* and thought, finally, there could be no doubt that this was the American Ladies of Jeddah meeting. He scanned the other book tables, studied their occupants from the corner of his eye, and was just about to ask about a cookbook called *1001 Recipes From Arabia* when a certain stall caught his attention. It had a display of paper art, yet was small among the others, and a reminder that sometimes in seeking the obvious one finds the subtle instead.

From the depths of a pocket, Nayir produced the yellow-patterned stork he'd found in Nouf's bag of possessions. He hid the damaged bird in the cup of his fist and drew closer to the stall, grateful that other people stood nearby to deflect from his massive male presence.

The stall's owner, a tiny woman in T-shirt and jeans, sat on a high, skinny chair. She was absorbed in her work. Nayir's first shock was seeing a woman so close; his second was seeing a woman unveiled, wearing tight clothes and apparently no undergarments. Immediately, almost, he reverted to habit and looked at her hands. They were nimble and quick, wielding scissors better suited to a mouse as they snipped tiny squares from a sheet of red paper. And then a glance at her face: green eyes, warm, ruddy cheeks, dry wrinkles at the corners of her mouth and eyes, odd on such an elfin, youthful girl.

Her artwork lay before her; its humour uncloaking her further still. From delicate coloured paper she had recreated a Bedouin teapot, the holy Ka'aba, a camel, some sheep, and an entirely too romantic desert scene replete with embroidered cushions and a hookah. Between these, Nayir saw a darker component: an obese prince on a throne, on his lap a whole tray of half-eaten origami hamburgers and McDonald's wrappers. Fat thighs spilled over the edge of

174

the seat. He seemed disgusted, stifling a belch. Another scene showed a man standing on a prayer rug with a GPS system embedded in it: 'Always pray toward Mecca!' But beside it a voice bubble quoted him shouting into his cell phone: 'I'm sick of these infidels invading our culture!' But the worst one of all, the one that made Nayir blush, was a string of origami men in white robes, holding hands like paper dolls. She had sketched their faces, and they were smiling lasciviously. A sign beneath their feet read: 'Men are more fun.'

He wondered if she was so wry about her own culture.

The other customers had wandered away and left him studying her work in a silence that suddenly felt unbreakable. She paused in her cutting.

He forced a look at her face. It was okay, this face. It invited a look. Americans did that. Summoning the English he'd learned from Samir's friends, and from his own dealings with desert tourists, he said: 'This is your work,' not sure if it was a question or a statement until she glanced at him and answered.

'Yep.'

The origami stork was now a crumpled ball in his sweaty fist. He set the stork on the table and attempted to straighten it.

The woman leaned forward and took the bird, studying it while adjusting its folds.

'A lovebird,' she said. 'For fertility. It looks like one of mine. Where did you get it?'

'Do you know a man named Eric Scarberry?'

She let her eyes linger on his coat. 'Yep. Sure do. Who's askin'?'

'Me.'

She saw that he was serious, and laughed, a sweet prickle of a laugh. 'Well alrightie.'

He had the sudden urge to satisfy his curiosity: to ask her name, why she was here, was she married, did she have children, and were they all like her, blonde-haired and boyish? What was she doing in Saudi, a woman like this, not really a woman but almost a man? Was America, in some general way, embarrassed by women like her, or was she normal? But what he said was: 'Do you know that Eric is missing?'

She set the scissors on the table, reflexively chewing her bottom lip. 'You a cop?'

'No.'

'What then?'

'An investigator.'

'A police investigator?'

'No, I'm just investigating for a friend.'

She nodded, reflecting, then suddenly shot him a devilish smile. 'Then you've got to explain the coat.'

He looked at her hands. 'How about this: if you answer my question, I'll answer yours. I want to know if you can help me find Eric.'

He dared another look at her face, right into her eyes, and found that she couldn't meet his gaze. She picked up her scissors and continued to clip, still chewing her lip. When she looked up again, it was exactly as if she'd veiled herself within.

'That's not a fair deal,' she said. 'Answering your question is going to have more implications than answering mine.'

'How do you know?'

She eyed him. 'Then you go first.'

'Only if you promise not to laugh,' he said.

She smiled, a mercurial spasm. 'Okay. I won't.'

'All right. I bought the coat because I wanted a . . . *tilasm*?'

'A talisman.'

176

'Something to help me when . . .' He looked up at the ceiling, unable to describe the thing he had not yet described, even to himself.

She set down her scissors and, leaning over the table, she extended a hand. 'I'm Juliet,' she said. 'And you?'

He stared at the hand, considered it, then cupped it with the same care he had taken with the stork. 'Nayir ash-Sharqi.'

'Nice to meet you.' Her smile was warm, curious, no longer so sexy.

'I gave the stork to Eric,' she said. 'Last year. I don't usually make storks – they're so cliché – but that's what happens when you fall in love. Every dumb cliché . . .' She wiped the paper scraps from her lap and stood up. 'But I really did want to have babies with him. Lots of babies. Like ten. Or twenty.' Her eyes betrayed a sadness. 'I'm too old now for twenty, but I could still do ten, if I got busy fast.'

Nayir gave a polite smile.

'And I don't really know where to find Eric,' she said breezily. 'We lost touch after we broke up. He used to live at Club Jed, but I've heard he moved in with his boy—' She froze, glanced at Nayir. 'Does that answer your question?'

'Yes, thank you.'

Nayir looked away and noticed the two men who'd come in earlier, the Arab men in George Bush suits. They were talking to a blonde American in a skimpy dress that might have been an undergarment for all he knew. It was clear that the woman was enjoying the attention, and that the men, slightly awkward, were trying to see how far they could go. Testing the Americans. A cultural study. And he was suddenly ashamed, of himself, of his pleasure in talking to a woman he'd known for only ten minutes, who could just as easily have fallen for the men in the suits. She was ridiculously free, Miss Shake-My-Hand and Watch-Them-Jiggle,

Miss I'll-Give-You-Ten-Children, and by the way what's your name?

'So you don't know where I can find Eric,' he said.

She didn't reply.

'Aren't you even curious—' he began, motioning to the stork.

'No.' She jerked up. 'I don't think I could take it.' A wave of the hand. An old wound, yet as soft as an overripe fig.

Nayir plucked the stork from the table. 'Well, the woman who had it is dead now.'

Juliet looked up. 'Who?'

'Her name was Nouf ash-Shrawi. Did you know her?'

She kept her eyes fixed on Nayir. 'No.'

'She died in the desert recently. She had the bird when she died, but it was in better condition. I crushed it by accident.'

'And you think Eric did it. That he killed her?'

Nayir shrugged. 'Eric may have known her. I'm just looking for him.'

She stared blankly at the floor, sifting through what seemed like messy emotions. 'I'm sure he had nothing to do with her death.' She laughed, nervously. 'If you're after him for sex crimes, believe me, you're after the wrong man.'

'I just need to ask him some questions,' he said.

'You're not going to arrest him, are you?'

He shook his head. 'I don't have that power.'

She started biting her thumbnail.

'Look, if he's innocent then this will prove it. I'll just get a sample of his DNA, and he'll be cleared. No problem.'

'How did you find me anyway?' she asked.

He explained about finding the cookbook. She seemed suspicious when he told her about Eric's apartment, but the suspicion gave way to a certain resignation.

Quietly, she began to gather her belongings. She folded

them flat, slipped them into plastic folders and stacked them in a briefcase. Others she placed in boxes – the little scenes, the Cadillac. He felt the impulse to assist but didn't dare; it would have been like touching her skin.

'Eric doesn't live on the compound,' she said. 'He keeps the apartment, but he's never there. He lives in the old town with a friend of his.'

Nayir heard an unpleasant emphasis on the word *friend*. 'Where does this friend live?'

She gave him an address. Nayir thanked her, but she'd become absorbed in her thoughts and only managed a distracted reply.

'Just don't tell him I sent you,' she said. 'And don't hurt him. I'm trusting you to treat him with respect.'

'Of course,' Nayir said, and he meant it.

17

The man who opened the giant walnut door, was in his forties, with greying blond hair and keen blue eyes. He looked Nayir up and down.

'May I help you?'

'I'm looking for Eric Scarberry.'

'I am Eric.'

'My name is Nayir ash-Sharqi. I'm a friend of the Shrawis. I'd like to talk to you, if you don't mind.'

Eric seemed to hesitate, but he stepped aside. 'Well, any friend of the Shrawis is a friend of mine. Please come in.' Nayir entered a cool foyer.

'What is this about?' Eric asked.

'The death of Nouf ash-Shrawi.'

Eric nodded sternly and led Nayir down an elegant hallway and into an enormous sitting room at the centre of the house. Broad cedar beams studded a majestic ceiling. The dark wood floors offset the white sofas and chairs, and a slanted skylight let in a touch of sun. The room might have been welcoming were it not for the books, thousands of them, each as dusty and ragged as if they'd been carried to the desert and back. They crowded the side walls, the tables, the chairs. They were stacked on the floor, emitting fungal smells. At their highest reaches, they loomed over the room threatening seismic collapse.

'Have a seat,' Eric said. 'I'll be right back.'

Nayir glanced at the books. Archaeology textbooks, every one of them. He had never seen so many in one place. As he picked his way through the intellectual remnants of one man's obsession with All Things Dead, the floorboards creaked dangerously beneath his weight.

The sight of a courtyard caught his attention. Slipping through a pair of French doors, he entered a cool grotto shaded by lemon trees and palm. The ground shimmered with the vibrant blue of medieval tile work, which rose to form a circular fountain in the centre of the patio. Nayir dipped his hands in the water and splashed his neck. How much of it would evaporate each day? Gallons, he thought. Only the super-rich could afford such waste. He wiped his neck on his sleeve and looked around. Most Ottoman-style homes in the old town were owned by royalty and Jeddah's elite families; the few that went to market cost millions. Yet this one, it seemed, was owned – or rented – by an American.

Nayir remembered how Juliet had referred to Eric's 'friend', and he wondered if Eric was gay. It seemed impossible and foolish – a gay American living in Saudi Arabia. Did he know that the kingdom executed gay men for breaking religious law? According to Nayir's friend Azim there were plenty of gay men in the Corniche district, but they were discreet, and the authorities tended to leave them alone. When the police wanted to capture gay criminals and make an example of them, they went after foreign men.

Eric appeared in the doorway and leaned against the frame, as lithe as a woman. Nayir kept his eyes on a sprawling mosaic that formed a geometric symphony on the southern wall while he studied Eric from his peripheral vision. He wore khaki trousers and a white linen shirt. His hair, swept back like sails in a breeze, shone despite the shade, and with that faint impatience in his slouch, he made Nayir uneasy.

'Tea?' Eric asked. 'Or coffee?'

Nayir faced him. He had trouble matching the svelte Eric with his previous image of a man who would live in a cramped hovel in Club Jed, only returning to pay his bills, and killing his bird out of neglect. 'Tea is fine, thank you.'

Eric nodded and disappeared. He was, Nayir thought, a terrible match for Juliet as well. She was far too open and friendly, yet there had been a genuine sweetness in her. Nayir didn't know many Americans, but he knew a jackal when he saw one.

He returned to the sitting room just as Eric entered with a pitcher of iced tea and two glasses. He set them on the coffee table and motioned for Nayir to sit in a powder-puff chair that looked to offer all the comforts of a Venus flytrap. Eric returned to the kitchen. Carefully, Nayir perched on the edge of the seat and watched with amazement as Eric came back with a large plate of meats, bean paste and breads, spinach pastries that blossomed like roses, broiled peppers and eggplant slices arranged like leaves. He noticed Eric's arms, reddened as if they'd been scrubbed clean to the elbow.

Eric poured a drink, sat in the opposite chair, and without formalities, invited Nayir to eat.

Nayir was unsure about the food. Although refusing it would have been awkward and rude, he half wanted to do it, just to see Eric's reaction. But he forced himself to eat a little.

'I always believe in treating guests as if they were kings,' Eric said, his nut-brown voice deepened by the food. 'It's one of the things I love about this country.'

'You're an archaeologist?'

'No, I'm an oil research analyst. My roommate is the archaeologist.' He motioned to the books.

'That's an odd combination.'

'Well, we do have the desert in common.'

'Where exactly do you work?' Nayir asked.

'In the mountains, mostly. The Arabian Shield. There are a number of different sites.'

Nayir remembered that the Bedouin map had shown a possible drilling site not too far from the wadi. 'I'd like to know precisely where they are, if you don't mind.'

Eric hesitated. 'Why?'

'Nouf was found in the desert not far from an oil research site.'

'You think I had something to do with it?'

'Did you?'

'Of course not!'

Nayir studied his face and decided that his indignation was real. 'How do you know the Shrawis?' he asked.

'They've funded my roommate's research in the past. They're very generous donors.'

'Is that how you met Nouf?'

If the question bothered Eric, there was only a slight unease to show for it. 'I really didn't know her that well.'

'I have it on good authority that you were helping her plan an escape to New York.'

Eric set his bread on the table. His mouth looked pinched. 'I have no idea what you mean.'

'I understand that you were meeting Nouf at the Corniche to arrange the terms of your deal.'

Eric drew himself up, but Nayir noticed that his hands were shaking. 'Listen – Mr Sharqi, is it? Are you with the police?'

'I'm doing this for the family.'

'Yes, fine. Then as a courtesy to the family I'll tell you this. I'm not in the habit of courting young girls from powerful families. If you think her death was suspicious, then I suggest you look into her life, in particular her family life, since that's probably all she knew.'

'According to my sources, she was meeting you in various places around the city to arrange a future for herself in New York. You were going to help her get a visa, an apartment, maybe admission to a university – everything she would need.'

'And your proof of this is . . . ?'

Nayir reached into his pocket and took out the origami stork. 'Have you seen this before?'

'I've seen dozens.'

Nayir set the stork on the table. 'You gave it to Nouf.'

Eric snorted. 'I suppose you can prove that.'

Unflinching, Nayir reached back into his pocket and took out the key that Mohammed had given him. 'And this? Does it look familiar?'

Eric blanched.

'It's a key to your apartment in New York. You also gave this key to Nouf. You told her she could stay there for a while until her own place was ready.' Eric was silent, so Nayir went on. 'I think you were helping her. She needed someone to arrange her new life, and she needed an American. You probably liked the idea of assisting. There was money in it. Probably a lot of money. Who knows, maybe you even liked her? She was young and sweet. It was the perfect plan – until you discovered she was pregnant.'

Eric sputtered in disbelief, but Nayir ignored it. 'That was trouble for you, wasn't it? Even in America. Suddenly, she wasn't safe any more, and you had to get rid of her.'

'I did no such thing.' Eric stood up. 'I think we're finished here.'

'If you value your roommate's funding,' Nayir growled, 'you'll sit down.'

Reluctantly, Eric slid back into his chair. He crossed his arms and waited.

'Nouf was probably kidnapped and taken to the desert. I'd hazard a guess that one of your drill sites isn't too far from the place where they found her, which makes you the perfect suspect.'

Eric didn't reply.

'You can either tell me the truth now, and trust me to be discreet, or I'll bring this whole matter to the family,' Nayir said. 'I'm sure they'll want to know all about it, even if it does ruin their relationship with your – roommate?'

'All right.' Eric exhaled with a noticeable tremor. 'I was helping her. She had no one, I was her only link to freedom. But I had absolutely nothing to do with her death. Why would I kill her? She was about to pay me close to half a million riyals.' He frowned at his guest. 'Now I have nothing.'

'So you went to all this trouble to help her, and she gave you nothing? Not even a deposit?'

'No – yes, yes, she gave me a little money for the apartment and the university registration. But it wasn't that much.'

'A million riyals,' Nayir said. 'That doesn't seem like a lot to you?' Mohammed had said it was a million riyals. Nayir was willing to concede that the figure might have been overstated, but Eric looked abashed.

'She did pay you,' Nayir said. 'Not half a million. A million. That's a nice bit of money – what, two hundred and fifty thousand dollars? But all the same, it puts you in a jam. Tell me, did she change her mind and ask for the money back?'

Eric scoffed.

'Of course you wouldn't have had to give it back,' Nayir

went on, 'since you probably didn't have a written contract, and nobody but her escort knew about the plan. But she could have threatened to tell her brothers about you. She could have made up a story about you stealing her money. It would be her word against yours, and who would they believe – her, or you?' An unpleasant emphasis on the word 'you' had the effect of unnerving Eric even more. He made an effort to look proud, but when he spoke, his voice shook.

'I'm sor – I'm sorry, but that never happened. It's true she could have revealed the plan, but that's not what she wanted.'

Nayir studied his eyes for signs of deceit. He seemed afraid of being caught, but whether because of his greedy financial dealings or because of murder it was hard to say.

'How much did she pay you?' Nayir asked.

'Half a million.'

'How?'

'In cash. But mostly gold. Like most women in this country, that was how she preferred to keep her personal assets. Tied up in chains, if you will.'

'How does a young girl get that kind of money?'

'Oh come on, her family's rich. Someone – I don't know who – gave her a large sum for the wedding, and the rest was probably hers.'

Nayir wondered who had given her the money, and if that person had discovered that it had not been spent on the wedding.

'When was the last time you saw her?' he asked.

'Two days before she disappeared. And I swear I didn't touch her. I didn't even know she was pregnant.'

'What happened at your last meeting?'

'Nothing.' Eric's voice was firm. 'We went over the details again. I gave her the key.'

'So you were still going ahead with the plan?'

'Yes, we were. Everything was fine.'

Nayir fought a sharp dislike for the man, but it wasn't the same as knowing he was guilty. He wiped his hands on a napkin. 'Where were you on the day she disappeared?'

'I was here, in Jeddah.'

'Were you at work?'

'Most likely.'

'Can anyone verify that?'

'Yes.'

'Then I'm going to need your office number and all of your drill-site information. But first, if you're as innocent as you claim to be, I'm sure you won't mind giving me a DNA sample.' He couldn't immediately determine the effect of his request. Eric sat fixed in his chair, staring curiously at him.

'Of course you can have my DNA,' he said finally.

Nayir managed to keep a casual pose, but his discomfort deepened. He tried to understand why he disliked Eric so much. There was a cockiness in his manner, and a snobbishness, too. Eric was, in some ways, the arch-evil American, the greedy man who comes to Saudi and does anything for money, wreaking havoc with society – in this case, with innocent virgins – and yet seems to have no idea that he's ruined lives. Nayir sensed that even if Eric had killed Nouf with his own two hands, he might fear getting caught, but he wouldn't regret his actions.

Eric gave an uncomfortable smile. 'How do you want it then?'

'A hair,' Nayir grumbled, and fished in his pocket for a baggie. Eric plucked out a few strands of hair.

'And the stork?' Nayir asked, picking up the object from the table.

'I gave it to her,' Eric said. 'It was our contract.'

'A stork?'

'A promise for a fertile future.' Eric waved a tired hand in the air, as if he knew there were no fertile futures. 'As you said, we couldn't sign a real contract; there was a danger it would slip into the wrong hands.'

'Of course,' Nayir replied. Eric's blasé wave of the hand disturbed him; it suggested that Nouf was a fool for believing that her dreams would ever come true.

'How did you meet her?' Nayir asked. 'I don't believe her family would have introduced you to their daughter.'

'No, they didn't.' Eric seemed to take no offence from Nayir's words. 'It was by accident, in fact. My roommate and I were visiting the Shrawis one afternoon. We went for a walk on the beach and who should ride up on a bright yellow jet ski but this beautiful young girl. She was modest, of course, and when she saw us she threw a scarf on her hair and wrapped it around her face. Ken – that's my roommate – said something polite. She seemed nervous speaking to us, but she asked if we were American, and we said yes. Then abruptly she left. We figured she thought we were dirty infidels, but as we were leaving the house, a young servant came after us asking for our phone number. Turned out he was her escort and she'd sent him to catch us when her brothers weren't looking.'

'And you gave him your number.'

'Why not? We had no idea what she was after, but—' Eric weighed his next words carefully, 'I was confident it wasn't of a – how shall I say it? An immoral nature.'

Nayir had the impression that Eric's first thought was that Nouf's intentions were indeed immoral. Perversely, he imagined that Eric had been disappointed to discover that she wanted something more businesslike from him. Nayir realized he was being harsh.

'One more thing,' he said. 'When you went to the Shrawi household, did you ever go beyond the sitting rooms? Into the men's bedrooms, perhaps?'

'No,' Eric sputtered. That this time he had taken offence was visible in a hardening of his face. A scarlet blush blossomed on his neck. It confused Nayir until he realized that the question had suggested sex.

'What I mean is . . .' He had meant to ask about Othman's missing jacket, but feeling flustered, he decided to drop it. Awkwardly, he stood up. 'Never mind.'

Eric seemed relieved that he was going.

The outside air was as cool as desert night. Nayir inhaled and slipped into his coat, which still smelled like the house. He had thanked Eric for the meal but gave an even greater thanks to Allah for the freedom of a street, for the right to walk away.

It was still early evening when he reached Mohammed's house. The escort was home, and he willingly gave up a sample of his hair. Nayir bagged it and went straight to the examiner's office. He didn't bother trying to find Miss Hijazi, he simply left the samples in a paper bag at the desk. The security guard promised to give them to her. When he asked if Nayir wanted to leave a message, he said no.

☽

He was doing what he always did when he needed to stop thinking. He was driving. In circles. There was precious little else in the way of alternatives. Saudi had no bars, no nightclubs, no discos or cinemas. There were underground hang-outs, of course, in the homes of the elite and certain members of the royal family, where a man could buy a glass of wine or a shot of whisky. There were even brothels, private residences where men could find prostitutes – all non-Muslim women, since it was *haram* to sleep with a Muslim whore. But Nayir had no interest in brothels and bars other than for their shock value, when he thought of what must go on in such places. However, there was plenty of one thing: at

52 cents a gallon, he could drive all he liked. So he did, along with a million other bored men. The traffic was so bad that he was forced to drive in ever-widening circles.

The city had no major intersections, only roundabouts. They branched off in ten, twenty directions. Open-air sculptures sat in the centre of each, conveniently distracting any driver with their enormous, sometimes embarrassing forms. Colossal Bedouin coffee pots. Flying cars wedged in a block of concrete. Body parts – a fist, a giant foot. But most of Jeddah's four hundred sculptures ranged from the abstract to the idiotically substantial without showing the human form.

Like many residents, Nayir spent much of his driving time seeking out roundabouts and giving their sculptures pejorative names. It was a habit he'd picked up from Azim – Azim who had gone to Palestine for an aunt's funeral seven weeks ago and hadn't been heard from since. Nayir entered the first roundabout off Medina Road with the Enormous Bicycle propped in its centre, its handlebars three times taller than a man. (He called it 'Made in China'.) He circled twice and cut east, zipping through the roundabout that held the first-ever Saudia Jet ('God Bless America for Infidel Technology') until he reached the clogged lanes around Mathematical Tools – compass dividers and a set square straddled by a protractor the size of an upended Boeing. He circled languidly, studying the sculpture from every side, but he couldn't come up with a clever name. Arab Inventions? What We Used to Do, Back When We Used To Do Something Important? What did they do, anyway? He'd forgotten.

His energy was gone, but he found it impossible to leave the roundabout. There were too many cars cruising around him. With a freak stab of panic, he imagined going round and round for ever. Desperately, he nosed right, and, after some honking, he broke free and away.

Gripped by a sudden urge to flee the city, he focused all of his attention on reaching the Corniche. There, he would have 80 kilometres of freedom. He'd take a ride down the coast, get away from the city and look at the stars. Maybe he'd sleep on the beach. Sometimes he thought of moving away from the city, living in a small cottage that was closer to the desert, but this was where his connections were, where he found new clients and kept in touch with the old ones. He couldn't leave his uncle – especially now that Samir was getting old. Besides, living on the boat was almost like living in the wilderness, if he went sailing frequently enough.

He decided he'd pull off the road and find a quiet spot. Just the thought of being close to the desert all by himself settled his thoughts, and with a burst of strength he switched on the radio. He tuned to Radio Jeddah and listened to an imam bleating about proper conduct with women. Usually, he didn't like this sort of angry noise, but tonight it was strangely comforting.

'Touching,' the imam growled. 'It is the fornication of the hand. You are not to look upon *na-mehram* women, do not look upon *any* woman who is not family to you, for that is the fornication of the eye.'

He thought about Miss Hijazi, and remembered their walk through the American compound. In one awkward moment, when he'd felt a terrible flutter in his stomach, there'd been something in her eyes – was it admiration? What reason would she have to admire him? He imagined Othman talking about him, painting a picture of . . . what? A righteous Muslim? A man who prayed five times a day, made a yearly Hajj, paid his charitable *zakat*, and conducted himself modestly in everything? He doubted that it would impress a woman like her. Maybe he was a heroic desert guide. A man who could shoot a jackal.

He passed the Blackpool Lights, Victorian-era streetlamps imported from England that were utterly jarring amidst the palm trees and dunes. His attention turned to the buildings, to the honeycomb mosques that flew past his windows and the Patriot missiles scattered between them, as menacing as hornets. Suddenly the scenery became plain again – long, empty fields broken by ugly housing complexes that looked abandoned in the dusk – and his thoughts shifted to Eric. What appeal did a man like that have for a woman like Juliet? He was too old for her, too prim and arrogant. Had they slept together? Nayir was jolted by a sudden memory of Nouf, but he shook his head to dispel the image.

Why would Eric help a girl like Nouf? For sexual favours? Because of his beliefs? Nayir suspected that his true motive was greed. Eric seemed to be doing all right, living in a house like that. Yet Nayir could imagine his insecurity – it was the 'roommate's' house; Eric was, in some sense, a guest. He still kept an apartment on the American compound. Perhaps his deal with Nouf was a way to insure himself, should his roommate ever decide to kick him out.

'And even the voice!' The radio broke into his thoughts. 'Its subtle contours can commit the fornication of the lips, the teeth, the very breath we use to praise Allah!' Nayir wondered what Nouf's voice had been like. Did she, like some women, put coins in her mouth to muffle the sweetness of her sound? Had she spoken through a burqa, or was she modern enough to show Eric her face? Eric was American, and Americans had a habit of annihilating the rules; when talking to one, it was sometimes okay to act as they acted. Nayir had seen it himself with Juliet, the way he looked right at her face. Nouf, who was rebellious enough to abandon her fiancé, probably did show Eric her face. She probably shook his hand and looked directly into his eyes, trying to prove she could be American, too.

The imam's voice, grizzled and mean, was a hazard to his driving, so he switched it off and rolled down the window, letting the air fill his ears. He tried to remember Miss Hijazi's voice. For a woman so brazen, she spoke with surprising softness. He'd suspected that she was trying to take the edge off her words, to appear modest when really she was not. Her voice hadn't been particularly lyrical or sweet, and he decided there was no shame in having heard it.

A larger thought was lurking, pushing its way into the light. Eric probably knew nothing about Othman's jacket, and even if he did, why would he steal it? It was a ridiculous idea: he undoubtedly had his own GPS and maps. Nayir felt foolish for even having asked. He saw now that he'd been hoping to avoid the fact that someone from the estate had kidnapped Nouf. He'd entertained the thought from the start. Samir had said it; all of the new evidence pointed towards it; and still he was ignoring it.

What would happen next? Miss Hijazi would process the DNA samples, but would she call him? Or would she do the right thing and talk to Othman first? If that happened, and if the samples revealed the identity of the baby's father, then he probably wouldn't see Miss Hijazi again. It would be a relief not to have to worry about his conduct any more, but in truth, he didn't feel relieved.

Turning back to the world, he found he was circling a sculpture he'd never paid much attention to before. It was a crude abstraction, a high steel pole notched like a spine. It was broken in half, and the top section hung over the street, clearly by artistic intent. Two words came to mind before he could stop them. *Viagra, Please*. And with a frenzied jerk, he cut through the traffic and tore into a darkened alley where he came to a screeching halt.

He'd reached a dead end.

18

It was the worst kind of noon, glaring and muggy and seared by a sun that had expanded to fill every inch of the sky. A steamy, breathless, penetrating air poured down like molten lava onto every surface, causing ripples of heat, sharp glints of light, and such mirages as might have lured an entire army into the very hottest part of hell. Katya waited for Ahmad in her usual spot behind the Coroner's building, but in the five minutes she stood there the soles of her new sandals melted, sticking like warm gum to the pavement.

When the Toyota pulled up, Ahmad saw her dancing on her toes like a yogi trying to cross a bed of hot coals, and he scrambled from the car. He tore strips of his cherished newspaper and laid them down one by one – testing them with his own bare foot to make sure they were thick enough to walk safely to the car. There was a stranger nearby, a Yemeni man in a long grey robe and a suit jacket. He rushed over to help, ripping his own newspaper and cursing the heat strongly enough to bring a rare smile to Ahmad's face. There was a friendliness in the stranger's gestures that made Katya feel it would be all right to thank him directly, and when she did, he smiled broadly and gave a generous bow.

Ahmad kept a potholder in his glove box for days like this, when touching the car door would cause a third-degree burn, when handling the steering wheel required fierce determination. He had the potholder in his pocket now – a large blue plastic glove modelled on something created by the Russian space programme – and with it he gently opened the door for her, cautioning her not to touch the door frame or the window.

The Yemeni man laughed at the glove. 'It looks like something you'd use to deliver sheep.'

Ahmad smiled delicately. 'This potholder belonged to my wife,' he said. 'I'm afraid she only cooked sheep with it.'

'Ah.' The Yemeni raised his eyebrows knowingly. 'I'm sorry,' he said.

Katya suddenly felt as if the exchange had happened on a distant world. It wasn't odd that such a casual conversation had led straight to the question of a woman's fertility, but she wondered how many such conversations she had heard over the years, and failed to recognize for what they were.

She climbed into the Toyota. Ahmad had left it running, and the air conditioner was at full blast. On especially hot days, he also kept a stack of towels in a cooler full of ice, and one of them was lying across the back seat now. But despite these luxuries, in the five minutes she'd stood waiting for him the heat had managed to permeate her body, and the relative cool of the car did not reverse the tide of sweat but merely seemed to stay the condition.

They stopped at the first shoe store they could find. Ahmad got out to buy her a pair of sandals and came back twice to ask about price and size. The sandals he bought were flat and sturdy with Velcro straps – and perhaps the ugliest shoes she had ever worn – but she suspected they would survive a trip to the sun. Gratefully, she put them on.

The freeways were crowded. It was lunchtime, and everyone had left work, but no one was going to leave the cool comfort of their cars. It took Ahmad and Katya nearly an hour to navigate their way out of the city, and when they finally reached the road to the estate, Katya leaned back against the seat and shut her eyes.

Work had been taxing. She'd gone to the lab early every day that week, but Salwa was always there, expecting her to do everything, so that in going in early, Katya had only managed to create more work for herself. Right now, she was supposed to be analysing traces for a spousal abuse case. A wife had killed her husband by setting his bed on fire. Katya knew little about the wife, but she suspected that this was like most husband-abuse cases: the woman had feared for her life.

She wished she could be more involved in the investigation – at least learn a little more about the murders – but her job was to analyse evidence, not uncover clues. On most cases, she was lucky to find out anything about the killers' motivations at all. The division kept promising that someday it would send women to conduct investigations. After all, there were female suspects, and shouldn't women interrogate them? But there were always excuses to keep the women cloistered. The division lacked funding. The government wouldn't approve. These days, everyone was watching the new team of female police officers, recently sent into the field for the first time. They weren't remarkable officers, but what could be expected from a group of women who couldn't drive cars or ride bicycles, and who didn't even have the power to stop a man on the street?

The car gave a gentle bump and Katya opened her eyes. To the right, the Red Sea glittered a brilliant blue, and she had the sudden, choking impulse to stop the car, run down the beach, and throw herself into the water, abaaya and all.

'Any chance we could stop for a minute?' she asked.

Ahmad shrugged nervously. 'I have another appointment in the city at two o'clock.'

Katya checked her watch. They didn't have time. *Just wait*, she thought. And then: *wait for what?* A day off. A day when the temperature was below 100 degrees. A day when her father was in a good enough mood to take her to the beach. Before meeting Othman, she had waited years for a husband. He would be the one to take her to the beach. He would drive her to work and escort her shopping. And now, a new twist: she had a fiancé, but she was waiting for the marriage. They still hadn't set a new date for the wedding.

Ahmad opened the cooler in the passenger seat and took out an ice-cold bottle of water. He handed it back to her. She flipped up her burqa, revealing a smile. 'Thank you, Ahmad.'

'Have you learned anything new about the Shrawi girl's death?' he asked.

She glanced at his eyes, reflected in the rear-view mirror, and tried to gauge whether her father had put him up to this line of questioning. 'One or two things,' she said. 'Nothing conclusive.'

'I was just wondering if you were bringing some news to the family.'

'No, this is just a visit.' She knew he was wondering why she hadn't waited until after work, but by evening the men would be home from work as well, and chances were the women would be preoccupied. 'I haven't seen them since the funeral,' she said. 'I just want to make sure they're doing all right.'

Ahmad nodded, apparently satisfied, and Katya cursed

herself for lying. She wanted to check on the women, of course, but another quest loomed larger in her mind.

Over the past few days, she had been able to determine that the DNA from the skin beneath Nouf's fingernails matched the DNA of the baby's father. So Nouf had seen the father before she died. Maybe she'd gone to him with the news of her pregnancy, and he'd been horrified. They'd fought . . .

But from there the story went in a dozen directions. Did they fight because he was ashamed of the pregnancy? Because he was married and unwilling to take on a second wife? Or because he knew she was engaged to another man? Nouf wouldn't have needed him to marry her. She was going to be with Qazi soon enough. She could have pretended the baby was Qazi's – unless, of course, the baby belonged to a different race. Blonde-haired, perhaps. Black-skinned or Asian. And what if she didn't want to marry Qazi? What if she wanted to marry the baby's father, and he said no? That might have created enough anguish to drive her away. A fight would explain the skin beneath her nails and the defensive cuts on her arms, but it didn't explain the head wound. That hadn't killed her, but it had been enough to have knocked her out. Could she even have run away after being hit like that?

What if Qazi was the father? Would he have become angry? Probably not. They were about to get married, what difference would it have made?

Despite Katya's efforts to be fair-minded, one possibility loomed larger than the others. What if Nouf had told the baby's father about her plans to move to America, and he had tried to stop her? That would have angered any man – Qazi included. Would she have told him something like that?

Katya sighed in frustration. She hadn't known Nouf well.

Most of the time, they had met in the women's sitting room, which was a public and slightly formal space. She'd spoken privately with Nouf on a few occasions, enough to realize that she was more vivacious than most of the Shrawi sisters. She had laughed easily and talked with excitement about her saluki dogs. One day, she had confided that she loved animals more than children, and that, if she could, she would have a family of dogs.

But as with the other women in the family, Nouf had a strange reserve and would fall abruptly silent in the middle of a conversation, often just when she was beginning to open up. Katya never knew what to make of those moments – they usually preceded a polite leave-taking, Nouf saying that she had things to do. Katya always felt slightly jilted. She had been drawn to Nouf, perhaps because she was Othman's favourite. Katya had never had a sister of her own, and she longed to be a part of Nouf's daily life, to be allowed into her bedroom just one time, to see the books she read, her trinkets or artwork or favourite stuffed animals. Was she sloppy? Neat? What sort of bed did she sleep in? What colour was the room? Did she have her own servant? Katya sensed that Nouf would be more relaxed in her bedroom, and she hoped that once she married Othman, the barriers of awkwardness or propriety would come down, and she could get to know her better.

As they turned onto the bridge leading to the estate, her throat constricted. From the beginning she had been eager to talk to the women, to ask them what they knew about Nouf's life. But since that horrible morning when she had identified the body at the morgue, she'd been unable to broach the subject without meeting a wall of silence and tears. Hopefully now, enough time had passed.

Ahmad rolled down the front windows, letting in a slightly cooler breeze. They were over the water now, and the estate was just coming into view. It still thrilled her to see the building's white walls rise up in the distance and to think that someday she would belong there. That is, if she didn't wear out her welcome today.

☽

She had spent enough time with the women to understand that they lived in the sitting room. They didn't cook, do dishes or laundry, didn't attend to anything but their society visitors, their prayers, and their comforts. The younger children played in distant rooms with two Filipino nurses, while the mothers and the older children spent the greater part of their lives in the air-conditioned sitting room, a white, well-lit space with cushioned sofas, screened windows, a television, and Quranic scriptures hanging on the walls. On the far side of the room, a row of windows looked out over the family's mosque. On the room's other side, double doors led onto a high-walled garden patio. The outdoor space was made lively by a fountain that seemed to have grown out of the rocky wall. Vines hung on a pergola above cushioned chairs and benches, and a neat row of potted lemon trees gave the air a cheery fragrance, but despite the fountain and the shade, it was often too hot to sit there, and the women remained indoors.

Nusra was in perpetual motion, always coming in with visitors and running off again to attend to the details of her household. Her sons' wives more often inhabited the room with their cousins or friends. When Nouf was alive, she and her younger sister Abir had spent most of their time there. The servants never left for long, they were always back to refill the coffee pots, take away the bowls, or replace them with new ones. Abir would torment the maids by setting herself up at the coffee table and playing with the food, while the maids stood by trying to decide whether or not to interfere.

It had taken Katya a while to become familiar with her in-laws' names, but it helped that they always sat in the same positions. There were four couches set in a square. The sisters-in-law occupied the side couches. Fahad's wife, Zahra, to the left, and usually her sister Fatimah beside her, either combing her hair or inspecting her fingernails or reading a book. The right-side couch was reserved for Nusra and her younger daughters. Muruj, Nouf's oldest sister, sat with her back to the door, while Tahsin's wife, Fadilah, sat across from her, taking the central sofa for herself.

Coming into the room this afternoon, Katya lifted her burqa and returned the chorus of greetings that broke out. From the silence, she could tell that she'd arrived between conversations. As all eyes turned to watch her, she imagined tripping on the hem of her robe or stumbling over Abir before she could reach the safety of a sofa. Moving carefully, she managed to seat herself beside Zahra. Coffee was being served, and she was grateful; it gave her something to do with her hands. She glanced around and saw that, as usual, the television in the corner was flickering with silent images of Mecca.

'Not working today?' Zahra asked.

'I took the afternoon off,' Katya said.

'You'll be doing a lot more of that once you get married,' Zahra replied with a wink.

Katya gave a soft smile, but nobody spoke. She couldn't tell if they were embarrassed by Zahra's comment or if she ought to have said something funny in return. She had nothing to say.

'So, Miss Future Wife of Little Othman,' said Fadilah, 'have you chosen a dress yet?'

Katya regarded her future sister-in-law. Tahsin's wife was so similar to her husband in build and manner that she seemed like a parody of him. They had the same round, jowled faces and succulent lips, the same languid eyes. They each wore well-tailored, impeccable robes, and sat in a watchful and imperious way, regarding their company as if they were courtiers.

Fadilah was asking about a wedding dress, and Katya hadn't even come close. The truth was, every dress that suited her style seemed either too boring or too cheap. Although it was her wedding, she felt a deep need to please her future in-laws, or at least not disgust them. A few weeks ago, Nusra had arranged for a professional dressmaker to come to the house, and the woman had arrived with twenty dresses, every one of them gaudy and overpriced, bedizened with sequins and Byzantine embroidery, gold lamé and tassels, heavy layers of satin and lace. Some had real bone corsets and others had monstrous hoop skirts, which made her feel like a roundabout statue, something to gawk at. Worst of all, the colours were appalling – mustards and hot pinks, chili greens and a hazardous, painful orange. She wanted to explain to Nusra just how garish the dresses were, but she didn't want to embarrass her or seem ungrateful. Katya would have preferred a quiet tamarind shade, or the simple red of a Bedouin blanket.

When Katya turned the dresses down, Nusra had been apologetic. 'I'm certainly not one to recommend a dressmaker,' she'd quipped, motioning to her blind eyes. Katya apologized, saying that she needed some time to decide what she really wanted.

'I still haven't decided yet,' she told Fadilah. 'I was hoping to find something simple and elegant.'

Fadilah shifted uneasily, the non-verbal equivalent of a harrumph. 'My sister is a dressmaker,' she said. 'Tell me what colour you like, and I'll have her make you a dress.'

Katya couldn't imagine anything worse than being obliged to wear a dress made by Fadilah's sister, a woman she'd never met. But something in the way the other women looked at her indicated that the offer was not the sort Fadilah made every day, and was certainly not to be refused.

'Thank you,' Katya said. 'I've actually got a dressmaker coming over this weekend. She's an old friend of my mother's. But I'll keep your offer in mind.'

Fadilah looked uncertain – perhaps she sensed it was a lie – but she nodded graciously and the conversation died.

As the tension lulled into one of the room's long silences, Katya felt more and more like a failure. She was not interesting enough to rouse any enthusiasm from these women. She sought desperately for a way to break the ice, to raise the subject of Nouf without being awkward, but her mind had stalled. Things were only made worse when the door opened again and young Huda came in. She was a Shrawi cousin who had come from Dhahran to perform the Hajj. In the two years since she'd arrived, she had done Hajj a dozen times. Far from growing sick of her perpetual visit, the Shrawi women spoke of her with superlatives, calling her the greatest pilgrim on earth and the right hand of Allah, while Huda, ever modest, never stopped thanking them for putting Mecca within her reach.

Huda's arrival caused a stir as Muruj leapt up to welcome her. Huda smiled faintly and announced that it was prayer time just as the call to prayer filled the room. It blared in the far window, which looked out over a steep rock wall that loomed over the family's mosque. Its loudspeakers were situated all over the island, but two of the largest ones pointed straight up at the women's sitting room, so that five times a day the room was filled with such beatific chanting that it was impossible to speak. Both Huda and Muruj went into an adjoining bathroom to perform their ablutions, while the sisters-in-law sat quietly, not looking at one another, slightly embarrassed to be left out and yet making no effort to join the prayer.

Katya waited, too. She had been in this position before. If Nusra had been there, or if there had been non-family visitors in the room, then everyone would have prayed, but when it was just the younger women, they did what they liked.

Katya studied the women silently. So much of her discomfort around them came from the stiffness she was seeing right now. Thus far, her whole relationship with them had been an elegant dance of pretend, of formal thank-yous and my-pleasures and *al-hamdulillahs*. But she was going to be spending a lot of time with these women, without Othman around. She had never believed in marrying a man because of his mother or sisters, although her friends did it all the time. The husband didn't matter so much. He was never home anyway, and if the household was big enough they wouldn't see him even if he was home. No, when you married you were marrying a mother-in-law, sisters-in-law, nieces. And Katya kept telling herself that they'd come to appreciate one another, that the relationships would grow warmer, or at least more tolerable, yet she had so little in common with these women. This was nothing like her own family, where Abu spent all day in the kitchen, cooking, smoking, reading newspapers and watching TV. This family never cooked or read papers; servants did it for them. Othman had promised her an apartment in the city, but he would still want her to visit the family frequently. She would spend her holidays here, bring her father here, even her children someday. She would see more of this room than she could ever imagine.

Now she wondered what Nouf had thought of them. Nouf, who'd wanted to live among dogs, to move to America, to go to college and have sex before marriage, how had she coexisted with women like Huda and Muruj? It must have been difficult having Huda move in – she was a year younger than Nouf but ten times more devout, the child any pious mother might have wished for. Or had Huda's presence been a blessing – a distraction that enabled Nouf to get on with her plans?

On the floor across from Katya, Abir was sitting cross-legged with a cold look on her face. She looked so much like Nouf that they might have been twins. Her house robe was a simple black, her hands were clasped on her lap in an unconscious attitude of modesty. There was an air of dis-gruntlement about her that Nouf hadn't had, or perhaps had done a better job of hiding. Abir was most like Nouf, not in temperament exactly, but in position. Young. Eligible. The family looked to these girls with a certain degree of sus-pense. How would they act? Who would they marry?

But whereas the women had treated Nouf as an adult, Abir was still the girl whose mother chastised her for playing with the food tray. Right now, she was eyeing the bathroom strangely, perhaps feeling pressure to join her sister and cousin, or perhaps silently scorning them for more cryptic reasons.

When Muruj and Huda emerged, they went to the corner window, unrolled two of the prayer rugs that were stacked there, and began their prayers. Katya watched them from behind, thinking how funny it was that Huda had come for a visit and never left. The family had practically adopted her, just as they'd adopted Othman years before, although his story was far more dramatic than Huda's. It was, Katya recalled, one of the first things he'd ever told her about himself.

The Shrawis had not really known Othman's father, but they knew that his name was Hussein and that he was a guest worker from southern Iraq. He'd been in Jeddah for only six months when the construction company that hired him had stopped paying his wages. Without the company's support, he couldn't renew his work permit, yet he didn't have the money to return to Iraq. Within a month, he'd taken to begging on the streets of Jeddah with his six-year-old son.

On his way to work one day, Abu-Tahsin saw them from the window of his limousine and called for the driver to stop the car. He led Hussein and his son to one of the family's charity homes, where he made sure they were fed and out-fitted with new clothes. He sent Othman to the local elementary school and even arranged to renew Hussein's work permit. He gave them enough cash to get by for a few days, and left them to their luck.

But two days later, while Hussein was walking around the city looking for work, he suffered a fatal case of heat stroke. He died that night.

Abu-Tahsin took such pity on the boy that he arranged the adoption papers at once. Katya often wondered what had prompted the decision. It wasn't rash exactly – the adoption itself had taken a year and a half – but it wasn't the sort of action that could later be revoked; it bound Othman to the family for a lifetime. What had Abu-Tahsin seen in the boy that turned his heart? Why was Othman different from any other homeless child? In any event, Katya mused, it was actually a story about Abu-Tahsin, and how rare it was to find such spontaneous passion coupled with such long-lasting generosity of spirit.

After the prayers were finished and the women had returned to their seats, Muruj suggested that they eat some fruit, and the women busied themselves. Zahra picked up the telephone and called the servants. Huda stacked the empty coffee pot and cups on the tray. Abir was idly picking lint from the couch. Katya wondered how Nouf's death had affected them, really. They seemed as composed as ever.

Zahra finished her call and turned to Katya. 'You seem

tired,' she said. The other women were chatting, and Katya felt comfortable giving an honest reply.

'I am tired,' she said. 'It's sad being here without Nouf.'

The name brought the other conversations to a halt. Even Abir snapped out of her daydream.

'It is sad,' Zahra said in a soft voice. The conversations picked up again, but without enthusiasm now. 'I've been wondering,' she went on, 'will you quit your job after the wedding?'

There was another lull and people turned to Katya, curious to hear her reply. She shrugged. 'I haven't discussed it with Othman,' she said.

'But certainly you'll want to have children.'

'Yes, we do.' She couldn't help blushing. She knew what came next, what Zahra would say if this were not such a formal sitting room: you'd better start having children before you get too old. You may be too old already! What is a job, compared to the value of children?

But instead, Zahra smiled and nodded. 'May you have as many children as Um-Tahsin.'

'Thank you,' Katya said, weighing whether her next segue would be in bad taste or not. 'How is Nusra? I imagine it's terrible to lose a child.'

'The worst thing in the world,' Zahra agreed.

There was a moment of respectful silence. Katya was dying to blurt out: *Do you think she ran away?* But it was Huda's soft voice that split the silence.

'Allah forgive her. She should have known better.'

No one knew quite how to argue with that. Katya glanced at the women, all looking at their hands. 'It's so strange,' she said. 'I thought for the longest time that she'd been kidnapped.'

Muruj snuffed loudly and sat up in her seat. 'No.' She looked straight at Katya with eyes full of scorn. 'I'll tell you what happened. My sister had a head full of fantasy. Ever since she was a child!' Her voice had reached an awkward pitch. The other women were in agreement. Fadilah gave the subtlest of nods, and Abir exhaled sharply as if to say: *Well, of course we knew that!*

'She ran off for the most shameful reason,' Muruj said. 'For a man! Probably a boy she met at the mall – or Allah help us all – through her driver. She fell in love, or *thought* she was in love, and when she ran off to meet him, he didn't show up. He left her out there in the desert to die.'

Fadilah shot Katya a look that said: *Why did you bring this up?*

'That driver ought to be fired!' Muruj snapped.

'If you have proof of this,' Katya said softly, 'then shouldn't the family try to find out who this boy was?'

'Any way you look at it,' Muruj ploughed on, 'it's the same old story. He damaged her and then he abandoned her. That's what you get when you don't have a marriage contract. Nouf wouldn't be the first poor girl to learn that!'

'Yes,' Zahra murmured. 'We are trying to find out who it was. Isn't Tahsin—?' She looked to Fadilah, who raised a hand to indicate that she didn't want to talk about that either, and was disgusted with the drift of the conversation.

In the face of scorn from both Fadilah and Muruj, Katya had to summon her deepest reserves of nerve to ask the next question: 'Nobody has any idea who it was?'

No one answered right away, but Huda and Muruj exchanged a meaningful look, which caused Huda to shut her eyes and plunge into a series of whispered prayers.

'Whoever did this to my sister will find his judgement in heaven,' Muruj stated flatly. And with that, all the scorn fell from her face, and she sat back on the sofa with a sad, defeated air that somehow seemed more honest than all the bluster that had come before it.

Only Abir kept her eyes fixed on Katya, but when Katya met her gaze, there was a knock at the door and Abir leapt up to answer it. Three women came into the room.

Katya felt a sinking frustration; there was no hope of continuing a private conversation. The new arrivals were obviously guests. When they shed their burqas, no one recognized them, and they greeted the company awkwardly. One of the women introduced herself, explaining that her husband had come to make a donation. The other women remained happily anonymous, but Katya guessed that their husbands were visiting the house, too. They were a well-dressed group; clearly their husbands were wealthy. The women's purses were Gucci, their high-heeled shoes revealed a daring portion of ankle, and most telling of all, their cloaks were silk and tailored to suggest the elegance of form beneath them. One woman even wore false fingernails with a bright red gloss. Compared to these paragons of fashion, the Shrawi women looked as if they'd just wandered in from the desert. They didn't wear make-up or silk cloaks or high heels, and they certainly never painted their nails. Abir was staring at the women's hands, but her expression was inscrutable. Was she offended? Disgusted? Envious? Before the door shut again, Abir slipped out of the room.

Muruj invited the women to sit, and Katya leapt up, offering her seat and politely rebuffing the protests. She seized the opportunity to excuse herself, saying that she had to get back to work. Fadilah looked at her oddly, and it was only when Katya was out of the door and halfway down the hall that she realized why: she'd already said she'd taken the afternoon off. She blushed just thinking about how blatantly she'd lied.

☽

At the end of the hallway she came to a corridor. To the left was the exit, used exclusively by women, and to the right lay the entire unexplored realm of the women's side of the house – their bedrooms, bathrooms, kitchens and sewing rooms. Katya had been there once, on a brief tour with Nusra, but she had not seen it since her first visit to the house. Abir had probably come this way.

No one was there now. Katya turned to the right and tip-toed down the hallway, listening for sounds of teenage activity. Would it be the scratching of a homework pencil? The faint strains of rock music emanating from headphones? Did she even have music? It was the only comparison Katya could come up with – her own life as a teenager, minus the technology.

She passed an open doorway and saw an empty bath-room. A few yards down the hallway was a complex of doorways. She took the first one and went into a foyer, a quaint box of a room with a tiny square table standing in the corner. On the table was a copy of the holy Quran.

Gently, she tapped on the bedroom door. There was no answer so she pushed it open and peeked inside. The first thing she saw was blue wooden letters spelling NOUF on the wall. Looking back into the hallway to make sure no one had seen her, she stole inside.

It was a spacious bedroom. The floor was carpeted with a cerulean blue rug, like a massive sea upon which the various pieces of furniture had been cast adrift. A white canopy bed floated between two matching dressers. The walls were smooth and white, undecorated but for the wooden letters. On the dresser, however, were a few family pictures in ornate golden frames. Two potted palm trees near the bath-room door looked real enough. Like flotsam in a harbour, all the room's smaller items, the stray shoes and stuffed animals and jewellery boxes, had drifted into a corner.

There were no windows, but two skylights let in the light. A lamp stood beside the bed, next to a small reading table with a magazine poking out of the drawer. Katya approached the bed. A heart design embroidered on the pillows and the softness of the white cotton sheets were touchingly virginal. The fluttery mosquito netting only added to the sense that this bed had held someone innocent and sweet and needing protection. When she opened the drawer to the reading table and took out the magazine, it was open to an article entitled 'The Seventy-Seven Words for Love'.

Instinctively, Katya looked back at the doorway. No one was there. There were doors on every side of the room; all of them were shut. Katya went to each of them and studied the handles, but none had a lock. Someone could walk in at any moment, from any direction. Nouf must have felt exposed here – and yet she'd been comfortable enough to leave an article like this one lying around. Her parents probably wouldn't have approved unless it had been titled 'The Seventy-Seven Words for Allah'. Katya sat on the bed and looked at the article. Perhaps with a blind mother, a teenage girl could do what she liked.

There was a sound and one of the doors swung open. Katya quickly stood up, shoving the magazine into her purse by some idiotic force of instinct. She instantly regretted it – now she was a thief.

Abir stood in the doorway. 'What are you doing here?'

'I, ah . . . sorry. I was looking for you, actually, and I found this instead.' She motioned to the room.

Abir glanced down and saw the magazine stuffed awkwardly into Katya's purse. 'Why were you looking for me?'

'Well, I got bored in the sitting room, and I saw you leave, so I figured . . .' She shrugged.

Abir eyed her as every teenager eyes an adult who seems to understand them, not certain that the understanding is genuine but fearing that it won't be, and repulsed in either case. Katya met her gaze. She was wearing a headscarf – she must have been praying – and she held a copy of the Quran, open and clutched to her chest. Abir was the same age as Huda.

'Which surah are you reading?' Katya asked.

Abir lowered the book, shut it, and set it on the bedside table. Awkwardly, she sat on the bed. 'Actually, I was only trying to read.'

Katya felt a bleakness steal over the room. She glanced at the photographs lined up on the dresser and noticed that Abir was not in any of them. There were four frames; two contained pictures of Abu-Tahsin and Nusra, one was a picture of Nouf at a younger sister's birthday party; she was cutting cake and grinning happily. The remaining picture showed a pair of saluki dogs, their tails wagging happily. 'I'm sorry about your sister,' she said.

Abir didn't respond.

'You must have been close,' Katya prodded.

Abir slid her hands nervously beneath her thighs. 'You saw her body, didn't you?'

Gently, Katya sat down on the bed beside her. 'Yes, I did.'

'So you know how she died?'

'Yes,' she replied, looking down at her hands. She had a sense where this was going. 'She drowned.'

Abir clapped a hand to her mouth. 'Oh.'

'I'm so sorry.' Katya could see that she hadn't known. Had her parents felt that she was too young for the truth? What was the shame of drowning, when the position of Nouf's body at the funeral had practically been an announcement of the worse crime of fornication? Or had Abir not noticed? Still, it was a kind of relief to learn that Katya wasn't the only victim of secrecy in the family.

Abir's hands were shaking, and she seemed to be trying

not to cry. 'They won't tell us anything. I know she ran away. She got lost in the desert and she died, but I don't know the details. And I have to know. I keep worrying—' She clasped her hands into tight balls and jammed them into her lap. 'I keep thinking she – what if she – what if it wasn't an accident? What if she ran away and didn't want to come back? Maybe she wanted to . . .'

'You mean, did she kill herself?' Katya offered.

Abir nodded and tears slid down her cheeks. 'I don't want to think that her soul is in hell. She was my sister.' At this, her voice trembled, and she started to cry harder. Katya resisted the impulse to wrap her arm around the girl's shoulders; she sensed it would be unwelcome.

'I don't know exactly what happened,' she said, 'but I'm fairly certain she didn't kill herself.'

Abir swallowed and glanced at her.

'She was hit on the head,' Katya said. 'It wasn't what killed her, but it may have knocked her unconscious, so when the flood waters came, she had no defence.'

Abir's face went white. 'But I don't understand. Who hit her? Was someone with her?'

'I don't know.' Katya hesitated. 'Listen, Abir, can you think of any reason why she might have run away?'

Abir shook her head. 'I knew that she was nervous about her wedding.'

'Why?'

She shrugged. 'She didn't know Qazi that well.'

'Did she ever talk about leaving?'

'No. Only sometimes, as a joke.' Abir wiped her eyes again. '*Did* she run away?'

Katya hesitated. 'I don't know.'

Abir seemed to regain her nerve. She sat up straighter and her shoulders stopped shaking. She wiped her nose on her sleeve.

There was an awkward silence, and Katya fumbled through it. 'I'm sorry I've been asking so many questions about Nouf. I don't mean to upset you. I know it won't bring her back.'

Abir nodded.

'I wish I'd had the chance to know her better,' Katya said.

Stiffly, Abir stood and went to a door in the corner. She opened the door, switched on the light, and motioned Katya inside.

It was an enormous walk-in closet stuffed with clothes – on racks, hangers, stacked in plastic drawers, clothes in trunks and lining the overhead shelves. Shoe racks were filled with shoes. Everything was clean and pressed. Katya stepped into the closet with amazement.

'Wow,' she whispered. 'Was she always so organized?'

'No, no. After the funeral, my mother arranged for everything to look neat.'

Katya was afraid to touch anything, but Abir began to hold the clothes out for inspection. A motley assortment it was: a pinstriped blazer rubbed shoulders with a siren red negligee. There was a slinky ball gown with sequins, a fluffy pink mohair sweater with a cable knit, and a pair of pink leather pants. Shorts and T-shirts were stacked on a shelf, and the undergarments seemed ridiculously skimpy, ribbon panties and see-through bras. For the first time, Katya felt that she was seeing some of the personality she had hoped to encounter in the room outside. This lavish closet – probably hundreds of thousands of riyals' worth of clothes – was a fantasy world where Nouf could actually wear a man's blazer or a pair of shorts. There were jeans, of course, and dozens of black skirts and blue button-down shirts, private school uniforms from the looks of it. But right beside them was a tremendous, white, floor-length coat made of the softest fur.

Katya stopped at the coat, struck with a fierce, instantaneous longing to have a coat like this, and a world to wear it in. It was something her namesake would have worn. On the hanger beside it were two gloves, a muffler, a scarf, and a large fur hat. She buried her fingers in the hat's furry pile. It was cool and smooth, and for the briefest second she was Nouf standing in the closet, reaching across the gulf of time and space to touch a clear lake of ice, or the very zenith of a glacier.

Turning, she saw Abir holding out a formal, hot pink gown. The skirt was wide enough so that the dress was almost able to stand up on its own. Katya realized what it was.

'Her wedding gown?'

'Yes.'

'It's extravagant.' Katya looked around. 'Wait a second, how much of this is her trousseau?'

'Everything on this side, and about a third of that.' Abir motioned to everything that was interesting in the closet. Katya looked at the fur coat again and felt a surge of disappointment. Nouf hadn't bought these clothes; Qazi had. What remained of Nouf's original possessions was a row of cloaks, a pair of jeans, some T-shirts and a dozen housedresses.

Katya motioned to the trousseau. 'I thought she'd chosen all of this.'

Abir shook her head. 'She didn't like pink.'

Qazi, of course, would have had no idea. Did he buy the clothes thinking that all women liked pink? Or was that what he wanted: a woman who belonged in it? Katya thought of her own trousseau. Othman was still putting it together, but she hoped he would avoid this order of clothing, tantalizing items whose only functional purpose was to symbolize what the wearer would never be.

When she looked back at Abir, she saw that the young girl was ready to leave. Katya followed her back into the bedroom. Abir's expression was cold and formal now. She picked up her Quran.

'I'd better go,' she said.

'Yes, of course.'

There was a moment of awkward silence before Abir turned to leave.

'I'm sorry,' Katya said again. Abir looked back and shook her head as if to say: *It's not your fault.* With a gentle rustling of robes, she left.

19

Katya peeked into the laboratory. It was lunchtime, and she'd joined the other women in the ladies' lounge for fifteen minutes before making a pretence of needing to use the bathroom. Slipping back through the corridors on her way to the lab, she'd gone unnoticed. The men usually left the building for lunch, and the place was deserted.

In the laboratory, she sat down at the counter. Over the past two days, she'd surreptitiously prepared the DNA samples, extracting the variable DNA and mixing it with a buffered solution of polymerase and primers. This morning she had put the samples in the thermal cycler. The machine always took a few hours to process the samples, and she had to be there right when they were ready so that nobody else would take them out by mistake.

There were two samples, one from Eric Scarberry and the other from Nouf's escort Mohammed. She watched the machine whirr into its final phase and glanced back at the door.

She had just enough time to put the profile printouts in her purse and hide the evidence of her work before Maddawi came back into the lab, followed by Bassma. The women sat down to resume their work, undisturbed that Katya was already there. They seemed happy and continued their lunchtime chatter.

Relieved, Katya went to work on blood samples from a case she'd prepared that morning. She glanced at her purse. She hadn't taken the time to look at the printouts, and now it was bothering her. Had either DNA been a match for Nouf's baby? She would have to wait until she got home to find out.

☽

That evening she was distracted. Abu noticed that something was wrong, but when he asked, she lied and said she was coming down with a cold. All through dinner, she thought about Othman and wondered how she would tell him what she'd discovered.

After dinner, she called Ahmad. Half an hour later he came to the door. Abu invited him in and the two men talked while Katya went to her room, put on her cloak and scarf, and made minute adjustments to her burqa. She hadn't told her father she was leaving, but if she let the men talk long enough, eventually Ahmad would tell him. It was harder for Abu to say no that way.

A while later, Abu knocked on the bedroom door. 'Katya.' He sounded angry.

She came out fully covered. 'I'm going out for a little while.'

'I know. Ahmad told me. Where are you going?'

'I've got to meet with Othman briefly. It's about his sister.'

Abu eyed her dangerously. 'Why can't you just call him?'

'It's not something I want to tell him on the phone.' She looked pleadingly at her father, but his frown grew even deeper and he might have stopped her from going had Ahmad not appeared at the end of the hallway.

'Ready?' Ahmad asked. 'Let's make this quick.'

Katya wanted to kiss him. He always knew exactly what to say.

Abu turned to his friend. 'You keep a good eye on her,' he said grouchily. Katya felt his stare on her back all the way down the hall. Ahmad nodded and with his best show of sternness, led her to the waiting car.

As they drove through the old town, Katya stared idly out the window at the souks, which were closing for the night, and at the buildings, which were made of coral quarried from Red Sea reefs. She had the impulse to reach out of the window and touch one, to feel its rough texture beneath her fingers, something to snap her out of her unending thoughts about people. Abu. Nouf. Nayir. Salwa and Abdul-Aziz. Othman.

When they pulled into the parking lot of the children's amusement park, she saw that Othman was already there. He'd driven the silver Porsche, and the top was down. He was wearing a blue button-down shirt, and his hair, thick and curly and black, was shorter than before, but it was the sight of his profile, his long arms, and something in the way his hand draped over the steering wheel that caught in her throat.

Behind him, the amusement park was shutting down for the night, and one by one the rides went dark, first the Ferris wheel, then the roller-coaster, then the smaller rides. Katya asked Ahmad to wait until the lights were out completely before pulling up to Othman's car. There was less chance they'd be noticed in the dark – and it was already suspicious, two cars in an empty lot exchanging a female passenger. At night, the religious police were scarce, but Katya felt edgy.

'Your father will want him to keep the top down,' Ahmad said. 'But not, of course, if you're going on the freeway.'

She smiled at him and got out of the car.

When she climbed into the Porsche, Othman pressed a button that brought the top over them. His eyes were dewy, as if he'd been crying, but she suspected he was just tired. She lifted her burqa. He clasped her hand and kissed it. 'It's so good to see you.'

She felt a flutter in her stomach. 'I've missed you,' she said, braving herself to lean over the seat and give his cheek a kiss. It always felt awkward. *It will become more comfortable,* she told herself, *when Ahmad isn't watching.*

He accepted the kiss and cradled her face in his hand.

'Are you all right?' she asked, running her hand through his hair.

'Yes.'

'I like your haircut.'

He smiled. 'Do you want to go for a ride?'

'Yes.'

Kissing her forehead, he released her hand and started the car. They turned out of the parking lot. Othman kept an eye on the rear-view mirror to make sure that Ahmad was following them, and they drove without talking, letting the growl of the car's engine fill the small space. Now in his presence, she was filled with affection. She couldn't remember why she'd doubted him and suspected that it had been only because of her own stress and the days of silence between them, however unintended they were. One fear rose inside her – the fragility of her loyalty, only now kept at bay by frequent glances at his steady hands, his melancholy eyes, the comforting presence of his musky smell.

Twenty minutes later, he pulled onto a darkened beach south of the city. There was a series of private beaches here. Like the others, this one had high stone walls on three sides and a small metal door at the corner. They went into the beach and shut the door behind them. Through the door's iron grate they could see Ahmad in his car, his face half-lit by the flickering light of his portable DVD player.

'What's he watching?' Othman asked.

'Bootleg reruns of *Hour el-Ayn*.'

'What's that?'

She was mildly surprised that he'd never heard of *The Beautiful Virgins*. 'It's a prime-time drama about the recent militant attacks on the American compound.'

'And it's called *Hour el-Ayn?*'

'It tells the stories of the people who died and their attackers. I guess there are some virgins in there, too.'

Othman smiled and shook his head and led her down the sand. There was a hut near the water, its door locked with a chain.

'Is this your family's beach?' she asked.

'Yes, but I haven't been here in years. We have beaches on the island now.'

'It's lovely.' She had been on private beaches before, but the protective walls had always extended so far into the water that nearby bathers couldn't reach them without swimming. The walls on this beach ended just ten feet shy of the water's edge, and although Katya heard no sounds of activity from neighbouring enclaves, the moon shed a stark light on the water and she didn't feel comfortable taking off her abaaya. Othman suggested they sit on the sand.

They sat close enough that their legs were touching. Draping his arms on his knees, he looked out at the water with what she recognized as a longing to go in. When he caught her looking, he bowed his head.

'Do you want to swim?' she asked.

'No. No, I'm exhausted.'

'Don't hold back on my account.'

He sighed. 'It's all right. I am genuinely tired. I've been in meetings all day. Always in meetings! I wish I could get away.'

'Can you take a day off?'

'Not this week. With my father still in the hospital, we're all working twice as much.' He shook his head. 'I don't know what we're going to do when – Allah forgive me – when the day comes that he passes away.'

The mention of his father brought her thoughts back to Nouf and the DNA samples. She didn't want to plunge right into the matter, so she let Othman talk. It was best to listen for a while, so she could judge his state. Othman went on about work, about one of their donors who made a habit of questioning every donation that the family made, no matter how small. She listened, laughing at the appropriate moments, but her mind was abuzz with a chatter of its own. *Talking about Nouf always makes him so sad. I'm afraid of displeasing him. I shouldn't be afraid! If this marriage is going to work, we have to speak openly. He should realize this is important. But I understand his grief . . .*

'You seem distracted,' he said finally. It wasn't an accusation but an impartial observation. She felt a swell of relief.

'I'm sorry. I've been worrying about work myself.' She noticed that he was looking at her hand. Idly, he took it in his own and began to stroke her fingers. 'I saw your sister Abir yesterday.'

He smiled. 'So I heard.' His finger was tracing spirals and brush strokes on her palm. It took her a moment to realize that he was writing a message. She spelled it out . . . W-A-N-T . . . T-O . . . M-A-R-R-Y . . . S-O-O-N? She smiled and grabbed his palm, to write her own message in reply.

Y-E-S.

He squeezed her hand. 'So what have you been worrying about at work?'

'Oh, my boss. The usual,' she said. 'Actually, I did some work today on Nouf's case.'

He stiffened so slightly that she almost missed it. 'Ah.'

'I'm sorry it's taken so long to get back to you. I've just – I've had to do a lot of the work off the clock.'

'You're not putting your job in jeopardy, I hope?' He frowned.

'Not really.' She saw that he didn't believe her. 'I was quick about it.'

There was an awkward silence. He dropped her hand and exhaled, running a hand through his hair. '*Ya Allah.* I never even thought about it—'

'No,' she said, 'don't worry.'

'No, no, I should apologize! I'm sorry. It didn't cross my mind that you'd have to . . . I don't know, sneak around and hide things. That's what you're doing, isn't it?'

She couldn't deny it.

'I'm such an idiot! Katya—' He took her hand again, more firmly now. 'I'm sorry.'

'Don't apologize. I want to do it.' She squeezed his hand. 'Listen, it's no problem. I was just trying to determine the DNA of the baby's father,' she said softly. 'I was hoping to match it with her escort.'

His grip went slack. 'Was it a match?'

'No.' She wanted to tell him about Eric, but it seemed too much to add. She felt certain suddenly that he didn't know about Eric. How could she explain what Nayir had told her? That Nouf had been making plans to move to New York. That she had been meeting an American. It was a dangerous thing to reveal, especially if Eric still had a connection to the family. *I can't say it tonight.*

'Do you have any other suspects?' he asked.

She gritted her teeth.

'No, wait,' he said. 'You don't have to answer that. I'm

sorry. It's not even really your job. I feel selfish for putting this on you.'

'No, please don't apologize.'

'Katya.' Suddenly his voice had an edge. 'As much as I appreciate your dedication to my sister, I think you should consider your job first.'

She felt abashed.

'I mean, not every woman has the courage to work,' he said. 'I know I've said this before, but I'm really proud of you. I honestly don't want you doing anything that will put your job at risk.'

'Trust me,' she said. 'I'm very careful.'

After an awkward pause, he nodded, but she felt him draw into himself. There was a look in his eye that reminded her of Nouf just before she would pull away.

Another silence ensued. He put his hands around his legs. The silence, his withdrawal, felt like a rebuke. She told herself that it wasn't personal, that he was grieving and this was how he grieved, but the mood was so dark that it poisoned the air, and she felt they'd never recover from it.

'I'm sorry,' she said.

He seemed to snap out of a reverie. 'Don't apologize. But listen. I'm grateful for what you've done, and for how much you care about Nouf. You've *proved* it to me. I *know* that you care. But what's done is done. Think of what this commitment might cost you. You can't bring her back.' He looked at her. 'I think this should stop.'

She was so taken aback that she didn't know what to say. 'What should stop?'

'This . . . all this work you're doing. I appreciate it. I want to find out what happened to her, too. But this is dangerous. And – and this thing about her child, I think it's only going to cause more pain. What will happen if you find out who fathered her child? We don't want to punish anyone; we don't want more suffering.'

Katya thought he might cry, and she realized just how difficult it was for him to hold his feelings in all the time.

'I know it's been hard,' she said finally. 'I don't want to cause you any more pain. But I was thinking that whoever fathered that child might have had something to do with her disappearance.'

'That might be,' he said, hands gripping the sand, 'but then what? Someone gets punished for falling in love? For breaking the rules?' His voice had gone up a pitch. She waited for a moment, letting the silence calm him. 'Look, my family is trying to accept her pregnancy right now. Any more news could be devastating. Meanwhile, you're putting your job at risk.'

'I'm sorry,' she said. 'It may be that I'm prying—'

'You're not prying.'

'But the father of her child may have hurt her, and wouldn't it be better if you knew who it was?'

'If my family has to believe that Nouf's death was accidental, then that's the way it should be for now.' He raised a hand to stop her protest. 'For *now*, I said. If you get caught doing this, I won't forgive you for jeopardizing your career.'

She looked away, fighting a turmoil of emotions. She wanted to say that he was acting suspiciously, that if he knew who the father was, if he was protecting someone, then he ought to tell her.

'Please don't ruin your life.' Othman took her chin and gently guided her face towards his. He looked straight into her eyes. 'Nouf is dead,' he said, 'but you are not.'

She nodded, understanding, if not his every statement, at least the impulses behind them. He kissed her softly and nuzzled her cheek, but instead of pulling away, he continued to kiss her with a growing passion. She felt a spasm of

225

pleasure when his hand slid around her waist, but they heard a noise behind them – it sounded as if Ahmad had rolled his window down; the noises from his DVD player suddenly got louder – and they both recognized it as a warning: *That's enough.* Othman withdrew his hand and sat up straight.

His words troubled her. Did he really think that she was pursuing this investigation to prove something to him? And why was he so upset that she might lose her job? *She* ought to be upset. What if, after they got married, she decided to stop working? She would probably want to have children one day. Would he forgive her for quitting? Would he understand? The sudden realization that they hadn't talked about children – at least not enough to satisfy her – made her tremendously nervous.

She also felt a creeping doubt. It surprised her that he'd been so adamant about her job. He didn't like talking about Nouf, she knew – he had always become withdrawn. By previous standards tonight had been practically a catharsis for him. Something had caused it, but she didn't want to speculate on what it was. It was late, and she was sick of guessing.

20

He was lying beneath her. Her long dark hair fell over his chest and face, tickling his cheeks. It was cool in the room, but where her skin touched his, he felt a pleasant heat. He'd dreamt about this woman a hundred times but never saw her face. Her hair, cascades of it, long and black, obscured everything, but just when he'd reach up to brush it back, she would pull away. It felt as if the reach were actually a push, and that the more strength he used the faster she'd disappear. He learned from the dream that the only way to catch her was to stop wanting her, to stop trying and let her hair drape him in darkness, let her body enfold him in a spell of sensation. Someday he'd see her face, but meanwhile he could enjoy the weight of her body, the softness of her skin.

Opening his eyes, Nayir thought he was still in the dream. His groin was throbbing and something tickled his cheeks, but the boat rocked around him and he realized that someone was above on deck. There was a clatter in the doorway. Pushing off the sheet, he scrambled to his feet and saw Miss Hijazi at the top of the ladder, the hem of her cloak clutched in her fist. 'Nayir?' she called. 'Are you there?'

He stumbled to the bathroom.

'Nayir? I'm sorry. I have to speak to you. I tried your cell phone, but it was off.' There was an awkward silence. 'May I come in for a moment?'

He shut the bathroom door and rubbed his face. It had been a few days since he'd seen Miss Hijazi. He'd been trying not to think about her.

'I'm coming down,' she said. He thought he heard a catch in her voice. Peeking back out the bathroom door, he saw her descend the ladder. He caught a glimpse of her ankle and shut the door again.

'Sorry to intrude,' she called out. 'Your neighbour was watching.'

'So you came *in?*' he asked.

'I told him I was your sister.'

'Oh, no!'

'I had no choice. Listen, Nayir, I've tried calling you. Why don't you turn your cell phone on?'

'I'm busy. Does Othman know that you're here?'

'This is important. I got the DNA you left. I was finally able to analyse it, and it turns out that neither Eric nor Mohammed fathered Nouf's child.'

Annoyed and unable to process what she said, he switched on the tap. The water was lukewarm and slimy. He stared in the mirror instead; he looked exhausted. What time had he fallen asleep? He'd been up all night studying maps of the desert, searching for Eric's research site.

'Did you hear me, Nayir?' She sounded breathless. 'Someone else was the father.'

Summoning his nerve, he took a robe from the door and put it on. Opening the door just enough to slip through it, he darted into the bedroom and shut the door behind him. From the corner of his eye, he'd noticed that she'd kept her back to him, and he was grateful for it. He stripped off his house robe, snatched a pair of pants from the floor, and found a shirt on the bed; both were rumpled. He put them on anyway.

'It means there has to be a third man,' she called out.

Moments later, he emerged from the bedroom and found her standing in the kitchenette. 'Well, it wasn't me.'

She spat out a laugh and clapped a hand to her mouth, which was behind a burqa.

He frowned.

'I'm sorry,' she said.

'You shouldn't be here,' he snapped. 'This is a *zina* crime, you know. Did you tell Othman you were coming here?'

'No, but—'

'And why aren't you at work? I thought you had a job.'

'I took the morning off. Look, I'm sorry to intrude.' She said it as if she meant it. He averted his gaze. Even though she was wearing a burqa, he still didn't like staring into her eyes. 'I need your help with something,' she said.

'What?'

'I want to investigate a site that may be connected to Nouf's death.'

'What do you need me for? You've got a driver. And a fiancé.'

She didn't reply. She turned to the window, crossed her arms, and gripped her elbows. Nayir waited, growing more tense by the second.

'Othman doesn't want me to do this any more,' she said, her voice unsteady. 'We talked about it, and he said I was risking my job.'

Slowly, Nayir sat down on the sofa and looked around for his shoes. 'Are you?'

'Not really . . . maybe a little. But I'm very careful, and this is about Nouf. It's about his *sister*. You would think he would take all the help he can get.'

Nayir was torn. He wanted to tell her that it was no use

229

complaining about Othman to him; he was Othman's friend and it wasn't going to change. He couldn't see her face behind the burqa, but her eyes were expressive enough to tell him that she was upset. Othman or not, he felt a pang of sympathy.

'I know that Othman wants to find out what happened to Nouf,' he said carefully, avoiding his next thought: *Maybe he just doesn't want you involved.* Perhaps Othman was finally growing uncomfortable with the fact that she had a job, with her boldness in regards to this case. He wondered if she'd told Othman that they'd gone to the apartment and the optometrist.

'Why do you think he asked you to stop working on the case?'

She sighed. 'I don't know. He seemed uncomfortable with it.'

'Did you tell him that I went with you to Eric's apartment?'

'I told him we did some investigating together,' she said. 'But I told him that days ago. It was just last night he got upset. He always gets upset when I talk about Nouf. Last night, I explained about the DNA. I think it upsets him especially to talk about her pregnancy, and this time he got angry. He said he was worried about me. I told him he shouldn't worry, but he insisted that I stop. He said that if I didn't, he would never forgive me for jeopardizing my career.'

It surprised Nayir, because even though he understood Othman's reluctance, this was obviously more than reluctance. It was suspicious. And something else was wrong: Othman was worried that she would lose her job. Did he really care? Did he *want* her to work?

She appeared to be waiting for his reply. While it flattered him, he was wary of the consequences of expressing his opinion. He stood up, opened the closet and took out his coat.

'I can't explain Othman's behaviour,' he said.

'But don't you think it's odd?'

He didn't reply. Perhaps Othman knew something about Nouf's disappearance, and he didn't want Miss Hijazi to know about it. It didn't mean he was guilty.

'You think he doesn't trust me,' she said.

'I didn't say that.'

'Your face said it for you.'

Although it made him uncomfortable, he was impressed that she'd noticed his face without looking directly at him. Her arms were still crossed in a defiant way, and he remembered her stubborn silence at the examiner's office. *She's not going to give up the investigation,* he thought. *Not even for Othman.* And he felt the same mix of indignation and grudging respect he'd had then. She was being defiant, but he couldn't disapprove of her reasons.

'I'll talk to him,' Nayir said. 'That's what you want, isn't it?'

She turned to face him, and he quickly averted his gaze. 'Yes, if you can. But more than that . . .' She faced the window again. 'I'd like to know that you're still in this.'

He hesitated. 'I want to know what happened to her. And I think so does Othman, whether he feels that way now or not.'

She seemed relieved, or grateful, and she uncrossed her arms. 'Then will you come with me right now? This is important. I need your expertise.'

He hesitated again.

'Tracking,' she said, as if that explained it.

After a pause, he nodded. 'Just give me time for morning prayers.'

☽

Miss Hijazi had told him they were going to an abandoned zoo. The night before, she had flipped open the newspaper to find an article ('Monkey Business?') about the illegal sale of pet chimpanzees in the Kingdom, a practice that had been banned but flourished nonetheless. The article also highlighted the deplorable conditions for animals living in Jeddah's smaller zoos. As she studied the pictures of hairless, bone-thin chimpanzees, she found her thoughts going back to the manure on Nouf's wrist and Nayir's uncle's discovery that whatever animal it had come from had probably been poisoned. She hadn't yet determined where the manure had come from, but what better place to start looking than the abandoned zoo?

So, following her Toyota once again, Nayir pulled off the freeway and drove inland, down a desolate strip of road that intersected a field of grey sand. With every mile came a deeper sense of guilt. Now they were truly sneaking around behind Othman's back. He told himself that Othman would approve of their reasons, despite what he'd told Miss Hijazi the night before, but in his heart he knew the truth: when she had asked him to come to the zoo, he had wanted to be in her company.

His mind kept returning to the fact that she had told Othman they'd gone to Eric's apartment, and Othman hadn't been upset. Of course he shouldn't have been – he trusted Nayir in matters like these. But it stung him to realize that it was the same trust a king has for a eunuch. He was worse than a eunuch; he wasn't missing a part, he was missing something else, a hidden seed that made him a man. He remembered Othman laughing at the jacket bazaar; he'd been laughing because Nayir was the last person on earth who should see a woman's body. It was as if the woman had flashed an ayatollah. The more he thought about it, the more disgusted he felt with himself for thinking about it at all.

He began an ascent up a broad, steep hill. Dust poured past the windows, obscuring the view, but when he reached the zenith, the panorama opened. Below, a dozen whitewashed homes dotted the valley wall; above, a rusted concertina wire formed the western perimeter of the abandoned zoo.

Nayir rolled down the window and took a deep breath. It wasn't camel shit; he knew that smell. This was definitely zoo smell. He had to admit that Miss Hijazi was clever to think of coming here. If Nouf had actually been to a zoo, she'd have had a dozen to choose from, but if she was meeting someone in secret, she'd have come here.

They parked in a vacant lot near a children's playground that looked to have been unused for a decade. He got out of the Jeep and saw Miss Hijazi dragging what appeared to be a toolbox from the Toyota's boot. Her escort assisted by fluttering around her, performing trivial tasks before she could get to them, first handling the toolbox, then shutting the trunk.

'Thank you, Ahmad,' she said with a trace of annoyance. 'This shouldn't take long.'

She joined Nayir and they approached the old entrance, a metal ticket cage tucked in the shadow of a palm. Beside the ticket cage was a metal plaque reading: *Children May Be Accompanied by Either their Mother or Father, but Not Both Parents. Boys over the Age of 10 are considered Adults.* Beside that was a timetable for men, women, children and school groups, so that the different species of humans didn't overlap.

Nayir glanced back at the driver and saw that he had returned to the air-conditioned car. His over-casual way of letting Miss Hijazi wander off with a non-family man rankled Nayir even though it had happened before. Ahmad, too, must think he presented no danger. He was trustworthy, but it was no consolation.

The turnstile was jammed, so Nayir climbed over and

turned to help her, but she handed him her toolbox and climbed over herself.

'You know, I can do this alone,' he said.

She stared at him fiercely. He actually blushed. Then, quickly, she took the toolbox from him.

Turning down a palm-sheltered avenue, they saw that the road ran past buildings and empty cages, murky fountains and broken benches.

'Nouf had manure on her wrist,' she said.

'Her escort also had manure on his shoes,' Nayir replied, remembering the smell on Mohammed's shoes.

'Oh. You didn't tell me that.' Seeing that he wasn't going to reply, she pushed on. 'What would you be doing, if you were Mohammed and you came to the zoo? Looking for someone? Meeting someone?' They stepped into the shade of a nearby building.

'The real question,' Nayir said, 'is what would you be doing, if you were Nouf and you came to the zoo?'

She gave him a nervous glance. 'Maybe you'd be meeting a man?'

A welcome cool enveloped them as they wandered beneath a row of palm trees overlooking a former Serengeti exhibit. A few animal bones lay in the deep wells between the cages and viewer platforms – perhaps the thin fragments of giraffe neck, the skull of a large cat. Lions, the kings of the jungle, were the wimps of the desert. The heat had killed them all.

No, Nayir thought, the *Saudis* had killed them all with their ambitions to build an outdoor zoo in the world's most inhospitable climate. They imported the animals, but the crowds didn't come. And why should they? Who would want to walk through the stifling heat to see a bunch of suffering beasts? Certainly not Saudis, notoriously scornful of anything lower on the food chain than themselves.

A faint breeze swept beneath his coat as they entered the reptile house. Here the bones were more interesting. He saw long spinal fragments within larger remains, as if a snake had eaten its cellmate, swallowed it whole before dying. Would the snakes have survived if the keepers had bothered to set them free? Rumour had it that they'd moved the easy animals to a local pet store and left the dangerous ones to die.

Nayir and Miss Hijazi crept out onto the avenue again, past crocodile cages and old aviaries covered with dried-up vines. In the distance, they could see the top of a mountain, an imitation Matterhorn, undoubtedly once populated by goats.

'Let's check that out,' she said. He grunted a reply.

The Matterhorn was as quiet as a tomb, and they approached it carefully. It was not as tall as it seemed from a distance, perhaps ten metres high. Its base was sprinkled with flowering plants.

'I think that's oleander,' he said.

'Yes,' she said. 'Odd that it should grow here, where the animals could eat it.' They walked through the bushes, stepped over the low gate that surrounded the mountain, and crossed a narrow field of grass, now dried to a crisp, its gullies filled with sand. Miss Hijazi set her toolbox on the ground and opened it. Extracting a baggie, she took a sample of the oleander and the dirt around it.

While she worked, Nayir circled the mountain. The shell was made of green and brown plaster, and the tip was painted white to look like snow. At the bottom edge he spotted a doorway. Pulling gently, he prised the door open and peered inside.

The interior was hollow. Through various cracks in the plaster, the outside light poured in, revealing a dirt floor, white walls, and a blanket bundled in a corner. The air was wet and heavy. Nayir studied the floor. Just past the doorway, he saw wide trails in the dirt as if someone had swept there recently. The trails spilled outside and onto the nearby grass. There were no footprints in the dirt.

'Find something?' she asked.

'A hideout,' he said.

She entered the room. 'It smells like . . .' she gazed hesitantly at Nayir, '. . . sex.'

'I know,' he said, then silently asked forgiveness for lying. He stepped inside and pressed his sleeve to his nose. A dozen alarms went off in his head. How would she know that? Maybe it was part of her job to know it, but how did they *teach* that? Another alarm went off, announcing that they occupied a very small, private space. That smelled like sex. He stepped back outside.

She came out holding the blanket. Carefully, she unfolded it, held it up, and studied its surface. 'I may be able to get something from this.'

Going back into the mountain, he switched on his penlight and ran it quickly over the ground, stopping once at a small piece of gravel but carrying on. She poked her head inside.

'Anything else?' she asked.

He shook his head. 'The floor is pretty smooth, considering what was going on here. Someone cleaned up.' He looked around one last time and, satisfied that nothing else was there, left the mountain.

'I'll take this blanket,' she said. 'If I'm lucky, I'll get some skin cells.'

Nayir shut the door in the Matterhorn's side. 'It may be no relation to our case at all.' He caught a smile in her eyes. 'What?'

'You said "our case".'

'I said *your* case.'

Amused, she went back to her toolbox, where she found a bag large enough to hold the blanket. They spent another half an hour scouring the grass around the mountain, but their search produced nothing. When they were done, they wandered out of the Alpine exhibit, past a long row of bird-cages and down a narrow dirt path that led to the perimeter fence. The fence was topped with barbed wire, but the gate was unlocked. Exiting the zoo, they followed a footpath down a very steep hill and into the valley on the zoo's south-ern side. The air was heating rapidly, and both of them were beginning to sweat.

'I need to know everything you've found out so far,' she said. 'Is there anything else you haven't told me? It's going to be easier if we both know all the facts.'

'I meant what I said: this is your case.'

'Fine. Is there anything else you haven't told me?'

'Did I tell you about the marks on the camel's leg?'

'No,' she said. With some embarrassment, he explained about the camel. She was walking in front of him, stumbling occasionally when the hill grew too steep.

'I've always thought it was odd,' she said, 'the idea of giving someone an evil eye. Personally, I think it's ridiculous.'

He didn't reply.

'And I think Nouf would have agreed with me,' she said. 'I didn't actually know her that well, but the few times I talked to her, she seemed very practical. I really don't think she believed in spirits and djinni and all that.'

'So who do you think made the sign on the camel?'

She shrugged. 'Who was with her in the desert? Who *could* have been with her? Everyone has an alibi. Her whole family was home. Othman tells me that her escort was shop-ping with his wife. What about Eric?'

'His alibi checks out; I made some calls last night. He was at work the whole day.'

She stopped at the bottom of the hill. 'The way I see it, there has to be a third man, someone we don't know about yet.'

They had reached a circular patch of land that marked the end of an access road, which he guessed led back to the main road. The first thing he noticed was the dark orange colour of the dirt. Scraping the ground with his fingers, he felt the hardness of clay.

'You know my uncle ran an analysis of the dirt from Nouf's head wound,' he said. 'I think this dirt is a match.'

Katya bagged a sample of the dirt. 'So she could have been hit here.'

Nayir turned to a scrubby row of palms, their branches dense enough to offer a bit of shade. Behind the trees stood a thicket of bushes, overgrown and tangled. It was a sad, forsaken place; the wind didn't even stir the leaves. But the dirt beneath the palm trees showed evidence of activity. He walked to the edges of the clearing and studied the tyre tracks.

'Stay off the dirt,' he said.

She set her toolbox down near the bushes and looked around. Nayir followed a set of footprints along the road. He tried to view them through Mutlaq's eyes, but there were dozens of tracks and he couldn't keep them apart. It seemed that cars and trucks came down the access road frequently. Footprints led away from the tyre tracks in all directions, but he couldn't tell which footprints belonged to which tracks.

One set of tyre tracks had stopped in the middle of the clearing. Careful not to disturb them, Nayir followed the tracks to the edge of the access road, where it seemed the car had spun around and headed back past the zoo. And there, at the furthest edge of the clearing, he noticed a metallic glimmer in the bushes. Moving closer, he found a tin can half-buried in the dirt. He picked it up, disappointed.

'Nayir?' Miss Hijazi's voice sounded strange. She was kneeling in the dirt, poking gently at something. 'I think you should come here.' Dropping the can, he went to her and saw that she had brushed the sand away from a crooked pink object. It was a shoe. A stiletto, squashed flat by a car's tyre.

'It's her other shoe,' he said, kneeling down and helping to pry it out of the dirt. 'She must have dropped it.'

'But wouldn't she have noticed if she'd dropped it? Wouldn't she have come back for it?'

Nayir nodded. She'd held on to the other one even in the desert, where it was entirely useless. 'I don't think she would have left it here on purpose.'

'Unless she was trying to leave a clue behind . . .' Miss Hijazi whispered. 'She must have been abducted.'

A thrill of potential discovery passed through them both. Nayir wanted to fuel the moment by telling her where they'd found Nouf's body, and about Othman's missing jacket, which implicated somebody from the estate, but he wasn't sure he could bring himself to say it, because it implicated Othman first.

He looked down at the dirt. 'Do you see any evidence of blood?' he asked. 'She was hit on the head, there must have been a lot of blood.'

'Not necessarily,' Miss Hijazi replied. 'Most of it could have been on her face and her robe. But here—' she pointed to a section of the road. 'It looks as if someone wiped the dirt. If there was blood, maybe they tried to clean it up.'

'Those look like drag marks,' he said. 'What if she was hit here? She would have fallen down. Her kidnapper would have had to pick her up, or drag her to the car.' He followed

239

the marks to the tyre tracks. 'If that was the case, wouldn't there be some blood along this path?'

'I don't see any,' Miss Hijazi said, 'but I'll take a few samples and check for traces.' She stood up and returned to the toolbox. With great care, she placed the shoe in a plastic bag, but instead of putting it into the box, she held it for a moment. 'It's strange that she was carrying the shoes,' she said.

'Yes. Why didn't she just leave them in the truck?'

'Maybe she thought they would get damaged by the heat?'

'People keep Qurans on their dashboards,' he said. 'And anyway, she could have parked in the shade.' Nayir continued circling the drag marks, looking for blood.

'Maybe she did leave them in the truck,' Miss Hijazi said. 'It could be that someone dragged her out of the truck, and the shoe fell out.'

He looked up. 'The other shoe – how did they find it?'

'What do you mean?'

'Did you see if she'd been carrying it in a bag?'

'No. There was no bag.'

'Then it must have been in her pocket,' he said. 'Otherwise, they would never have found it with the body. The flood was strong enough to knock off the shoes she was wearing.'

'Yes,' she said thoughtfully. She set the shoe in the toolbox and wiped the dirt from her cloak. 'Let's say Nouf came to the zoo to meet someone she trusted enough to meet alone. How did she get here? The truck. She drove it down here and waited.'

'Why wouldn't she park in the lot?' he asked.

'She probably parked here to be discreet. She was a woman, so even if she was wearing a man's robe, someone might notice the outline of her body. The person she was going to meet arrived in his car, and they both got out of their cars. Here.' She pointed to the footprints around the tyre tracks. 'All of these footprints are pretty small. It looks like the person she was meeting was relatively small.' She took a tape measure from her box and measured the prints.

Nayir wandered around. 'You know, these could all be the same prints.'

'They're not all the same pattern, but they're similar.' She looked up. 'All size thirty-six. And they look like men's shoes.' He handed her the mangled stiletto, and she measured it, looking at him dolefully. 'Also thirty-six.'

'If she was going to exchange the shoes, they probably didn't fit.'

'Maybe she was lying,' Miss Hijazi said.

'I have the shoe she was wearing in the desert,' Nayir said. 'It's on my boat. I'll measure it tonight. What about the camel? It seems to me that the kidnapper would have brought it—' He stopped, feeling that the rest was obvious: that if the kidnapper had brought the camel, then he had been to the estate, and he knew enough about the grounds to know how to steal a camel and a truck.

Miss Hijazi looked uneasy. 'Well, we don't know that the camel was here.'

'I doubt that someone would kidnap Nouf and then go back to the estate to steal the camel with her body in the car.'

'All right.' She snatched a handful of vials from her tool-box and went back to the drag marks. 'The truth is, we don't know what sort of relationship Nouf had with the kidnapper. She might have brought the camel herself, as part of some ... arrangement they had. Who knows?' She sounded breathless. Kneeling down in the dirt, she scooped up two samples and sealed the vials. 'Maybe she *was* running away, and someone was trying to stop her. If she was hit here, she still could have run off on her own after the fight. She might have been mobile, but disoriented. It might even explain how she lost the shoe, and then later the camel.'

'It's possible,' he said, 'but it wouldn't explain the missing truck. They still haven't found it. If she drove herself to the desert, the truck should have been near the wadi.'

'Someone could have stolen the truck in the desert.'

He refrained from pointing out that such a thing was extremely unusual. It was best not to argue about the truck at all, since they had no evidence. He watched her take the dirt samples back to the tool kit. 'If someone else met her here, and knocked her out, then one car would still be here. Where is it?' he asked.

'Maybe the kidnapper left it here,' she said, 'and then came back later to get rid of it.'

It sounded flimsy, but he let it pass. 'How did she even know about this place?'

'Would her escort know? He didn't mention the zoo, did he?'

'No,' Nayir said. *But he smelled of manure.* He walked around some more, studying the prints.

She shut her toolbox. 'There's evidence that other people were here,' she said, 'but it's not necessarily connected to Nouf. I think you should go back to Mohammed. He would be able to tell us how she knew about this place, and whether she came here more than once. He might also be able to explain the shoes.'

'I already asked him about that.'

'But think about it – Nouf kept the shoes. Maybe she really was going to exchange them. She would have needed Mohammed to do it, and maybe that's why she brought the shoes here. She was meeting Mohammed.' She looked warily at Nayir. 'You have to talk to him again. I'll come with you.'

'No,' he said.

'Yes.'

'*No.*' From the look in her eyes, he could tell he was only making matters worse. 'It would be better if I went alone,' he said, his voice softening. 'He trusts me, and I have the feeling he'll open up again, which he won't do if you're there.'

Grudgingly, she agreed. For a moment they stood facing each other, too hot or too tired to speak. The sun bore down on their heads, and the air was heavy with dust. In the distance they heard a bird's angry screech. Nayir realized that he was staring at her burqa. He didn't feel like avoiding her gaze just then. It felt all right to study her eyes, to watch her hands move, and to notice the outline of her body through her cloak. The fabric was thin, and in the sunlight he could almost see through it. She had shapely arms and a narrow waist. For a very brief moment he indulged in a fantasy that she wasn't Othman's fiancée, she was just a woman he'd met. He wondered if she had fantasies about him, and he looked at her eyes for a clue, but she was studying his face with suspicion.

'I'll have to tell Othman about this,' she said.

He felt an unpleasant jolt. 'What?'

'About the shoe.'

He nearly exploded with relief. *Allah forgive me for my sinful thoughts.*

'It's not the kind of thing we can hide,' she added.

'I'll tell him if you like.'

She turned and squinted into the sunlight. 'That might be better. Why don't you just tell him it was your idea? In fact, don't mention me at all.'

'I can't do that.'

She turned back to him. 'No, you're right. I don't want you to lie.' She rubbed her forehead. 'I appreciate you coming out here. I hope this doesn't make things awkward for you with Othman. I don't want to cause any trouble between you.'

Too late, he thought. 'Don't worry.'

'You know he talks about you a lot. You're like a hero to him.'

He didn't know what to say.

'Maybe it would be best,' she said, 'if we both told Othman what we found here today. It might make a difference if he hears it from you, too.'

He nodded. With a tired sigh, Miss Hijazi shut the toolbox, stood up, and turned back toward the hill. 'I have another hour and a half before I have to be at work. We should talk about what we're going to say. Ahmad has to leave soon. Would you escort me to lunch?'

He could think of ten reasons to say no, but he couldn't force down the eagerness rising in his chest. However, as a matter of principle, he frowned. 'I don't see how that's possible.'

'I know a place,' she said. 'Just follow me.'

21

Nayir climbed out of the Jeep into a heat that felt dangerous. The humid air gagged him with its industrial stench.
They had parked in the last two spots in a tiny lot near al-
Barad. The lot, surrounded by tall apartment buildings, was
half in shade, but it hardly made a difference. The afternoon sun warped everything like a desert mirage – the cars,
the pavement, the billboards overhead. A lone, dry fountain
at the head of an alley seemed to be dripping with waves of
heat. Only the buildings were immune, sturdy limestone
structures heavy with casements and lattice screens that
kept out the heat.

A woman scurried by, darting across the lot into the
entrance of an alley, glancing around to make sure no one
was following her. Nayir felt a familiar twinge of alarm at
seeing a woman alone in the streets. How did they do it, he
wondered, walk so fast with their faces covered? She
slipped into the alley and slowed her pace. Perhaps she was
only hurrying because of the heat.

He crossed to Miss Hijazi's car, and by the time he
reached it his shirt was soaked and his pant legs were sticking to his ankles. He wished he'd worn a robe.

She was taking her toolbox from the trunk and saying goodbye to Ahmad. The driver gave Nayir a stern look before climbing back into the car. The look was half a warning to treat her with respect, the other half an acknowledgement of solidarity.

'I'll carry that,' Nayir said, motioning to the toolbox.

'I'm fine.' She took off, heading down an alley. He followed awkwardly. Walking behind her made him feel like a child, but she was leading, so he couldn't very well walk in front. He would have to walk beside her, although that didn't feel right either. He imagined Othman seeing them together. Even husbands and wives didn't walk side-by-side; the woman would hang back as a sign of respect.

He drew up beside her just as they left the alley. She turned right and slowed, gazing around, her head swivelling with every turn since the burqa clipped her vision. 'It's here somewhere,' she said.

'Where are we going?'

'It's one of those family buffets where you can take an unmarried woman to lunch.'

He'd heard about such places – cafés where women and men could dine together without being confined to 'family' sections. It was a family restaurant, yes, but women were not expected to veil their faces, only their hair. More surprising, women could dine alone – but men could enter too, as long as they had female company. Nayir heard that men hired Filipino girls for the sole purpose of helping them gain access to these 'family' cafés. Once inside, they could flirt with any girl in the place. Basically, they were pick-up joints, and he hoped to Allah that this wasn't one of those. How would he ever explain that to Othman?

As they walked past storefronts displaying perfumes and trinkets, his palms began to sweat. He felt foolish searching for a café that the authorities had probably shut down just as soon as it had opened. But after a few more paces, they spotted a metallic sign hanging over a doorway: *The Big Mix – Families Welcome!*

'This is it,' she said, suppressing her excitement.

He stopped walking. 'I don't think this is—'

'Don't worry,' she said, looking slightly amused. 'It's not what you think.' Before he could reply, she turned into the doorway and began to climb a flight of narrow wooden stairs. He followed, wondering if she was leading him into a trap. He imagined a plot: she had decided he was lonely, inept at meeting women, unlucky enough to have no family to arrange a marriage for him. So she'd come up with a plan to drag him here, hoping a spark would catch. If that's what she was thinking, then she didn't know how misguided she was.

At the top of the stairs they entered a glass-walled waiting room. 'A friend of mine has been here before,' she said. 'She told me the food was excellent.' A maître d' greeted them and motioned them into the dining hall.

The room was an enormous glass-domed atrium with a splashing fountain at its centre. Filtered through the windows, sunlight dappled the blue carpets and the glass-topped dining tables in the middle of the room. Beyond those, a set of regal stairs led to separate seating areas, where more tables, large and small, were placed for privacy, each shielded by potted palms. The maître d' told them they could sit where they liked, so Miss Hijazi led him to the top of the room, where a table for two seemed waiting to receive them. Nayir cast a quick glance around. There were a few men in the crowd, but they were far enough away, and busy eating.

Miss Hijazi laid her toolbox on the floor, sat down at the table, and raised her burqa. Having no other choice, he sat across from her and wondered how he would survive a whole lunch with her exposed face in front of him. But she wasn't looking at him; she was staring at the crowd – men, children, women with their faces revealed. 'I almost don't believe it,' she said. 'I've wanted to come here for the longest time just to see if it was real.'

Nayir, too, took in everything, scrupulously avoiding the exposed female faces, looking instead at the men. There didn't seem to be a single bachelor in the crowd: all of the men were sitting with wives and children. They looked happy and relaxed, not concerned that their wives' faces were exposed in public. Daring a glance at one or two women, he noticed that they were conducting themselves modestly. Most wore cloaks and headscarves and kept their attention focused on their families. He felt a relief, mingled with surprise that a restaurant as modern as this one would be filled with good people acting appropriately.

From his periphery, he noticed Miss Hijazi grinning. She'd been oohing at the silverware and admiring the chandelier, and he was pleased to realize that for all her independence, she was, in some ways, still a sheltered woman.

Then he realized that this was the first time he'd ever been with a woman in a restaurant. It was a milestone, somehow, but it was too fraught with guilt to appreciate fully. He slid a hand into his pocket and touched his misyar, the fake marriage licence. He would have to pencil Miss Hijazi's name into the box, in case they were caught, but even that felt like a guilty act.

'What do you think?' she asked.

He withdrew his hand. 'It's a nice place.'

'It's cool, too,' she said. 'Not cold, like so many stores you go into. And now comes the best part.' She stood up. 'You can actually get your own food.'

'I'll be right there.'

She gave him an odd glance but headed down to the

buffet. Once she was gone, he took out the misyar and reached into his pocket for a pen. It occurred to him that he'd had the misyar for years, had anticipated its use as a momentous occasion, and now it was happening without warning, and with a woman who was completely unavailable to him. It felt like a sin to put her name in the box. It wasn't what he had wanted.

He folded the misyar, put it back in his pocket, and went down to the buffet.

He spent twenty minutes exploring the dazzling selection of fruits and pastries, hot sandwiches, skewered meats, vegetables, rice. Yogurts and ice creams. Ten kinds of tea. Coffee – black or American style. Hot chocolate. Cold chocolate. Ice – ice! – in buckets on every display. When they finally returned to their table, Miss Hijazi was silly with excitement.

'I could come here every day,' she said, whipping open her napkin and picking up her fork. Nayir tried to picture her there with Othman. She was so happy that it might infect him, too. And perhaps that's what he liked about her – this carefree side to leaven his dour moods. Nayir imagined them coming here years from now, their young children sitting at the table around them, and he wondered: *Would she still be this happy then?*

He dared a glance at her face and saw a child's excitement in her eyes. He imagined that a joy like that could last. She smiled, not at him exactly, but in response to his attention, and somehow he allowed the future to become his own. He was sitting at the table with her, surrounded by his children, himself the recipient of that generous smile. It thrilled him, and it choked him. *Allah, forgive me. I am a sinful, selfish man. This wouldn't happen if I had a wife.*

'I think it's safe to assume she was kidnapped,' Miss Hijazi said, returning to the subject of Nouf.

'Maybe.'

'But who did it?' She took a bite of her lunch. 'Maybe we should think of it this way. What did Nouf do that was most outrageous? She got pregnant. Now who would that upset the most?'

'Her family, if they knew.'

'Let's say they knew,' she said. 'Qazi would have found out on their wedding night that she wasn't a virgin. He would have divorced her. So maybe the family took her out to the desert just to spare themselves the shame of a public discovery of her condition.'

'It's not likely,' Nayir said.

'It's not quite an honour killing,' Miss Hijazi went on, 'it's an honour abduction, except they don't take the blame. If they make it look as if she ran away, then it's all her fault, and people will say that *she* was trying to avoid the wedding.' She fell silent, chewing.

'But how could they do that without killing her outright?' he asked. 'There would always be a chance she would find her way back, and then what?'

'You're right.'

Her speculation made him uneasy. She seemed to notice, because she ate in a silence for a while. Nayir had considered the 'honour abduction' theory in the desert, and again with uncle Samir, but every time he tried to imagine it, it seemed ridiculous, a piece of comic theatre in which a few neatly polished upper-crust gentlemen attempted to haul a camel into the back of a pick-up truck without sullying their expensive desert boots, in which they managed to smash their sister over the head with a pipe and drag her out to the desert without splattering their designer shirts with blood. He didn't think they had it in them to murder their sister, especially not for 'honour'.

'Nayir,' she said, 'what do you really think about this case?'

Caught off guard, he wasn't sure what to say.

'Oh come on. Doesn't anything bother you?'

'Well, yes.' It took him a moment to organize his thoughts. 'Nouf was going to marry Qazi just to leave the country. That bothers me. She was going to abandon him on their honeymoon.'

Her smile vanished. 'I know it's awful. I think she must have been desperate.'

'Can you imagine what would have happened if she *had* managed to dump her husband and run off with some American guy? Her family would have gone crazy. Who knows what they would have done to Mohammed? He would have lost his job, at the very least. The family would probably have sent someone out to find Nouf and bring her home. Don't you think he knew that? Don't you think Nouf knew that?'

Miss Hijazi nodded. 'It seems her escort cared about her more than he cared about himself.'

'Or he was getting something out of it.'

'What if he just felt sorry for her?'

'Why?' he asked. 'She had everything. Her family let her ride around on a jet ski. They gave her an escort so she could go shopping. And I know she had money of her own.'

Her face showed how little she thought of his assessment. 'But she couldn't do the one thing she wanted! They didn't like the idea of sending her to school, and I doubt they would have approved of her having a career – particularly one working with animals. You really have no idea, do you? Nouf had everything her father *let* her have.'

He wiped his face with his napkin. 'Most people would be glad to have half of it.'

'No. Most people wouldn't be happy.' She spoke quietly, and he recognized the change in her speech: the quieter the voice, the stronger the statement. He braced for it.

'Imagine if you couldn't go to the desert,' she said. 'You

251

couldn't even leave your house without someone's permission. You'd have money and things, but if you wanted to *do* anything you wouldn't be allowed. The only thing you could do is get married and have kids.'

Nayir wanted to tell her that that *was* the thing he really wanted, but it was beside the point.

'I don't think they would have forced her into marriage,' he said, trying not to become heated. 'She chose to accept the wedding arrangements.'

'But that doesn't matter,' she replied. 'If she didn't marry, she still wouldn't have been able to fulfil her dreams. She was allowed to fulfil only the dreams her family had for her – being a good daughter or wife.'

'And that made her angry enough to run away?'

Miss Hijazi had stopped eating and was toying with her food. 'I think it probably did.'

'Then it's especially vindictive that she was planning on abandoning her fiancé. I suppose it was her way of spitting in her parents' faces.'

She said nothing.

'Instead of simply leaving the country,' he said, 'she was going to drag her fiancé into the whole mess. She didn't care if she broke his heart. She didn't care if she disappointed her parents. You know, she could have left the country on her own; she had enough money. She could have paid someone to smuggle her to Egypt. It would have taken her less than a day.' He realized that he was letting his anger show, and he stopped for a minute, took a breath. 'What she was planning seems cruel.'

Eyes lowered, Miss Hijazi nodded. 'You're right. She could have left another way.' She stared down at her water glass. They were silent for a while, and her speechlessness frustrated him. He marvelled at the way it seemed to cast a pallor over the entire room.

252

Slowly, they resumed eating. His attention wandered to her hands, and he had a sudden image of them stroking Othman's cheek. He felt a deep tremor of shame.

He looked around at the other diners, men like himself. People only acted decently on the outside; inside they were probably all just like him, longing for things they shouldn't. He was ashamed of himself for admiring her hands. It just went to show that men and women were not meant to be friends. Wasn't that the whole idea behind all the rules and laws? That men and women had different places in the world? It wasn't human design, it was God's message, and the basis for systems of philosophy and law. Who was he to reject it? Some kind of infidel.

Miss Hijazi seemed to sense the change in his mood; her eyes flickered nervously across his face. 'But don't you feel the least bit sorry for Nouf?' she asked.

He nodded. 'I do, yes. But I don't think that makes what she was planning okay. Would *you* ever do that – marry a man just to get an exit visa?'

'I don't know.'

'Come on, make all of those elaborate arrangements, for what . . . to go to *school*? They have women's schools here, you know.'

She struggled with her next words. 'I would marry a man if it meant I could have all the freedom I wanted. If I were Nouf, I suppose I might have done what she was going to do.'

Nayir wondered if that was what she was doing – marrying Othman so she could have the freedoms Nouf had had, the money and escorts and lavish shopping sprees. He wondered, too, if she would wind up like Nouf, dissatisfied with her wealth, hungry for even greater liberties, not caring any more about her family or her husband, only for herself and her insatiable appetites. That's what they were, he realized now, Nouf's *appetites*.

'You could be wrong,' she said. 'Maybe Nouf really loved someone. Maybe she loved the father of her child and she was just trying to be with him.'

'Do you think so?'

'You know, going to America, that just means that she wanted to be like American girls. It doesn't mean she was a whore.'

'Bu—' he sputtered. 'She was pregnant.'

'Maybe with a man she truly loved.'

'Okay, maybe she was in love,' he said, 'and she wasn't running away to go to school, but if that's true, then she wasn't as oppressed as you'd like to believe. Maybe she wanted to be a wife and mother after all.'

By the look on her face, he could tell that this idea astonished her, or perhaps her own inconsistency surprised her. 'Well,' she said, 'just because a woman wants to be a wife and a mother, it doesn't mean she gives up her dreams of a career.' She gave him a steady look. For a second, their eyes met, but he saw a plea for understanding in her face, and all at once her defiance seemed like a clumsy front for a vulnerability that he hadn't noticed before. As he recognized it, he felt a sudden instinct to protect her.

'Is that what you want?' he asked, looking away. 'To be a wife and have a career?'

'Yes,' she said. 'That is what I want.'

'What if your husband doesn't want you to work?' he asked.

'I want a husband who respects my work.'

He hesitated before asking the next question. 'What if he doesn't? What if he tells you he likes it and then, once you're married, he changes his mind? Says he wants you to stay home and take care of the kids?'

She gave him a careful look. 'Maybe I'd want the same, once I had kids. I want to have the option.'

She didn't seem disturbed that he was talking about Othman. Instead, she resumed eating, and Nayir fell silent, lost in ugly thoughts. Othman was doing what every groom did: promising his fiancée anything she wanted. A coat. A job. An expensive home. Nayir couldn't count the times the men he knew had described the deceptions they'd contrived for their wives: the little lies, the bribes, the apologies, excuses. It made him nervous the way they talked. 'The old cow, she doesn't ever shut her trap.' And: 'I'll just give her another baby, that'll keep her busy.' Or: 'I'll bring home a second wife, see what she says then!' If his friends' version of women was correct, then all they did was complain all day. They felt stuck at home, and it made them boring and frightening. When their husbands came home, the women attacked them with everything: pleas and entreaties, lavish meals, the promise of sexual favours in exchange for a ride, for some money, shopping, picnics, outings. Some wives didn't moan about it, they were happy with their lives, but there were plenty of bad marriages, and sometimes it seemed that his chances of getting into one were enormously high. Yet he had observed that the men who complained most vehemently were not men he admired. All their lying and manoeuvring certainly lowered his opinion of them. He resolved never to act that way with a wife.

It didn't surprise him to think that perhaps he didn't want to get married, that maybe his bachelorhood was a choice after all. What surprised him was the sudden discovery that a look at Miss Hijazi's face dispelled his inner turmoil. She was munching away, animated by some interior reflection. He had the urge to ask her what it was, to pry deeper even as another attack of guilt was starting to dissuade him. *Allah, it would be nice to be able to ask her. Just this once, and not to have to worry about what it means. I want that choice.*

'Options,' he said, surprising himself by speaking out loud.

'Yes, options,' she replied, giving him a grateful smile. 'I think that's what Nouf wanted, too.'

'Did she think that America would give her more options?'

She shrugged. It occurred to Nayir that they could speculate in the quiet corners of their minds until they were dead but never get any closer to the truth. It saddened him to think that perhaps *no one* knew. What if the father of her child didn't love her, didn't know she was pregnant, or didn't care?

'You never told me whether there was any evidence of unwillingness – on the body, I mean.'

She paused in her eating. 'No, there was no sign of rape.'

'Why didn't you say so at the examiner's office?'

'I thought you would judge her,' she said, shooting him a nervous glance.

He nodded, amazed that he'd been correct about her intentions. 'Is there anything else you haven't told me because you thought I might not approve?'

She hesitated slightly. 'Nothing I can think of just now.'

The hesitation stung him. She thought he was harsh, but he was a rational man, thoughtful and decent. If he seemed judgemental, it only stemmed from a belief in the virtues of tradition. It stung him, too, that when she glanced at his face, she seemed to withdraw.

'You think I'm being judgemental,' he said, 'but don't tell me that you don't have any faith in this system. I think you do. It's designed to *protect* women. All the prescriptions for modesty and wearing the veil, for decent behaviour and abstinence before marriage, isn't the goal to prevent exactly this sort of thing from happening?'

'Yes . . .' she said. 'In theory, I agree. But you have to admit that those same prescriptions can sometimes *cause* the degradation people fear the most.' She was nervous now. She couldn't seem to still her hands, so she folded them awkwardly and dropped them on her lap. 'That is, I think, what happened to Nouf.'

It amazed him to realize that she didn't look down on him, as he'd thought. She feared his judgement. It meant, somehow, that she cared what he thought. A great rush of guilt coursed through him, and he wanted to apologize, to take back – not his words, but the sternness and the coldness with which he'd spoken them.

'I'm sorry,' he said.

She looked up.

'You're right,' he said. 'Nothing is perfect – not the system, not the rules.'

She was speechless. She nodded. He felt, somehow, that she understood the apology. But a moment later she looked at him. 'What about you? Is there anything else you haven't told me about the case?'

Instantly, he thought about Othman's coat, and he hesitated, not certain he could say it without making Othman seem guilty, or without upsetting her.

'There is something,' he began, hearing the nervousness in his voice already. 'It could be important.' Fighting his discomfort, he told her about the wadi and about Othman's missing coat. Miss Hijazi listened with a calm expression on her face, but when he finished, she frowned.

'How long have you known this?'

'Ah,' he said, flustered. 'A few days? I don't remember exactly.'

She eyed him and looked away, obviously hurt. He felt terrible.

'You don't have to hide things from me,' she said. 'I'm doing this because I believe I can handle the truth. It's important to me.'

Nayir realized she was right. She was ambitious in this pursuit, and not for herself. She was going against Othman's wishes, possibly jeopardizing her job, and making commitments of time and energy for which there was no compensation *except* the truth. He felt impossibly dumb and flashed on the idea that people this stupid shouldn't be investigators.

They finished eating in silence. She seemed preoccupied with her thoughts, and he wanted to know what they were even as he begged Allah's mercy for the sin. *Forgive me for this. I am allowed my sins, am I not? But these are dangerous sins. Forgive me.*

After paying for lunch, he walked her back to the Coroner's building, where they said an awkward goodbye. Only after he'd left her did he realize that they hadn't talked about what they would say to Othman.

22

Just as soon as Ahmad pulled onto the island, Katya felt the exhaustion of the day overtake her. Ahmad stopped at the entrance to the estate, but she didn't move.

'Would you like me to take you home instead?' he asked her.

It wasn't just the day, she realized, it was the past two weeks. Ever since Nouf had disappeared, she'd been frantic, trying to go about her daily life as if nothing had changed, although everything had. Her feelings for the family had grown into a dark knot of suspicion, generating a constant stream of doubt and worry that was, she saw now, a source of distraction. If Nouf had not been a runaway bride, then someone in the family knew exactly what had happened. Katya's mind circled back to the one person she knew well enough to judge: Othman, who, apparently, had known his sister best. The spectrum of possibilities sprawled across her mind: he had kidnapped Nouf, seduced her to the desert, and engaged in an elaborate cover-up. He had hired someone to kidnap her. He had discovered she was pregnant and conspired *with* her to make her disappear for a while. Evidence? Any of it could have been planted –

the mud, the missing jacket, the shoe. If Othman had orchestrated the kidnapping, he had thought of everything. But the one piece of evidence that couldn't lie was just within her reach.

'Kati?'

'I'm sorry. No, I don't want to go home yet. I need to get something, but it shouldn't take long.' She opened the door and got out. Ahmad got out, too, to retrieve her toolbox from the trunk and give her one of his impossibly sympathetic looks. 'Thanks, Ahmad.' She took a few baggies and swabs from the toolbox. 'I'll be right back.'

Nouf's younger sister Jannah met her at the door. She smiled demurely and led Katya to the women's sitting room, where Nusra was having tea with a group of women. Katya recognized a few as Othman's aunts, but Zahra and Fadilah were not there.

'Katya,' Nusra smiled and stood to greet her. Slightly unsettled by Nusra's instant recognition and by her glassy eyes, Katya greeted her awkwardly and struggled to find a place for her hands. The women were staring indulgently at her, no doubt imagining what a fool Othman was for marrying a woman as old as she. Twenty-eight and she was only a few years away from the youngest of them, but she didn't look nearly as ruined as they did. They were grey and wrinkled, obese, most of them, sitting idly on the sofas. Their fat hung in layers from their waists and arms; they looked like sofas themselves. Katya lowered her eyes, embarrassed by her thoughts.

Nusra led her into the circle and offered her tea, which she couldn't refuse. She sat quietly on the edge of a sofa until one of the women turned to her. 'So, Katya, are you excited about the wedding?'

For a weird moment, the question presented ominous possibilities: What if she said no? What did they mean, excited? About the promise of money? Sex? Or did she mean the wedding itself, the food, the pomp? They would be scandalized if she told them the truth: that the excitement had been muffled by Nouf's death and Othman's reaction to it all. She was beginning to doubt that the marriage should happen any time in the next few months. Othman needed time to grieve; he shouldn't be forced to celebrate now. But she couldn't say it; they would think she was crazy. A woman her age should take whatever she could get.

'Yes,' Katya replied. 'Yes, I'm very excited.'

'It must be hard for you, having it now after the tragedy?'

'Well . . .' Katya looked at the women's faces, sceptical all. 'Yes, Nouf's death has put a weight on things. It's been difficult for everyone.'

'Don't think about that,' Nusra said. 'It's over now. There will be plenty of time to grieve when you are older. Now, your life is opening.' She spread her hands like a flower. 'Be happy for that.'

Katya smiled and somehow found herself blushing. 'Thank you.'

Slowly, the women's gazes shifted away, back to the invisible centre of the circle, and they continued their previous conversations about their children and grandchildren and the unending stream of trifles and problems that seemed to plague every group of mothers. Katya sat back on the sofa, feeling as if she'd survived something. As the women chattered on, her mind returned to its sequence of unanswerable questions, and she began to realize that the things that concerned her – evidence, crime scenes, difficult motives – would possibly never concern these women, and what interested them might never interest her.

She thought back on her lunch with Nayir and on the

careful way he'd dealt with her, and she marvelled at how her opinion of him had undergone a shift. Instead of an imposing, overly righteous ayatollah, he now seemed like one of those men who, aware of their own physical power, develop a kind of masculine grace which, in Nayir's case at least, had become a grace of personality as well. She could see now why Othman liked him. He wasn't overbearing; he was kind, thoughtful, smart and reliable. And right now, he was the only person she trusted with information about Nouf's case.

A servant came in with a tray of date cookies, and tasting them, one of the aunts laughed with delight. 'You amaze me, Nusra, these are delicious!' she crooned.

There'd been a time when Katya had found this family's lifestyle appealing, but the more she got to know the women, the more she realized that she didn't want to become like them: insular and boring, consumed by the ridiculous minutiae of their easy lives. So far, they seemed to accept that she worked, and one of the aunts had even asked about her job, although she'd lost interest and quickly changed the subject back to her children. Katya tried to think of Othman; he nurtured and supported her choices. She imagined that he liked her precisely because she was nothing like the women of his family.

'You don't look well,' said one of the elderly aunts.

'No, I'm fine.' Katya sat up. 'I'm just tired.'

'I hope it's not nerves,' someone else said.

'No, not at all.' She set her teacup on the table and turned to Nusra. 'I'm sorry to have come when I have no energy. I just wanted to see how you were doing.'

Nusra, typically so adept at polite repartee, pressed her lips together and nodded sternly.

'I'm so sorry,' Katya said, feeling the weight of a terrible gaffe, even if she wasn't sure what it was.

'I take no offence that you should stay so briefly,' Nusra said, 'but I don't want to send you back out into the world as exhausted as you seem. Why don't you rest here for a while? I can have one of the servants take you to a spare bedroom.'

'Oh no, that's too much trouble.'

'Not at all.' Nusra rose to her feet and snapped her fingers at the maid who was waiting by the door.

'Please, don't trouble yourself,' Katya said.

'Nonsense. Aaliyah, bring Katya here to one of the spare bedrooms and make sure she has everything she needs.'

'Yes, *Sayeeda*.'

Katya sighed. 'Thank you, Um-Tahsin.'

'Of course.' Nusra clasped her hand and motioned her towards the door.

Gratefully, Katya followed the maid into the hall and shut the door behind her. 'Listen,' she said. 'I'd like to hang my cloak, if that's possible.'

'Yes, I'll take it.' The maid held out her hand.

'No, no. Let me do it. That way I'll know where it is when I want to leave.'

'Yes, it's right this way.'

The maid led her down the corridor towards the men's entrance. Just off the foyer, a small door led to a cloakroom. The maid switched on the light, revealing dozens of cloaks and scarves arranged on hangers. She turned to help Katya out of her cloak.

'Actually,' Katya said, 'I can do this myself. What I'd really like you to do is fetch me a glass of water.' She leaned closer to the maid and whispered: 'I have to take an aspirin.'

'Ah. Yes, of course.' The maid smiled delicately, gave a little bow, and left the room.

As soon as she was gone, Katya shut the door and locked it. She set her cloak on the floor and looked around. The men's cloaks were hanging on one side of the room, the women's on the other. She went to the men's side. Getting on her hands and knees, she scanned the floor for hair. She found plenty, and swiftly bagged it. It didn't matter who the hairs belonged to, she just wanted a collection of samples from all the men who were in the house or who had been there recently, servants included.

Neither Mohammed or Eric had fathered Nouf's child. There were no other leads. The collection of hairs from the cloakroom floor was her best hope. It might not yield a name or a face, but it would prove that the man had been to the house, and if she could prove that, she could begin to ask Othman about the family's visitors over the past few months.

Standing up, she finally confronted the hanging cloaks. Until now, she had studiously avoided any hint that one of the brothers had impregnated Nouf. It was terrible to think of it, but it felt equally wrong to dismiss her darkest suspicions simply because she didn't like them.

She didn't know what the men of the family wore at home, but she knew their scarves and cloaks on sight. Tahsin had the perfect white cloak with the pompous gold trim, Fahad wore a dingy old thing, and Othman's cloak was a pale shade of blue. She found the first two, and quickly scanned them for hair. She took samples from each, and bagged and labelled them. When she came to Othman's cloak, an acute self-consciousness forced her to hesitate. Was this a betrayal of her loyalty to him, or was it just that she feared his involvement?

This ought to be easy, she thought. The DNA would prove he was innocent. She found three hairs on his cloak and slid them into a bag.

After hastily sorting and labelling everything, she snatched her cloak and unlocked the door. The hallway was empty. Deciding not to worry about the consequences, she darted for the front door.

'Katya?'

Stopping short, she turned and saw Nusra standing by the cloakroom door.

'Katya, what are you doing here?'

Katya briefly entertained the idea of pretending to be someone else. But it would never work with Nusra.

'Yes, Um-Tahsin, I'm sorry. I got a little lost.'

'Where is Aaliyah? She was supposed to take you to a room.' Her voice was soft and questioning.

Katya felt obliged to explain herself. 'I'm sorry. I just wanted to get away from the sitting room for a while. I sometimes feel very intimidated in there.'

After a pause, Nusra came closer and put out her arm. 'I understand,' she said. 'It must be hard for you. But you have no reason to worry. We don't judge you.'

Katya felt an immense relief. But just then, the front door opened and they heard men's voices. Katya whipped the tail end of her scarf out of her collar and held it across her face, leaving only her eyes exposed. Othman came in with another man. Othman glanced at her briefly and turned to his mother.

'*Ay, ummi?*'

Nusra smiled and opened her arms to him. He gave her a kiss on the forehead and introduced his friend. Katya stood rigid. It occurred to her slowly, and then with a terrible punch, that Othman hadn't recognized her, and had probably mistaken her for a servant. She watched him fiercely, certain that he wouldn't dare to look at her eyes, not in front of his mother. Did he not recognize her eyes, or the hand that held her scarf, or even the purse on her shoulder? He didn't give her a second glance. She wanted to be pleased, knowing he was not the sort of man who would look at strange women, but her heart had stopped, and she watched as if seeing him for the first time. He was sweeter, softer, more boyish in his mother's presence. There was an openness in him that he had never demonstrated with her, and it stabbed her deeply. Nusra was transformed too. Her voice was higher, her whole face uplifted. Most striking of all, her gestures were awkward and fumbling, as if she had been blind for only a day and relied on her son to guide her.

Katya waited for Nusra to say something: *Look, Katya is here* or *Don't you recognize your fiancée?* But instead, she walked off to escort Othman and his friend to the men's sitting room, leaving Katya standing frozen in the hall, her heart split in half and lying on the ground, her mind torn between wondering who was more blind, Nusra or her son.

They were gone. She turned abruptly and marched straight for the door, hoping desperately that no one would see her leave. Her head was light, but her body felt like an anvil. Some murky emotion was gathering within her, horror, sadness, the urge to laugh until she cried. As soon as she reached the car, it came pouring out.

Ahmad leapt out, put his arm around her, and held her, letting her cry on his shoulder while observing his usual silence. When she was done, he used his *shumagh* to wipe her tears, and then helped her back into the car.

☽

The coffee table was big enough to hold all the evidence, and she laid it out in neat rows: the mud samples from Nouf's wrist and from the zoo; the cedar flakes and dirt from Nouf's head wound; skin cells from the blanket they'd found at the zoo; DNA samples from everyone, and all the corresponding chemical and trace analyses, printed out on white paper. Before sitting down, she changed into her favourite house robe, made herself a strong cup of coffee, and pinned up her hair. She was ready to work. With a pen and paper, she began to catalogue the evidence, trying to develop yet another picture of the events surrounding Nouf's death.

The dirt from the zoo was a match to the dirt on Nouf's arm; both carried traces of oleander toxins. There was no evidence of blood mixed in with the dirt, but the presence of manure was enough to show that Nouf – not just her shoe – had been at the zoo before she disappeared.

The blanket they had found at the zoo was more interesting: on it, she'd found cells from two people: Nouf and the baby's father. A perfect match. So Nouf was having sex at the zoo, but not with Mohammed or Eric . . .

She turned to the DNA samples she'd collected at the Shrawi estate. Feeling urgent and slightly reckless, she'd run them in batches at work. Salwa and a few other workers were home with fevers, so it had taken only a day and a half to finish all of the samples. This afternoon, she'd stuffed the last batch in her purse before looking at them. Later, riding home in Ahmad's comforting presence, coming back to an empty house – Abu was out playing cards with his friends – and eating a leisurely dinner, she hadn't been able to summon the nerve to study the results. Now they were burning a hole in the table.

Setting her coffee cup down, she reached over and picked up the stack of papers. Ten different hairs from the Shrawi cloakroom, and seven were from men. Surely something from this last batch would give her the answer she sought.

23

Nayir woke to the sounds of a sailing day. The clatter of footsteps on the pier. Boats gunning their engines to leave their slips. Weekend voices calling out orders, and bottles clinking against ice in metal coolers. In the occasional lull he could hear the familiar whipping of a small flap of canvas against the ~~Fatimah~~'s mast, signifying a stout wind and the promise of a perfect day at sea.

With vague notions of sailing, he rose and made coffee, propped himself absently against the stove and took in his surroundings. The cabin was a mess. His water tank was low, and his monthly mooring fee was two days overdue. He knew without checking that he had no clean clothes. On top of everything else, his thoughts were in such a state of disarray that he couldn't remember why he had to talk to Nouf's escort again, or what exactly he and Miss Hijazi had discovered at the zoo. The whipping canvas above his head began to sound like the drumbeat of military discipline. Forgetting his coffee, he performed his ablutions at the kitchen sink, grabbed his prayer rug, and went up on deck to pray.

He spent the morning tidying up the cabin, doing laundry, and taking care of his debt. The cool air actually made it possible to enjoy the confinement, and as he straightened his living quarters, his mind found an organizing principle of its own. The evidence he had gathered over the past week began to make some sense. Only one question nagged at him: why had Nouf put the stilettos in her pockets?

To answer this, he realized that he first had to figure out when she had changed into the white robe. When she was still on the island? She had to change before she got into the truck. In a black cloak, the chances were too great that she would have been stopped on the freeway. But if she left the island in the truck, wearing a white robe, then why didn't she just put the shoes on the seat beside her? Why in the pockets?

Perhaps she had to sneak around the island in the white robe, and she didn't want to be seen carrying the shoes. Nayir took her belongings from their plastic bag and laid them out on the sofa. The white robe had pockets, and it was possible to fit the stilettos inside, although the heel stuck out slightly and the fabric was so thin that the hot pink showed through. It was probably better than carrying them around, but why not put them in a plastic bag?

Did she put them in the pockets and then forget about them? From his own recent experience, he knew it was difficult to forget about a six-inch stiletto in your pocket. Even if she did momentarily forget them, why didn't she then take them out when she got to the zoo – or while she was driving? They would have been a nuisance. To prove it, he put one shoe in each pocket of his house robe and sat on the sofa, but he had to stand up quickly to avoid any damage.

The shoes made no sense. More than anything else, they argued for her running away – he couldn't imagine a kidnapper going to the trouble of shoving pink shoes into her pockets.

☽

That day, Nayir drove back to Kilo Seven. As he pulled into the alley in front of Mohammed's house, he saw the Sudanese women vendors folding up their blankets. After inching the Jeep into a shady spot, he got out and glanced at his shadow on the road. It was a short shadow, pointing southwest. Zuhr prayers would start soon. He turned quickly toward Mohammed's house, hoping to find him home.

Mohammed answered the door as if he'd been standing right behind it, preparing to leave. He wore slick, expensive trousers and a blue satin shirt. When he met Nayir's gaze, he turned bashful. The shyness became piety; the piety, remorse – until it seemed that he belonged in a different suit entirely.

'*Marhaba*, Mohammed.'

'I was just heading out.'

'Nothing's open but the mosque. You're a religious man, aren't you?'

'Yes.' Mohammed swallowed hard. 'Of course.'

'Then let's pray, shall we?' Nayir began walking. Reluctantly, Mohammed shut the door and followed.

'I found Eric,' Nayir said.

'What did he say?'

'We've cleared him for the time being.'

'I see.' Mohammed seemed edgy. The muezzin's call broke through the air, and Nayir followed the sound, leading his companion through a series of narrow alleys, where vendors were pulling down their metal grates and turning off shop lights.

They found the mosque squeezed between a barber's shop and a ramshackle tenement building, both of which seemed to have fallen asleep long ago. Men were entering the mosque in oppressive silence, mopping sweat from their brows as if it were blood. Taking off their shoes, Nayir and Mohammed went inside. They cut through the crowd to reach the fountain, mumbling their own versions of *niyyah*. The fountain was crowded, so they had to wait.

When they finally reached the water, Mohammed motioned for Nayir to dip his hands in first – perhaps a gesture of respect, Nayir couldn't be sure. Other men were nearby, absorbed in their thoughts. When he finished cleaning his face, Nayir said: 'I've been to the zoo.'

Mohammed continued to rinse, but Nayir saw him hesitate.

'I found the second pink shoe there,' he went on. Mohammed still had nothing to say. Nayir dipped his fingers in the water and wiped his ears. 'I also found the room inside the mountain.' He stood up and saw that Mohammed's hands were shaking. His barb had hit the mark; when they entered the prayer hall, Mohammed's face was bleak.

The prayers couldn't quiet Nayir's thoughts. He felt guilty doing the work of Allah by sabotaging ritual. But no matter, he told himself, Allah would understand. Beside him, Mohammed's voice seemed loud in recitation. 'Forgive me with your Forgiveness and have mercy on me. Surely you are the Forgiver, the Merciful.'

When they said the last of their *salah* and rose to leave, Mohammed again waited for Nayir to lead. They returned to the fountain in the antechamber, where men were congregating to talk. Mohammed seemed to think that Nayir would steer him outside, but reluctant to leave the mosque entirely, Nayir led him to a niche behind the fountain, where they sat on a stone bench built into the wall. Other men stood nearby, but the splashing fountain muffled their conversation.

'Someone was meeting Nouf at the zoo,' Nayir said, 'and I believe it was you. I smelled it on your clothing the last time we met.'

Mohammed blanched. Nayir knew he wasn't the baby's father – the DNA tests had proved it – but he wanted to push him anyway.

'I know she used to go there,' Mohammed muttered.

'To meet with you.'

'No,' he whispered.

'Someone was having *sex* with Nouf at the zoo,' Nayir said more loudly. 'That's probably where she became pregnant.'

'I swear it wasn't—'

'As far as I know, you're the only person who even knows about the zoo!'

'It's not what you're thinking!' Mohammed blurted. Two men looked over, and he lowered his voice, fighting to compose himself. 'All right. I used to meet her there, but only because she wanted me to run errands for her.'

'You didn't take her there?'

'No.' Mohammed crossed his arms. 'She went by herself.'

Nayir felt a terrible excitement churning in his gut. 'Then how did she get there?'

'She had a motorcycle. She knew how to ride. She used to ride with her sister around the estate all day.'

'And she just rode away from the house, in plain sight?'

'No, she kept a motorcycle on the mainland beach. She'd jet-ski off the island, dock on the mainland, and use the motorcycle from there.' He glanced nervously at Nayir. 'She wanted that freedom being out on the motorcycle, otherwise I would have given her a ride.'

'How did you know when she was going to be at the zoo?'

Mohammed sighed deeply. 'She would call me in the morning and tell me when to meet her. Usually she needed me to keep up her alibi. If she told her mother she was going shopping, then I had to show up at the zoo with some shopping bags full of stuff. She didn't care what it was. She wasn't materialistic. She wanted to ride her motorcycle more than she wanted new clothes.'

Nayir nodded coolly. At least it explained why Nouf had taken the shoes to the zoo. 'She was going to give you the pink shoes,' he said. 'You were going to exchange them for her.'

Mohammed nodded glumly.

'So you saw her on the day she disappeared.'

'No, I didn't!' Mohammed hissed, looking nervously at the men standing nearby.

'She called me that morning and told me to meet her at the zoo, but when I arrived, she wasn't there.'

'What time was this?'

'I was supposed to meet her at eleven o'clock. I got there a little late, and there was no sign of her.'

'If you didn't meet her, then why did I smell the zoo on your clothes?'

Mohammed shuddered involuntarily. 'Since she disappeared, I've gone to the zoo a few times to see if I could find anything that would help me understand what happened to her.'

Nayir sat back and crossed his arms. 'Did you find anything?'

'No.' Hands folded in his lap, eyes cast down, Mohammed looked like a boy who'd been punished and shamed. 'I didn't even find the shoe.'

'It was on the access road behind the zoo, buried in the dirt.'

'I looked there!' he whispered.

Nayir had to remind himself that Mohammed wasn't the father of Nouf's child. Yet he knew about Nouf's trips to the zoo; he'd met her there secretly; he'd been lying to the family for months, perhaps years, and when Nouf disappeared, he hadn't told anyone the truth. He couldn't have

273

been more guilty. At his apartment, Mohammed had given a subtle impression of righteousness; he felt he'd been keeping Nouf's secret in order to protect her. He couldn't possibly believe he was being virtuous, not knowing all of this. He must have been getting something out of it. The chance to share a secret with a beautiful woman. The chance to rebel against the Shrawis, whom he didn't like. Or perhaps it was more practical than that: if Nouf didn't need him, he didn't have to show up for work.

Nayir stared at the fountain, thinking. He realized suddenly why Nouf would have kept the shoes in her pockets. She'd been riding a jet ski and a motorcycle. There was probably no storage compartment on the jet ski, and it was safer to keep the shoes tucked away than to have a bag dangling from her wrist.

'What about the motorcycle?' he asked. 'Where did she keep it?'

Mohammed shook his head. 'That was her secret. I went looking once or twice, but she changed the location.' Wiping sweat from his chin, he fell into an uneasy silence.

'How did she get the motorcycle to the mainland in the first place?'

'Allah forgive me.' He shut his eyes. 'I have no idea. Look, I don't know where she kept it, I don't know how often she changed the location. The family owns a lot of beach property, and that's all I know. I asked her about it, but she wouldn't tell me. She just *wouldn't*. She said that only one other person knew about it – probably one of her brothers. I mean, how else would she get a key?'

'A key?'

'To a private beach.'

'All right. Did she say who gave her the key?'

'No,' Mohammed frowned. 'I think it was Othman.'

'Why?'

'I don't know. It's been bothering me. I've thought about it for weeks now, but it has to be Othman. He's the only brother she ever talked to.'

Nayir rubbed his chin. 'She wore a man's robe when she went out on the bike?'

'Yes. And a helmet, so no one saw her face. And gloves, to hide her hands.'

'Didn't someone notice her leaving the estate dressed like a man?'

'No. She always left the house in her black cloak. It was only on the mainland that she changed into the robe. Look, we had conversations about this. I told her it was dangerous, but she said she would only do it once in a while, for fun. And anyway, she never listened to me.'

'And you didn't tell her family.'

Mohammed crossed his arms and compressed his lips into a line. Nayir already knew the answer – Mohammed would not have told the family about Nouf's business any more than he would have told the police. Yet his silence made Nayir angry. An escort's job was to *guard* a woman, not to spoil her. A favourite phrase of his uncle's came to mind: *If you cannot harden your heart, you cannot raise children.*

'Why didn't you tell them?' Nayir asked coldly.

Mohammed wiped the sweat from his forehead. 'When I got to the zoo that day, her motorcycle wasn't there. I waited at the service entrance for an hour, then I went into the zoo itself, but she wasn't there either. So I left. I thought she'd changed her mind, and I figured if she needed me, she'd call.'

'Yes, but later, when you realized she was missing – you don't think the family might have wanted to know where she was supposed to be, even if you didn't think she'd been there?'

Mohammed flushed. 'Look, I checked the whole zoo;

she wasn't there, and there was no sign that she'd been there. I didn't see how it would have help—' But his voice cracked, betraying his regret. 'I honestly didn't think she'd even made it there that day.'

Nayir bit back his frustration at the boy's selfishness and idiocy. 'What made her go to the zoo in the first place?' he asked.

'She liked looking at the old exhibits. I told you she loved animals.' His voice quavered. 'I swear I didn't see her there that day. I swear it in front of Allah.'

Nayir barely suppressed a snort. People were inclined to swear a good many things in front of Allah, most of them sincere, but this felt dirty. Mohammed was the one person Nouf had trusted, yet he'd done nothing to find her. If he'd just told the family about her trips to the zoo, they might have been able to put the pieces together more quickly. There might have been a chance to have found her alive.

'She trusted you,' Nayir said. 'She must have told you who she was meeting that day.'

Mohammed's blush was slow but harsh, it burned a streak down his neck. 'Eric, I thought.' He tried to look cool, but his voice trembled with anger. The meaning of the anger struck Nayir like a punch. Mohammed wasn't just concerned for her safety, he was jealous, and he feared that she'd been sleeping with Eric.

'So perhaps she did meet with Eric when you couldn't keep her in your sights.'

Mohammed looked furious. Nayir remembered his beautiful wife, their baby, the apparent domestic bliss. He couldn't imagine that Mohammed had slept with Nouf, but now he knew that Mohammed had loved her, or believed that he did. He certainly glorified her and let himself be swayed to assist her in all sorts of potentially dangerous acts: running away, riding a motorcycle, meeting strange men in remote places. It was no longer a shock that Mohammed would lie about Nouf's secrets; what amazed him was Mohammed's possessiveness. How could he expect honesty from Nouf, when he was, in some way, lying to his wife?

Suddenly, Nayir felt ashamed to have brought this kind of conversation into the masjid. He rose abruptly.

'I'm sorry,' the escort said. 'I should have told you everything before.'

'I am not your judge.' Nayir motioned for him to stand up. Mohammed rose and followed him out of the door.

By the time they reached the street, Nayir's thoughts were so busy that he could hardly focus. He forced himself to turn to Mohammed. 'Did your wife know about your feelings for Nouf?'

The escort's twitch of embarrassment answered the question.

'I see,' Nayir said. *'Ma'salaama.'*

He was halfway down the block when he remembered one last thing. He turned back to find Mohammed still standing by the mosque, looking bereft.

'Why would Nouf want to buy a pair of glasses with no prescription?' Nayir asked.

Mohammed's look of shame turned to one of self-loathing. 'For her costume,' he muttered. 'She had a small bag of clothes that she was going to wear when she got to New York. She was going to leave Qazi at the library, so she bought a suit that made her look like a librarian.'

'What else was in the bag?'

'A wig, a brown suit, some high-heeled shoes. She was going to wear the glasses, too.'

Nayir gave him one last disgusted stare and went back to his Jeep.

☽

Nayir left town and drove south toward the Shrawi estate. The sun was blistering the road, and to his right the ocean seemed to laze in the heat. Following the coastal highway, he drove past the bridge road until he came to a white, expansive beach that was popular with windsurfers. It was just south of the estate. On his boat, during summer excursions down the coast, he'd passed it many times, but the presence of so many small boats and surfers had always prevented him from getting a closer view.

He parked the Jeep at the edge of the beach near an outcropping of palms. The water was gentle; no one was surfing. To his left, the sand extended as far as he could see, but to his right stood a strange rocky region, beyond which lay a series of private enclaves, each sectioned off by high stone walls. The walls reached a good ten metres out to sea. Families came here seeking privacy so that their women could enjoy the water. There were no homes nearby; the beaches had thick iron gates and padlocks.

It seemed logical that if Nouf had jet-skied from the island, she would have come here. Not only would the currents have favoured it, but this was the closest shore for a landing. The rest of the nearby coast was rocky. It also seemed unlikely that she would have hauled the jet ski out of the water – much easier to leave it in a quiet spot, behind the confines of a stone wall on a private beach.

To access the restricted areas, Nayir had to cross the rocky part of the strand. It took him a good fifteen minutes of stumbling to navigate the field of jagged black stones. These were obviously imported, although for what purpose he couldn't imagine. Perhaps the wealthy beach-owners were hoping to thwart an attack of windsurfers. When he finally reached the first stone wall, he was winded, scraped in a dozen places, and nearly mad enough to abandon his

Jeep altogether and swim back to his boat, never mind that he was wearing his coat.

The stone wall was in a state of mild disrepair. Large stones were missing in places, and an amalgam of sand, dust and guano quilted the upper half. First he walked up the shore and inspected the gate. It was locked and impenetrable, a sheer slab of iron. Then he went back down the length of the wall, searching for a hole large enough to squeeze through. No place was suitable, and besides, squeezing into anything had never been his forte. His would have to be a vertical assault.

Because of the wall's jagged design, heaving himself up proved easier than expected. When he reached the top, he stood up and looked around. A series of identical walls spread out before him, each neatly sectioning a thirty-foot-wide portion of beach. Directly below him was a private enclave.

The scale of his task quickly became apparent. It would take him a whole week to investigate every beach, climbing up each wall, down the other side, snooping around in search of . . . what? A hut? A small pier? Quite possibly each beach had one or the other. And even if he did have a whole week to waste, he doubted he could scale so many walls.

He climbed down the wall into the first enclave. The beach was empty, but he looked around anyway. Nouf might have chosen this enclave. It was at one end. To the north, the other end pressed up against the bridge road that led to the estate. She wouldn't dock there; it was too close to home. She would have had to use the main road to reach the highway, and that would be risky: anyone driving into the estate could see her. She would have chosen this end of the beach. At least, this was where he would come, if he were Nouf.

Finding nothing in the enclave, he scaled the next wall and looked down. A small skiff, looking as if it had been untouched for decades, was tied to a metal hook in the wall. Next to this was an old shack, timeworn and somehow friendly. He began to get excited. In his mind he could see Nouf's slender black form, waspish and intent, buzzing across the waves on a yellow jet ski and docking at this beach. He climbed down the wall.

Inspecting the sand, he found a chaos of footprints, some of them small enough to have been made by a woman. He worked the pink stiletto out of his pocket. A rudimentary comparison proved that at least three pairs of the footprints might be Nouf's size. Many of the prints ended at the shack.

The shack's door was held firmly shut by a combination lock on a metal hasp. Nayir walked around the shack looking for another way in, but there weren't even windows, so he went back to the door. The lock was stubborn, but when he yanked it there was a crack of wood and the entire metal plate – hasp and all – fell into his hand, leaving the door swinging free.

Gently, he opened it and peered inside. What he saw made him whistle with delight. It was just as he'd imagined. In the centre of the room sat a shiny black motorcycle, propped elegantly on its kickstand.

Beside the door he found a camping lantern, which he used to prop the door wider. Sunlight flooded into the narrow space, which was spartan, dusty, and smelled vaguely of sunscreen. A basket hung from a nail in the wall, and in it he found a tube of lipstick, some powder, lotion, and a small box of cardamom-flavoured Chiclets. Beside the basket, a white robe hung from a hook, and a helmet hung beside it, with a pair of gloves tucked inside. On the floor, half-hidden beneath the robe's bottom hem, was an old city map. He picked it up and read the scribbles in the margins. It was a graceful script, in a woman's hand. *Second left after stoplight* and *right on the first dirt road after that*. Someone had circled the zoo.

Nouf. He rubbed the back of his neck against a quick chill. He had imagined her many times, but he'd never quite had this feeling before, as if at any moment she would step into the room. He went outside and looked around, half expecting someone to be there. The beach was empty, but the eerie sense of her presence remained.

He ran a hand down his face and went back inside. The motorcycle was slender and elegant. He circled round the bike, but in the shadows behind it his foot hit a soft spot, and with another loud crack the floorboard splintered and his foot dropped into the sand below. He eased his foot out and saw an edging of black beneath a thin veil of sand. Bending over and prying out the floorboard, he found a hollow space, almost a compartment. In it lay a small black book, no larger than his hand. He was so surprised that at first he didn't touch it; he just stared as if waiting for it to resolve into an old brick or a rotten slab of wood. But no, it was a well-worn, leather-bound book. Gently, he brushed the sand from its surface and took it out.

In the empty compartment, a hint of light came from the left, and putting his face as close to the floor as possible, he saw that the compartment was an arm's length away from the sunlight. Someone had probably slid the book in here from the outside.

When he opened the book's cover, he discovered a journal, as densely packed with text as a Quran commentary – written text, in this case, in the same elegant script that he'd seen on the map.

'Allah forgive me.' Turning to a page at random, he began to read.

In the name of Allah, all-merciful, all-knowing, I almost killed myself today, but I was too frightened to do it. I didn't have the courage to see my own blood. So I got on my jet ski and rode like crazy, I rode and rode until I ran out of gas and I was all alone in the middle of the sea. I could still see the coast, but it was getting dark and I thought I would die by accident then, because THEN I realized I didn't really want to die, I just wanted to get away. I was so happy to realize it, and so, so scared to realize that I MIGHT die, because of stupidity. But then, like an angel's messenger, he showed up on the boat. He came with the spotlight and the horns and somebody else, and he pulled me out of the water. Allah, forgive me, I held on to him and cried and I didn't let go until he took me home. And I never even asked how he found me.

Nayir skimmed the next few pages and read another passage at random.

Allah, please forgive me, I know it's wrong to love him, I know it would chain me and make me miserable for the rest of my life, but my whole body yearns for him. I can't stop thinking of him. I remember every little thing he does. I wish I could always see his smile, hear his voice, so soft, so secure and intelligent. I long for his touch and he KNOWS it, but he doesn't act. He can't. Neither can I. It would lead to so much pain, so much danger for me – and for him, too, I know it.

He tore his eyes away. Who was she writing about? Someone with a boat, or access to one – but that could be anybody. Sailing was a popular pastime, especially on summer nights when being on the water was the only way to cool down. What sort of man would have followed her out to sea?

Miss Hijazi was right; there had to be a third man. Nayir

282

skimmed a few more pages but found no mention of a name, only a vast outpouring of frustrated longing. He decided to read the journal later, when his mind was clear. He tucked it into his pocket.

Then he got up to inspect the bike. It was covered in a fine coat of sand. The glove compartment was unlocked but empty, and much too small to hold a pair of shoes. He peered at the handlebars, the pedals, the seat, any place she might have touched, if only to make sure that he'd covered all the bases. There was a heavy coating of sand on the tyres, caked into the treads. He stuck his finger into one of the grooves and scraped the sand into his palm. It was a fine grain, the palest beige. Most likely it had come from the desert.

As he stood up, his eye fell on the chrome logo on the gas tank. A Honda logo. His fingers traced the familiar design: a bird with a single wing spread to the side. Each feather was deeply grooved. Then he saw it.

'Allah, what a fool!' He touched the logo again. Five feathers, as neat as the stripes on the camel's leg. Looking closer, he saw a trace of blood and hair on the logo. It was probably from the camel.

In a rush, it came together. So *this* was how the killer had returned from the desert. Nouf had arrived at the zoo on the motorcycle. The killer met her there, knocked her out and put her in the truck. He squeezed the motorcycle into the back of the truck with the camel, then he drove out to the wadi. The heat must have turned the logo into a brand – thus the marks on the camel's leg. Once the killer had abandoned Nouf, the camel and the truck in the desert, he hopped on the bike and rode back here.

Nayir left the shack and stared at the sand. Ten dozen pairs of footprints led down to the water, and another five dozen led up to the gate. At least one thing was obvious:

after ditching the motorcycle, the killer could have gone in any direction.

He took a miswak from his pocket and began to chew. Although the killer hadn't left obvious prints in the sand, he had left a curious print of sorts: the fact that he'd returned the motorcycle at all. Clearly, he knew Nouf well enough to know about this beach and its shack, just big enough to hide a bike. It was just what a person would know if he'd been following her around, on a boat at sea. But once he returned the bike, which way had he gone?

Nayir walked down to the water's edge. There was no jet ski there, only the small boat. He looked around for a pair of oars but saw none. Mohammed had said that Nouf used a jet ski to get to the beach. According to Othman, the servants had found her jet ski at the island's dock on the same afternoon she'd disappeared, so whoever had returned the motorcycle here must have taken the jet ski back to the island. Did he do it to get rid of the evidence that Nouf had been at the beach? Or did he do it because it was his only way to get home?

Nayir looked down at the maze of footprints and decided it was time to call Mutlaq.

$$\supset$$

Later that afternoon, the two men climbed over the wall. When Mutlaq saw the sand, he gave a low whistle.

'An awful lot of activity,' he said, rubbing his hands with relish.

Nayir followed him around, listening to every *hmmph* and trying to divine its meaning from Mutlaq's face, but his friend wore a look of intense concentration.

'You were here,' Mutlaq noted. 'And so was your friend Othman. But not at the same time.'

Nayir struggled to understand how Mutlaq would know

that, then he remembered that Othman's prints had also been at the campsite in the desert.

'He was here before you,' Mutlaq said. 'These are his prints, very recent, too.' The prints were deep, and once Nayir had isolated them from the dozens of others, he saw something else.

'He came here with someone?'

'With a woman, I think.' Mutlaq pointed to the other prints, which were smaller but also deep. 'It's a strange fact that people make deeper prints in certain types of sand at night.'

Nayir thought Othman must have come here with Katya, although perhaps he'd come with one of his sisters. 'So you think they were here in the evening?'

'I'd say it was pretty dark.'

'Do you recognize any other prints from the desert?' Nayir asked.

'Yes. Othman didn't come here with the girl from the desert. But she came here before him. Here.' He traced a different set of tracks leading from the jetty to the shack, and another set from the shack to the gate. Apart from shoe size, the two sets looked nothing alike. When Nayir pointed this out, Mutlaq merely shrugged. 'So she changed her shoes in the shack. From the shack to the gate, she was walking with a motorcycle – here are the tyre marks. She probably needed sturdier shoes to ride the bike.'

Nayir didn't know what to say. He trusted Mutlaq.

'In any case,' Mutlaq said, pointing to the prints near the motorcycle marks, 'these are the same footprints we found in the desert.'

'So let's say Nouf left here with the motorcycle,' Nayir said. 'Who brought it back? It's in the shack right now.'

Mutlaq wandered around. He was able to isolate the motorcycle's return, but the footprints beside it had all but been obscured by more recent markings. There was only a single print, and it was Nouf's.

Mutlaq walked around the print, studying it carefully from a variety of angles. Then he knelt down and got very close to it. He even pressed his cheek to the sand and inspected it from the side. When he stood up again, wiping his cheek, he said: 'It's Nouf's print. She brought the motorcycle back.'

Nayir was stunned. 'Are you sure?'

'Yes.'

'Do you see any evidence that she was kidnapped here?'

'No. Nothing yet.' Mutlaq continued to inspect the sand, squatting down in places, tracing outlines with his finger, touching the heel prints, toe prints, feeling for firmness. Nayir watched with admiration. He was like a search and rescue man who knows a terrain well enough to know its secrets, only Mutlaq's terrain was a landscape in miniature, the hills and valleys of a footprint ridge. *In the fact that Allah sends down sustenance from the sky, and revives the Earth after its death, and in the change of the Winds, are signs for those that are wise.* Allah could be known by His signs, and the scenery of world was one of the biggest; but Mutlaq's scenery, being smaller and man-made, held its own divine secrets.

Mutlaq made no other discoveries but was able to re-affirm what Nayir had already learned: that Nouf had not been kidnapped there, and that she was the last person to have returned the motorcycle to the shack.

Nayir felt a terrible, desperate sinking of hope and began scrambling for alternative theories. 'Is it possible she was meeting someone here?' he asked. 'Maybe she brought the motorcycle back and then got into a car with someone.'

'There is no sign of it. In fact, her freshest footprints lead straight down to the water. I think she got into a boat.'

Nayir thought back to the short section of the journal he'd read. Nouf had met a mysterious man on a boat. It was possible that her kidnapper had arrived on a boat, but if that was the case, then where was the jet ski she'd used to get to the beach in the first place? Had her kidnapper disposed of it? Or had she in fact gone back to the island?

It was all becoming muddled, and his one good theory – that Nouf had been kidnapped at the zoo – was about to collapse under this new evidence. Mutlaq noticed his concern. As soon as Nayir explained it, Mutlaq offered to accompany him to the zoo for another look. Gratefully, Nayir agreed.

24

The next day, Nayir pulled onto the Shrawi island armed with a box of dates from the Balad souk, where they still rolled them by hand, layered them in geometric patterns, and wrapped them in decorative gold foil. He parked in front of the house and carefully lifted the dates from the seat. The box was heavy and warm, and he wanted to keep it, not because of a sudden appetite for dates or because of the sparkling box, but because his mission today was not generous at all, and the giving of such a fine and simple gift smacked of deceit.

A woman met him at the door. She wore a black house dress and a black burqa through which he could just see her eyes. Glancing at her hands, he saw that the fingernails were modestly short and that a chain of prayer beads was wrapped around her wrist. She quickly bowed her head, tucked her hands into her sleeves, and welcomed Nayir with an *Ahlan wa'Sahlan*. He averted his gaze.

'I'm sorry,' she said, her voice low and humble. 'I can take you to the sitting room.'

'No, no. If you would be so kind as to tell one of the brothers that Nayir ash-Sharqi is waiting at the door.'

Nervously, she took a step back and whispered: 'Please, *Ahlan wa'Sahlan*. Make yourself at home. If you know your way to the sitting room, you're welcome to go there yourself.' As if embarrassed by her own forwardness, she quickly turned and skittered down the hallway.

He watched her go. Once she disappeared, he stepped into the hallway and shut the door. As he tiptoed down the hall, he wondered if she would be considerate enough to inform the men of his arrival.

Ten minutes later, a veiled and cloaked woman appeared in the doorway bearing a coffee service. The woman seemed nervous, hesitating at the door, her unsteady hands gripping the edge of the service tray. Instead of leaving it by the door, she entered the room and attempted to bring it to Nayir, but she was short, and the tray was heavy, tilting under the weight of glass cups, a bowl of dates, and a brass coffee pot. To make matters worse, pillows were scattered about, and someone had left a book on the floor, another coffee service, and a deck of cards. Nayir leapt to his feet and reached out to her but couldn't prevent her from stepping on a pillow.

'*Ya'rub!*' she yelped, stumbling. He caught two cups before they slid off the tray.

He saw her hands and realized she was the same girl who had met him at the door. She extended the coffee service to Nayir, and he took it, giving her time to raise her burqa. When she lifted the black veil, Nayir stood back.

She was the very image of her sister, Nouf.

Blushing bright red, she took the service back and bowed her head. Nayir blinked a few times and glanced away, but his eyes were drawn uncontrollably back to her face. He had only seen a picture of Nouf, but his memory of the examiner's office was clear enough.

'Pardon me. You're . . . a Shrawi.'

'Yes. My name is Abir.'

'Nouf's sister.' *The one on the jet ski.* He thought she was the same, but he couldn't be sure. She was the only other sister close to Nouf's age. His eyes wouldn't move; he couldn't take them from her face, and the longer he stared, the easier it became to keep his eyes there, to trace the curve of her temples, her chin, her jaw, scanning for an aspect that would prove she wasn't Nouf. At least that's what he told himself. Even though it was foolish, he felt that he knew her, and that, in some way, she should know him, too.

After a moment, the girl summoned her nerve, kicked the pillows aside, and laid the coffee service in a clearing on the floor. She knelt down and poured him a cup of coffee. When she handed it to him, she blushed. He realized he was staring.

She tucked her hands into her lap. 'My father said you were an honest man.'

His whole being shouted: *I am an honest man!*

'A desert man,' she added, glancing quickly at his face. Suddenly, his heart fell. Yes, perhaps she was just like Nouf, a woman who would marry an honest man so she could dump him for a fantasy. The thought sobered him, and he picked up the coffee cup, grateful for something to do with his hands. Whatever she was like, he knew that her presence offered him a chance to learn something about Nouf, but he couldn't think of a single good question; the ones that came to mind all seemed terribly improper. When he looked back, he saw fear in her eyes.

'Forgive me,' she whispered. 'I never approach men like this. Please believe me, I'm only doing this because I have to. Our lives have changed so much since Nouf died. We've been confined to the island, we can't go to the mainland any more. My brothers are afraid we'll turn out like Nouf. That's what they say, but they're really afraid that we'll learn something we shouldn't.' There was panic in her voice, and it raised his protective instincts.

'What is it?'

'I'm sorry, it's just – I heard that you were investigating what happened to her. I wouldn't ask you otherwise, and I'm sorry to bring this up, but . . .'

'No, go ahead, Miss . . . Shrawi.'

She took a deep breath. 'Miss Hijazi was here asking questions about Nouf. I wanted to tell her what I knew, but I couldn't.' She looked down at her hands.

He wanted to know why she'd withheld information from Miss Hijazi, and chose instead to reveal it to him, but he was afraid to break the spell. As the silence went on, he began to get nervous, so gently he said: 'What do you know?'

The girl's eyes flickered wildly from the coffee service to Nayir's knee, as if she were struggling to contain a rising horror. 'The day Nouf disappeared,' she said, 'she had a fight with my brother.'

He felt his stomach harden. 'Which one?'

'Othman.'

He tried to remain neutral, but his heart was pounding.

'It was a bad fight,' she said. 'They were in the kitchen, arguing about something. I didn't hear it, because they were whispering at first. They were going to walk the dogs, but then suddenly they started screaming. It made no sense to me, what they were saying. Nouf ran back to her room. Othman was standing there. He looked stunned. Then he followed her.'

'What happened then?'

Her hands were shaking and she glanced back at the door. 'It started out quiet, they were still arguing in a whisper, but then it got louder. She was screaming, and I don't know what he was doing. I stood outside the door, so I didn't actually see them.'

'What were they saying?' Nayir asked.

'Something about . . . I didn't understand it. Something about not letting this happen. She told him something, and it made him angry. I got the impression that she wanted to do something, and Othman didn't want her to do it. I don't know what it was. *He* was angry. Nouf sounded scared.'

'And what happened? How did it end?'

'Nouf came running out of her room, and then Othman came out chasing her. She—' Miss Shrawi faltered and pressed a hand to her mouth. 'She had blood on her arm. She ran out of the house – through the kitchen door. I think she went down to the beach with the dogs. My mother came in and wanted to know what was going on. Othman said it was nothing, Nouf was nervous about the wedding. And she believed him.'

'And you didn't tell her the truth?'

'She wouldn't have listened. Not when it's my word against Othman's.'

Nayir sat back, hit by a cold confusion. Othman had told him none of this, and it was difficult picturing his friend so upset. He must have had a good reason. What had Nouf told him? Had she confessed to her pregnancy? Her plan to go to New York? Why would she?

'I can see why you wouldn't tell Miss Hijazi,' he said. 'That was considerate of you.'

She nodded nervously. They heard a thump in the hallway and she quickly stood up, but no one came in.

'May I ask you one more thing?' Nayir said.

She looked anxiously at the door. 'Yes.'

'Did you ever see Nouf go into Othman's room? In particular, did she ever talk about his jackets?'

She blinked in confusion. 'No. Not that I remember. Why?'

'Othman's jacket is missing.'

She squinted, cogitating. 'Now that I think about it, I remember that he was looking for it. One of the servants asked us if we'd seen it. I never saw Nouf go into his bedroom, but it's odd: she did mention his coat once before she left. We were talking about her trousseau. She was eager to see the jackets Qazi had chosen for her. She said something like: "I hope I get a desert jacket like Othman's." At the time, I thought she was just excited about her clothes. She wanted one of everything, even if she would never wear any of it, but it does seem strange now.'

Nayir sat forward. 'Was anything else missing besides the coat and the camel?'

'Yes.' She glanced at his face but quickly looked away. 'She took her gold. That's why I thought she ran away.'

'How much was missing?'

She paused. 'My brothers don't know any of this.'

'I won't say a word.'

She nodded. 'Nearly two million riyals' worth, including the gemstones.'

Nayir froze, startled by the amount. Two million riyals was enough for a person to live comfortably for years. 'Why haven't you told your brothers?'

'I thought she took it, and I didn't want to make matters worse for her. I was afraid that it would betray her somehow. Then later, when I found out she was dead . . .' She swallowed audibly and spent a moment composing herself. 'I was afraid to tell my brothers, because I began thinking, what if she didn't run away? What if someone kidnapped her, and stole her money? I was even afraid to tell my mother because what if she told my brothers . . . and what if Oth— . . .what if he knew what had happened to Nouf? I know this sounds crazy.' She straightened her shoulders and whispered: 'You can't tell *anyone* what I've told you.'

'I won't,' Nayir assured her. 'But let me ask one more thing. How would Othman get access to her safe?'

She was trembling, unable to speak. He watched in horror as the tears began to slide. He fished in his pockets for a tissue even though he knew he had none to offer her.

Just then, they heard footsteps in the hall. Miss Shrawi flipped down her burqa just as the door swung open.

Tahsin entered with Fahad on his heels. Nayir tried to compose himself, but no one took notice. Tahsin looked as if he'd just eaten and was ready for a nap. He glanced at the mess, but when he saw Nayir his face lit up slightly.

'Brother, how are you?' He crossed the room, casting a cursory glance at his sister. She scurried to the door, but Fahad grabbed her arm.

'Hey!' he snapped.

Tahsin turned. 'Who is that?'

'Your sister!' Fahad kept a firm grip on her arm. 'What are you doing here?'

'Serving coffee,' she murmured.

'A hundred servants in this house and *you're* serving coffee?' Fahad reached for her burqa but she wrestled free and ran out the door. Fahad went after her. Their voices echoed in the hall.

Did you show him your face?

I was only serving coffee and dates!

What other sweet things did you put in his lap?

Tahsin turned to Nayir. 'I'm so sorry, please have a seat.'

'Thank you.'

'Be comfortable.'

Nayir took the box of dates from the table and handed it to Tahsin, who accepted it with a slight bow.

'I know how much you like the candied ones,' Nayir said. 'But these are new. They've got peaches inside.'

'Thank you. Please, sit.' Tahsin pursed his lips and opened the box. 'They look magnificent. Please try one.'

Nayir took a date and chewed mechanically, his mind abuzz. Fahad came back and ate a few dates, and Nayir learned that Othman wasn't expected home for another few hours. Suddenly he was grateful to avoid him. The remainder of the conversation was light, and as soon as he could, he took his leave.

25

Unbelievable, the mind of a girl. He pushed the book away and stood up from the dinette table, rubbing his eyes. The journal was possibly longer than Quranic commentary and single-mindedly obsessed with love and romantic notions of her future. He had read it with his own obsessive interest, quickly and thoroughly, hoping to finish as soon as he could because it felt like an intrusion, invading the privacy of the dead.

He had seen only snippets of her before; she'd walked through his head like a woman on the street. Now he finally heard her voice and was able to picture her moving and thinking. He saw her as short and wiry, and imagined that her gestures would have been soft but firm. She liked peppermint candies, black ribbons for her hair, and she didn't mind getting dirty. She loved animals – all kinds, but especially her dogs, Shams and Thalj, whom she kept in the stables and walked every day. She was occasionally fastidious: she drew pictures of her dogs and labelled their parts in an elegant script. She also took copious notes about their behaviours, a scientific study that would have made Samir proud.

The great part of her writing was about the mysterious

man who had rescued her on his boat, but there were not enough clues to reveal his identity. Even though she was careful not to mention the man's name, she managed to describe him. He was smouldering, secretive, intelligent. He was practically a superhero when he saved her on the boat. Yet he was not someone she spoke to in confidence, rather someone she kept secrets from and saw infrequently. It scarcely sounded like Mohammed. Nayir had the sense that Nouf talked to Mohammed, that they were comfortable together and knew each other well. The man in the journal was a romantic stranger.

Despite the outpourings of lust and frustration, there was still something missing, a sense of what had turned her girlish fantasies into actual recklessness. When it came to many things – her heart, her secret meetings, her plans for the future – she was far too trusting. She had been paying Eric, but there was no mention of a contract, only 'friendship' and 'trust', and she had given him half the money up front, plus little extras here and there. Why was running away to New York the only answer? Couldn't she have found a better way to fulfil her dreams, closer to home, in a safer place? Was she just hopelessly romantic? Or was it that home truly wasn't safe?

There was no mention of her secret phone calls with Qazi, which was odd considering that she wrote down all of the other details of her illicit affair. If her lover was Qazi, then the phone calls would have been the least of her sins. Unless Qazi was lying and there had been no calls, only secret meetings. But Nayir's instinct was telling him that Qazi was not her lover. The only mention of him came in the latter part of the book.

I accepted Qazi's offer of marriage today. It's scary to think of marrying him, but it's the only way . . .

The only way to what? Leave the country, he supposed. And why? Because Qazi was just innocent enough not to suspect her schemes, trustworthy enough to keep his promise to take her to New York.

It was disorienting to see such calculation amidst such cloying romanticism. Yet there was one thing about the journal he found diverting. At the top of a page she'd written 'The 77 Words for Love', and in her elegant script she'd listed the words along with all of their explanations. There was *Hubb*, which meant love, and also seed; *Ishq*, entanglement, and an ivy that strangles a tree; *Hawa*, liking, and error; *fitna*, passionate desire, also chaos; *hayam*, wandering thirsty in the desert; *sakan*, tranquillity; and *izaz*, dignified love. Then the list grew darker, from captivation to confusion and affliction, even to depression, sorrow, and grief, culminating in *fanaa*, non-existence. The page stood out as a work of art, with flourishes in the corners and a perfectly symmetrical 'In the name of Allah, most righteous, most merciful' written at the top. Each word had been copied in a perfect hand, each diacritic mark stood in its rightful place. It was odd that this page contained the journal's only overt reference to Islam, and also its only philosophical look at love. So she wasn't wrapped up entirely in adolescent dreams.

What struck him most was the title. Although there was some disputing that all seventy-seven words could be called words for 'love', they could certainly describe the condition of lovers. And such a wealth of vocabulary only reinforced his own sense of romantic poverty. How could there be so many kinds of love, and a man could die without knowing half of them? After staring at the page for many minutes, he came to think that that's what Nouf had wanted – to know all the kinds of love, even if some of them were better left alone.

He stood in the kitchen now, waiting for the coffee to

boil. While taking breaks from the journal, he'd sat at the ~~Fatimah~~'s dinette table surrounded by his navigational charts, his desert charts and sea charts. Often, when he was bored or simply too tired to do anything else, he stared at his maps and found good memories there, as well as a certain peace of mind that only such emptiness could inspire. But tonight he had assembled the maps to help visualize Nouf's journey into the wilderness, as if by plotting the points of her departure and death, he might find the missing piece.

He'd determined that she could have left the estate by jet-skiing around the island's west side. That way, she wouldn't have passed beneath the women's sitting room, and the women wouldn't hear the buzz of the jet ski. She docked on the mainland, and changed her clothes, taking the shoes from the pockets of her black cloak and transferring them into the pockets of the white robe. Then she'd gone to the zoo on her motorcycle, her joyful burst of freedom.

Mutlaq's trip to the zoo had confused everything. He'd found Nouf's footprints on the service road, and there was evidence of a struggle, but the chaos in the dirt made it impossible to say if there'd been an attacker. It seemed as if Nouf had fallen down near the bushes – that was probably when she lost her pink shoe. The drag marks didn't seem connected to Nouf, because at some point she had got back to her feet and gone to the truck. Had she suffered a fainting spell of some sort – perhaps from the pregnancy? More confusing still, Mutlaq found motorcycle tracks on the service road just beside those of the truck, made by the same model of motorcycle as the one at the beach shack.

Mutlaq had also found Othman's prints at the zoo, but they were not on the service road. They were outside the Matterhorn. There were another man's prints there as well, but Mutlaq didn't recognize them.

So Othman had been to the zoo, but Mutlaq had been unable to tell if he'd been there when Nouf had been kidnapped. The ground by the Matterhorn was dry and dusty, not as easy to read as the dirt on the service road. Maybe Othman knew about Nouf's trips to the zoo, and he'd gone to investigate. It wasn't something he was obliged to tell Nayir, although it might have been useful. Explaining why Nouf was at the zoo might have led to uncomfortable questions about her activities, and Othman would have wanted to protect her. It made sense anyway.

But nothing else did. Judging by the tracks, Nouf had gone to the zoo on the motorcycle. But then she'd returned the bike to the hut. From there she'd probably jet-skied back to the island. It looked ever more likely that she'd stolen the truck from the house herself. But then she'd gone to the zoo again. Mutlaq felt confident that the truck and motorcycle tracks had been made on the same day. Why would she go back to the zoo? Was she looking for her lost shoe? Nayir gathered from the journal that she went to the zoo frequently, by herself, to read the signs that described the animals. Perhaps she had gone there for privacy or comfort.

But it was also where she met her lover.

Taking his coffee to the table, he looked again at the map. He paused at the wadi and thought of all the things that were missing from the crime scene. Nouf's bag of librarian clothes – Mohammed still had them. Her glasses, which she hadn't yet picked up. The key to the apartment in New York. If she was running away, he ought to have found one of those items somewhere near the body. Instead, he had found the pink stiletto, her alibi for leaving the house. She had left with the shoes in the morning – then she'd gone back to the house, stolen the truck and the camel, and driven back to the zoo, all the while toting around a single shoe. Why the shoe and not the other items?

Nayir went to the bathroom and rinsed his eyes. It felt as if someone had rubbed sand in them; they were red, and now his vision was blurry. *Maybe*, he thought, *I should go back to the crazy eye doctor.*

He sat down again and picked up the journal. The last third of it was mostly observations of her dogs' behaviour – no mention of her plans to run away to America, no mention of names. Although the romantic passages had grown ever more painful, they were less confused. She seemed sick of her unrequited love. She had turned her attention to animals instead, finding comfort in their mysteries. Every so often she mentioned love again. 'I saw him today, and the way he looked at me sent me to the darkest realms of hell. I know I'll die if this goes on.' *If what goes on?* Nayir wondered. *This oppressive flirtation? With* whom?

He turned to the very last page of writing. There were only two paragraphs. The handwriting was sloppier than before, almost frantic.

I'm not a girl any more. I've done it, WE'VE done it, and the strangest thing of all is that I don't regret it. I feel so stupid when I think of all the fear I had. Allah, I almost committed the biggest sin, I almost killed myself! I realize all of the things I feared are only the beginning of something beautiful. I feel alive for the first time. And the crazy thing is that I didn't know it would happen. I thought that it was almost over between us. He was avoiding me, and when I'd see him, he wouldn't even look at me. I thought he'd given up. But when I got to the zoo, he was waiting near the mountain where they used to keep the goats. I was shocked! I asked him how he found me. I never tell anyone! He said he figured it out himself, but he didn't say how. I was nervous, too, but he hugged me. I almost fainted from surprise, and then he kissed me!! I tried to say no, but he said: 'My heart tells me you don't mean it.'

He told me that he wouldn't ever stop loving me, no matter where I went, no matter who I married. I started to cry, and he took me in his arms and brought me into the centre of the mountain. It was cool, and dark. He kept apologizing, because it was not expensive or romantic, but he knew that I love this place, and nothing would be better.

Slowly, Nayir closed the book and set it on the table. He shut his sore eyes, and a deceptive tear streaked down his nose. Although she had died young, at least she'd learned one of the words for love.

A sudden shifting of the boat announced an arrival above. He blinked, wincing, and clambered out of the dinette to peer up the ladder. A black shape swooped around the hatch, and he knew before he saw her that it was Miss Hijazi.

'Nayir?' she called. Her voice sounded pinched.

He checked his cabin clock; it was 9.30 – not too late to pay a social call, but unusual nonetheless. He climbed up the ladder and caught sight of her eyes, red and tear-stained in the glow of the cabin's light. 'What's wrong?' he asked. She stumbled, and he reached out to keep her from falling. 'What happened?'

'Can we talk?'

'Yes, come in.' He descended first and stood below her, in case she stumbled again. To his surprise, his heart was thumping.

She stepped into the cabin and seemed to collapse. He managed to grab her around the shoulders and steer her towards the sofa, where she landed with an impact he wouldn't have expected from such a thin woman. Folding in pain, she put her face in her hands.

He chewed his lip and looked around. He was supposed to comfort her, but how? Going into the kitchen, he considered making more coffee but decided on tea, and set the kettle on the stove. Behind him she had curled into a ball – knees up, arms wrapped around her legs, face buried in her cloak. She was sobbing quietly. When the tea was ready, he took her a cup and set it on the table.

'Drink something,' he said, sitting on the sofa beside her.

She took a deep breath and raised her head. After a few moments, she lowered her legs, straightened her cloak, and sat up. She lifted her burqa and took the teacup.

Nayir turned away so as not to embarrass her.

'I found the baby's father,' she said.

He couldn't help it; he looked. The expression on her face told him everything. *Othman.*

'He's not really her brother.' She gave a dry laugh. 'But I never thought—'

He was too stunned to speak.

'I also found his skin cells and blood beneath her fingernails. Remember those defensive wounds she had? It was someone else's blood.'

'His?'

She nodded and broke into tears again. Nayir took her teacup and set it down. His own calm surprised him. Gently, he put an arm around her shoulders, half-expecting her to flinch or pull away, but she turned and curled against him like a child. 'Othman was sleeping with his sister!' she wailed. He raised his other arm and enclosed her. It wasn't as awkward as he'd thought it would be. She sobbed unabashedly, and he waited, wondering if he smelled like garlic, if he should have said something different, wondering how it would end. He marvelled at himself. He was unable to remember why he'd been so harsh to her before, which is what it seemed now: his own harshness, not hers.

303

She was shaking and he rocked her back and forth, whispering *ism'allah ism'allah* in her ear. In that blinding instant when she'd burst into tears, all the barriers between them had ripped apart.

At last she stopped crying and slowly, very slowly, she pulled away. 'I'm so sorry,' she said.

'Don't be.' He withdrew his arms and watched as she unwound the lower portion of her scarf and used it to wipe her nose.

'You know what my mother used to say?' she said. 'When you see a woman blowing her nose with her veil, divorce her.'

He gave a crooked grin.

'You know what's funny? My father didn't want me to marry Othman.' She wiped her nose and tucked her scarf back into her collar. 'I guess he was right. I was saved just in time. If I'd married him, he wouldn't have loved me. Maybe he'd have killed me, too!'

'It doesn't mean he killed her.'

'How do you explain his skin beneath her nails?'

'Maybe they fought before she was abducted.'

'And someone else abducted her? Come on. He had motive – he had to cover up the pregnancy. He was jealous because she was marrying someone else. I'll bet he found out about Eric, about her plan to run away, and it drove him crazy. He knew enough about her to kidnap her and make it look like she ran away. And he knew enough about the desert to know where to take her, because he was too cowardly to kill her outright. He wanted the desert to kill her so he wouldn't feel the *guilt*.'

Nayir had a hard time imagining Othman kidnapping Nouf, banging her on the head, driving her out to the desert. But Katya was right: he did have the motive and the opportunity. Yet why, if Othman had kidnapped her, was he so eager to find her abductor?

'Have you spoken to him yet?' he asked.

'No.' She sniffled. 'I'll do it tomorrow, once I've calmed down.' He nodded. 'I'm sorry to come here and dump this on you,' she said.

'I would have found out anyway.' His mind went back to the journal and he understood why Nouf hadn't written the man's name – the people most likely to read the journal would have been scandalized if they had found out. In fact, most of the journal would have upset them, but Nouf had protected Othman's identity.

It made his skin crawl to think of it.

He glanced at the journal sitting on the table. He wanted to tell her what he'd read, but he didn't want her to read it. Not tonight, maybe not ever. Standing up, he gathered his maps and charts and slipped the journal between them. He took everything and set it on the captain's desk in the kitchen.

Katya lifted her feet onto the sofa and wrapped her arms around her legs. She seemed to be nestling in for a while. He found a box of tissues in the bathroom and placed it on the table. He brought a pillow from the bedroom. She thanked him and clutched the pillow to her chest. He went into the kitchenette and took his time preparing more tea. When he brought the teapot, she forced a smile.

'Thank you, Nayir. I realize this must be awkward for you.'

'No,' he said. 'It's not awkward at all.' He sat down at the table and poured the tea.

☽

An hour later, he climbed up onto the deck. Below, Katya slept soundly on the sofa. She'd fallen asleep, and he'd decided it was best not to wake her. He'd brought a few old blankets from below, and now he laid them on the deck, making a pillow for himself from a ratty old life jacket. The boat bobbed rhythmically, and except for the gentle splash of water on the hull, the world was incredibly quiet and calm. Everything slipped behind him now – Nouf, Othman, the unborn baby. All he could think about was Katya.

26

Ten minutes later, Katya's driver came tramping down the pier, calling her name. Almost at once, she clambered up on deck, clapping a hand to her mouth.

'I'm all right, Ahmad! I'm so sorry, I can explain!'

Nayir stood up and glanced at the neighbours' boats. No one was in sight, and he hated himself for feeling so relieved.

'*Kati*,' Ahmad spat, barely able to contain his outrage. 'I have been trying to call you!'

She climbed onto the pier. 'I'm so sorry.'

'You said you'd leave your cell phone on. Your father is terribly concerned. It's a good thing he hasn't called the police!'

'*Wallahi*.' She whipped out her cell phone and called her father at once.

Nayir watched the conversation and tried to ignore the driver's nasty stare. 'Nothing happened,' he said finally, 'if that's what you think.'

'I don't think,' the driver snapped.

'I wouldn't do anything—'

The driver snorted and strode back down the pier.

☽

Once Katya had gone, he realized that sleep was impossible, so he made coffee and sat at the table, uncomfortably alone with his thoughts. The image of Othman making love to Nouf racked him with disgust. He could imagine them meeting accidentally in the quiet recesses of the Shrawi estate, terrified, awkward, scurrying quickly away from each other as if the mighty force of their attraction had been reversed. He could see the capitulation of desire, the two of them meeting at the zoo, filthy with dirt and sweat and sex, a consummation. And then the final twist: Othman's discovery of her plans to flee, his own desperate plans to ruin hers – a blow to the head, abandonment in the desert. At the very least, he had lied and cheated. At the worst, he had killed her. And yet for all its horror, the fact brought Nayir an unpleasant relief. Katya certainly wouldn't marry him now.

Forgive me for these wicked thoughts! He shut his eyes and tried to envision this as an isolated event, not a deeper darkness in Othman but rather a single failing that could have happened to any man. Othman was in a difficult situation. When a man falls in love with a sister, he is locked into her life. He cannot avoid knowing her; he cannot so easily avert his gaze. It would require a measure of self-control that even Nayir would find daunting. He had known Katya only a short time, but already he was having licentious thoughts about her. If he had to live with her, knowing she was not a sister by blood, it was possible that he, too, would fall into sin.

Yet Othman had been such an archetype of decency, so modest despite his immodest wealth, that Nayir's disappointment was fierce. Was goodness only on the surface of a man – the part that you could see? Was the heart always wicked? Even the most decent men were always on the verge of losing control. And Katya – did he trust her only

308

because he wanted to, because his body drove him to? If he couldn't trust a man like Othman, how could he trust a woman?

It struck him that she was gone, maybe for good. It would be awkward to contact her now. Just when she'd been liberated from Othman, she was less available than ever.

))

A sleepless night was followed by an aimless day. Nayir was too tired to go out, but at lunchtime he walked to the parking lot and bought a schawarma from the marina's vendor. He managed to avoid seeing Majid, but the quiet return to the boat, and the stifling isolation that met him there, only made the day stretch emptier than before. He had never felt quite so purposeless and dull, and it took him a while to realize that he was experiencing the vast and immobilizing dread of knowing that he had to talk to Othman but feeling he'd rather throw himself into the sea. Yet until he saw Othman, he would accomplish nothing else.

Later that afternoon, he drove to the estate. A butler met him at the door and took him to the sitting room, where Tahsin was sitting in state with a nervous-looking Qazi. It was curious that Qazi was there. Was he close to the brothers? He had told Nayir that he had come to the estate only once during his courtship with Nouf. Othman never talked about him, in fact had never once mentioned him until Nouf's disappearance.

Sitting across from Tahsin's bulk, Qazi looked like a reedy boy. He held a shaking teacup on his lap but was too nervous to drink, and his forehead glistened with sweat. When he saw Nayir, his face became eloquent with relief. Perhaps he had come to pay more personal condolences to the family.

Tahsin greeted Nayir and invited him in. Nayir shook

Qazi's hand and sat beside him, wondering at the cause of his distress.

'We were just discussing the future,' Tahsin said.

Qazi smiled nervously, sloshing his tea. Nayir was inclined to believe what he'd said about his reasons for loving Nouf – that she wasn't stiff or formal. In the sitting room, he seemed uniquely out of place.

'We can continue this later,' Tahsin remarked.

Just then, the door opened and Othman appeared with Fahad, the two of them escorting their father, Abu-Tahsin.

Tahsin got up to clear the pillows from the floor. With steps as slow as a clock's minute hand, the three men shuffled into the room. Abu-Tahsin's decrepitude was painful to see. In the course of a few weeks, this lithe and gregarious man had withered like a dried plum. His chest and arms were shrunken, and a host of new wrinkles netted his face. He could hardly stand on his own, and with each step his expression grew more taut. He didn't notice his guest until he was practically beside him.

'It's Nayir, father,' Tahsin said. 'Nayir ash-Sharqi.'

Abu-Tahsin's voice climbed out of the depths of his throat. 'Ahhmm.'

Nayir was shocked. 'Abu-Tahsin, I'm at your service.'

'Hahhhhmmm.'

Nayir stood back to let him pass. He cherished a single memory of Abu-Tahsin standing above Wadi Jawwah near Abu-Arish, aiming his rifle at a flock of white storks with a gleam in his eye. It was late afternoon and the sun fell on him in a golden haze, deepening the sable colour of his skin. Nayir remembered the sudden crack of the shot, the stork's unearthly skirl, the powder floating in the air like lines of white silk. Abu-Tahsin had turned to him and said, his voice deep like a rumour, 'The birds in the sky are not to be counted, and yet every one of them follows a pattern. Do you think this is a sign for prudent men?'

Nayir had said yes, it was probably a sign. At the time he thought only of the obvious meaning, as it says in the Quran, that Allah's existence can be known by His signs, the mysterious structures of the Universe. Yet here in the sitting room was another sign of sorts: the decrepitude of age, as dark and predictable as night.

Othman glanced at Nayir, his gaze inscrutable, and he whispered in passing: 'The doctor says he has to walk. Around the house three times a day. It keeps the blood from clotting.'

Nayir nodded sadly. The old man's spirit was gone.

Tahsin motioned for Fahad to let go of Abu-Tahsin, and he took his father's arm. The two brothers led him through the terrace door.

A moment later, Othman came back. Everyone turned, expecting perhaps that Abu-Tahsin was coming behind him. Othman regarded them awkwardly, and, to distract from their obvious discomfort, begged them to sit. It made Nayir nervous, and he realized that – for himself at least – their friendship was vanishing, replaced by the cold formality of the sitting room. Othman seemed to sense it, too. He avoided Nayir's gaze, and everyone sat.

Nayir tried not to stare but couldn't help it. Othman hadn't shaved; his clothing was rumpled, his skin dull from lack of sleep. Fahad asked Qazi about his father's business, and Qazi began to talk about shoes, account books, employees and foreign trade. Nayir waited, growing more anxious as the minutes went by. He felt ridiculously inferior, unable to participate in the conversation, or even to understand it. He had to keep reminding himself that Othman was the fraud, the one who had lied, the one who should be ashamed of himself.

Abruptly, Othman reached forward, picked up a box of dates and extended it to Nayir. 'Please have a date.'

'No, thank you.' Nayir touched his stomach.

'No, please. Just one.'

Nayir raised his hand. 'Really, I'd better not.' Beside him, Qazi and Fahad were absorbed in their conversation.

'You're looking pale,' Othman said.

Nayir plucked the front of his shirt from his chest. 'It must be the heat.'

'Would you believe, in a heat like this, I found my coat?'

'Where was it?'

'At the back of the closet.'

'Had you checked there before?' Nayir asked.

'I thought I did.' Othman seemed to lose his interest. He took a handful of dates and stood up with a grunt. 'Anyway, you're hot. Shall we walk?'

Appalled by the indiscretion of having admitted that he, Nayir ash-Sharqi, expert desert tour guide, was actually *hot*, he mumbled a vague protest as he followed Othman into the hallway. Silently they traversed dark passageways and cut across vast, empty rooms until they reached a terrace door. Othman led him out onto a narrow loggia that overlooked the sea. Nayir suddenly felt disoriented. He'd never been to this part of the house before. The ground sloped dangerously down towards the cliff. Only a stone wall at the patio's edge protected them from a hundred-metre drop to the rocky beach below.

Othman motioned him along the loggia and through a narrow doorway. 'Watch the stairs.'

They descended a dank metal staircase barely wide enough for Nayir's shoulders. The air had a tacky, industrial stench. Eventually, the stairs became shiny glass steps, and a blue light filtered up from below. Nayir walked carefully, fighting dread. Suddenly, he spotted movement beneath his feet, the undulating rhythms of kelp and sea anemone, the sudden flicker of a brightly coloured fish. At the bottom of the stairs, they stepped into an aquarium.

They were standing in the centre of an enormous glass cavern, easily as large as the house itself and glowing in a phosphorescent halo of light. On all sides the ocean stirred with luminous creatures sunk in sad isolation. It was cooler here, but Nayir still felt clammy, and the undersea pressure seemed to weigh on his chest. He felt as if he'd entered a dungeon.

'It's impressive,' he murmured. 'Did your family build this?'

Othman shook his head and began to walk. They wandered in silence, studying the vast assortment of fish. Nayir recognized a masked butterfly fish. Othman called his attention to a blue-spotted stingray. He watched politely as it glided away, but his mind returned to an image of Othman from Nouf's journal, rescuing her at sea. Then it switched to the opposite images: Othman grabbing her by the wrists, smashing her over the head, dumping her body at the bottom of a wadi. It was horrifying, and selfishly, Nayir felt betrayed. A man doesn't know a friend until he knows his friend's anger.

Could Othman, with his strict sense of tradition and family honour, really have done it? Fornicated, kidnapped, possibly killed? The man standing in the aquarium looked as if he'd been kidnapped himself.

'Have a seat.' Othman motioned to a metal bench that faced the widest glass panel. They both sat down. A school of black-spotted sweetlips shifted nervously in the glittering light. Othman watched them but seemed to retreat into himself, brooding.

Nayir crossed his arms to hide his unsteady hands. 'I thought only the King had an underground aquarium.'

'This used to be a royal house.'

'Ah, yes.' He smoothed down his shirt. He could feel a confession coming on.

'Brother, I'm sorry to have involved you in any of this,' Othman said. He sounded sincere, but something in his tone made Nayir turn his head. 'I talked to Katya this morning. She told me . . .'

Nayir hesitated. 'I'm sorry. I meant to tell you that I'd seen her.' Othman eyed him strangely. 'We had lunch,' Nayir said, which wasn't as hard as his next admission: 'And we went to the zoo.'

'Ah. The zoo.'

'I realize I should have told you earlier.'

Othman gave a sad laugh. 'You don't owe me any apologies. My sins are so much greater than yours.'

Nayir agreed, but felt the urge to console him anyway. 'A sin is a sin.'

'I appreciate everything you've done, Nayir.' The words sounded remote, empty, as if he were profoundly tired of formality. Nayir sensed that something was about to break, that it would take only a nudge to shatter the wall of restraint.

Othman kept his eyes on the sea creatures. 'I used to come here with Nouf.' He laid a hand on his mouth, and for a moment he looked regretful, but when he dropped his hand, his face was bitter and closed. 'Before she got engaged.'

Nayir's eye twitched. 'That must have been hard on you.'

He didn't reply; perhaps he felt it was an obvious remark. Eventually, Othman raised his chin. 'She loved it when I told her about the different fish. There was one fish here, we used to see it all the time. It's a grouper of some sort, and the thing about groupers is that they're all born female, and when they get older, some of them turn into males.' He gave a dry chuckle. 'She loved that. She said she wanted to be just like the grouper, so when she grew up she could act like a man.'

Nayir felt the same pervasive sadness he'd felt in the beach shack. He sat still, waiting.

'I actually told my father about it,' Othman said, giving a dry laugh. 'What a mistake. I told him I wanted to marry Nouf. At first he thought I was joking, so I played along, but I think he began to suspect that it was the truth, and he was disgusted by it. So disgusted that, when Katya came along, my father didn't care that her family wasn't like us; he didn't care that she was older. He just wanted me to get married. So we made the arrangements. But with Katya I made the biggest mistake of all.' He paused, struggling with his next words. 'She was a friend to me, and I didn't tell her what was truly in my heart.'

'That you didn't really love her?'

Othman shook his head. 'Not as I loved Nouf.'

Nayir experienced a poisonous admixture of relief, guilt, and crippling anger. The idea of Othman being in love with his sister was not so disgusting any more; it paled in comparison with Othman's behaviour to Katya. He had used her – first, to keep up appearances with his family, and second, as a comforting presence, someone to soothe his broken heart, never mind that he was going to break *her* heart. Perhaps he had even used her to punish Nouf, who had dared to get engaged to somebody else. Nayir flashed on the jacket bazaar and a heap of sad, empty wedding coats destined for a forgotten closet somewhere.

'So your father knew about your feelings for her,' Nayir said.

'Sort of. I didn't tell him everything.'

'He knew you were the father of her child?'

'I think he suspected it.'

Nayir knew Othman's next words would answer the deeper question that disturbed him – whether Othman had actually kidnapped her. He was afraid to ask, but he had to know.

'Is that why you paid for a private investigator – to prove to them that you didn't kidnap her?'

Beside him, Othman sat immobile, as if catatonic. Nayir knew he had to say it.

'You did kidnap her.'

Othman shut his eyes. The tears fell then, down his cheeks in a line on either side. Nayir looked away.

'I'm sorry,' Othman said. 'I know what you think.' After a painful moment when even the fish seemed to slow in their world, he raised his head. 'It's true that I loved her, but brother, believe me, I don't know what happened. I've been crazy, *crazy* trying to figure it out. It leads nowhere. I've found nothing—' His voice cracked, and he stopped. 'I paid for the investigator because I didn't know what happened, and that's the truth.'

'Nouf had bruises on her wrists.'

Othman shook his head. 'I didn't kidnap her.'

'We found your skin cells around the bruises.'

He seemed confused. Perhaps it was the word 'we'. But if it caused him pain, he didn't show it. 'Nouf and I fought just before she got kidnapped.' He swallowed hard. 'She told me she was going to run away to New York. I couldn't believe it.'

'So you grabbed her?'

'No, I was thrilled. I told her I wanted to plan a life with her. I told her we could move to New York together; I'd give her anything, let her do anything, but—' He paused. 'She didn't want to. She wanted to start over.'

'How did you end up grabbing her wrists?'

'I begged her, *please*, please don't go! She'd be ripping

316

out my soul. She was crying, too. She started to hit me. I grabbed her to make her stop, but it was hard.' He unbuttoned his sleeve and rolled it up, exposing a series of faint discolorations from his wrist to his elbow. They might have been from scratches that had happened two weeks before. 'She got me, too. I had to stop her. She was frantic. I didn't realize I'd hurt her.'

'Why was she so angry?'

Othman rolled down his sleeve with a steady hand. 'When I realized that she was telling the truth, that she didn't want me to come with her, I said something I shouldn't have. I told her I would stop her. I didn't mean I was going to kidnap her; I only meant that I would tell my father about her plans.' He covered his face with his hands and shook his head. 'I apologized. I told her I didn't mean it – and I *didn't* mean it. I just didn't want her to leave.'

Nayir nodded, not certain what to believe but stirred anyway by the sincerity of Othman's words. 'So you were meeting her at the zoo.'

'We met there, yes. It was private. She liked it.'

'How often did you meet there?'

He hesitated. 'Once a week.'

'She went to the zoo on the day she disappeared,' Nayir said.

Othman looked at him. 'Are you sure?'

'Yes. We found her shoe – and her footprints – on a service road behind the zoo. We also found evidence on her body. The dirt in her head wound matched the dirt from the service road. There was also some manure on her wrist. But there's something I don't understand. She fought with you that morning, and she went to the zoo after that. Why would she concoct a lie about needing to exchange her wedding shoes and then go to the zoo instead, when you weren't going to be there?'

Nayir waited, but Othman sat rigidly staring at the fish. 'I don't know,' he whispered.

'Is it possible she went there to meet somebody else?' Nayir asked.

'No, that's ridiculous. She probably went to . . . I don't know, maybe it reminded her of us.' He brought his hand to his eyes and pressed them hard. 'Maybe she went there to say goodbye.'

'But who else would have known about the zoo?'

Othman sighed. 'I don't know. Maybe she told Mohammed. She told him everything.'

'What about someone in the family?'

'She didn't tell anyone in the house – it was too risky.'

'Did she have any friends?'

He shook his head. 'She did have friends, but she wasn't the kind of person who would confide something like this to anyone. She was more comfortable with the dogs.'

'As far as we can tell, you're the only person who knew where she might have been going that day.' Nayir tried to keep the judgement out of his voice, but his thoughts were spiralling in on themselves. It seemed obvious now. Not only was Othman the only one who knew about the zoo, he was the only one with a motive to follow her that day. They'd just had a fight; she'd stormed out of the house. He had probably gone after her to rectify things – or to stop her from going to New York.

'Where did you go after the fight?' Nayir asked.

Othman crossed his arms tightly over his chest. 'I was too upset to stay here,' he said. 'I went for a drive. When I came back later that afternoon, she was gone.'

'You were alone in the car?'

'Yes.'

'I see.'

'I know,' Othman said. 'I wish I could offer you some

proof, but I can't. And your surprise about this mess – I have felt it myself, I still feel it. But I never actually looked at the *thing itself*.' He pinched his fingers together and poked the air with each word. Nayir saw the shame and anger in the gesture. 'I never had the guts. She never let me in. I spent months trying to open her up, trying to make her happy, to make her *trust* me.' He pressed his lips together to contain a sharp rage. 'After it happened, after I told her I loved her, she pushed me even further away. And dammit—' His voice cracked. 'I still loved her.' He turned away, angrily wiping tears from his cheeks.

Nayir turned back to the glass. A clown fish swam by, urgent and paranoid. Somewhere above them, a generator switched off, and silence descended. Nayir, feeling himself uniquely inept at discussing matters of the heart, became absorbed in his thoughts. He waited, too, for Othman to speak.

'I would never have hurt her,' Othman finally said. 'Disgusting though it may seem to you, I loved her, and she was carrying my child.'

☽

Nayir returned to his Jeep. He could feel helplessness sinking into him like sand in an hourglass, filling him, weighing him, and he wanted nothing more than to return to his boat and set out to sea, perhaps to a quiet spot down the coast. Drop anchor. Fish. Yes, he would fish, and lie in the sun, and watch the windsurfers and the gulls and the boats passing by. That was all he needed. Just a few fish and a quiet place to forget the one thing that was bothering him: Othman hadn't asked what else he'd discovered about the case. There were too many lingering questions. Why had they found her body so close to the old campsite? Why were the camel and the motorcycle together in the back of the

319

truck? Could Nouf have even done that by herself? Where was the truck? If Othman was genuinely perplexed by her kidnapping, wouldn't he want answers to these things as well?

Just as Nayir was climbing into his car, he caught a glimpse of black and saw a woman emerge from a nearby Toyota. It was Katya. He was struck by her courage, coming to face Othman so soon. When she saw him, she flushed and averted her gaze.

'Hello,' she said.

He greeted her, but she seemed at a loss for words, and an awkward silence deadened the space between them.

'Thank you,' she said, 'for everything last night.'

'You're welcome.' He felt the urge to say something – anything – but nothing seemed right. He felt unbearably self-conscious. Not knowing what else to do, he said good-bye and turned back to his car. She turned just as quickly and walked towards the house.

27

The boat bobbed quietly on the waves. Nayir sat on deck, fishing rod in hand, staring at the expanse of sea. From the left, he heard a buzzing, a jet ski no doubt, and sure enough, a moment later a strange woman came zipping over the water. She was wearing a bikini that looked like scraps from a tailor's floor, something that would rip if she sneezed. She was also pressing buttons on a cell phone, the other hand on the skis, steering recklessly. Defiantly, he didn't avert his gaze. He waited, watching. How long would it take her to realize he was staring? But she didn't notice. She was absorbed in her phone call. Her sleek brown thigh failed to arouse him. All he could think of was the fish she was scaring off.

Two days on the water had managed to put some distance between him and the events of the past few weeks. This morning he had finally been able to think about his conversation with Othman. It seemed absurdly false from a distance. Othman had hit Nouf on the head and dragged her out to the desert and left her there. So what if they hadn't found his prints on the service road at the zoo? They could have been obscured in the struggle. Even Mutlaq would admit to that.

But why had Othman done it? Had he needed to release his rage? Why not some other kind of release – a forgetting, moving on? *Those who believe, and suffer Exile and strive with might and main in Allah's cause, with their goods and their persons, have the highest rank in the sight of Allah.* That was true jihad, the giving up of goods, hopes, desires, when life demands it, when *not* to give up would lead to wrong. But Othman hadn't given up, and he'd become a liar. His love for Nouf – was that a lie, too?

The only question now was what to do about it. In theory, Nayir should take the whole thing to the police, to the judges or the mosque and the men in charge of law, but since the examiner's office had already closed the case – decided, in fact, that there was no case to close – then what hope did he have of stirring up justice from a system so easily corrupted by the rich? Even with the evidence that he and Katya had collected, there was not enough proof that Othman had actually kidnapped his sister or delivered that last blow, the one that had knocked her unconscious and allowed her to drown in the wadi. Nayir acknowledged that he could be wrong about Othman, and his mind circled relentlessly back to this hope.

It was possible, of course, to try Othman for *zina*, specifically, for sex out of wedlock. But the family would issue a punishment for that, which would probably be the same as no punishment at all – or, perhaps, a punishment for everyone. Nayir could imagine the look on Nusra's face if she ever found out that Othman had been intimate with Nouf. Personally, he hoped to spare her the knowledge. Othman could be tried for incest, but that didn't seem fair either. It wasn't really incest in a technical sense – he wasn't her blood – and even if a court could establish that he was her brother under law, and *mehram* to her, Nayir didn't think it was humane to punish a man for being in love, or for thinking he was in love, if that's what it was.

There was nothing he could do but engage in his own time-honoured practice of jihad: a giving up of his friendship with Othman, a silent but perhaps strongly felt protest against his friend's behaviour.

Forgiveness is incumbent upon Allah, it says in the Quran, but only when a man commits a sin in ignorance, and immediately repents. Forgiveness is not incumbent for those who go on committing the same sins until death puts an end to them.

Yet the Quran also says that Allah forgives all sins, and is all-merciful.

The jet ski faded away, and he heard a ringing below. It was his cell phone. Annoyed, he took his time laying the rod aside, climbing down the ladder, and fishing through the junk on his desk to find the damned thing. It continued to ring until he flipped it open and heard a crackling.

'Nayir? It's Katya.'

'Hi—'

'I'm sorry to bother you, but I've been thinking about your question. You know, the one you asked me at the restaurant – whether I would deceive a husband like Nouf was going to do? That day I told you that I probably would, and I still think I would, if I were desperate enough, but I'm not. That's the thing – I don't think I'll ever be.'

He wasn't sure what to say.

She sighed. 'I'm sorry to call you like this. You must think I'm crazy. It's been bothering me. I think you would have to be desperate to deceive someone. Nouf was deceiving Othman. She didn't tell him anything about Eric or her plans to go to New York until the very last minute. And that's what angered him, that she'd been hiding it. But here's the thing: I think she was leaving *because* of him, because she was so ashamed of her feelings. She could have had that life here – everything she wanted. But Othman would be here, and no matter who she married, no matter what she did, she would always have to see him.'

Nayir remembered a passage from the journal. Shuffling through the papers on the desk, he found the notebook, opened it, and flipped through the pages. There it was, a short, simple passage that hadn't made much sense to him before:

I can't stay here any more. I can't bear it. It will always be here, this feeling. I'll never escape it, not here.

When he'd first read it, he had thought she was referring to a general sense of oppression, but Katya was right. It was probably specifically about her feelings for Othman.

'What exactly are you saying?' Nayir asked.

'Nouf was desperate enough to run away to New York, but that was just an admission of the fact that she truly loved him. It scared the hell out of her.'

'All right.'

'She was desperate enough to run away, but I don't think Othman was desperate enough to kill her.'

Nayir closed the book and sat down. He had an image of Katya sitting at a desk somewhere, just as he was sitting here now, both of them pondering a way to absolve Othman. He knew what she was thinking – hoping, demanding – that Othman loved her, that he didn't love Nouf. It was sad. He couldn't help feeling sorry for her – more than for himself – because at least he had managed to face the possibility of an awful truth.

She gave an empty laugh. 'Othman wasn't enough of an animal, does that make sense?'

He didn't reply.

'Believe me, he's not.'

He realized that he hadn't told her about the journal yet. And he couldn't, not right now, maybe not ever. In the journal, Othman wasn't an animal exactly, but Nouf's words

painted a picture of a desperate man, someone who followed her around at sea, to the zoo. An uneasy silence hung
between them. He couldn't find a single word to break it.

'Nayir.'

'Yes.'

'Please tell me what you're thinking.'

He hesitated. 'There are things that can make men turn
into animals,' he said, 'even if they're not normally animals.'

Another pause seemed to last for ever. 'You think I'm just
trying to excuse him,' she said. 'I'm not. Think back. He
was the one who hired that private investigator. He sent you
to the desert.'

'But he was also the one who tried to stop you analysing
the DNA.'

'That's just it,' she said. 'He didn't want me to find out
that he was the baby's father – it's obvious why. But he
wanted to find out what happened to Nouf in the desert,
because *he didn't know.*'

Nayir had to admit that it explained the inconsistency.
'You may be right,' he said, fighting a strange mixture of
excitement and disappointment. Perhaps Othman wasn't
guilty after all. 'Then who killed her?' he asked.

'I don't know. Who was desperate enough?'

It felt as if he'd been over this too many times before.
Who wanted to silence Nouf? Who had a reason? There was
no evidence to direct his thoughts. Once again he was adrift
in the sea of his own imagination, floating further and further from an understanding of things.

'I talked to Othman,' she said, a hesitation in her voice.
'He apologized. And I think he really meant it.'

'I would imagine.'

'But we decided to call off the wedding.'

Nayir's stomach rose into his throat. 'I'm sorry to hear that.'

'Yes, well . . .' She gave a resigned sigh which was meant

to convey strength but which managed only to convey how lost she truly felt. Or so it sounded to him.

The remainder of the conversation felt awkward. They talked briefly about fishing and the weather on the sea. He told her about finding the motorcycle at the beach shack, and the inconsistency of the footprints they'd found at the zoo. But as he fumbled along, he had the sense that they were supposed to be talking about Othman. Maybe he was failing to ask certain questions, to ride fearlessly into those territories of the heart that he didn't understand. But revealing that ignorance terrified him; he was glad she wanted to know about fish. Only after he hung up did it occur to him that perhaps she didn't want to talk about Othman at all, and that their chatter about the weather had provided her with comfort enough. At least, that's what he hoped.

That night he lay on deck, bobbing gently on the sea. Thinking about Fatimah, he realized that the thing he most resented was her cloaking of truth, her failure to tell him that she was entertaining other men while she courted him. Othman's own lies of omission were not quite as personal, but they stung in their own awful way, and Nayir wondered whether he was doing it himself, lying to others. What *wasn't* he saying to those he cared for? His own jihad against Othman seemed cowardly then, and he stood adorned in a dishonourable silence, plumped and feathered with false piety. A passage from the Quran sprang to mind: *We have bestowed garments upon you to cover your shame as well as to adorn you, but the garment of righteousness is best.* It was said that Allah created man free of evil and shame, but that once man was touched by sin, his thoughts and deeds became garments that covered and revealed him, showing him for what he was. Nayir knew that if he was an honest man he would stop veiling himself to hide the shame of Othman's naked sin; he would have to confront him.

28

Standing in front of the Shrawi estate, on a white marble courtyard flushed salmon with dusk, Nayir watched the red womb of sunset enclose the world. The front of the house was most beautiful now, when a pale vermilion streaked the clouds and the sea shone the colour of its namesake. He marvelled at the details he had missed before: the elegant curve of the tiles on the roof, the complexity of the cliff wall, the fine grain of the marble beneath his feet.

A breeze flapped the hem of his pale blue robe, raising the scent of manure from the stables below. It was a comforting smell. A prayer came to mind, and he whispered it to himself.

> *By the heaven, and by the nightly visitant!*
> *Would that you knew what the nightly visitant is!*
> *It is the star of piercing brightness.*
> *For every soul there is a guardian watching it.*

He hoped for a guardian himself.

Turning, he crossed the courtyard in front of the main door and crept past the windows until he found the side path that led down to the stables. He wanted to see the camel one more time. *And this*, he thought, *might be the last time*. It was darker than he'd expected, but he had his penlight, which was enough to guide him safely down the stairs.

The lower courtyard was empty. Overhead, houselights lit the scene, so he switched off his penlight and crossed the court to the stable door. It was open; he slipped inside. After a minute, the penlight came out again, this time cupped in his hand. Nothing stirred. He made his way down the stalls until he reached the last one on the left. Peering through a crack in the wood, he saw that Nouf's camel was sleeping. He hesitated then, not certain he should wake her. She might startle and wake the others. But he heard a gentle shifting behind the door. He pressed his lips to the crack and gave a soft blow. Ever so soft. Peering back inside, he saw that she had moved.

Just then, he heard a rustle behind him. He spun and aimed his penlight down the long corridor, but nothing moved. He waited. Hearing no further sound, feeling no other presence, he turned back to the stall.

The camel was awake. Gingerly, he opened the door and stepped inside, reaching out to rub her ears. She nuzzled his arm, and he moved his hand down her neck and back. Eventually his fingers found the burn mark on her leg, and he probed it again, feeling its shape. It was, indeed, the Honda logo.

He continued stroking the camel, who grunted merrily for the attention. Outside, he heard the rustling again. It sounded like the swish of a robe. He turned and listened. Curious, he crept out of the stall, and shut the door. The rustle came again. When he stopped, the sound stopped with him. He felt a presence now. Someone stood on the straw between him and the door. He flicked off his light to let his eyes adjust, took a hesitant step, then another; the rustling continued. He walked toward the sound, keeping as close to the stall doors as possible. The intruder was closing. As soon as he felt the warm aura of body heat, he flipped on his penlight and caught a woman full in the face.

She winced and shrunk back. He recognized the camel-keeper's daughter; a large brown bruise above one eye was faded but still visible. Although her head was covered with a scarf, her face was fully exposed. She didn't turn away but stood patiently while he stared. His modesty took hold and he lowered the light, but his eyes didn't leave her face.

'How did you get that bruise?' he asked.

Her face tightened with what he thought was anxiety. She raised a shaking finger and beckoned him closer. He stared in surprise, but she was backing up, gesturing. *Come, follow me.*

He went after her, swept on by curiosity. Halfway down the corridor, she stopped at a stall door and put her hand on the latch. She waited for Nayir to approach with the light.

She swung the stall door open so that Nayir stood on one side and she on the other. He was left staring into an empty stall while she waited on the other side of the door, four fingers wound around its edge.

'What . . .' He cleared his throat. 'What do you want me to do?'

He imagined he heard a sigh. 'Look inside,' she whispered.

With a flash of embarrassment, he looked into the stall. He shone his penlight on the walls. At the back of the stall hung a thick grey tarp, but otherwise, nothing was there.

'On the floor,' she said.

His light caught a metallic glint on the ground. It was a handle, a trapdoor. Bending over, he brushed the straw away. The latch came up with a gentle squeak, and he raised the door slowly, revealing a small compartment. He shone his penlight inside and found a black velvet bag, as large as a woman's purse. He picked it up and loosened the drawstring.

The bag was full of gold. There were rings and bracelets, earrings and necklaces, all 24-carat. Rubies and diamonds glinted in the torchlight. Most of the gold items were stamped with the letter 'N'. He shut the bag and left the stall.

The girl's fingers were still clutching the door. Although he wanted to see her face, he thought it best to keep the door between them.

'Who put this here?' he asked. She didn't reply. 'Tell me. Who gave you that bruise? Did he knock you out the day Nouf disappeared?'

Silence. He almost swung back the door, but he didn't want to scare her.

'Who was it?' he asked gently.

'I don't know,' she whispered.

'But you trust me.'

She didn't reply.

'You trusted me enough to show me this, so trust me now.'

Her fingers disappeared, and he heard her walk rapidly back toward the stable door.

☽

In the courtyard in front of the house, Nusra ash-Shrawi stood in a penumbra of shadow between the night and the brightness from the foyer within. When she heard his footsteps coming up the side path, she turned to the sound.

'Nayir,' she said.

He kept the velvet bag close to his side and hoped that Nusra wouldn't hear the faint clinking of jewels. 'Good evening, Um-Tahsin.'

'Where were you?' she asked. 'I heard your Jeep, but then you didn't come.'

Nayir stopped beside her. 'I went to see the camels first.'

She chuckled softly, groped for his arm, and steered him toward the house. 'You may not be Bedouin by blood,' she said, tapping his chest, 'but you are in spirit.'

'Thank you,' he murmured.

'I will take you to the sitting room.'

He stepped through the door with trepidation. If Um-Tahsin knew he was here, then who else had noticed?

Inside, she released his arm and motioned for him to follow, but instead of the familiar path to the sitting room, she led him deeper into the mansion, down corridors as dark as her blindness. Nayir was forced to slow down and fumble his way through. He wanted to ask where she was taking him, but he didn't have the nerve to break the silence, and for a terrible moment he wondered if she was leading him into a trap.

Abruptly, they entered a high-walled courtyard where the starlight twinkled. The air was moist from the spray of fountains. Nusra motioned him through another door, into a narrow hallway and through a spacious gallery that seemed to have no purpose except as a vast, almost desert-like space for the servants to cross. With a quickness that startled him, she halted.

She took his arm, and her grip was firm. 'I may not be able to see,' she said, 'but I know the workings of my household better than most.' She leaned closer, so close that he could feel her warmth. 'I knew you were in the camel stalls.'

He didn't move. The glow of a nearby candle cast long shadows on her cheeks, deepening her scowl. 'I heard you go down there, and now I can smell her on your clothing,' she hissed, tightening her grip. 'Her name is Asiya. And if you're going to ruin her, you'd better marry her.'

Nayir, who had been holding his breath, let out an imperceptible sigh. 'Please, Um-Tahsin. I'm an honest man.'

She raised her chin sternly, and he felt himself blushing. 'It's about time you married anyway.'

He couldn't speak. After a long, painful wait, she released his arm and stood back, drawing herself up and restoring her usual dignity. 'Speaking of marriage,' she said, 'did Othman tell you our news?'

'No, what is that?'

She turned and led him on. 'Our daughter Abir is going to marry next month.'

'Congratulations.'

'She is marrying her cousin, Qazi, the young man who was supposed to marry Nouf.'

'Ah. That's convenient.' That must have been why Qazi had been at the house that day. Nayir thought of the boy's face, so young and uncomfortable.

'Yes, and prudent as well.' She stopped short at the sitting-room door. 'Abir will be right for him.'

Her words hung ominously in the air. Was Abir more right than Nouf? Um-Tahsin opened the door and motioned him inside. 'I don't believe Othman is home yet, but I will check. Meanwhile, I'll have a servant bring tea.'

Without another word, she left.

Nayir looked around the room. Two of the window screens were gone, and a bank of white candles flickered on the windowsills, casting a golden light. He took a seat on the sofa and waited uneasily, imagining Othman's arrival, the awkwardness to which he knew they would both succumb. Everything he had planned to say seemed too harsh now. *I know you killed your sister. You hit her, took her to the desert, and abandoned her. You wanted her to die.* Wasn't this certainty, in the absence of proof, just another kind of sinful pride?

Reaching into his pocket, Nayir took out the bag of gold

that had belonged to Nouf. It was possible that Othman had stolen the gold and hidden it to prevent Nouf from leaving. But how had he got the combination to the safe where the gold was kept?

Allah, I need your help. Guide my thoughts. Nayir's mind turned back to the sites of his discoveries: the zoo, Eric's apartment, the shack at the beach. Had he overlooked something? A small detail that was quietly out of place? *Help me, Allah. Help me see the detail.* He shut his eyes and tried to clear his mind, but his thoughts were racing. What if there was no detail? Perhaps the killer had left no trace, nothing to direct him.

One image persisted in his mind: a map, the city map he'd found in the shack, half hidden beneath the bottom hem of a robe. *What is it?* he thought. There was nothing unusual about the map. Nouf had used it to find the zoo. He reached into his pocket and touched his prayer beads. Shutting his eyes, he continued to pray, a long prayer that unspooled like a mesmerizing dream and that found its refrain in a simple stanza:

> *Oh Allah, my Light, my Guide*
> *Show me the kernel of the truth*
> *Give me the heart of a lion*
> *And a falcon's eye.*

He was on his fifth repetition when the door creaked open and a woman entered. Nayir's eyes sprang open. In amazement he stared at the black robe, the burqa, and finally the hands, which belonged to Abir. He stood up.

This time, she set the coffee service on the table. Keeping her veil down, she poured a cup and handed it to Nayir, spilling only the slightest drop. He was surprised by her new confidence.

'I've been practising,' she said. 'Please be careful, it's hot.'

He took the cup, sat down again, and found himself staring at the sleeve of her robe. All of a sudden his thoughts clicked into place. It wasn't the map – the map meant nothing – it was the robe that had obscured the map.

A man's white robe had hung in the shack.

At the time, it had seemed natural. Nouf wore the robe when she went out on the motorcycle; she had to dress like a man. But Mohammed had said that Nouf wore a black cloak when she left the island, then changed into the white robe when she got to the beach. She was wearing the white robe when she died, so where was her black cloak? And why was there another white robe in the shack?

Who else would wear a white robe, and then leave it at the beach?

Nayir was stunned by the discovery, empowered by it even as he marvelled at his ignorance. He looked up at Abir, wondering suddenly why she'd come. Did she want information, or was she afraid he was going to say something to Othman?

'I think I know what happened to your sister,' he said calmly.

Abir stood back and wrapped her arms protectively around her chest, but he saw a frown in her eyes.

'And I think you might know, too,' he added.

She bowed her head, a gesture he now recognized as a feint of modesty. 'How would I know that?'

'I found this.' He set the black bag on the table. Abir looked at the bag with mock-confusion, then tried to let recognition seep slowly into her eyes, but the result was a look of childish stagecraft. 'Is that Nouf's jewellery bag?' she asked, her voice a hoarse whisper. Unfolding her hands, she quickly knelt by the table, lifted her burqa, and pried

334

open the bag. Seeing its contents, she rolled her eyes and let out a moan that managed to approximate authentic grief. 'Why would she leave it at the house?' she asked, clutching the bag to her chest.

'How do you know she left it at the house?'

She paled.

'I think you can stop pretending now,' he said. Abir's puzzlement held a touch of hostility. 'She never took it out of the safe in the first place,' he went on, energized by the sudden clicking-into-place of his thoughts. 'You took it out. You had to make it look as if she ran away, and you knew that if she disappeared, someone would check to see if her gold was gone. My only question is: why didn't you find a better place to hide it?'

'You think *I*—?' she sputtered unconvincingly. Abir swallowed, blinked, and shook her head as if to chase away a fly. Her face wore a brief look of fear, but it resolved to the cold, well-mannered aspect that belonged in a Shrawi sitting room. 'You're wrong about this,' she said bluntly. 'I have no idea what happen—'

'Stop.' He raised his hand. 'Lying will only make your sins grow greater. I know what you've done.' He imagined she'd seen the flash of excitement in his eyes; she struggled to compose herself. Carefully setting the bag on the table, she tried to stand up but seemed unable. She was trembling.

'You don't know what you're talking about,' she said, but her eyes were fearful.

'I hear you're getting married,' he said, 'to Nouf's fiancé.'

'He's not her fiancé.' There was more vehemence in the comment than he expected.

'He was going to marry her.'

'But he didn't love her,' she spat. 'And she didn't love him.'

Nayir saw the anger in her face and decided to take a risk. 'She had everything, didn't she? Everything you wanted.'

'I don't know.' She scowled.

'You were jealous that she was going to marry Qazi. You wanted to marry him, but you couldn't. She was older, so she got first choice.'

'She didn't love him.' She clutched herself and started to shake, her eyes welling with angry tears. 'I knew what she was doing, sneaking around and having sex with Mohammed.'

'Did she tell you that?'

'How else did she get pregnant? It's disgusting what she did! The only reason she wanted to marry Qazi was because he was going to be rich some day, and because he wouldn't care if she cheated on him.'

No doubt she was telling the truth, as she knew it; her high emotion was like a furnace, and the tears burned honestly down her cheeks. But from here, the rest of his theory was guesswork, based on too few clues and his own imagination.

'Why don't you tell me what happened?' he said. 'The Quran says there is forgiveness for those who repent.'

She looked at the floor and, shutting her eyes, declined with a proud shake of the head.

'All right,' Nayir said. 'Here's what I think. You planned it. It must have taken a while to figure everything out – how to get her to the desert, which truck to use, how to steal the camel, everything. It was a lot of work. But I think you knew that she was meeting someone at the zoo.'

She opened her eyes and regarded him with a mixture of curiosity and fear.

'Did it sicken you?' he asked.

'She was seeing *Mohammed*,' Abir spat.

'I have news for you,' he said. 'She wasn't seeing Mohammed. She was sleeping with someone else.'

'Who?'

Nayir held back, enjoying the fact that he finally had some answers, even as he was unwilling to give up Othman. 'Let me go back a little bit,' he said. 'You wanted to get rid of her so that you could have Qazi to yourself—' Seeing her eyes flash, he raised his hand. 'Or so that you could protect Qazi from her. And the only way to do that was to make it look as if she ran away. The best place to take her was the desert. No one would ever find her out there. But in order to make it look like she went to the desert, you had to steal a camel.'

She replied with a look of disgust that he found oddly encouraging.

'It's hard to steal a camel, especially in broad daylight, but you knew this camel; she was Nouf's favourite, and the camel probably trusted you. It wasn't actually too difficult getting her into the back of a pick-up truck. What did you do – make her walk up a plank? The same plank you later used to roll Nouf's motorcycle onto the truck?' At the mention of the motorcycle, Abir's rigid countenance showed a mild crack of fear, but she kept her jaw firm.

'Anyone could have stolen that camel,' she said.

'Yes, but it's a big feat for a girl your size. I was just wondering about the practicalities. She's a pretty docile camel, but still.' Seeing that she wouldn't offer up an explanation, he went on. 'I think a plank would be the easiest way. There were planks in the courtyard. You brought the truck around from the front lot. Pretty easy to steal a truck; your brothers keep the keys in the cloakroom by the front door. So you stole a truck from the lot. You drove it around to the back courtyard and got the camel into the back. You also took a pipe from behind the stable door. And nobody noticed except the keeper's daughter, but you just hit her with the pipe. It probably knocked her right out.'

She seemed oddly pleased, but then she lowered her

gaze – well-trained, he imagined, not to show her pride. Her quiet self-satisfaction irritated him; he must have made a mistake.

'No, of course . . .' he said reflectively. 'You were smart enough to know the best time to steal the camel – when no one was around. The keeper's daughter caught you when you were hiding the gold?' Abir's eyes flashed with anger and he knew he was right. 'Was it the same day you kidnapped Nouf?'

She didn't reply.

'No matter,' he said. 'You got the camel in the truck. You had a weapon – the pipe. You put the wooden plank in the truck. All you needed was Nouf, and you knew where to find her. She must have told you about her meetings at the zoo.'

'I found out about those myself,' Abir said.

'How?'

'Just because I knew about her behaviour,' Abir said, 'doesn't mean that I killed her.'

Nayir forced patience. 'How did you find out?'

'I followed her to the beach hut one day and found her map to the zoo. When she came home, I went back to the beach and took the motorcycle and went to the zoo myself.' Her chin jutted forward with an unmistakable look of righteousness. 'I found condoms in the motorcycle.'

'But you still didn't know who she was seeing.' He looked for a reaction and saw only the façade of moral justice. 'You got to the zoo before she did,' he said, 'and waited for her. Once she pulled up on her motorcycle, you knocked her out. How?'

She was silent.

'Now that I think of it,' he said, 'how could you be certain that she wouldn't be with her lover? I don't think you intended to kidnap both of them.'

'You see,' she said, a wicked satisfaction showing in her eyes, 'your story doesn't make sense.'

'You must have planned to get there either before her lover arrived, or after he was gone. You knew already that Nouf went to the zoo by herself, those moments of freedom she cherished on her motorcycle . . .' Nayir watched her face carefully. 'You knew that she met Mohammed there, and you probably also realized that he ran errands for her, to keep up her alibi at home.'

'He was stupid,' she said.

'Did she come home with shopping bags full of clothes she never wore?'

'She came home smelling like an animal.' The hostility in her voice gave him a brief, wicked thrill; it carried all the reckless anger that had driven her to kill her sister. Even if her composure didn't crack entirely, this small fracture was a satisfying marker of her guilt.

'So you suspected that at some point Mohammed would leave to do the shopping,' he went on, 'and Nouf would be alone. You were lucky to arrive when she was alone, probably before Mohammed got there. But I'm still wondering: how did you knock her out? Her motorcycle would have been parked on the service road, and it would have taken no time at all for you to haul it into the back of the truck. Then what? Did you wait in the bushes and spring out at her? Or did you actually talk to her?' He studied her face for a clue but saw only reserve. 'I can't imagine that you did. How would you have explained the fact that you were there, not to mention that you were driving a truck with a camel – and her motorcycle – in the back? No, you must have surprised her. You came at her from the bushes—' He touched the spot on his temple that coincided with Nouf's head wound. 'That's why she was hit on the side of the head. You certainly knocked her out; she didn't even wake up later when it started to rain. But I'm getting ahead of myself. You knocked her out. She fell. We found drag marks where you pulled her body to the truck.'

Abir looked as if she were tolerating the inane rantings of an elderly uncle.

'It's funny,' he said, 'my footprint specialist confused your prints, so it looked as if Nouf had stood up again. But those were your prints we saw. Those were your prints at the beach, too.'

'Your story is ridiculous,' she said.

'It's your story, too.' He saw the heat on her cheeks, and he plunged ahead: 'Your next problem was getting to the desert,' he said, 'but you'd planned for that, too. You'd stolen your brother's jacket with his desert maps and his GPS systems, and you figured out how to use them. You had to find a place to take her where she wouldn't be found, so you thought you'd head out to the last campsite Othman had gone to, because the GPS would be able to lead you there and back, wouldn't it? It was already programmed, and although it's a pretty high-tech machine, it wasn't so hard that you couldn't use it. Once you were out there, you could head away from the camp and dump her body where no one would find her. That way, she was stranded in the wilderness, but you were not, because you could follow the wadi back to the campsite and navigate your way back to the estate, thanks to the GPS. The campsite wasn't that hard to get to anyway, was it?'

She gave him a cold look, and he imagined he'd insulted her. Her pride was showing through now; the only trace of modesty left was the tight way she clutched her torso, hands tucked into her armpits.

'Once you got to the desert, you could drive the truck right up to the wadi's edge, and then it was only a matter of pushing Nouf out of the front seat into the wadi, maybe not realizing it was a wadi at all. It was just a convenient dip in the ground where people would be less likely to notice her.'

'I know what a wadi is,' she snapped.

'So you pushed her out of the truck, dropped her in the wadi. Then you drove – where? Maybe further upstream? You had to find a place to dump the camel, far enough away from Nouf that she wouldn't be likely to find her.'

Abir maintained a stubborn silence.

'Then you drove back towards the city, but you had to get rid of the truck. You obviously picked a clever enough location; it still hasn't been found. From there you climbed onto the motorcycle and drove back into the city. It was clever, I think, using her motorcycle. That's how you got home. Except you left behind some evidence. The motor-cycle logo burned its brand into the camel's leg.'

Her face showed another quick tremor of fear. 'So?'

'I think it's obvious proof that the camel and the motor-cycle were at close quarters,' he said. 'Somewhere extremely hot.' She looked as if she would speak, but she didn't indulge him. 'The whole trip took only – what? – three hours? Half an hour to the zoo, an hour to the desert, half an hour dumping the body, and another hour back to the beach. You were back before anyone noticed you were missing, and when you rode up on your jet ski, I'm sure they thought you were just out skiing. When I think about it now, it's pretty amazing that you did all of that by yourself. You're just a young girl.'

'You don't know anything about girls,' she spat.

The comment struck him harder than he would have liked, but he pushed it aside and focused on her face. He saw there the hardness he expected in a murderer. Whether it came from the Shrawi upbringing or simply her personal-ity he couldn't say, but it sickened him. She had barely protested at his reconstruction of events, and although her outburst had betrayed a motive of jealousy, it was her silence that disturbed him. It accepted his story. Judging by the remoteness in her eyes, she wasn't facing guilt; she was hardening herself, cloaking the truth behind the curtain of her femininity, the right to remain silent.

'I congratulate you,' he said, bitterness chopping his words. 'It's amazing that you managed to pull it off and confound everyone.'

'People are stupid.'

He sat still, holding his anger in check. 'If people are stupid, then that includes you. There were a lot of details you had to work through, but you forgot one thing.'

'Oh?'

'Clothing. When you drove back to the hut, you had to get rid of your white robe, the one you wore to disguise yourself as a man. So you hung it on the hook.'

The pride and defiance left her face.

'If Nouf ran away,' he said, 'wouldn't her black robe still be hanging on that hook?'

Abir quickly conjured her smugness again, draping it over her face like a veil. 'That could be anyone's cloak.'

'I think it proves that someone was in the hut after Nouf disappeared. That person stole her black cloak to hide the fact that she was there. But they left a white cloak that shouldn't have been there. Who would want to do that?'

'I don't know.'

His temper was rising, and he sat forward, lurching close to her face. 'You would. You left her in the desert to die. You might like to think it was an accident, but your blow to the head left her unconscious, and when the rains came she didn't stand a chance. She drowned. Do you tell yourself that it wasn't your fault? That it was her fault for not waking up in time to get out of the wadi? Let me tell you that even if she had got up and out of the wadi, the heat and the sun-light would have killed her anyway. You didn't leave her a camel, or a truck, or even a bottle of water. You left her out there to die.'

Abir wore a sneer that equalled his own, but she kept her mouth shut.

'I am ashamed to say it,' he said, 'but I never considered that a woman could have done this. It was my ignorance, of course. I couldn't imagine it.' He took a breath, trying to calm himself, but it didn't work. 'And this was all about Qazi? I guess that means you didn't know that she was plan-ning to abandon Qazi on their honeymoon.'

Abir made no effort to hide her shock.

'Yes,' he said. 'She was making arrangements to live in New York. She'd even found someone to put her up for a while, until she could find her own place.'

'That's not true!'

'It is.' There was no satisfaction in seeing her horror; it only angered him more. 'She didn't want to be with Qazi. She wanted someone else – and something else.'

Abir bit her lip so hard he thought she would puncture it. 'She was only marrying Qazi for the money,' she said, but without conviction. 'She wouldn't have left him so easily.'

'Are you so sure?'

Fear flashed across her face, but his anger roared through him and he couldn't find pity in his heart, only a vague dis-gust. Had the sisters tormented each other enough to stoke this kind of hatred? He'd heard nothing about it until now. Katya would know better, but he guessed that Abir was just uncommonly self-serving. Averting his gaze, he sat back on the couch and stared at the coffee service.

'I don't believe she was seeing someone else,' she said. 'You're just saying that to upset me.'

'There was someone else,' Nayir said. 'Someone she

loved much more than Qazi. But I won't tell you who it was, because I think it would only cause more pain.' *And give you the chance to blame someone else*, he thought.

'But she was still using Qazi.' Her voice was shrill now. 'Still lying to him and sleeping with another man!'

Nayir nodded once, a grudging agreement. 'But I don't understand why that meant you had to kill her. I don't think there's any sense in it, when you could have stopped the marriage simply by telling Qazi about her behaviour.'

She was sitting on her haunches, hands gripping her thighs, fingers pinching into the fabric brutally. Something in the jerky dance of muscles on her face indicated that this was the most disturbing question of all. Nayir sat forward with new interest.

'Or was it that he wouldn't have believed you?' he whispered.

'Of course he would,' she said lamely.

'Maybe he loved Nouf so much that he might not have even cared?'

'That's not true!' she cried. 'He wouldn't have believed me, but that's only because he doesn't think ill of people.'

'But you're not so sure,' Nayir went on. 'What if you told him and he said to himself: *That Abir must be crazy!*'

'I'm not crazy!'

'Only one thing could be worse,' Nayir said. 'What if he believed you, but chose to be with her anyway?'

'He wouldn't do that!'

'But it's bothering you, isn't it – not knowing what he would have done?'

She sat glowering at him with all the malice in her being, but he felt immune to it now.

'Did you ever talk to Nouf about this?' he asked.

She let out a dry laugh. 'You can't *talk* to Nouf. She doesn't care about anything but herself.'

He found her use of the present tense strangely disturb-ing. 'Did you ever try?'

'Yes,' she snapped. 'I tried, but she *didn't listen*. She was going ahead with the marriage no matter what.' Her mouth twisted into a sneer. 'That's when I told her I knew what she was doing, and I wanted to marry Qazi, and she had no right to marry him, and do you know what she did?' Her gaze was challenging. '*Nothing*. She didn't *care*.'

'So you hated her.'

'Yes.' Although she was holding herself rigidly still, she spoke with a frankness that touched him and that prompted a sudden pity. He could understand her feelings, but the actions that resulted he did not understand; he didn't even come close.

'In a way, I am more blind than ever,' he said, squinting at Abir. 'I see the truth now, but I still don't know what's right.'

Abir's neck was rigid, her whole body tense. 'You won't turn me in,' she said. 'You know what they'll do to me.' Abruptly, she stood up. Her hands were still shaking, and carefully, she lifted the velvet bag from the table. 'Besides, you have no evidence,' she said. Lowering her burqa, she turned towards the door.

'Wait.' Nayir stood and reached into his pocket. 'I meant to leave this with the family.' He took out Nouf's journal. 'I found it in the hut at the beach.'

She eyed the journal with horror.

'It's her journal. I think they would want something to remember her by.'

Abir reached for it, but he drew it away. Their eyes made contact. 'This is not for you,' he said.

Turning, she stumbled from the room. He made no effort to stop her, feeling certain that she wouldn't go anywhere. His only regret was not seeing the final look on her face.

Once her footsteps had died away, he reached into his pocket and took out the last item: the origami stork. He touched its tail. It still had its shape, despite having spent so much time in his pocket. He had wanted to return the items to Othman, but now he didn't feel comfortable leaving them here, where Abir could get her hands on them. He put the book and the stork back into his coat.

The candles had burned down. Outside the window, he could hear the ocean crashing against the rocks below. Funny that he'd never heard the ocean before, not from this high on the island. He opened the terrace door and stepped into the night.

In the distance, he heard a jet ski's engine cranking to life. He felt the urge to tell someone, to call the police, perhaps even call her fiancé and explain the whole thing. That would at least put an end to her marriage plans. But he didn't have the heart. He felt weakened by what she'd said, because despite the shock of her ruthlessness, despite his anger and disgust, she was right: he knew what they would do to her. But what stopped him was knowing what it would do to her family.

Something greater was crumbling inside him, the wall that held the strength of his beliefs, and it hurt to feel himself weakening, to feel this much sympathy for women like Nouf who felt trapped by their lives, by the prescriptions of modesty and domesticity that might have suited the Prophet's wives but that didn't suit the women of this world, infected as it was by desires to go to school and travel and work and have ever greater options and appetites. He tried not to feel that the world was collapsing, but it was collapsing, and there was nothing he could do, just watch with a painful, bitter sense of loss.

Stepping up to the marble balustrade, he reached into his pocket. There was another item there. His old misyar. The box for the bride's name was still empty; his own name was fading from the groom's box. He studied the document, ran a finger over its embossing, and admired the seal. It looked so authentic. It was a very nice misyar.

The jet ski's engine grew louder as it passed below. He could see the headlight cut a crescent on the water. He watched it spin a loop, going round and round, its buzz echoing in the night. He took out a lighter and held it beneath the misyar, feeling the flame's soft breeze rustle the paper. He hesitated once, knowing how difficult it would be to replace. But he knew the truth: he would never use it.

With a steady hand, he held the flame close and watched the paper catch fire, watched it crumble and begin to fall apart. He let go, finally, when the wind caught the charred remains and floated them over the balustrade and down to the sea.

29

In the blistering heat of a weekday afternoon, the children's amusement park was never full. His friend Azim had told him about it, saying that it was the perfect place to take a woman. The other funfairs on the northern Corniche were strictly segregated, but this one was for families, and people would automatically assume they were a couple. It was a bit boring, but they'd be able to talk, and from the top of the Ferris wheel they would have an excellent view of the sea.

After two days of sailing alone, Nayir had docked at the marina and switched on his cell phone to find that Katya had called him twice. The first was a simple, formal-sounding message: 'Please call me back.' The second betrayed a craving for food: 'How about that family buffet?'

At first he was shocked that she had called at all, but his indignation had melted like summer ice. He was excited to hear from her. When he called her back, she sounded very pleased, which made him nervous and happy. They made arrangements to meet at the children's park. He insisted that they arrive in separate cars and that Katya be accompanied by her driver.

At one o'clock the next afternoon, Nayir stood at the

entrance to the park. A few families walked by, on their way out. It was getting too hot for the children. The women's faces were shrouded in black, but all of the women were accompanied by men. It occurred to him that the men might not be their husbands or brothers, and he studied the couples for indications about their relationships. Sometimes children called them 'Mummy' and 'Daddy', but there were couples without children, and he watched them closely, memorizing their postures, their gestures, their tones of voice. He noticed that most of them weren't speaking. They looked wilted, ready to leave. One man talked to a woman with an ease that suggested familiarity. Another man spoke almost carelessly to his wife, not even bothering to look at her face. Nayir tried to imagine talking to Katya that way, but he couldn't.

Katya finally arrived, stepping around the iron entrance gate. Nayir recognized her form even before Ahmad came into view, and for a split second he panicked, thinking that Ahmad hadn't come after all. But the trusty escort appeared, his grey hair shining brilliantly in the sunlight. As Katya drew closer, he could tell that she was smiling behind her burqa.

'Hello, Nayir,' she said. 'It's nice to see you.'

'It's nice to see you, too.'

Ahmad approached and shook his hand. The three of them headed for the Ferris wheel, but Katya stopped at an ice-cream stand, and Nayir stopped with her. Ice cream was a wonderful idea. The only problem, he realized, was the time lapse between buying the ice-cream cone and getting to the place where Katya could lift her burqa to eat it. It might take three minutes, if they contrived it correctly, to buy the ice cream, buy their tickets, climb into the cage, and wait for the Ferris wheel to lift them up and out of sight. But in three outdoor minutes, no frozen substance stood a chance of survival.

Nayir explained the problem to the ice-cream vendor, who took some time to understand, but when he finally did, he assisted by lending them his portable cooler and a bag of ice. They nestled their cones in the cooler and, promising to return it, they headed for the Ferris wheel.

Three minutes later, Nayir and Katya sat alone in the open carriage, side-by-side. One car behind them, Ahmad sat reading a newspaper. The attendant, who seemed accustomed to odd, childless couples acting like children, said he'd let them ride until they shouted to get off, and he wandered away, giving Katya the privacy to raise her burqa.

Once the wheel started going round, a light breeze blew over them and they took out their cones. When Katya flipped up her veil, Nayir couldn't resist glancing at her face. It didn't seem different from the last time he'd seen her, but he'd expected more sadness.

He waited nervously, unable to eat his ice cream, watching it dribble down the back of his hand. One of them had to say something, but nothing came to his mind. As they rode to the zenith, Nayir studied the view of the sea, and as they descended, he studied his ice cream, sea and ice cream, sea and vanilla, until finally Katya plucked up the courage to say: 'So have you seen Othman lately?'

Even though his ice cream was melting, he kept his eyes fixed on the view. 'I haven't seen him since that day we met in the parking lot.'

'Ah.' A slight pause, followed by more licking and another pause. 'Are you two still friends?'

He had to consider the question – first, for the spirit in which it was asked (Curiosity? Jealousy?), and second, for the answer, improbable though it was. 'Yes, I still consider him a friend.'

'But you're not – close.'

He noticed her ice cream tipping dangerously over the cone's edge. 'Why do you say that?'

She shrugged. It was the falsest attempt at nonchalance he'd ever seen, but it managed to topple her ice cream, which bounced down her leg and landed on her shoe. '*Ya Allah!* I can't believe it.' She shook her foot and the ice cream flew out of the carriage. It sailed over the attendant's booth and hit the pavement with a splat.

He wasn't sure whether to laugh or frown, but she looked abashed, so he offered his cone. After a delicate hesitation, she took it. 'Thanks.'

He rubbed his fingers on his robe, but it only seemed to make them stickier. A silence fell. He had already told her about his conversation with Abir, but on the phone she hadn't betrayed much of a reaction other than bafflement. He wondered how she felt about it now, but was too afraid to ask.

'By the way,' she said, 'the division has decided to reopen Nouf's case.'

He glanced at her. 'Really?'

'Yes. I showed my boss the work we'd done and all the samples from the body. She took them to her boss, and he put in the request. The division chief just approved it.'

'So what's going to happen now?'

'They're sending police to question the family.' She shrugged. 'The Shrawis are powerful; they might try to cover it up again, but I've already spoken to Nusra about it.'

He looked at her with curiosity. 'What did you say?'

'I told her what we discovered at the zoo – the shoe, I mean. I also told her that we had reason to suspect Abir, based on the cloak in the beach shack and the missing gold.'

'I'll bet Abir hid the gold again.'

'I don't know,' Katya said. 'But when I talked to her,

Nusra had no idea what had happened, and she promised to cooperate with the investigators.'

Nayir was filled with admiration not only for Katya's courage in turning over their evidence but for speaking to Nusra, who had already lost one daughter and now stood to lose another. 'You amaze me,' he said.

She suppressed a smile. 'My boss also took the liberty of calling Qazi to warn him that his fiancée was under investigation.'

Nayir grinned. 'That's creative justice.'

'I think so, too. I don't know what's going to happen to Abir if they do find her guilty. She'll probably spend some time in jail.'

'It would be well-earned, I think.'

'I also wanted to mention,' she said, 'that the division could use an investigator like you. Have you ever considered working for the government?'

His eyes popped open. 'No.' Was this why she had asked to see him?

'Why not?'

'That's not a good idea.'

'Oh come on! You're good at detective work. You're better than some of the—'

'I don't like dead bodies,' he said quickly.

She stopped licking. 'Oh, that's right. I forgot about that.' She smiled.

'That's generous of you.'

'But you could get over *that*.' She stifled a laugh.

'Listen, I can't stay too long.' He was flustered, and he took a piece of ice from the cooler and used it to wipe off his hands.

'Why not?' She seemed disappointed, and he felt glad.

'I've got an eye appointment,' he said finally.

'Oh! Well, I'll come with you. Is it with that doctor?'

'Yes, and you don't have to come.'

'But I'd like to.' She eyed him – strangely, he thought – and licked her ice cream. 'Think of me as a professional escort, in case any women should throw themselves at you; they'll think I'm your wife.'

He felt himself blushing. Idiotically. 'Women don't throw themselves at me.'

'Yes, they do. You just haven't been paying attention.'

☽

'I'm so happy you've come back!' Dr Jahiz led them down a carpeted hallway and into an examination room. 'Did you say that the desert was troubling your eyes?'

'Yes.' Nayir guided Katya to a chair near the door and then spent an awkward moment climbing into the patient's seat. 'I think it's the dust, aggravating my vision.'

'Of course.' Jahiz dimmed the lights and switched on a lighted wall chart of letters, arranged into columns. 'Let me tell you, it's always the dust!'

Nayir studied the chart but found that he couldn't read any of the letters. 'Actually, I have the most trouble seeing in the city, I don't know why. I can see everything in the desert.'

A phone rang in the outer room, and the doctor slumped. 'Excuse me, I'll be right back.'

When he was gone, Katya raised her burqa, crossed her legs, and laid her hands together on her knees. *She wants something*, he thought. He wondered how he knew that. It wasn't an action he'd seen her do before, but it felt universal, like the gesture for 'I'm choking.'

'I wanted to invite you to dinner next week. My father and I are planning a little party, just a few people, and I'd like you to come.'

Nayir raised his eyebrows politely, but his gut yanked

353

him hard in the opposite direction. Dinner? With *her father*? No, no, he wasn't ready. Not for that.

'It would mean a lot to me,' she said, looking rather sheepish. 'I know it might seem strange, but other people will be there, and my father would like to meet you.'

Nayir nodded, although it might have been a tremor.

'And like I said, other people will be there.' Katya raised an eyebrow.

In the antechamber, Nayir could hear Jahiz's aggravated voice. *Well you'd better stop the drops at once! No, don't apply heat, it's swollen, ya'Allah! Who ever heard of putting heat on swelling?* Katya was waiting for his response. There was no way around it. Not only did she want him to meet her father, but she wanted him to meet *her father's friends.* The sleeve of his robe got stuck on the arm of the phoropter and he spent a slow, grateful moment prying it free. Jahiz's voice filtered in. *Yes, go ahead and put some ice on it. I'll tell you what, if you can find a cube of ice in this whole damn desert that will stay solid long enough to reduce the swelling, then next time you come in, I'll give you a pair of Gucci sunglasses at a discount price . . . Yes, you have my word. Gucci!*

'Which evening were you going to have this party?' Nayir asked.

'Thursday night.'

'Aaahhh, I have dinner with my uncle on Thursdays.'

'Oh.'

'I'd like to come, but it would upset my uncle. He has no one else, and . . .'

'I understand.' She nodded. 'I do.'

Instead of relief, he felt bad for having disappointed her. 'Let me talk to my uncle,' he offered.

'All right,' she said, smiling.

The doctor returned, and Katya flipped down her veil. Jahiz sat in a swivel chair and kicked himself toward Nayir like an energetic crab. 'Now remember to breathe calmly,' he said. 'This won't hurt.'

Gratefully, Nayir turned his attention to the doctor. Aside from the occasional discouraging remark – *My goodness, a negative five in the left eye!* and *Must be hard to read anything, eh?* – he found the process relaxing. It was dark, and still. The complex instruments, handled delicately, and in reverential silence, gave him a sense of universal well-being. The doctor could fix his vision. Thanks be to Allah, *anything* could be fixed, in the proper hands.

A negative five!

He remembered the camel's leg, and it made him think of Othman, of his desperate love for Nouf, and of Nouf's feelings in return. *She wanted to be like the grouper.* But the Nouf of his mind was free already, jetting down the freeway on a Harley-Davidson. She wore a scarab-like helmet, alligator gloves, and a man's white robe. The robe whipped around her ankles as she skirted tractor-trailers and SUVs, some lunatic Bedouin on a space-age camel.

Jahiz stood up and closed Nayir's chart. 'We'll get started on your glasses, it should only take an hour. While you're waiting, perhaps your sister would like an examination, too?'

Nayir glanced at Katya. Her head twitched in what might have been a 'No.'

'No, thank you,' Nayir said, getting out of the chair.

'You know,' Jahiz's eyes had a cunning look. 'Not many women get their vision corrected. Men prevent them from doing it. It is only the strong and *liberated* woman who comes in for an exam.'

Even though she was veiled, hands tucked into her sleeves, Nayir could read her sudden hesitation. Slowly she turned towards him as if to say: *Not a bad idea!*

'After all,' Jahiz went on. 'With veils on their faces all day, women only want to see the world, you know. And clearly, my friend, *clearly*.'

Nayir looked at Katya's burqa, rising gently with her breath. She wanted to say something, she was thinking about it . . .

'I think,' Nayir said, 'that she already has perfect vision.'

He imagined he saw her smile.

AUTHOR'S NOTE

The title of this novel is taken from an important event narrated in the Quran and the Hadith, the oral traditions relating to the words and deeds of the Prophet Mohammed. A celebrated occasion in Islam, the mi'raj is the second half of a miraculous night-time journey during which Mohammed ascends on his winged horse al-Buraq to the heavens, and there in Paradise is presented before Allah.

The mi'raj is both a physical journey and a spiritual climax – a moment of revelation for Mohammed. In this book Nayir's journey to learning the truth behind Nouf's death is, for him, a physical and a spiritual discovery too. With this in mind, I have given Nayir's story the title *The Night of the Mi'raj*.